T.L. HU

MW01137550

SEARCHING
FOR
PARADISE

3/2/2016

T.L Hughes

outskirtspress

DENVER, COLORADO

Searching For Paradise
All Rights Reserved.
Copyright © 2016 T.L. Hughes
v3.0 r1.0

Outskirts Press, Inc.
http://www.outskirtspress.com

ISBN: 978-1-4787-6570-7

Library of Congress Control Number: 2015916133

Outskirts Press and the "OP" logo are trademarks belonging to Outskirts Press, Inc.

PRINTED IN THE UNITED STATES OF AMERICA

I think back
Through all my life
To all the friends I've known
Different faces
Distant places
All Circles

The good times we had
We'll have them once again
We left each other's company
To live our lives in vain

Why to lose the friends we had
For others just the same
Man rolls his dice
To sacrifice
Those Circles

For Collette

CHAPTER 1

It was a cool air summer night and palm tree silhouettes tripped the moonlit sidewalks. We were riding the line of chance as we packed up Lucas Coppens's '64 Ford Fairlane and prepared to leave Huntington Beach, the people, the beaches, the whole West Coast behind us forever.

Culminating in dirt roads and desire, I found my life at a crossroads. Like any twenty-five-year-old blue-collar kid from the East Coast drawn by the rich songs of The Beach Boys and The Mamas and The Papas and all else that was California in the sixties and the seventies, I had gone there for the girls, the beaches, and, of course, to be in the movies. But now, I had to leave.

I thought back now to the very first time I had ever heard "California Dreamin'" by The Mamas and The Papas, my being in that quintessential moment in Lowell. I remembered thinking then that I had to find a way to get to California. Even though I had never been there before, all I could imagine as I heard that aching flute solo was beautiful beaches, cool and clean, unlike the blowing bitter wind of our New England coast, and beautiful women everywhere; their fine lines and soft words forever surrounding me in endless reverie.

It had been three hard years of conflict and struggle though.

Of my slumming Hollywood Boulevard working meager no-pay production jobs in my spare time and going to dive motels on The Strip to pick up still no-name directors with British accents while they opened up their trash in the backseat of my red Mercury Comet, I worked the clutch and the three-on-the-tree shift on the Comet's steering column while I chauffeured them around from La Cienega to Sunset, back to La Cienega, and finally back to the studio. One loser left all of his food trash all over my backseat as I scurried him between production sets. I finally had had enough.

And my starving all of the time, raiding abandoned friends' apartments who had since given up and moved back to Ohio or the Northeast, searching their empty refrigerators for meat but satisfied with the bread and the condiments, only to get through another few days before that meager production assistant check had arrived. I had so gotten used to condiments sometimes being our main course, like packing ketchup sandwiches for our lunch while we worked for free for the students at the American Film Institute, that when we were lucky enough to find meat, it almost made me hurl at first. It was funny how a whole loaf of white bread and a large bottle of ketchup could hold us over for three days. When you hurled, the Ohioans referred to it as "horking."

The only rewards were short-lived, like sucking down those two Budweiser tall cans after our long day working at the Scientology building, helping more rich kids do their student films so they could get a good grade for their parents. But I couldn't do it anymore. I remember this one Scientologist guy with two big Dalmatian dogs hanging around the hotel lobby set trying to talk us into his religion, but as hungry as I was, I didn't seem to care any about Scientology. I had read *The Martian Chronicles*, and even thought to myself after his empty lecture that everybody knows there isn't anyone living on Mars . . . It was just a good story.

I had even tried to sell reclaimed energy, just so I could make some money to break back into Hollywood again. It was 1984, and nobody was really serious about conserving energy though. I always believed that the world would eventually dry up; oil was a finite resource, just like gold and chocolate and coffee, but as soon as the fuel prices in America came back down again, no one really cared about reclaimed energy. Supply and demand; cheap and expensive; that is what they taught us in school. I felt really sorry for myself; down on my luck, completely out of it, the flame was flickering. I looked at my life as one big riddle that still wasn't solved. It was always raining in California, and although I still wanted to chase my show biz dreams, I needed to do it elsewhere now.

So after borrowing about a thousand dollars off of my sister Ciara in Massachusetts and moving in with Declan Brady and Lucas Coppens in Huntington Beach and working an office job for a few months to try to save back up my cash reserves, we all began crafting a great expedition.

All three of us had the same and different mind-set. We snuck out at midnight in late August, Lucas, Declan, and me, northbound to San Luis Obispo, stealing away inside an hour where half the world was asleep and the other half was using up all of its energy.

I'd miss Huntington Beach, I thought, even those crazy oil derricks pumping midnight oil everywhere about our existence, the soft monotone of their grinding mechanisms, their heads dipping with indifference, accepting their blue-collar roles, seemingly not caring, not wanting to ask why as they sucked the fuel out of the ground below the quaking beds in which we slept.

It was really funny though that one of the oil derricks, the one in our backyard rental cottage lot, the digger that Luke had mounted to ride before, so quickly did come to a grinding halt like some sort of premonition. After pumping for who knows, maybe years endlessly, this giant grasshopper machine just stopped dead in the night as if it too was trying to tell us something, that maybe something had changed. It left the still backyard in the beach night eerie. The background hum we had become accustomed to for so long was gone. Like the grandfather clock in my grandmother's kitchen that ticked endlessly throughout my childhood, the one that had suddenly stopped dead on the day of my thirteenth birthday, the oil derrick had also stopped. Declan ran in from the back porch with a few others to tell everyone who was huddled in our empty kitchen for the going away party what had happened.

"She's stopped! The oil digger in the back lot has stopped! I think she wants to come with us!" he exclaimed laughing with animated wide eyes and the big white Declan Brady mouth filled with Brady teeth that all the Brady family seemed to have.

We had said our good-byes to the handful of misfit orphan friends, because in California in the eighties, even people with parents were orphans, all of them friends that we had collected over the past few years. We drove the Ford down to the end of Sixth Street and took a right on Pacific Coast Highway, heading north away from the pier and her ever-fainting lights, out past the concrete county of Los Angeles and into the darkness ahead of us.

We drove all night. After a good while, the three of us had been reduced to twenty-minute driving shifts, twenty minutes being all we could take before the road turned blurry and the divider bumps, bursts of reality within someone's foolish dreaming, woke each of us up behind the wheel, and we resigned to pass the wheel over to the next driver. It was crazy dangerous to drive this way, we all knew it, but we were being pushed by some foolish, reckless desire to find ourselves, to somehow find a way to get to where we were supposed to be.

Up, through, and beyond Santa Barbara, we managed to pull off California 101 and into Pismo Beach around four o'clock, maybe five o'clock in the morning; the night was still dark.

Right off the 101, the old Ford climbed up to a house on a hill that overlooked the highway and the rolling sand dunes of Pismo Beach. It was a planned first stop, as thought out as a notebook plan of zigzag stops across the whole North American continent could only be. We just hadn't planned on being so doggone tired and having such a tough time staying awake in order to get there on our maiden leg; after all, it was only our first four hours of liberation.

Pismo was my "friend" stop. The dots we had placed across the map were the respective contacts we had collected amongst the three of us, most of whom had some place in our past, be it a high school or college acquaintance or a family member or somebody else's relative. This was the plan so we wouldn't have to outlay tons of cash on our trip across the great continent.

Zane, now living in beautiful pink-sanded-reflections-of-sunset Pismo Beach, was originally from my old neighborhood, Christian Hill, in Lowell. We went to high school together, and both lived at Paradise Beach in New Hampshire for many summers, first at the MacNamaras' green, two-story boarding house and then renting our own place, "The Penthouse," with a few others. It was at "The Penthouse" that Zane had put a few holes in the drywall while suffering through the pain of an apparent heartache. That was before any of us knew what it was. The pain manifested itself with karate chops; he put them right through the moaning drywall between his bedroom and mine, the result being an irregular window in the partition wall. I remember being seventeen and driving in the maddening rain in the October nights with Zane in an old Buick that was sicker than we were as we headed from Paradise west into Nashua to take those karate lessons. And then back at Paradise Beach, he'd be throwing a twenty-five-pound plate into a green army backpack and running down the beach with it at the crack of the next beautiful dawn. One day, Zane and his girlfriend Maureen all up and moved to California. We had all graduated high school by then, and he wanted to move on. I guess they had both listened to all of those same songs from The Beach Boys and The Mamas and The Papas like I had.

CHAPTER 2

Zane and Maureen had been expecting us. I had called ahead from a phone booth just north of Santa Barbara, and they both were wide awake and waiting for us with big hugs. We rolled in late and threw our things down and crashed right in their living room.

"Spending all this time in Los Angeles?" Zane said, "You'll never catch me down that way unless I'm driving through on my way to Mexico . . . and Lowell? I'm not ever going back again!"

He seemed content to just stay right there on the beautiful golden Central Coast and maybe live in a trailer someday and hunt wild boar with his crossbow in the beautiful oak tree hills that covered the grade around San Luis Obispo. Zane wanted to live off of the grid just like a hermit and never have to pay taxes again.

But for me, I felt that I needed more than that. Life was still one big riddle that needed to be solved. Notoriety, happiness, security, love, comfort, faith, it was all connected somehow. I was determined to figure it out before it was all over. Perhaps Zane already had figured it out.

Declan, Lucas, and I were driving cross-country until the road ran out, and then we were going to jump on a plane with a one-way ticket to London and then maybe backpack across the whole European continent until we found our dream jobs working in the entertainment industry somewhere along that path; a music video production job in England would be great.

When we all awoke at Zane's the following morning, Zane and I talked about New England and all of the vivid memories that went with it. Aidan Maloney, God rest his kindred soul, lived at the MacNamara boarding house with us on the New Hampshire coast back during those high school summers. Aidan "Lones" (as we called him), Robert Hillyard, and I shared a little room off of the front porch of the MacNamara main house when we were all about fourteen in 1973. Lones was an arcade hand for the summer at the Paradise Beach Casino; Hillyard was a busboy, and I was a dishwasher. Zane was sixteen then and lived in another room in the back of the MacNamara house where he had his own door and no under-age eleven o'clock curfew to fear. But Lones loved going out with Zane and the older guys and used to sneak back into our off-porch closet room through an open outside window every night around one o'clock in the morning. I remember one night Mrs. MacNamara busting into that little room after curfew and throwing that light switch on right in the nick of time to catch Aidan crawling through that side window after he had been out all night drinking with Zane and the older kids.

"Aidan Maloney! I'm calling your mother in the morning and sending you home!" she screamed.

"No, please, Mrs. MacNamara, please don't send me home! Please, please, Mrs. MacNamara!" Lones begged her.

Zane and I remembered Robert Hillyard (who is now a priest). Robert Hillyard, sitting in that rocking chair at the MacNamara house at eight o'clock the next morning just eating his plain toast with butter in the corner of the front porch, rocking away, just like he had never been woken up the night before.

"Beautiful morning, isn't it, Mrs. MacNamara?" Robert asked her as she passed through on her way to her yard.

"Not if your name is Aidan Maloney!" she snapped back at him.

I had seen my first concert with Zane. It was Roy Buchanan playing that sweet blues sound at the Paradise Beach Casino the summer after we graduated high school in 1976. I had never heard someone make sounds like that from a guitar, sounds that truly touched the soul. How come I had never heard of this guy before? And he was doing it all as drunk as a fool. He walked to the end of the stage that night at Paradise Beach and fell off it just like he had walked over the edge of a cliff, and the show was over, and that was it. Roy Buchanan, plastered, lay on the floor, and the show was cut short. There was no catcher in the rye for Roy that night. Crazy, mad, and beautiful life; it was everywhere.

How I wanted to play that sweet sound just like Roy Buchanan, or Jeff Beck, or Keith Richards of The Rolling Stones. I wanted to be that good but didn't want to put the time in with guitar lessons, and could never get past the first few weeks of calloused fingers. That was too much time, so that was that.

Unbeknownst to me and the world back then, but Roy would cut another thing short a few years later in 1988—his life. He hung himself in jail after getting arrested for driving under the influence in Pennsylvania. All that sweet talent only with us mere mortals for such a short time and then gone forever. But everyone doubted that he killed himself. His captors did it to him, they said.

The *American Graffiti* movie had put that dream of California in me too. Even though it had been released a few years before, I finally got to see it with Zane in that summer of '76 at the Paradise Beach movie theatre. I imagined myself someday cruising some beautiful California boulevard, chasing beautiful blondes like Suzanne Somers in a white T-Bird and the Beach Boys and The Mamas and The Papas singing everywhere.

After I graduated college in 1980, one night while the summer Massachusetts night air blew through the screens in my bedroom on Eighteenth Street in Lowell, I had my first vision of her, my sweet Colette. The fireflies briefly lit the bushes running our concrete driveway while my thoughts looked past the open window into the blowing trees of a soft summer rainstorm. The lyrics of Led Zeppelin played aloud on my bedroom turntable and told me that I would find her there, out in California.

It wasn't until the following year in 1981 that the journey out west did come to pass, though. I was driving a truck for the *Lowell Sun*, my third three-month job since graduation, when my friends Richie Clark and Sal Caprissi approached me at a men's softball league party outside Charlie McIntyre's Pub and asked me if I wanted to move to Newport Beach with them.

"Newport Beach, Rhode Island?" I asked, "What do you want to go there for? Isn't that where all of the rich people live? Huge houses, rocky coast, shipbuilder descendants, tales of prohibition bootleggers and whalers from *Moby Dick*?"

"No, California!" Richie said with his eyes lighting up the August twilight. "You know, Beverly Hills! We're gonna be movie stars, Mike!" He screamed aloud and began singing the jingle from TV's "*The Beverly Hillbillies*." After this, he just let out one of his characteristic loud, infectious laughs, and Sal and I laughed with him. We planned to leave three weeks from that night.

But there was a hiccup. Richie had always been a lady's man, tall, good-looking; he even kept two girlfriends at both ends of the state, both of them named Sarah, so when they called he wouldn't mix them up. That was, until the day that he *did* mix them up. He thought he was talking to one of them instead of the other and really screwed things up and one of the Sarahs consequentially broke up with him. Because of this, Richie wanted to postpone the trip for a month or so and see if he could work things out with the Sarah's, but Sal and I thought differently.

Sal Caprissi and I, after already quitting our jobs, couldn't wait for poor Richie. We jumped into my red Mercury Comet with the "three gears on the tree" on the date that we had planned and headed west with Taboo. Taboo was Sal's sweet, amicable-as-long-as-you-knew-her pit bull. We drove for a week on the Auto Club highways of America until we finally got to the other side. California! We put up at Zane's near San Luis Obispo. We stayed with Zane for about a month but found no work in the sleepy sixties hot tub college town, so we packed up our stuff (and Taboo again) and headed south for Los Angeles.

Back then, poor Zane was probably glad to get rid of us, for he was out of work and only trying to be as hospitable as his own money could stretch in accommodating his two jobless friends. But that's what people did when you were friends; you'd let them overstay their welcome, maybe for months at a time, before finally booting them out.

One morning, with all of the stress that Zane was under, he drained the oil out of his new Honda and put brand-new oil in the transmission fluid reservoir and his car seized on him while going up Questa Grade. It was that very afternoon that Sal and I left.

Three years later, Declan, Lucas, and I were here at good old Zane's again. Colette had left me just months before in Huntington Beach, and I needed to leave the beautiful coast through the same open door that I had come in from.

Zane and I reminisced some more about the Paradise Beach, New Hampshire, days. We talked about another Lowellian, Larry Bordeaux, who left Lowell for San Diego in the summer of 1979.

"Whatever happened to Larry? He seemed to disappear forever," I said.

"Remember Larry tying himself to the chimney before he got into his sleeping bag those nights we used to sleep on that slanted third-story roof of The Penthouse in Paradise Beach?" Zane laughed. His heavy laugh started at his mouth and soon took over his whole face as he threw his head back. Passing his eyes, the laugh changed the color of his skin a warm red all the way back to his jet-black Native American hairline.

"Yeah, Larry was afraid of sleepwalking off of the edge. He didn't want a surprise three-story ride!" I told Declan, Lucas, and Zane's girlfriend Maureen.

"It's a good thing Roy Buchanan never slept on that roof with us!" Zane laughed.

We had nicknamed that apartment "The Penthouse" because it sat atop two stories of a shingled, dilapidated beach house with a rickety staircase going up on the outside. We had even bought red and black silk-screened T-shirts that advertised the party palace to all of Paradise Beach as we walked to and from our restaurant jobs. During that particular summer, I was seventeen and Zane was nineteen. Nothing was in our refrigerator back in those days save for a few bricks of processed cheese that had been stolen from the restaurant we both worked at . . . Cheese that kept us from starvation some of the days; we seemed to subsist on cheese and beer.

I remembered waking up on that Penthouse roof beside Larry one morning who was tied to the chimney in his sleeping bag. A rooftop of sleeping bags, we all watched that huge red ball of sunrise pushing up through the water of the deep Atlantic Ocean. Zane was tapping me on the shoulder and pointing to the sun's magnificence, with no spoken words, just all of us watching it happen; the sun itself coming from an eleven in the morning London tea, or somewhere else out over that same curved horizon that once mesmerized the Native Americans.

Here in California, I had watched that same beautiful sun set so deeply over the Pacific on its way somewhere else. It was time to find out where it was coming from, that magnificent, warm ball of light.

That morning in Pismo Beach, Zane and Maureen took Declan, Lucas, and I to brunch at a roadside restaurant right off the 101 where a giant cowboy sculpted from a redwood stood at watch out in the parking lot looking westward. The wooden cowboy looked out toward the Pacific Ocean; consternation appeared in his face, as if he was frustrated that he had come all this way and run out of west. For him, there were people everywhere, college students, and no more open land. This was San Luis Obispo, where Cal Poly "Dollies" roamed the streets of yesterday's hippy girls; where hot tubs and freethinking, hairy armpits clashed with upturned-collared Izod Lacrosse shirts and sweet daddy's money.

"Tell Zane and Maureen your sleeping-in-the-refrigerator-box story," Declan said at breakfast.

"All right then," I obliged. "There was a late-night party in Covina a few months ago where our friend Henry and one of his ex-marine buddies had asked me to come along," I began. "I fell asleep in the back of Henry's friend's Z28 before we even got to the stupid party, so Henry and the marine just locked the doors of the car to let me sleep. They went off to the party somewhere down the street on their own. Around one o'clock in the morning, I awoke in the back of the car to the sound of someone peeing all over the Z28 door! It startled me. And then, as I jumped up, the guy bolted!" I said. "This guy didn't know someone was in the car he was pissing on, and I scared the crap out of him. I was so disoriented that I got out of the car in a stupor and automatically locked the stupid door behind me, leaving my dungaree jacket behind. I walked the streets up and down but couldn't find the party my friends were at. I was freezing in the windy Covina night! Full of weary despair, I pulled an empty refrigerator box out of a flatbed truck in the alley and dragged it behind a garage to get warm, to find sweet sleep, because that is all I wanted to do. While I lay in the box with an opening for my face to look out, all of a sudden, another guy was peering in at me! He said that he had watched me from his window and asked if I wanted to get warm in his apartment until my friends came back. It was cold, and he kept insisting that I sleep on his couch inside. I hesitatingly accepted and lay there wide-eyed on his couch for a few hours as my observer paced the floor of his apartment. Wondering all sorts of crazy things that might happen to me, I abruptly jumped to my feet, and bolted out the door and back to the side of the car in the early-morning light."

"Once the little creepy guy had seen me gone, he quickly found me again beside the car and was back to try to convince me to come back in," I told them. "But it was all too freaky, and I was spooked now. I had seen too many scripts where this wasn't going to be a good ending."

"It was a few more hours before Henry and the ex-marine ever returned laughing and wondering why I hadn't just stayed in the car. I told them about the guy first peeing on the car, then the empty box maneuver, and finally the little guy that had coaxed me upstairs."

"'Where does he live? Let's go rough him up,' the ex-marine laughed, but I wouldn't point out the place to them. I wouldn't have it. I didn't want anything bad to happen to the poor little guy; he probably meant me no harm," I said to Zane and Maureen.

"Things that would happen only to you, my friend," Zane laughed.

I looked over at Maureen's pretty face, her sweet smile, her long, dark hair and her beautiful curvy body and thought at that moment of just how lucky Zane was.

We talked of all kinds of things before we left them: Tina Turner on the radio, the beautiful Aegean Sea, and the Greek Isles. Zane wanted to sell his earthly possessions and join us for a minute, but then what about hunting wild boar and his own vision of paradise? He had to stay in Pismo. We talked about random things like Vanessa Williams, pretty girls, and how many chin-ups we could do, but in the blink of an eye, we were back on the road, and

Zane and Maureen were gone. It was two forty in the afternoon, and we headed north out of Pismo. Lucas got out of the car one last time to adjust and readjust the bungie cord on the Fairlane, the bungie cord that held down Declan's surfboard on the top of the car, just to make sure the surfboard wouldn't vibrate too much on the ensuing drive up sweet rocky California Route 1 just south of Big Sur.

CHAPTER 3

The surfboard was a statement of sorts. Declan and Lucas wanted it to stay affixed to the Fairlane roof all of the way across the country. We had envisioned driving through Kansas with the surfboard on our car.

Declan fooled with the radio trying to get some music . . . anything. A weak "Tijuana Taxi" by Herb Albert and the Tijuana Brass came through momentarily but fell out to a mixture of airwave static and someone speaking in broken Spanish. I remembered as a teenager getting that same album as a birthday gift with Herb and his band standing in a huge field of yellow flowers on the cover. I wondered what had ever happened to that album now, for it was no longer with me. I thought about how my large album-filled apple crate that I had dragged out to California was now heading back east again to my parents' house on a United Parcel Service delivery truck. But Herb Albert hadn't been in that crate collection for many years; he was lost.

The California coast keeps going on, I thought, as we passed through Atascadero State Beach with waves hitting the shore endlessly, mostly unwatched. The waves pounded the hard sand to the left of us as shiny aluminum-roofed farmhouses sparkled on our right, glimmering like the shiny pop-can sweet ocean itself does in the hot, forever sailing sun. Behind the tin-roofed barns was a mountain curtain backdrop, with mountains all in a row, rising up from the two-lane highway we rode upon and stepping back into America.

"Tijuana Taxi" came back for a few more minutes and then statically mixed into a song from a group called Ambrosia, "Holdin' on to Yesterday," which caused me to reflect, once again, upon losing Colette. What a miserable wreck I still was three months after the break-up. Lucas told us that this song was about Billy Pilgrim, Kurt Vonnegut's time-traveling eccentric in his novel *Slaughterhouse-Five*. Billy had been kidnapped by aliens and taken to the planet Tralfamadore. The Scientologists and Shirley MacLaine believed that aliens walked amongst us all.

Music had become a part of my being, my soul, for after all, I was a Beatles-generation kid. Music was important to all of us who had grown up in those baby-booming times; it was woven into our days, reminiscent of all of the good times that we had. I was an imaginary rock star and dreamed often when my mood was down. But after losing Colette, it was those songs of love gone wrong that really brought me down.

As a kid, Declan had taken piano lessons from a nun when he attended Catholic school in Ohio. I, myself, had taken clarinet lessons for eight long years. Once a week, I took the bus to downtown Lowell to Bob Noonan's Music Studio on Central Street; the place was upstairs from the old Rialto Theatre. The Rialto had been converted into a bowling alley before those times. Bob Noonan was probably in his fifties back then but had the thickest gray hair I had ever seen on a human being. He used to use this crazy hair-thinning comb while I sat there practicing my clarinet trills. It was funny because I was already starting to lose my hair, yet Bob Noonan had too much of it.

During my weekly lessons at the music studio, I learned how to play "Flight of the Bumblebee," trilling those clarinet keys fairly well. I guess I was pretty good at it. At least my father thought so as he sat in the waiting room and listened to me sometimes. He thought I was so good that he would make me take the clarinet with us on our Sunday trips to see his aunt, Auntie Sister, where our whole family had to sit around and visit her in these big, huge, stale rooms of the nun convent. The convents always smelled of mothballs and bleach back then. I remember the big, scary mansion rooms of the Julie Country Day School, where Auntie Sister was mother superior. I'd have to break out the clarinet around midvisit and play for them all in a big, echoing room, with lots of nuns inviting themselves in to hear me as I sat there drilling the woodwind to "Flight of the Bumblebee." It nearly killed me. When I got into high school and told my father Frank that playing in the marching band wasn't really cool and asked him gingerly if I could quit the clarinet, he reluctantly said okay. It must have secretly killed him. I quit the band, and Bob Noonan, the clarinet teacher, died of a heart attack shortly after that. Poor Bob Noonan left all of that thick hair behind.

After quitting band, I began running track because running (from things) was something that I was always really good at. I wrote things too. It was around that time that I wrote this song, "Reincarnation of a Rock Star" after playing air guitar one day to The Stones in the parlor on Eighteenth Street.

The days, he stays inside
He isn't trying to hide
His dreams are heavy screams, alive
They allow him to survive

His tools are vocal jewels, he sings
A harvest, running springs
A band silhouettes the stage
A lion on his cage

While lights go on
Fingers born, the frets are worn

The days, he stays inside
He isn't trying to hide
No social suicides
No more

I loved dreaming. I could be a world-class surfer in my dreams. Right down the street from Bob Noonan's Music Studio was The Strand Theatre where I first saw the 1966 *Endless Summer* documentary with my friend Ray Champeaux. I was mesmerized watching these guys chase the summer around the world, surfing the oceans of our crazy earth. It made me realize that it could always be summer for me. And while these surfers chased the sun, the sun was always warm. I truly wanted to feel the warm sun forever as I surfed upon these oceans of life. How comfortable and crazy it all seemed to me now.

Our own surfboard was now knocking its bungie bondage as we passed the long, distant beaches on our left. I felt like I was James Thurber's Walter Mitty, living the life of a double agent, secretly leaving Colette or whatever else I was leaving in Los Angeles and slipping away to a top secret assignment somewhere in the East.

I was a singer in a rock-and-roll band. Back living in Huntington Beach, I occasionally sang with a group of Vietnamese guys that I worked with in the circuit board factory. Minh Nguyen and Bang Tran played the instruments, and I sang with them in their garage some-where in Garden Grove. I knew the words to Billy Idol's "White Wedding," and I could sing it in perfect English, which was good enough for them at first. Declan tried to sing it one evening with me, and that's when these Vietnamese guys decided not to invite us back for practice. They decided that they would rather learn the English words themselves because Declan and I could hardly carry it; they were getting better, and we weren't. I always thought that I was a great singer, but isn't that the way that these things always go?

And so it had come to pass that all three of us, Lucas Coppens, Declan Brady, and I, looking for something more, had planned to collectively move on till we found it. We would go together or separately. It was planned that August 24th would be the day we all would quit our jobs, and we did. Declan quit his newspaper ad sales job at the *Daily Pilot* (he always referred to the paper as the Daily Planet). Lucas quit his job as a mechanical engineer with the government, and I left my temporary job at the circuit board factory. We were off across the zigzag country and on to Europe.

"No more conventional jobs! No more 8 to 5! No more break rooms filled with ciga-rette stench and coffee cups!" Declan yelled aloud as Lucas rolled down his own driver-side window in order to let out a shrill, seemingly everlasting, scream from the meandering roads that skirted the cliffs just to the south of Big Sur.

Declan finally gave up on the radio and pulled out a cassette tape from Lucas's amassed collection. Changing colors moved both above and below us; there was all of this turquoise water, the greens, and grays of hills above, and the rocks so far below. Waves crashed on the hard coast thousands of feet beneath us while the cassette deck played the Rolling Stones's "Tattoo You." The song "Heaven" came in with the crescendo of the waves that skirted the coastline. I sensed the waves below rolling to the beat of the music. I heard Jagger's overlaid, calming, psychedelic voice and rare guitar play hitting the soft shore with Bill Wyman and Charlie Watts backing him up.

Sal Caprissi and I, God rest his soul, with Taboo, the pit bull, had "Tattoo You" playing on our tape deck all of the way across country on our way out to California in 1981 because it was the only tape we had with us. The Stones were touring that year, and Sal had bought the tape before we left Lowell. During our traveling dizziness, we changed the words in every song. We made every song about Taboo, the pit bull. For "Little T&A," Sal would sing and dance with Taboo's paws in his arms. The dog sat in his lap in the front seat of the Comet as Sal tried to drive, almost going off of the tired road sometimes. Sal really loved his dog. When Sal and I had left Zane in 1981 and landed in Orange County, in order to get an apartment to live in, Sal had to give his little rock-n'-roll pit bull away. After that, Sal Caprissi was never the same again. He thought back to the happy times that he shared with Taboo in the Dracut apple orchards, Taboo lying in the cool breeze on her golden stomach. Sal wondered after that if Taboo was happy. Had he done the right thing for her? Three months after he had to give Taboo away, Sal Caprissi packed up his things and hitched a ride back to Massachusetts, homesick and dog-less. He left me a large loaf of white bread and a large bottle of ketchup in the empty refrigerator.

It wasn't long after that I began rooming with Declan and Lucas, all of us college graduates and California orphans in the 1980s, all of us looking for something that we couldn't put into words.

Driving north now, our day was filled with Caribbean colors, with the waves still assaulting the cliffs below us as we drove on. We listened to more rock and roll. During a stop, Lucas seemed undaunted in his demeanor as he stood on the edge of a 1,000-foot cliff overlooking the ocean in order to scream a shrill scream once again, a ledge he had crawled to like some Native American spirit, to get one last look at that great western rock-breaking ocean before traveling eastward home. The smell of Pacific pines awoke my closeted camping memories as the keenest of my senses brought them in deep again and then in a bright flash of day, the whole Pacific was gone.

Eric Clapton was on board with us in the Fairlane as we drove. Derek and the Dominos belted out the classic "Layla," with the beautiful soft keyboard instrumental ending it all; it ended the same way every time; it was amazing. How did he do it? There was the slow bleed of the guitar that quietly faded in and took it all over. It was such a sweet song that accompanied my driving dream.

East of the Pacific Range, as I awoke momentarily, we encountered the August brown Northern California hills; giant, golden, short-haired pit-bull-skin hills. They appeared to have been formed by the drop of some giant ruffled pit-bull-skin blanket. I imagined a giant Taboo waking up and turning to confront us on the winding roads, almost like Clifford, the red cartoon dog, turning our little car with the surfboard on top over with her nose and then pounding away to go look for Sal Caprissi elsewhere.

"He isn't here," I said to the giant imaginary dog outside of the car window. "He went back to Massachusetts two years ago, regretfully, without you. I'm sorry. It was probably my fault."

Taboo was upset at me. If it wasn't for me, Caprissi would still be with her, running in random apple orchards and lying in the cool, late-summer breezes of rural Massachusetts, both of them scratching their ears in the Dracut meadows and watching the puffy-shaped clouds blow by.

We got into Sunnyvale, at the bottommost part of the San Francisco Bay, right next to the heart of Silicon Valley around nine thirty at night. Roni, my friend from Lowell High and UMass, and her friend Elizabeth from San Jose (and Elizabeth's basset hound, Cloey) were at the house anxiously waiting for us. We were the three weary travelers that had called ahead with our mad plans just a few days before. For this big trip, we had called ahead and asked everyone we knew, all of our past acquaintances who were all spread across our great continent, if they might have a place for us to stay for a night or two.

CHAPTER 4

The girls had made dinner for us: baked chicken, wild brown rice, fruit salad, and pumpernickel bread. As we sat there around Roni's kitchen table and talked into the calm California night, we wondered aloud where we were really going and what we were leaving behind. We tried to explain to the girls why we had just up and left Southern California in the manner that we had. We were out of our gourds. Part of *my* reasoning, of course, was the whole Colette thing. We talked and talked and all the while dreamed in table conversation about what we all intended to do once we got to Europe. We were going to make music videos.

From Roni's kitchen table, I suddenly looked around to find Declan, for now he was gone.

On the side of the room, away from the dinner table, Declan was bouncing around in a late-night fit of rejuvenated energy, already aching to move on. He was road restless, he said, as he yelled over to the rest of us who still sat around the table talking. That was Declan—he loved everything about the moment—but now he couldn't sit still for we had started talking about Europe again. Declan screamed that he couldn't wait until the morning when we could push onward. This was the most incredible journey of a lifetime!

But what if the three of us had just made the biggest mistake of our lives?

Lucas and I told the girls what had happened at the going away party back in Huntington Beach, which was already a few days behind us. We caught three guys stealing our beer off of our back porch cooler. On Lucas's first alert of the raid of our cooler, the three of us ran out the front porch door, running down the back alley across the street and cornered the three bandits in the dark. They were our parallel lives, I thought. We cornered them in a dead-end garage door cul-de-sac. I confronted one of them dead-on as the other two threw full bottles of beer at me; they were whizzing by our heads like giant cocktail missiles. Just then, the guy I had cornered went into a roundhouse kick and hit me square in the chest, knocking me on my ass. Ooompff! . . . And how I tried to get back up and give him a roundhouse kick in response, remembering my Nashua karate lesson days with Zane and the maddening rain, but I failed to connect with the guy and landed square on my ass again!

I lay there on the dark alley ground thinking, *Oh no, maybe this is where I get my nose broken!* Like the time it happened in the cold, icy driveway of a fraternity night brawl at UMass, someone just kicking at my face on the ground while I lay on the bottom of the pile.

But these three guys were more frightened than I was, and with me on the ground, they ran by all of us, right out of the alleyway. Declan talked of the sheer comedy of all of life after watching me fall. He laughed in the alleyway at me, holding his stomach and falling with his back against a garage door. He forgot about everything else during that moment.

On the way out of the alley, we all laughed in relief when Lucas spotted the getaway car just a few houses down from our dilapidated porch. Lucas had seen them arrive in the car, so he knew what it looked like, he told Roni and Elizabeth. But the beer bandits were nowhere to be seen. Their car, however, sat in the dark on the curbside. Opening the hood of their car, Declan immediately went to work and pulled the distributor cap off while Lucas disconnected all of those blue wires that go to the spark plugs. With our work done, Declan slammed the hood and wiped his hands clean while Lucas carried the wiring with him back up to our porch.

"This is great!" Declan screamed. He told Roni and Elizabeth, "It was the next morning that one of the guys had to come back with the tow truck! Lucas and I stood on the front porch laughing at the guy!"

"The guy flipped us the bird," Lucas added while he chuckled.

"Hope you win the big one!" Declan yelled back to the guy as the poor soul just sat in the tow truck looking at them both. "Karma will get you every time!"

Back in high school, Roni was a cheerleader and had been the girlfriend of one of my high school friends. She always had a boyfriend through high school, and come to think of it, even college. And, of course, everyone was always secretly falling all over the cheerleaders in high school; they were beautiful, all of them. Roni was the prettiest of them all with the kindest of eyes; she never seemed to be down, I thought. She had like this weird sense of confidence, like she knew how life was going to turn out in the end—an eternal positive attitude—it was always going to turn out perfect for her. This glass of life was more than half-full.

Ah, the cheerleaders. Back in high school, Jerry Russo had me laughing all over myself as he teased the cheerleaders while taking a test in art history class one day. He showed me a question on the test and how he had answered it, just to be funny.

"Who is Ra?" the question asked (we were studying early Egyptian art and culture).

"THE GOD OF THE CHEERLEADERS!" was his answer.

Seeing this written answer on his test, I broke out into crazy laughter in the middle of class. Jerry laughed aloud with me. The teacher came over and pulled both of our tests and that was the end of it all. We both got Fs.

"No more conventional jobs!" Declan yelled to us from Roni's living room. He was back to bouncing around.

"No more endless nightclub scenes off of Beach Boulevard! No more paying five-dollar cover charges to be suffocated in cigarette smoke, beer-drenched carpets, and deafening music!" Lucas added. "How can you meet anybody that way?"

In Southern California, we had all been victims of this pitiful nightclub existence. There didn't seem to be any other way for shy nerdy guys to meet someone, so we went to that slaughterhouse every weekend night. Snaggletooth the DJ played the latest '80s stuff while our friend Brian Kelly shrieked the corn dog whistle in the corner at passersby. He'd tell us that if the girls turned to look his way while he shrieked that whistle, they were certainly corn dogs!

Everyone always seemed so desperate to find a girlfriend in these places, but nice girls didn't go there! Hah! If they did, it was by mistake. Declan admitted that he wouldn't miss these clubs any, but would sure miss the great sound of KROQ that Snaggletooth always seemed to play from her booth. KROQ was Declan's and this other friend, Vandy Vanderkampf's, favorite radio station. KROQ boasted the new sound of alternative rock that was slowly taking over the eighties. Declan told us he'd also miss KROQ's morning Southern California surf report, for he loved to surf, especially when he was supposed to be working. He had an outside sales job, selling ad space for the *Daily Pilot,* but he managed to get a few hours in every day on the surfboard, the same surfboard that was now bound to the Fairlane roof, without the *Daily Pilot* ever knowing anything about it.

We talked and talked around Roni's table that night. It was around twelve thirty in the morning when we all decided it was time to finally sleep. Declan, Lucas, and I, just like the night before at Zane's, slowly found our respective spaces to crash, either on Roni's living room couch or her floor while Elizabeth (and her dog Cloey) headed home. The girls both had to work in the morning. Hah! They had to work!

We all agreed that night that if we ever came back this way, Lucas Coppens, Declan Brady, and me, that we would have to all have dinner with Roni and Elizabeth again. Maybe we would have great stories to share about our great journey throughout the romantic European continent. Maybe we'd all be married someday.

Morning came quickly. Lifting an eyelid, I caught Roni trying to slip out quietly to work at eight thirty without trying to wake us. She worked as a sales manager for one of the big hotel chains (either the Marriott or the Hilton) and had to be there by nine. From the front door, Roni whispered to me across the great space of her living room as I still lay on her couch—"Good-bye, Mike!" Her warm smile brought a smile back to my groggy face as she told me in loud whispers to help ourselves to breakfast and showers, but to be sure to lock the door on our way out! And then, just like that, she was gone.

Before we left that morning, though, Lucas, Declan, and I ran a couple of miles through the Sunnyvale neighborhoods to get in one more short morning workout before our next stop. Then I left Roni a thank-you note on the same table that we had crowded around the night before. I noticed that the table had been completely cleared of the wineglasses and beer bottles that we had left all over the place the night before. In my note, I thanked her again for the dinner and everything.

It was ten in the morning now. Our next stop was San Pablo, which was a town just due east of the San Francisco Bay. San Pablo was where one of Declan's Ohio State friends, Mary, now lived. It would only take us a little over an hour to get to her house, a very short trip in the grand scheme of things, but we had to stop and see her just the same, because after Mary, there would be no more friendly faces until Aspen.

We all secretly hoped that the money we had each carefully saved and took with us would hold out throughout our entire journey, wherever we all may end up. Before quitting our jobs . . . before we left Huntington Beach, we had carefully plotted this course across country. It was a crazy zigzag route that included a lot of our families and our friends; there were some college buddies too—just about anyone who might take us in. Lucas had graduated from Kansas, KU; Declan graduated from Ohio State; and I had graduated from UMass. We were giving ourselves some time to get to Boston; actually about a month, and there were even two weddings to go to—one that was along the way—Lucas's sister in Aspen and then my friend Billy's in Lowell. After Billy's wedding, we planned to jump on a big aluminum cylinder all loaded up with jet fuel and fly across the great Atlantic Ocean. Our tickets to London would only be one-way tickets, of course, for we never knew if we would ever make it back.

And from London, who knows . . . We needed to find ourselves in this beautiful life. Maybe we would get jobs in the music video business, or television, or movies because of our collective Hollywood experience. Maybe we would go to Amsterdam, or maybe Munich. If things got so bad, we could go straight to the Greek Isles and drink ouzo and lay on the beach with beautiful women in the warm Mediterranean sun. Maybe it would be like the *Endless Summer* documentary; we would chase the sun, and it could always be warm. I would write about everything we did; I would record the whole journey in a crazy journal. We were destined to find happiness if we persevered. I imagined that there had to be a formula for happiness, because life was full of formulas. If you followed the formula, everything could be pretty easy. We'd forgive everyone who had ever wronged us or who had never given us a chance if we did ever make it. All of my writing, all of our ideas, all of our crazy scripts, all of our poetry and song lyrics, even the "You Can't Harpoon-a Generic Tun-a" song Eddie Kinsley and I wrote—everything would be published someday. We were leaving Hollywood to invent Hollywood somewhere else. There was so much irony in the whole mouthful of it. And Declan had all of the reckless ambition crazy luck that might allow us to stumble into it all. Lucas was more balanced than Declan and I; he could reel us back in if we ever got into any real trouble along the way. And that was the plan . . . so we thought.

"Did you know that about one in every three people in Los Angeles is writing a screenplay?" was always the chatter in the west. It wouldn't break me, though, for a great screenplay was still in us all, I knew it!

Colette was gone. I had lost weight over it. I discovered that I was down about twenty pounds in just three months after weighing myself on Roni's bathroom scale after our morning run. The scale needle barely registered 140 pounds.

Weeks before we left Orange County, I had secretly camped outside the hotel where

Colette worked. Quietly lurching in my Subaru, I tried to catch a glimpse of her one last time. Was there someone else? Maybe I would jump from the car and beg her to take me back if she appeared, just like in the movies. Was I stalking her? I just didn't want to let her go. Why had she dumped me?

But Colette never appeared in the hotel parking lot that day. Fate had decided it all for me. I was left with no other choice but to leave the place that reminded me of her, to move on. I had to leave Southern California. I was too consumed with it all. I had to forget it.

I had been in love one other time during a teenage summer in New Hampshire, but I was a kid then; I was only seventeen then. Everything was different now; the sadness had left a lot quicker back then. But this feeling now . . . Nothing had ever hurt this bad.

Declan's surfboard had survived the night on the roof of the car without anyone messing with it. The bungie cord was taut and in place, and we pressed on to San Pablo. The waves of the inner depths of our great North American continent, cornstalks and grass fields, were now ahead of us; we would surf for the next 4,000 miles. The odometer read 69,968 miles in Sunnyvale. We had traveled 468 miles already. I put $14.70 in the gas tank for 13.2 gallons of gas. Numbers meant everything to me, for they really helped to pass the time.

Going north on the 880 Freeway we saw three guys our age in the car right next to us with shirts and ties on. Hah! This was a foreign concept to us all now, an alternate world that we had just exited from, a broken mirror image of the immediate past. It didn't make too much sense. Everyone had to work a shirt-and-a-tie job just for money to fuel their dreams, doing things they didn't want to do, wasting the best part of the day. We were never going to wear a shirt and tie again, we vowed, because white shirts and dress ties were symbols of the eight-to-five business world where you always had a boss. We were artists. Artists didn't have to wear white shirts and tight neckties.

"Who-hoo! No more conventional jobs!" Declan shouted our road mantra.

Lucas rolled down the window and shrieked his characteristic ear-piercing shriek again. The three lost souls looked over at us briefly and then continued to talk amongst themselves in their moving car bubble. We were no great distraction to them; perhaps we didn't even exist!

Lucas had worked as an engineer for the government. Dedicated as he was, he really hated those few years that he did it. He used to wake up first thing in the morning and realize after a great sleep, "Crap! I'm back here again!" This thought of his was so funny to me. Work was such a downer that he hated to even exist. Naked on the door stoop of life, Lucas imagined himself as an alien in an objectionable place where buttoned-down necks with loud ties choked his freedom. But now he was finally free. Like Moses, I guess, he had been spared; the fleeting Fairlane was his basket of freedom, and he was now floating with the current of the river, hoping to come aground in some new exotic place and be given a second chance.

We pulled up to Declan's friend Mary's house and saw her in the open garage. She worked meticulously on the freehand lettering of a sign for one of her customers, UHAUL. Mary painted signs all summer, Declan told us, and taught elementary school in the winter.

"Declan!" Mary cried and ran to him, giving Declan a huge hug after putting down her brush on the long prep table at the side of her garage.

"Why, hello, Mary!" he smiled with that big Declan Brady smile, all of those teeth showing again.

Mary, with her own booming and heavy laugh, brought the three of us immediately inside and had us all take a seat at her wooden kitchen table. She talked quickly, running to the refrigerator to pull out four cold bottles of Coors beer. It wasn't even noon yet. She sat down across from us all, bubbles and happy, recanting her past shenanigans with Declan at Ohio State. After graduation, she had crossed the great Northwest across the plains by herself . . . with no sleep and in the vast hours of an approaching dawn, she came across the Great Salt Lake in Utah much the same way as the Mormons did, not knowing at first from a distance whether it was water or a dancing hallucination of light bouncing off of the desert floor. Mary was gifted with stories, talking on and on from our moment of arrival, from the seagulls of Utah to her motorcycle daredevil grandmother who lived in Florida and who slept with a forty-five under her pillow. She laughed and laughed and hugged Declan like he was her little brother.

CHAPTER 5

Mary was a big, tall girl. She had a beautiful face and reminded me of Mama Cass. "What do you mean, I'm a big girl?" she laughed at Declan. "What do you mean by that?"

We drank more beers as Mary told us more stories. Mary and Declan and another of their friends, Max, from Ohio State, had gone on spring break to Hawaii their senior year. They went rafting on the ocean while they were out there. Mary laughed as she told us, "Declan and Max weren't afraid of sharks because they told me that my butt was dragging deeper in the raft than their butts were, and I would be the first (and the last) to go, because I was a big enough meal for any great white!" She laughed. "Can you believe they said that!"

"The sharks would be full after Mary!" Declan laughed aloud with her.

After drinking for about three hours, we headed out with Mary to the San Pablo BART (Bay Area Rapid Transport) station. The train took us under the water of the great bay to the beautiful tip of San Francisco. In the city, we rode the cable cars to Chinatown and then down to Fisherman's Wharf where we looked out over the bay at a moving barge whose deck for one moment held so perfectly the abandoned prison of Alcatraz. But Alcatraz escaped, slipping off the back of the barge, back to her isolated island rock perch, alone and cold. A yellow sailboat, glistening in the afternoon sun, came toward us from afar, cutting zigzag across the ever-widening gap between the barge and the prison. Alcatraz seemed so close to this incredible city, but the white-crested ripping currents and the supposed shark-infested waters, increased the distance by a lifetime. No one had ever escaped from Alcatraz and its ghostly walls, walls that now welcomed curious tourist travelers. I tried to look out from those walls one time when I was out there, as if I too were a forgotten ghost, looking past the choppy white water at the big hilly skyscraper city, dreaming of a day when I would run free again.

On the wharf I watched the countless, nameless, and sorrowful faces of the homeless pass us by; some of them with bitter determination in their look; some gazing at the dead space right in front of their eyes. We walked around them, tourists and businesspeople shunned them, as if ignoring God Himself. There were so many of them here; they all had such desperate and tired eyes; different faces all with such sad passion, all of them isolated in their own prisons, all of them seemingly so lonely, so forgotten. Why were they all here? Why not somewhere warmer? Or did they not know? Were they ill? Were they schizophrenics who fell off their medication and had just been abandoned by life? Maybe some had been people who had come here chasing a dream and had just run out of unstoppable West to move against, coming to a dead halt at the Pacific Ocean and finding nothing more but those icy, choppy waters. Some wandered aimlessly like driftwood now, abandoned by society. This had been the beat of Kerouac's *Dean Moriarty* and *Sal Paradise*, who, in my mind, still paced the wooden docks around us asking for loose change. I imagined them continually traversing these aching city hills. And I thought on how this big, mysterious city with all of its ghostly chills had swallowed many. My eyes were an open movie camera recording the speed of life now; there was a living video unwinding before me. I watched the open-ended script tell its story, people darting everywhere while the homeless moved at a slower speed. There were thousands of stories to be told, all of them going off in all different directions, and I wondered in amazement how anything could ever have a common end.

Every life pulsating, walking on our earth today and all the way back to the beginning of time, all had these plot points, I thought, like a script, points that turned our living souls in certain directions, ones that ultimately set the beat of the rest of our lives. Like any living being, I could see all the points in hindsight, after deep reflection, after a great expanse of time, but why was it so hard in the moment to find them? To identify the one point that will change and define our very being, to see it in the now. Maybe this walk on the wharf was the turning point.

We left to go eat ice cream cones, and I immediately felt the pain of past months-gone-by kidney stones. I chowed down a giant salted pretzel with caked on mustard from a street vendor, and we drank more beer. At least we were eating right, I thought. Through all of the San Francisco street madness, Declan's friend Mary continued with her endless stories. The chill in the air of this mysterious city still wrapped around us as we walked along, taking in everything. Mary's voice was coming in and going out of range; it was all a part of a dream. I watched beautiful women in business suits on Market Street; I saw a small group of people on the corner at Union Square speaking French; a black man was playing an alto saxophone near the small park there; he looked just like the great wailer, The Big Man Clarence Clemons himself. He motioned to the tourists (who kept on snapping pictures of him) with the bell of his horn to feed his weathered open and empty sax case with their silver coin.

"I Left My Heart in San Francisco." The sweet sound of the sax swooned in the swirling air around us with a background hum of Mary's voice.

"If you want to take a picture, you've got to put some money in my case," the sax player stopped his song abruptly and pleaded to the French tourists beside us. "Don't any of you people realize that there ain't no such thing as a free lunch!" He looked over to us and then rolled his eyes in the direction of the tourists before puckering his lips again and blowing on the mouthpiece one more time.

Wasn't this the first law of thermodynamics? How did the sax player know about this law . . . "*No such thing as a free lunch?*" I had learned this law in college physics, and it had to do with energy going from one place to another. Maybe he had learned it in physics too.

Lucas threw a handful of his loose change into the poor man's case.

"God bless you, Lucas!" the jazzman tipped his hat to my friend.

From there, we took a bus to the center of town and then boarded BART again and headed back to Mary's in San Pablo. I slept in the train. I heard Mary's voice in my half dreams as I slept. These were the broken speed bump dreams that had been left there from our ride all of the way up the California coast. Colette was about 400 miles behind me now. Huntington Beach was gone. The distance was starting to settle in. No more dress shirts and striped fabric ties, I dreamt. No more disgusting break rooms littered with cigarettes and coffee cups. In the dream, the break room was empty. Broken images crashed in with Mary's mumbling voice. A homeless man we had seen at the BART train station who sat huddled in a fetal position with a worn plaid blanket bundled around him changed into a giant caterpillar in a cocoon, Kafka-like, and I dreamt that I was desperately trying to wake up the caterpillar. The noise of the train was loud and coming in. Would we ever find our way under the bay?

Going up the stairs of the station back to our car on the other side of the bay, I thought of Colette's song.

The candle
Needs oxygen to burn
Takes in everything to learn
To grow

The wax begins to soften
As the grains fall through the glass
Impressionable to something
When the wind quiets to pass
Or blow

Its candor
A plaid chair made of whicker
Soft light may always flicker
Although

The wax turns into liquid
Intrigued without a doubt
Impressionable as something
I tipped it to pour it out
To know

Its tallow
The rising tide is not forgotten
In a mold for twisted cotton
And so

The candle
Needs oxygen to burn
Gives us light in her return
And we grow

The four years since my college graduation had come and gone like a song through Billboard's Top 40 charts. Everyone always said that the older you get, the faster the years go by. At eighty years old, a year is one eightieth of your life, whereas at four years old, a year is a whopping one-fourth of your life. Einstein talked about this. A train traveling at the speed of light doesn't allow you to enjoy the scenery at all, and everything goes by in a flash, and when you get back to your original destination, those who saw you off are gone forever.

I wrote down in my notebook . . .

A life and a song,
The comparison wrong,
To view them from the outside we see,
That when a song ends,
It can be played again,
A life can't be.

So maybe life was more like a movie script then. A song seemed way too short to compare it to.

It was late afternoon in San Pablo, and I began to notice that I was losing my hair quickly now. There were falling clumps in Mary's rusted shower drain. I scratched my head and thought how beautiful Colette was. She was the most beautiful girl I had ever met.

I thought of her constantly. I wanted to physically touch her again; hold her hand and feel the warm rush of life in her. The light of God himself touched and highlighted the space she occupied; it was such a stark contrast to the impending darkness of the unknown that lay ahead. Ah, Colette—was there anything ever more beautiful? My heart remembered, trembled in the shower, how nothing could ever be more perfect than the night we saw James Taylor at the Irvine Amphitheatre. If I could have just that moment back, to live it forever, there would be nothing more that I would ever long for again.

CHAPTER 6

I woke up on Mary's couch at eight the next morning from a deep sleep. Sleep was the great escape from everything. It was August 28, 1984, the fourth day of our journey. Mary had prepared fresh squeezed orange juice and sliced avocados in the kitchen and directed us to her outside patio table. Once we were seated, she brought out three plates of scrambled eggs, with bacon and thickly buttered toast. A large, potted, jade-colored cactus cast a shadow toward us from the far end of the wooden deck. My head ached from the day before. But the orange juice began to revitalize me. It was life to me. I wanted to swig it down so it would pour over the sides of my mouth and drip off of my chin onto my T-shirt.

"Nectar of the gods!" Declan exclaimed, downing his large glass of juice quickly, and then jumping up and instantly heading back to the house on the hunt for more.

From the kitchen window, Mary talked to us as we ate. She talked about wine-tasting tours in Napa, forty minutes north of San Pablo. "They make you take the tour before you can taste test at Christian Brothers," she told us. That was a bad idea for Mary, for all she really wanted was to drink the wine.

Looking beyond the large, jaded cactus toward the smoky emerald city of San Francisco that hung like a mirage on the horizon, I thought back to all of the lonely souls down by Fisherman's Wharf that we had encountered the day before. The sax man had said to Lucas, "God bless you," when Lucas threw him his loose change. He called out to Lucas by name . . . like he knew him as if Lucas had been wearing his name on his shirt sleeve or something. Lucas and the sax man were brothers, two kindred souls in a chance meeting on the sidewalk of life.

"Do you think that the homeless are closer to God?" I asked Lucas.

"Some are, I guess," Declan answered. "They have no one else to turn to."

I ate my cut mango slices with the avocado before eating the scrambled eggs. This was a theory I had picked up on proper food combining from crazy Delores who I worked with at the Southern California circuit board factory. She was such an attractive lady for being over forty but was kind of nuts and always preached crazy diets; she believed in crystals, wind chimes, and the signs of astrology. She was an honest-to-goodness hippie girl that had been thrown forward out of the sixties simply because the sixties had to get ready for the seventies and the eighties. Poor Delores didn't know how to leave that era behind. But her theories on food combining seemed believable, at least, and it had really helped me, I think, when I had to pass kidney stones because I didn't have any health insurance. Dolores read that the key to good health was that fruits must always be eaten first, lest they ferment in your stomach on top of the rest of the stuff and never get digested properly.

She was a polytheist. "I believe in any deity but God," Dolores used to say to me, "because that would give too many born-agains the excuse to talk to me!" She was high on herself, and I guess it's okay to be that way if you are healthy and always practicing proper food combining techniques and you have lots of gods to save you.

"For the homeless, it is their only way out of this mess," Declan responded to me again, coming back from the kitchen with a third full glass of his God nectar.

At the circuit board factory, Amid, the Palestinian engineer, would get into discussions with Dolores about how he wasn't afraid to kill a person. He saw life differently than the rest of us. Life had been cruel to his people and his family in Palestine; they had lost their whole hillside farm full of olive trees when the Six-Day War between Israel and Egypt ended. They had gone from wealth to poverty in one quick swat. Because of this, Amid was angry all of the time, and the rest of us were afraid. Even Delores was afraid of Amid.

But unlike Amid, I was one of the many who absolutely feared death; it would always scare me.

When I was a senior in high school, we saw a poor old lady get killed at the Bridge Street Bridge. It had been in the dead of winter when it happened. My old friends Gordon Scott, Billy Caldwell, and I were walking home, just coming off the icy bridge into Centralville, and we saw this car whack her. The hard impact sent the lady flying about twenty feet before she landed on the sidewalk in the freezing footprints of others. It was awful. Gordy, Billy, and I ran to her side, but she was lifeless. She was lying there with blood coming out of the side of her mouth. I couldn't help but think as I stood there how she was someone's grandmother and no one at this moment but us three strangers knew that she was dead. It was this chilling thought that stayed with me for a very long time. Just like that, she was gone.

In San Pablo, we sat in the beautiful California sun having breakfast, looking out over the lower hills of Berkeley, the glimmering mackerel scale water and the distant purple city across the bay. I adjusted my vision, like a TV camera zoom lens, with the spiny big-armed cactus first in focus and then out of focus as my gaze went beyond it and rendered it a blur. I was in and out of the conversation taking place on Mary's patio. It was already eleven in the morning and Declan and Lucas were discussing our plan for moving on. Mary would come with us to Lake Tahoe it was decided.

Jeff Beck's song, "Cause We've Ended as Lovers," played from somewhere beyond Mary's kitchen, and the sound actually stopped time to overtake me. It was a beautiful song, an electric guitar instrumental, with the guitar crying, throbbing out like a baby. I knew this song well, for I owned the *Blow by Blow* album. The song title alone said it all, and that was fine; for Jeff Beck's version had no lyrics, unlike the original that Stevie Wonder had written for his sweet Syreeta. I heard Jeff Beck's guitar try to sob those same haunting lyrics. Lost love was a crazy, winding labyrinth of emotion through the course of falling sand grain time that we all shared for someone different; it tore at the core of our very beings all in the same way. The pain kept us prisoner until we could find a way out.

I loved the sound of the electric guitar when it cried. Carlos Santana was another great, and his song "Europa" did the same thing to me. How did these guys write this stuff? Where did the inspiration come from? Beautiful music moved everyone's soul, a common chord within us all.

All of my rock-and-roll albums sat packed up in an apple crate back in Newport Beach. I had a number of packed up boxes that I couldn't take with me, the balance of my earthly possessions, all sitting at Ingrid's house waiting for the UPS delivery guy to ship them back to Lowell. Ingrid had let the three of us stack all of our boxes in the pebbled entryway of her bungalow right there on the Newport Beach peninsula. Lucas had learned after calling Ingrid on Monday that the day had passed without UPS ever showing up.

"Maybe Jesse can help us and find out why the UPS driver never showed," Lucas said to us. Jesse was another of our old roommates who stayed behind in Huntington Beach.

We had all lived next door to Ingrid in Newport Beach but moved at the start of the summer to Huntington Beach because the owners of our beach castle rental wanted the summers for themselves. When we had first moved to the coastal castle in Newport Beach in 1983, Declan, in his friendly way, knocked on Ingrid's door and invited her up to our place for spaghetti. It had become a weekly thing where we would invite close friends over and cook up all of this pasta for mass consumption because it was cheap. Friends would bring beer and dessert. We got to throwing a new item in the sauce each time we made it; one week avocadoes, another week a little beer, a third week raisins, just about anything that was edible. Ingrid came on the night that Declan decided to throw an avocado pit into the sauce to see if anyone would find it. It was too big to choke on so, he assumed, it was all safe; and Ingrid found it. That night, Ingrid told us the great stories of her long life, filling the evening with the colors that spanned sixty-five years. After that, she was our friend forever. She was of Latvian heritage and had lived in Newport Beach as a professional painter. She sold in the local galleries after studying art at UCLA, painting beautiful local landscapes fused sometimes with industrial complexity. After years of painting on the Newport Peninsula, Ingrid developed some sort of respiratory condition from breathing in all of that oil-based paint and had to give it all up. The corridors of her home were lined with her works; the bright blues, the pinks, some landscapes intermingled with civilization's mechanisms and gears; sharp lines against soft edges, turning wheels against ebbing tides, the faces of the Back Bay, the lonely oil derricks. Some of her stuff took me back to high school art history again with Jerry Russo and the cheerleader god Ra. Ingrid's stuff was reminiscent of the impressionist works by Guillaumin. Some looked like the pond lilies of Monet. My favorite work of Ingrid's was a painting of the old Newport Beach fish cannery sitting up on that rectangular pier with the boats docked in the foreground and the sunlight highlighting the Western Cannery Company logo in a large iron red circle, a circle high on the structure. I saw it clearly in life, the orange brown reflection off of the old tin roof and the mustard yellows of the building. Ingrid once gazed at it from the other side of the peninsula at dusk in a moment of time. She painted the greens and the light blues of the floating boats; a white yacht, the Juanaloa dwarfed a fisherman's dingy in the foreground. The water in the bay was a green, white, blue, and brown reflection that appeared to be shimmering like multicolored ice.

Ingrid was a young soul in an old person's body. I once imagined her in her beautiful youth, the wrinkles and the gray hair gone, a young Grace Kelly or Ingrid Bergman; it was a snapshot stolen from the past. She once had been young like us too, and we too would be old like her someday. Ingrid told us on the night of the spaghetti dinner that the mind is an eternal spirit and every day is another chance to live something beautiful for in the history of time; a life goes by quicker than the burning of a match.

Alan and Lisa lived below us at the coastal castle and complained to the landlord on the night of our big dinner. They cried that we were making too much noise. They always called the landlord on us. Declan called Alan "Mark" all the time. Declan told us he called him this because he looked like someone who should be called Mark. Alan had to correct Declan and tell him that his name was not "Mark" but "Alan."

"Okay, sorry, Mark," Declan replied.

Alan and Lisa called the landlord in Los Angeles just about every weekend after that to complain about us running up and down those back steps. Alan was a nurse, and Lisa was beautiful, and I never could understand how someone as toxic as Alan could ever be with her.

"Okay, sorry, Mark," Declan replied each weekend until the end of May when we had to move to Huntington Beach for the summer. And here it was the end of August and, God-willing, we would never see Mark again.

I picked fresh mission figs from the fig tree in Ingrid's backyard just days before we left Southern California. I had even brought some to Colette when we met at the Rusty Pelican Restaurant in Irvine that last time. I had finally gotten a hold of her and convinced her to see me. I looked into those big green eyes and wondered about it all.

Collette told me that night that she had a new boyfriend. It took me down. It made me wonder why I had ever come out to California at all. In my old vision where I had looked out toward the dark west through the screened bedroom window on those humid New England summer nights, the fireflies that once lit the bushes along the driveway below me were now nowhere to be found.

There was that very last vision of her. She was beautiful standing there, red plaid shirt and blue jeans, country like, the beautiful Orange County setting sun studying the perfect lines of her face. How I longed to touch those lips one more time just ever so softly with my index finger, to touch her beautiful cheeks as she closed her eyes gently, run the bridge of her perfect nose forever.

Back in the San Pablo kitchen, with her sewing machine, Mary closed up an armpit hole in the green long sleeve striped jersey that I had been wearing for three days now. I wore jeans, tennis shoes, no socks, and no underwear; I wanted to conserve my change of clothes for the long road ahead of us.

Lucas was firing up his Fairlane out in Mary's driveway. It was time to move. Mary crawled into the backseat of the car, moving the gift-wrapped cookbook that was illustrated with Norman Rockwell's paintings aside. It was a wedding gift that I needed to send from the road to Spooner and Bethany.

"That's a wedding gift that I'm going to send to some people back East as soon as we find a post office in Reno," I said apologetically to Mary.

"Ask Mike if he pulled it off of a wedding register," Declan said.

"No, I didn't pull it out of any wedding register! Everyone likes Norman Rockwell, don't they?" I asked Mary. "Shouldn't that count for something?"

"Well, I guess it's the thought that counts!" Mary said with a very big laugh looking up to the front seat at Lucas and Declan with her big rolling eyes.

"I think that's definitely one that might be regifted!" Declan chuckled, and then he rolled down the front window as we headed eastward on the freeway. "I'm on vacation," Declan laughed and yelled out at all of the moving people around us. He cracked the aluminum stem of a can of Coors Light, taken from a small cooler of beer beside him in the front seat, and proclaimed to the wind, "You can't fly with just one wing! We're on vacation!"

Lucas paid forty cents for the toll at the Vallejo Bridge and from there, we pushed toward the majestic Sierra Mountains and the high California state line.

Mary talked on as we traveled the winding 50 Freeway through the California Sierras and the El Dorado National Forest. She talked about hitting the casinos when we arrived; she would play it by ear; roll with the moment; pull the slots and play blackjack, and then she would hop a bus back to San Pablo when she ran out of casino cash. Our plan from Tahoe was to continue north to Reno and then on to Salt Lake City, leaving Mary and her sweet California life of teaching school and painting ice cream parlor windows in the Sausalito summertime behind. Someday, she would paint canvases of scrambled eggs and sliced mangos and avocados in the patio foothills of Berkeley, foothills that had been weak for the lost set of the *Summer of Love*.

Mary laughed when Declan reminded her of Max from Ohio State; Max the teddy bear. He lived in San Pablo for a while but had returned to Ohio back in March. Lucas and I had met Max back in January. Burly, curly Max always had an open twelve-ounce can of beer in his hand. Declan even said it was that way back in college too.

"The guy just wouldn't look right if he was empty-handed," Declan said laughing. "'You can't fly with one wing!' was his signature announcement every time he opened up a new can of beer! Good ole Max!"

Mary reminded us of Max's incredible pot pipe, and its uncanny will to always seek out and find its rightful owner—Max. The story was that back in Columbus during college, Max was walking through some random meadow by the Old Mill; he was high, of course. It was a place that he had never been to before, and he stumbled on the lost pot pipe that he hadn't seen since Akron (which was hours away) more than two years before. Max absolutely believed that this pipe had some magical will to find him. It was so powerful; otherwise, this random appearance never would have happened. So before he returned to Ohio from San Pablo in March, Max purposely left the pot pipe with Mary to test its will again. Mary now handed the pipe to Declan to bring it back to Max in Columbus. Declan laughed and tucked it away with his things, promising Mary that he would deliver the magical pot pipe when we got that far.

I looked out the backseat window at a single oak tree atop the huge, brown grassy hills of disappearing California while Bruce Springsteen's "Thunder Road" played on the cassette deck. Just like those summer nights on Christian Hill back in 1977 when Richie's eight track tape deck blared the sound out of the open windows of his green Mustang as we rolled the back roads of Dracut, the harmonica slowly opened that all-too-familiar tune.

Springsteen was on tour now. It was an election year; Reagan was on his second term running against Minnesota's Walter "Fritz" Mondale. Mondale had selected Geraldine Ferraro, the first female candidate for vice president ever in our history as his running mate. "Fritz and Titz" was the conservative bark. I felt bad about never registering for an absentee ballot, but I had no idea where I was going to be on November 6th. Besides, none of the three of us (Lucas, Declan, and I) had a house key anymore.

Through the high Sierras I drifted in and out of my visions of *Dean Moriarty* and *Sal Paradise* and wondered if Neal Cassidy and Jack Kerouac, with all of their back and forth, to and from San Francisco, had traveled this very same road we were on, maybe even in Kerouac's *Dharma Bums*.

More oak trees on grassy hills soon became pine trees on rugged mountains as we made our way slowly toward Lake Tahoe. On the approach to the beautiful deep lake, we looked down on it in all of its blueness from our higher ground, Tahoe was an Ingrid painting of just nature alone, frigid alpine blue surrounded by office calendar mountains. People were parasailing too, sky skiing over and around the lake. It was a real live Monet of a later day, with the freelancers' orange chutes the only unnatural thing visible to my naked eye. Although it was now late in the day, the sun was still hot and the smell of the tall Sierra pines through our open windows took over my senses.

"What do you think the distance is across the lake?" Lucas asked us aloud.

"Probably thirty miles," Mary guessed.

"Well, the lake itself is about twenty-three miles long, but from where we are all the way out to the tops of those mountains on the other side is probably about fifty miles," Lucas said.

"The naked eye can't see for fifty miles, can it?" Declan asked.

"Of course, it can," Lucas said. "The moon is surely more than fifty miles away!"

"Are you sure about that?" Declan asked him. "You know, fifty miles is an awful long way."

Declan had to go swimming in Tahoe. It was one of the many goals that he had penciled out for himself in his little notebook before leaving Huntington Beach. He had to swim in every famous body of water we drove by or crossed; he had to get in every tourist's family picture he possibly could; he could never wear a tie again; he could never carry more than one key on his person ever again. And so his list went on and on.

We pulled off the road as we got closer to the lake and let Declan run down to the water like a crazy animal to do his thing.

"Aren't you guys going swimming?" Mary turned to Lucas and me in the car.

"It's too cold, Mary!" Lucas laughed in his characteristic big smile laugh that told you everything about why we both thought that her friend Declan was actually crazy.

When Declan returned about fifteen minutes later, we saw him coming up the road from afar with a pretty girl. He had met her on the raft about 100 feet offshore. Declan came up to the car with her and introduced her as "Gilda," although I embarrassingly called her "Glenda" twice. Gilda was from Oregon; she worked in Tahoe as a waitress, and Declan told us that she would be going to school in Boston in January of '85.

Declan had dragged poor Gilda off of the raft and back to shore and all the way up the small road to where we were parked just to get her to meet someone (me) from the Boston area. She had the look in her eyes of someone who didn't know why she was there; she had been taken hostage. There was a lot of awkward silence. This crazy maniac had just talked her off of her life raft and up this long wooded road, and she had followed him.

"Hey, Mike! Meet Gilda! Can you believe she is going to school in Boston! Boston College in January! Mike's from Boston, Gilda, I told you I was going to introduce you to someone from Boston! What do you think of that, Mike?"

Gilda stood there in the cold mountain air, shivering goose bumps, and after a few long minutes said to the three of us in the car, "Hi, nice to meet you. Good-bye!" and slowly turned back down the road to find comfort again on the cold floating raft out on the lake.

"Good-bye," we all said to Gilda, turning to Declan and shaking our heads as if to ask, "Why did you make her come all the way up to the car?"

"Hope you win the big one!" Declan called after the girl. Gilda, already a good ways back down the road, courteously half-turned to wave to us one last time.

"Poor thing!" Mary laughed.

"I think I must have freaked her out," Declan admitted, "But she sure was a cute one!"

We quickly found Caesar's Palace; it appeared like a giant lit beacon in the panoramic Nevada sky. It called out to Mary and all of us as if to say, "Bring me your money!" Inside the casino, we watched Mary for a few hours go crazy playing the slots, sometimes working two machines at the same time, with her bucket of quarters and big frame going seat to seat, pumping the machines continuously, with Mary always putting in five coins at a time. Declan, Lucas, and I were resolved not to spend any of our own money like this because of the simple notion that we might lose it all.

When Mary grew tired of pumping the bandits, she had us drive her over to Harrah's, where she was going to play blackjack for a few hours before catching the last bus back to San Pablo.

"Can't you guys stay for a while and gamble with me?" Mary begged.

"Sorry, Mary, but I'll send you a postcard from England!" Declan told her. "We really have to move on."

"Good-bye!" We left her sitting at a blackjack table. Mary talked away to the dealer and the other patrons as we walked toward the entrance. Her voice went from clear conversation, to a distinct murmur above the laughter, to eerie total deafening silence as the rest of the world around us once again filled with mad noise.

Before I walked out the casino door, I exchanged two single dollar bills for two silver dollars at the cashier window. I found a dollar slot machine close by the cashier and threw the first coin in. Spin, Good-bye. Before dropping the second one, I closed my eyes and visualized bells going off and coins pouring out of its greedy little mouth. I focused and pulled the large lever toward me. Spin, Cherries, Cherries, Orange, Nothing. Good-bye. It was seven o'clock.

We gunned the Fairlane and headed toward Reno. It was my turn to drive. Lucas had me pull over right outside of Tahoe so he could scale a roadside cliff that taunted him. I leaned against the car and watched him climb, taking in the quiet night.

Outside of Carson City, at another stop, Declan jumped atop the surfboard of our parked car for a chronicled photo opportunity.

Spin, Cherries, Cherries, Orange, Good-bye.

CHAPTER 7

Had I gone mad traveling across country with these two lunatics? Most twenty-six-year-olds were already settling into the sweet life by now . . . saving for a house; in a meaningful relationship with someone; working toward the future. Hah! But were they truly doing something they loved? You see, we didn't want to be like the oil derricks. They grind endlessly, work tirelessly, spending all of those minutes up and down, up and down, until the life that they are looking for eventually is sucked completely dry—and then life is gone.

Viewing the lakes and the valley below from the winding mountain road I noticed how the beautiful but forlorn terrain abruptly turned rust brown and dead as we got closer to the city. Carson City was exactly how I had envisioned it, a stereotypical western town. We arrived at dusk with the sun at our backs, just like Clint Eastwood did in the movies, and we drove through Carson City without stopping, lest we be ambushed again by the casinos and the one-armed bandits that hid in the shadowy hills around it.

I always loved this time of the day. Even the word "dusk" itself was not quite day and not quite night; it was a time of day when the western setting sun does funny things with the light from its low-to-the-horizon vantage point, making building façades wave dreamily at you and turn all different colors of purple and gold, as if you were driving on the set of an alien world, perhaps on Mars.

"Don't you think 'dusk' is a cool word?" I asked Declan and Luke.

Reno's casino lights lit up the eight o'clock sky as we passed straight through there too, with all of those ringing slots crying to reel us in, but our determination to lock with Interstate 80 and move on toward Utah would not waiver. Perhaps we'd drive all night until we hit Salt Lake City. We were suddenly alone. There were no friends or family to see until we got to Aspen now.

It was a great vast desert sky, and the music that we brought with us opened up that sky warmly with memories of the friends and the times that once had accompanied those familiar sounds; comfort flooded in from spaces unknown. There was an endless supply of cassette tapes in the car that really helped us pass through the many miles. Dave Mason's "Feelin' Alright" ripped the very heart right out of me; James Taylor sang about fire and rain and how Suzanne had committed suicide; Cat Stevens swam on the devil's lake. We tore across a silhouetted mountain range to our north while fiery bottomed clouds in a fading orange-to-gray sky crawled forever behind us. I experienced déjà vu moments where this whole trip had already been taken on a perfect day in a distant time.

A little bit further on in the night, I had Declan's small flashlight going in the backseat as I poured over the highlighted zigzag map of the trip ahead.

"Are we only just now in Lovelock?" I had to wonder why our journey of the past few hours had taken us barely a quarter of the way into Nevada. Declan was driving, and Lucas was asleep. If we wanted to be in Salt Lake City by the morning, we were going to have to take turns fighting off this angry sleep. Man, these were big states out here! Huge states to drive through if you didn't know anybody.

We stopped in a small Nevada casino town off of Interstate 80 to get gas, Winnemucca, Nevada. It was late. It was a true ghost town in my night of dreams. A few lonesome gamblers crossed a street under construction in front of us without even looking up to see the surfboard on the car. Declan shouted to me, "Who would ever live here and why?"

"Who would have put a pushpin in this section of the map?" he asked.

"Those that were probably born here," I replied calmly, talking like a zombie.

"But what about the first person who came here?"

"I don't know, maybe they came for the gold."

"Was there ever gold here?"

It surely looked like one of those painted red towns out of an old Clint Eastwood movie, maybe *High Plains Drifter*, or *The Outlaw Josey Wales*. I envisioned the building façades suddenly falling down behind the road construction and the moving night gamblers, throwing up a huge cloud of dust as the reinforced plywood-painted buildings crashed on the hard ground, exposing a full-on production crew, bright lights and a wide-open Utah sky hundreds of miles in the distance.

"This reminds me of *The Outlaw Josey Wales*," I said aloud.

"Yeah, where Clint spits right on the dog's head with his tobacco spit," Declan chuckled.

I took my shift at the wheel about midnight and was happily relieved by a refreshed Lucas about two in the morning. I crawled into the back of the comfortable Fairlane and stretched out as best I could.

Then it was suddenly four o'clock in the morning, and Declan and Lucas were waking my sprawled out carcass from the backseat of the car as they stood out on the shoulder of the road.

"You gotta see this, come on, wake up, Mike!" they said. "You'll be sorry if you don't."

Groggily I stepped out of the back into the open night air. There wasn't a human sound other than that of the soft wind in my eardrums for tens of hundreds of miles, and the incredible beauty of the lighted sky hit me with a cracking wake-up punch that lifted my senses to an everlasting high. It was a sky so completely illuminated by eons and eons of just arriving fresh starlight. I had never seen so many glimmering lights before. Every star ever identified by the history of mankind; every nebulous cloud; every faint light that had ever graced the face of our earth . . . all of it now stood above us in a complete canvas exhibit of the endless heavens. The vaporlike gases that formed the outer stretches of our galaxy dispersed among the stars in a cloudlike line. We stood out there in sheer amazement for at least a half hour, pivoting in circles as we looked up, our feet imprinting the salt flats that we stood on. When I tired of standing, I lay down on the desert floor. I identified the big sauce pan of the dipper and followed it across to Polaris like I was a little kid again. We guessed possible constellations; we discerned the distinct yellow light of planets compared to the blue light of the stars; we saw distant blinking satellites crossing the star dust and tens of shooting stars that dove toward the horizon all at once. This was the night sky before the electric light had ever been invented; the sky of the great oceans and the Sahara; the sky of Antarctica and Siberia; the sky of our past; the sky where men of long ago sat around crackling fires and talked of what it all might be . . . Those crazy blinking lights that came out every night and revolved around that single shimmering light that pointed due north; these were the night fires of the gods.

I made a wish on a shooting star
I made a wish in a speeding car

People in jars
Stay away from the stars
'Cause they're airtight

I wondered if where we now lay was the Great Salt Lake Desert. I looked at the white flats beneath me, I felt the cold moisture from the ground through my clothes, and I followed the desert plain with my eyes forever toward the horizon until my eyes met up with some dark shadowed mountain ranges, mountains only discernible because of the star-filled sky beyond them. I wondered how many souls before me had seen these silhouettes from this exact vantage point.

Civilizations' nighttime city lights had drowned out the skies of the Native Americans. I imagined the incredible wonder that the ancient peoples must have experienced staring up at this incredible canopy every single clear night of their lives.

A totally acoustic version of Pink Floyd's "Mother" played in my head, strumming soft strings, over and over again. It must have been the last song on the tape deck while I was sleeping with my friends already out in the flats looking up at the night.

We were in Utah for sure. It was August 28th, 1984, and only the fourth day of our travels. The Lord had created these heavens, with millions of tiny lights that flickered in and out of the endless abyss of earth's night. It became clear to me that the day was always meant to be separate from the night. Exhilarated about life again, I crawled into the backseat of the car to sleep some more. One hour and a half later, I opened my eyes and looked up at the upholstered ceiling to realize that the engine wasn't running, and it suddenly scared me. We were stopped somewhere again, and the other two were gone. I abruptly sat up and looked out at the now grassy fields off of the interstate to our south and saw that Lucas and Declan were running through the fields like kids toward a single mountain out in the plains about two miles away. The scarecrow and the tin man were running through the poppy fields toward the distant skyline of Oz, and it was barely the light of dawn.

I fell back asleep, too tired to care, and dreamt about Herb Albert and The Tijuana Brass. They stood in perfect yellow flower fields with their golden horns on a video album cover. I awoke again a half hour later and got out of the car. Where were they? Atop the distant mountain I heard two barely audible yells that sounded as if they were beckoning me to run out and join them. I could hardly see them at first, and only when they moved, did I imagine that it must be them on the very top of this steep treeless amber hill. So it was settled in my mind that the naked eye could only see for two miles at best. I wanted to sleep some more, and I did. It would be a long time before they'd return.

I woke up with them knocking on the car window and laughing at me. The scarecrow and the tin man were back. They talked of views of grassy fields for miles and miles.

It was my turn to drive. A while later, as we neared the Great Salt Lake with the other two asleep now, I watched the big orange morning sun rise right out of the east from the side of a grassy hill in front of me. The sun disappeared behind the adjoining hill as the car bottomed out in the valley and then quickly rose again above the whole range. Sunrise, sunset, sunrise again, it all occurred in the course of ten minutes.

Once the mountain range was behind us, the road set upon some sort of salt marsh now; grassy marshland lined up on both sides of the car. The salt air smell through my open window brought back memories of Paradise Beach and the coastal wetlands of my native New England.

When I was young, we drove the back road border towns into New Hampshire in our family station wagon on our way to Tidebrook and Paradise Beach. It was my father and mother in the front with three or four of us in the back. I'd be looking out of that bubble as we drove through the side streets of Tidebrook. My father always tried to cut through the old town to avert the vacation traffic on the main roads. There were stretches of tidelands everywhere that reached into the shantytown of Tidebrook; blue water canals that ran through miles of green marshy grasses. On a dirt road that had been laid above the marshland right off of the paved street that we traveled on, a row of dilapidated shacks skirted the edges of the swamp and disappeared around the bend. I was maybe ten years old when I first noticed this young teenage girl in the back of one of the shacks that was closer to our paved street as we slowly roared by her. She was hanging rag clothes on a rope clothesline that was tied to a tree. I remember that people called them all the "Brookers" who lived in these rows of poor houses. Rumor had it that the Brookers were all inbred; brothers marrying sisters and cousins with their lines running across only one or two families in the entire community. A fictitious phone book that only consisted of two surnames in the whole book of 200 pages.

There was so much sadness in that moment with the poor girl hanging out her family's old laundry. I tried to look for her the following year but saw no one. I wondered why these poor people had to live this way and what they thought of us—we tourists who passed along their roads . . . beach bound, heading for the Coppertone sunshine, fresh fried clams and summer rental cottages. I remembered how the girl had looked back at me with her fallen eyes as we drove by; our eyes locked for a moment, and for that moment in time, our thoughts crossed into a common barrier as we both tried to comprehend each other's world.

We had poor folk in Lowell too, like the family that lived behind Smitty's Barbershop. Old Smitty had cut my father's, my grandfather's, and probably every uncle in Lowell's hair for three generations. The houses behind his shop were in terrible shape. Smitty would leave the back door to his shop open on those hot, muggy summer days; days where the air hung thick with nearly visible droplets of humidity. As my father sat in the big moving chair and talked to Smitty about all that was wrong with the world, I'd stand at the back screen door and look out onto the backyards of the poor. I watched the sad-faced kids come up to the locked screen door and look up from the stoop at me. I was probably eight years old. Their mother hung clothes on a makeshift clothesline that was tied to a post in the yard. Why were they always hanging up their clothes? I guess my mother had done that too before my grandmother had bought us the new clothes dryer.

Now the road in Utah that I drove on was under repair. Declan and Lucas still slept. The whole area looked to be flooded by an expanding Great Salt Lake. On one side, I looked off into the distance at a lone mountain where the floodwater from its base came all the way up to our road. It was a good mile of it. On the other side of the road, an oversized structure that looked like a giant plastic castle sat alone. It was about a half mile from the road but was also surrounded by the engulfing tidewater. Was it a deserted boat marina out here in the middle of nowhere? But where were the boats? It was a ghost town castle memory of happier days that had since gone by. Nothing else existed. With the early-morning haze about us, the stage setting was completely surreal, like we were driving again in some eerie music video made on some distant planet. The Ford Fairlane with the surfboard atop it drove through the last days of the world, I imagined, with me and my companions, the sleeping tin man and the snoring scarecrow. Where was Dorothy? Would I ever find her? And Toto (Taboo the pit bull?), he was gone too. It was just the three of us now.

CHAPTER 8

In the quiet of the morning light, I snuck up on Great Salt Lake from the southwest. Surrounded by mountains, it was different from Tahoe in that the low-lying desert hillsides around it were less rich and more barren than the hillsides of the Sierras. As I eased into the city of the great Mormon, Joseph Smith, I saw that both Declan and Lucas still slept soundly. We had been traveling for five days now. It was the 29th day of August.

The great surreal salt crystal city was just as I had remembered it from my trip there in June of 1983 except that the June snow on the surrounding Wasatch Mountains was long gone. It had that same feel to it of robotic perfection that it had years before. As we entered her gates, I drove by her giant white Mormon Temple, then by the proud statue of Brigham Young and the Miracle of the Gulls Monument (two big bronze seagulls atop of a tall pole) and eventually pulled up close to the Art Center which was right across the street from the Marriott (where I had stayed before). After I parked, the guys awoke, and we all ran free from the car, working our legs again, taking some of our blankets with us to sleep on the green lush Art Center lawn. It was daylight now, and we didn't care what anyone thought of us; we were anonymous in this spotless city of Barbie and Ken; we were homeless and uninhibited. Restless and unable to sleep, I got up from the lawn after a while and headed over to walk the nearby mall by myself. I wandered the outside shops for about an hour watching the passing perfect blond haircut smiling faces. With every face that passed, I took the dark comfort of knowing that not a single being in the whole city and for hundreds of miles in every direction, save for the two transients asleep on the lawn, recognized me.

When I got back to my friends in the afternoon, we all wandered a few blocks toward the great Mormon theme park to take in the traditional Mormon tour. On our tour, we tried to grasp this Mormon version of Christianity that they tried so hard to sell to us. Same as the Scientologist guy with his two big Dalmatian dogs hanging around the hotel lobby set back in Los Angeles trying to talk us into his religion. I had read *The Martian Chronicles* and thought to myself again after the tour that everybody knows there isn't anyone living on Mars . . . It was just a good story. But that all aside, the architecture of the wooden tabernacle and the surrounding buildings was truly incredible; I was impressed with the majestic granite temple, the tight, clean façades, and the whole concept of what human minds that are driven by sheer faith can ultimately accomplish. On the tour, we had been lined up and drawn into a moving conveyor belt like it was a ride at Disneyland. There was no turning back or getting off of this ride. It was a story full of entertainment, but after it all was told, a story that somehow I could never truly believe.

"Beware of the cult!" the people said back in Southern California.

Raised Irish Catholic by a catechism passed down through generations of laborers and centuries of poor farmers tilling the soil of Ballynahown, I constantly wrestled with my own faith. What was truth and what was story? As a child, I questioned my father Frank's wisdom all of the time. Did Jonah really live in the belly of a whale? But how? And how, genetically speaking, could Adam and Eve ever have propagated the entire human race? That would mean brothers marrying sisters, wouldn't it? My own father chided that someday, if ever I might be so lucky, I would be humbled at the feet of Jesus Christ himself in the great expanses of purgatory and heaven, repenting for my sin. "How dare you talk that way, Mike!" And we argued on and on about this very thing called "faith" for many of my teenage years.

It wasn't always like this. I had started out at a very early age convinced that God, in fact, did exist; convinced because I heard him all the time talking to us above our heads when we went to weekly Mass.

When I was five years old, we attended Saint Matthews Church with the eleven-fifteen being the most popular Sunday Mass. So many people went to that one service that the church had to have simultaneous services in both its upstairs and downstairs halls. The larger Mass was held in the huge glorious upstairs main church, and the spillover Mass was held below in the lower ceilinged church hall. Every week, Frank, my father, parked on the side street in the rear of the church, and we would attend the downstairs service. As regimented as Catholic Masses always were, the people in both halls stood, kneeled, and sat at approximately the same time as the gospel was read. We all stood in unison as one giant body when the priest sang "Glory to God in the highest!" with the altar boys ringing their brass rows of bells during the priests' laments.

It was there in the downstairs hall that I first heard those magnificent rumblings of thunder above my head, unbeknownst to me at the time that it was the sound of the people rising to their feet in the main church above us, precisely at the time that both priests in both Masses uttered the words "Praise be to God!" For the longest time I had always believed those sounds to be none other than the acknowledging voice of God himself, acknowledging all of us, thanking us for being there, as we stood up to sing and to praise him. It was him! I was so, so sure it was him!

But sadly, the day came when I asked my father about this, and he chuckled and told me that the sound was not God, but merely all of the people upstairs standing up or sitting down.

"If God was that vocal, then, of course, everybody would believe in him!" Frank said to me.

"But why wouldn't God want everybody to believe in him?"

"Because we need to have faith first in order to be saved," Frank would say.

I wished after that day that my father had never told me the truth. It was easier to believe in God when he made noise. How would anyone ever be able to debate the existence of God if he always made noise? But after that day, God was silent.

On our Mormon tour, a beautiful Barbie Doll talked to us from her side of the partitioned conveyer belt. She told us that their "guy" was the same guy as our guy, but he had come over to the Americas after he died on the cross in Jerusalem. I wondered then why the Native Americans didn't tell Miles Standish about this occurrence. And she told us how Joseph Smith found these golden plates in the ground in upstate New York, but they got lost. If these golden plates were so sacred, why didn't he take better care of them, I wondered. Why are religions always losing their sacred things? Was it God's way of testing our faith? There were cobblestones on the streets of Boston older than Joseph Smith's golden plates. I just couldn't buy this whole "golden plates" story and Jesus traveling through the Americas, especially with all of the early American colonists' accounts that never mentioned this. The Native American spoken word stories would have surely included them.

"People ask that question a lot, the plates were returned to the Angel Moroni," Barbie said to me. I saw in her kind blue eyes that her blind faith was un-rock-able. She had been weathered by that question from many of us on the other side of the conveyor belt, but she would never waiver, because defection was so rare; she would never, ever, cross over to the moving sidewalk of the doubters; she would never question her own faith the way that so many Catholics had questioned theirs.

The tour was abruptly over. We moved on down that exit walkway while the Angel Moroni and Joseph Smith sat in some little room in all of Salt Lake City's collective mind working Joseph Smith's seer stone inside a grand magician's hat deciphering those invisible golden plates.

Leaving the building, we found a phone booth on the squeaky clean street, and Declan tried calling a phony number that he had come across on one of the mall bulletin boards. It was for some Salt Lake City movie production job. It was a wrong number; the person on the other end had no idea what he was talking about. It was nothing more than an illusion according to Lucas, "Just more golden plates." Lucas then called our old roommate Jesse back in Huntington Beach to check on the things we had left behind. Jesse told him that he had weighed all of our packed up boxes that had been left at Ingrid's entryway for UPS to pick up, just as we had instructed. He didn't know why UPS didn't pick them up unless they were waiting for the one hundred forty-eight dollar payment first. We grabbed workout clothes from the parked car and settled on a local gym to get a quick workout in before moving on. Talking to the desk agent up at the front of the gym, we posed as prospective members and Declan convinced the guy to let us try the place out. We got in a pretty good bench press workout, then showered, shaved, and quietly slipped by the front desk while the attendant was stacking towels. He never got our signatures.

Lucas loaded his KROQ mixer tape into the Fairlane tape deck, and we were fit to drive again, saying good-bye to the clean temple skyline architecture dwarfed by the creviced Wasatch Range.

When we got just south of the city, driven by mad impulse, Declan suddenly veered off the road after seeing signs for a closed copper mine and tried to find it. But we found no access to it without our having to get out of the car to look for it, so we abandoned that idea immediately. Declan was crazy again, and he headed west on another small road so he could swim in the Great Salt Lake, but when we got there, the dirty water on the flooded shoreline made this idea terribly undesirable. Even Declan decided not to swim in it. I had remembered seeing a picture of the Great Salt Lake in some old school textbook with clean-cut Mormon people from the fifties floating in it so effortlessly. Maybe it had just been cleaner in the fifties, I thought. We stopped at a small convenience store and picked up some groceries before we finally headed south on Interstate 15.

Declan wrote out a check in the Fairlane to UPS and sent the check to Ingrid special delivery from a post office we found a few miles away in Midvale. I mailed the Norman Rockwell picture book to Spooner and Bethany from Midvale too. Declan chuckled as he watched me stuff the large illustrated book into a post office padded envelope as best as I could. It wasn't the greatest wedding gift wrap after all.

I thought about Colette frequently. I was fighting off sleep and in and out of five-minute naps on the road; my head bobbed in the backseat. Languid and listless, my legs hurt from the run in San Jose two days before. I felt the hard pain of shin splints in my tibia bones. We were soon screaming southeast bound on Interstate 6 toward Price. I caught my crazy receding hairline in the rearview mirror once, the moving sun hit it, and I painfully realized that I looked balder than ever before. This was such a fleeting trip, this whole trip called life, and all of a sudden, I was sad again. The disappearing hairline had followed me from mirror to mirror over the last four years, and it always brought on the sadness. I dreamt of having hair again; I dreamt that I had long hair, lots of it; I dreamt of patches and patches of it falling and caking up Mary's shower drain in San Pablo. I was suddenly falling off of a cliff. I caught myself with a quick gasp of breath. It was a quick flash in the ever-encroaching night of life, and then I was awake again and looked out the tempered glass window of our moving car.

On my left I began to notice how our country seemed to be getting more mountainous as we pushed the eastern border of the Utah state and the foothills of the mighty Rockies. There were dusk-blown silhouettes of fading purple ridges that traveled the road beside us as the day now turned to night and the night turned to the darkness that I was always so afraid of.

Later on, Declan got pulled over going sixty-five miles per hour on Interstate 6. We sat on the shoulder, me in the passenger seat next to him, and I watched the trooper slowly strut up toward us in my side mirror. I frantically kicked at the empty beer cans at my feet with the back end of my heels trying to bury them under the bench seat. The aluminum cylinders crushed as they met resistance against the seat. *Crack!* I hesitated to move my feet lest one might come clanging back. I cranked down the window to let the officer lean in.

"Can you get out of the car, young man," the officer pointed at Declan. "Can I see your license and registration?"

"Mike, can you look in the glove compartment for the registration?" Declan called to me from outside the car, crouching to the window and reaching toward the jumble of papers I now held in my nervous hands.

"Luke!, I can't find the registration. Where is the registration?" I called back to Lucas who was asleep in the back, but Lucas wouldn't wake up at first.

"There it is." Declan pulled it from the stack of paper. But the name on the piece of paper wasn't Lucas's. It was the old lady's that he had bought the car off of.

"That's not it." Lucas was awake now and reached to his wallet to pull out a temporary registration that was issued to him. Everything checked out with the temporary registration. Never noticing the crushed cans that stay jammed at my heels, never saying a word to us about the crazy surfboard atop the vehicle, the trooper issued Declan a warning. "Son, you need to realize that the speed limit is fifty-five all over the U.S."

I thought of Kerouac's infamous *Dean Moriarty* and that beautiful Hudson going back and forth between Virginia and New York and Dean getting pulled over and arrested for breaking the speed limit. We were transients with no ties to anyplace now, crisscrossing America sort of the same way that Kerouac had done forty years before, without a worry in the world. But the alcohol abuse could overtake you like a thief in the night; there had to be a balance. I didn't want to die alone at forty years old on the side of the railroad tracks in Mexico, all overdosed on drugs and overexposed to the elements, dead from absolute kidney failure.

Roy Buchanan left his talent on the stage at the Paradise Beach Casino before he fell off that night. Years later, he hung himself in a Pennsylvania jail cell. Poor guy constantly walked the tightrope of genius and insanity at the end of his life. Was it the genius that took him up to the edge? Or was it the insanity? When do you know where to catch yourself before you fall off of the stage? And Salinger wasn't even in the rye anymore. He was a recluse in New Hampshire and didn't want to talk to anyone. How was anyone ever going to figure out genius on their own? We needed them around.

Maybe about an hour later, Declan pulled over for all of us to sleep. We would try to make Colorado tomorrow. The banana nut bread that Mary had given us was finished. We were still hungry but had nowhere to go. We were near Price, Utah. Declan decided to sleep outside a few feet off the shoulder of the road with a blanket he pulled from the back of the car. Lucas slept on the warm hood of the Fairlane out in another beautiful open star-loaded night, and I had the whole backseat to myself again.

CHAPTER 9

August 30th, Day 6.

I awoke in the early-morning fog and found Lucas sleeping in the front seat of the car. It was eight thirty a.m., and we were right outside of Price. Lucas stirred, sat up, and rolled down the passenger-side window to yell out to Declan who still slept about thirty feet away on the cold hard shoulder of the highway. Like a dumped body from some kidnapping gone wrong, Declan's flannel shirt and crazy pink shorts were partly visible under the poorly but tightly wrapped cocoon cotton blanket cover. His snoring body lay beyond the noise of the passing cars and the chill of the outside world. Declan, at first, didn't move at Lucas's beckoning.

"Hey, Declan, want us to leave you here?" Lucas shouted out again to him.

In the morning light, there were medium cool mountains of stratified rock around us. I noticed that the layers of rock ran at angles; they were bands of petrified rivers shaded with reds, grays, and browns. I marveled at the fossilized matter, strangely visible in the roadside cliffs as we began our drive again. These layers of rock had once been sea-level mud, I imagined, pushed up and hardened over the eons from a combination of earthquakes and continental drift. We slowly moved southward and eastward, pushing toward the distant border of this mysterious state, inch by inch. On the expanses of road along the valleys, I witnessed rows of butte-topped mountains in the distance that had been scraped by the march of retreating glaciers millions of years before us. Their distant blue stillness gave the appearance of being just painted out there, but I fathomed the slow but sure movements they had made over time. It was a glacial graveyard of beautiful giant ranges that continued to grow around us. These buttes were part of the pathway that would eventually lead us to the majestic peaks of Colorado.

It was hot. Tugging on my size thirty waist jeans, I looked down at my flat belly and my fading California tan. A freight train pulled boxcars west just about 300 yards off of the interstate. Humming the tune to The Allman Brothers "Melissa," I watched those empty boxcars going back to where we had come from just days before. I questioned myself as I watched them if I would be living a gypsy life forever. These trains crisscrossed the plains of our great West. I wondered if the train I now looked at was ultimately heading back to the port of San Francisco in order to load up again on containers from Asia, only to head back east all over again. Supply and demand; the cars had to always be full, for they had to always feed our growing American appetite with stuff. We all ran like they did on predetermined tracks over and over again. I fathomed myself as a timeless gypsy and continued to hum aloud alongside the beautiful Allman Brothers' love song.

I had weighed myself at 138 pounds on a Utah drugstore scale with my soaking shoes on. Sadly, I realized that I had lost another five pounds since San Francisco. I had still lost my appetite over Colette. Would I ever be fat again? We were homeless; Luke, Decky, and I, without a key to our names other than the one that started the engine of that sweet beige beast that now carried the three of us home. We had left Huntington Beach behind and were riding the beautiful line of mystery and riddle searching for something that we all called paradise.

Veering on to Interstate 50 and ultimately Grand Junction bound, we listened to something obscure; Declan's McGuffey Lane tape. They were a band out of Columbus that had toured with The Allman Brothers and the Charlie Daniels Band, Declan told us proudly. I wasn't particularly fond of it, though. Off the road, the train's container cars continued to slip westward silently beside us, eventually getting smaller and smaller as the mountainous landscape slowly engulfed them.

High red rock plateaus now rose on the horizon above us. It took me back to all of those Roadrunner cartoons I used to watch as a kid. The rock was all pinkish and gray, just like in the cartoons. I observed those omnipotent monoliths around me; they were huge sleeping giants, nature's Stonehenge casting midmorning shadows back toward Nevada in this big beautiful American West.

The colors of the landscape kept on changing as the hours began to roll by. Turquoise hard-faced rock buttes surrounded us now; they were sculpted, chiseled by centuries of ancient wind. I noticed that their red brick bases were laden with crumbled rock debris. The smooth rock of their upper plateaus drew stark contrast to their broadened rough rock pile bases. It was a kingdom of interstellar castles on their individual pillars, as if the castles had been built up there in my imagination amidst my own islands of fictitious clouds. These were the fairy-tale fiefdoms of the badlands of Utah. It reminded me of the artwork on a distant album cover. I saw on the Rand McNally road map that these were the forlorn lands where our great Native American brothers once roamed so comfortably—their descendants now confined to a great reservation on the left-hand side of the highway. This was the land of the Uintah and Ouray.

We took a detour on Route 191 after seeing a sign for Canyonlands National Park. There were several miles of a bumpy, hard-packed dirt road at first. A lone hawk flew all the while overhead, tracking us like wounded prey, its large wingspan marking a cloudless blue sky as it followed us into the Utah wilderness. When we stepped outside of the car at the park's entrance, the silence of the earth was all at once deafening and relieving. We all marveled at the smooth-faced cliffs around us as soft winds breathed faint whisperings of ancient voices into our ears. I could hear the voices talking amongst themselves.

"Do you hear that?" I said. "It sounds like someone is talking."

A huge rock topped a tower of smooth rising stone almost as if God had placed it there himself. Although still and balanced for centuries, the large boulder looked as if it might teeter-totter at any time and come crashing down to the valley below it, crushing us and forever rendering anything lying in its rolling path extinct.

There were outcroppings of subflora of blue green and yellow bushes throughout the rocky landscape as we walked about the scenic trails. On a sideways rolling plain, the desert plants intermixed with some larger green bushes; there were lazy-eyed Susans and brown green grasses everywhere. This complete picture reminded me of a western landscape of pastel colors that would have been so pleasing to the painter Ingrid's eye. But there were no industrial complexes like the Newport Beach Cannery or oceans of water in this desert wilderness for Ingrid to paint.

I dreamed as I walked, imagining a distant fictitious time on the ground upon which I stood, where an ocean raged above me, and the grasses and flowers around me were sea flora, with all kinds of invisible ancient marine life swimming amongst us.

A bird chirped; a fly buzzed about me and sensed the moist humidity of my being. The dry hot air smelled of the dust that sometimes precluded summer thunderstorms, with dark browns, red browns, and shadows of the impending afternoon consciously forming in the unraveling landscape before us. The breeze was suddenly soft again and reminded me of the girl I used to know.

That long, sweet guitar riff and Greg Allman's familiar song of "Melissa" moved back into my head; the memories of sweet Colette roamed comfortably in my soul.

We found our way back to Highway 70 and drove ninety quick miles into Colorado. The mountains got bigger, and then booming greens suddenly appeared everywhere. Trees as I once knew them filled the surrounding hills.

This was the upper Colorado River Valley. We joined the great river as it passed through a small town along Interstate 70 called Fruita. This was the mighty Colorado, I thought, as it raged beside us in the opposite direction; this was the river that would eventually cut through the great canyons of Utah and Arizona in order to get down to the gasping sands of Baja, where it would drip-drip into the Gulf there. I wandered in and out of a half sleep while this greenish, murky river ruffled like a ribbon beside us. It was a hot summer day.

I floated out of the moving car for a moment and up into the thin atmosphere. It seemed as if I was attached to a giant rubber band, a tethered umbilical cord. I saw the surfboard atop the tiny Fairlane below me; the magnificent Rockies were ahead of me. I saw the snow-veined mountaintops reflected in the surfboard's yellow fiberglass shell. I saw our three lost souls beneath the yellow shield meandering through the valley of the great river and Aspen bound. I snapped out of my sleep.

The 1969 road map we were using didn't list some of the sparse towns along the inter-state like Silt and New Castle on our approach to Glenwood Springs. At Glenwood Springs, we picked up Highway 82 and headed east to Aspen. We drew within the hour to Luke's sister's house.

"How about those Mormons!" Lucas spoke with feigned intonation. He was bored. "It's all an illusion, Mike, isn't it? John Smith found golden tablets out in the forest after wandering around when he was twenty-four years old? It's an illusion, right?"

"Wild mushrooms will do that to you!" Declan laughed. "He ate them right before he probably found those tablets!"

Lucas read a lot of stuff written by people like Krishnamurti and Richard Bach. He often wondered aloud if the past was nothing more than an illusion to all of us that never lived there.

"Everyone's looking in from all these different angles," Lucas mused. "And everyone's point of view is individually so different. Whose point of view writes the school textbooks? I think it's sad that history is written by the conqueror with the poor people who are conquered left only to be suppressed and either blended in or eventually exterminated. Therefore, don't you guys agree that the past is nothing more than an illusion?"

"What if Hitler had won the war that your dad fought in?" he asked me.

"I'd still know the truth," I said.

"But what about your children? The history books would all be different if Hitler had won, and those that knew the real truth would eventually die and be forgotten," Luke said.

When I was a kid, my father told me his war stories over and over again. He talked of the children in France bumming cigarettes from their liberators. "Cigarette pour mama?" and the Chinese trading tattoos, embroidered dragons and beautiful swords for cigarettes from the sailors like Frank who walked the streets of Shanghai.

My father, Frank Hogan, had served on a minesweeper with the U.S. Navy. During the war in the South Pacific, he told me, they once docked on a deserted beach and saw the heads of U.S. Marines cut off at the neck and nailed to the palm trees. Ghost beach, he called it, he had seen this horror firsthand. This gave him nightmares for the rest of his life.

"Okay, but then, how were the thousands of scrolls that eventually became the Bible preserved if the Christians were the persecuted, Luke?" I said.

"They were secretly hidden away, I think," Declan spoke up. "Some are probably still hidden, you know."

I realized that it was Declan that said this. Decky, the same guy that had streaked through a Christian Revival tent during a service in the big park across from our house in Huntington Beach just a few weeks before we left California.

Don't get me wrong. Declan's Catholic faith was rock solid, regardless of how crazy he got like running naked through that tent. Declan believed.

"Your faith is a gift," I said back to Declan in the car as we wove our way down Highway 82 toward Aspen. Declan felt real good. He smiled and nodded his head in affirmation.

Maybe Luke was right. Even my childhood seemed mostly an illusion to me now. I barely remembered anything that happened in my first five years of life, I got to thinking, yet I still existed. I remembered when JFK was shot. How could anyone forget that? I remembered all of my teachers crying at kindergarten at the Tenth Street School on the day that it happened; my grandfather and my mother waited for me outside the classroom in that giant shiny hardwood floor lobby. I saw it all again; all of the classes were dismissed and all of us little people spilled out into that great big room to wonder why our mothers were there waiting for us. I knew something was different that day. My mother never came to the schoolhouse to get me. My grandfather was the city engineer that inspected all of the public buildings, so he was at the Tenth Street School a lot. On the days he came to school, my teacher, Miss Lansing, would be all smug when he walked in. But Miss Lansing was crying on the day that JFK was shot, even with my grandfather standing there. My grandfather died real soon after that, at the age of sixty-two. He had a massive heart attack in the middle of the night. It was crazy. JFK and my grandfather both dying around the same time, and Miss Lansing crying that day in the hallway. Somehow, I thought they were all related. What happened to my grandfather was that he awoke in the middle of the night with this terrible pain and asked my grandmother to get him two shots of whiskey to help him get back to sleep, so she got him the whiskey, but he never woke up after that. I remembered at suppertime he used to love eating those big hunks of butter.

As I thought more about kindergarten, I remembered Ethan Rigby who pointed behind me on April Fools' Day to say, "Look, there's a horsey in the window!" That was kind of lame even for those times, but Ethan always was a little different. But what had happened to all of those months between JFK's death and April Fools' Day? They were gone. I envisioned all the other memories as the lost scrolls, slowly suppressed by the conquerors.

And right after that, God suddenly fell silent.

Luke, Declan, and I stopped just outside of Aspen to refuel and find a phone booth. Still thinking about my grandpa, I washed the bug-splattered windshield with a wet squeegee sponge at the gas station while Lucas went into a phone booth to call Kerry, his sister, but when the operator asked him to deposit one dollar and thirty cents more in coins, he frustratingly hung up the phone and clamored back to the car. He didn't have that much change on him. Declan ran up and jumped into the booth now, pushing back through the accordion door, to suddenly call our friend Ingrid; he remembered to tell her about the check for UPS that he had mailed to her earlier from Utah.

My memories of California were still alive, of course, but slowly fleeting. On the day we dropped off our boxes at Ingrid's house in Newport Beach, she had served us chocolate chip cookies, raw macadamia nuts, boysenberry juice, and ripe, sweet figs from her beautiful tree. Ingrid's bungalow sat in the shade of her sacred fig tree just like the tree in Hesse's classic masterpiece *Siddhartha*. I remembered sitting on Ingrid's comfortable sofa that night. I wanted to gulp the purple juice down so fast that it might even pour over the sides of my mouth and drip all over my shirt to stain it. I wanted to drink in all of this sudden sweet freedom of life.

"I am sad to see you all go off, but I want you to know that you will always be like sons to me," Ingrid told us with a tear in her eye.

It was that night that Ingrid and Lucas talked about the crazy theory that the Apollo missions had stopped because there was already another life-form up there mining the moon's precious metals.

"Come on now, you don't believe that, do you?" I asked.

Lucas talked on about the electrical physicist Tesla, who, at the turn of the century, was ridiculed in the United States because of his crazy inventions and ideas. He said that this guy Tesla had a laboratory that had some of the most amazing inventions of the century in it, inventions that had uncovered many of the electrical laws of the universe, but the government never believed in his work and labeled him as mad. One invention when raised to a certain level even caused the human body to urinate.

"Isn't that invention called beer?" Declan asked.

"It's always a paradigm," Ingrid said to Lucas. "All new theories are usually dismissed by the authorities as those of lunatics and skeptics, until the masses of our humble humanity eventually discover them and bring them to the front of public awareness. It is only then that thought and reason shift."

Declan and I were invisible to them both.

Ingrid was Ingrid, and Lucas was Lucas, and without them, the world would never be complete. If they were the yin, then Declan was always the yang, pulling me back from the more spiritual existence to the rigidity of Catholicism. I was always hopelessly lost somewhere in the middle, though, swinging like a pendulum, back and forth, always searching for an acceptable answer.

One cool evening, Ingrid and her older friend Howie were huddled under her fig tree like two crazy teenagers and caught me looking out at them from the window of our upstairs apartment. "Why, hello, Michael," Ingrid called up to me when she spotted me, never failing to embrace Howie as I tried to duck away.

"Hello," I waved sheepishly, pretending to fix something on the shade of my window.

"Don't be afraid!" Old Howie yelled up to me. "Fear only exists in our heads! Life is too great, too beautiful! Don't ever try to lose a minute of it!"

Youth may always be fleeting, but seeing those two like this helped me to realize that the soul had the ability to stay forever young, enduring everything. Our bodies were just a means to get us through this world, like a car going zigzag across the country, with eternal spirits inside for the duration of the trip, but at the end of it all, able to transcend to a place called heaven.

In Newport Beach, Ingrid had introduced Lucas to a controversial book called *Seth Speaks*. Jane Roberts wrote it in a trance, channeling this spirit named "Seth" while her husband sat there and recorded the whole mad dictation on tape. Lucas read Ingrid's copy of the book first and then passed it on to me several weeks before we left California. Although I didn't finish it, I tried to read as much as I could before returning it to Ingrid.

Seth seemed to have a rational explanation for everything. Science and religion fit together in his narrative; Seth even talked about Jesus. According to Seth, we can create our own reality. That's where Luke got his whole "*everything is just an illusion*" theory from. The present moment is the place where we can effect change. It is also where we have the ability to create the future. Every action, every choice, every random thought that is acted on is how we do it.

I wondered if it was Jane Roberts who believed this, or was it really the spirit Seth? Was Seth real or just a convenient alter ego? Was Jane Roberts the wizard behind the curtain?

"That stuff is just too crazy for me," Declan stood his ground.

Sitting there in the car outside of Aspen, I wondered if all of the religions and theories on life had a common thread. What if Jesus did come to America? What if there was a truly peaceful afterlife for all good people of the world, both religious and nonreligious; a place where there was no more fighting, just beautiful, warm, comfortable beaches with pictur-esque sunsets and everyone we ever loved with us forever? That would truly be heaven for me. Perhaps even the sandpipers were there.

It seemed funny that all the religious skeptics seemed to always blame the zealots for the sins and the faults of faith. But it was actually our own free will that was the wild card that got every one of us into trouble. Anyone who died in bloody battle in the name of Christ did it on their own time, not God's time. Gosh, it wasn't Jesus Christ's idea. People blamed the Crusades on religion, but it was men themselves and their own warped interpretation of the Bible that led to the Crusades and the Inquisition and all of mankind's crazy wars. Why was everyone always blaming God for everything?

"It is people who kill people. God doesn't tell them to do it!" Frank would say at the kitchen table. "God is peace. He gives us free will to make the right choice. How you react is a test of your faith. It's an absolute sin to think any misfortune is God's fault!"

The simple mention of the word "sin" would scare me silly too. Irish Catholic guilt al-ways weighed heavy on my conscious when I heard that word "sin."

But I had to keep asking questions until it made sense to me though; the giant riddle needed to be solved. I needed to figure it all out before I died, for the wrong choice might not sit too well if I missed out on those big pearly gates of forever. And forever sure seemed like a really long time.

When I was twelve, my father and I had an intense battle at the kitchen table one night debating how Jonah could even breathe if he was sitting in the belly of a whale. Frank would get so mad when I threw science back at him; his face would get all bloody red. That night, while we were both immersed in the heat of the argument, we suddenly heard my mother and my sisters scream from the living room. A terrified bat had flown out from the front hallway and through the living room straight into the kitchen where we sat. My father jumped up from his seat immediately to get on the trail of the thing. He dashed over to the broom closet in the pantry to grab a broom in order to swat at and chase the erratic flying bat from one side of the kitchen to the other. When the bat finally tired and took cover in the corner behind a vertical radiator pipe, Frank took the handle of the broom and whacked at him, pummeling the poor creature to death. He killed it clean and then picked it up by the wing to throw it out with the garbage. The event had ended the argument, and I often wondered after that what the meaning of it all was. Surely it all had to mean something when a bat flies right into the middle of an argument.

Luke, Declan, and I pulled into Aspen in the late afternoon. Aspen was everything I had always imagined it to be as I looked out now at the small, quaint, Hollywood setlike town with all kinds of friendly looking shops everywhere. We cruised down Main Street surrounded by a postcard mountain backdrop that breathed fresh, clean air and beckoned to us to roll down all of the Fairlane's windows. The pristine mountains were reaching for the heavens all around us it seemed, rising from an already-established base of about 7,000 feet high.

Lucas made another attempt at calling his older sister Kerry, but still got no answer at her house.

"She's probably still at work," he came back to the car shaking his head in frustration.

We tried a place that Luke thought Kerry's office might be at, but it wasn't there anymore. A cleaning lady told us that someone by the name of Kerry had worked there three years before our arrival, but she had no idea where the office had moved to. We stopped at a Greek deli and had shaved lamb on pita with salad while Tina Turner sang from the jukebox. There were travel posters of Greece hanging all over the walls inside of this deli. We looked up at them as we sat there and marveled at the true blue color of the Aegean Sea. We fathomed lying on the pristine beaches and exploring the whitewashed buildings on these hillside posters someday. We talked about how these pueblo-like dwellings seemed to fill up and cover all of the rolling bumps of these beautiful Mediterranean Islands while the picturesque Rockies secretly looked back at us through the large restaurant windows the whole time.

When we walked out of the deli it began to rain. The fresh smell of rain on pavement came up and took me; it hit me and triggered more memories. Hah! It was a paved street in Paradise. I thought of past times again, to the summers I had spent so long ago at Paradise Beach, New Hampshire. I remembered running from the beach with Linda O'Toole in the sudden summer rain with those same fresh rain smells, with bare feet and soaking wet towels and both of us jumping the puddles of those everlasting beach streets, dripping wet, without a single care in our ever-widening world. I remembered the simple comfort once again of a crackling fireplace in the living room of Mrs. MacNamara's boarding house at the end of a beautiful simple day. This was the whole world to me, I realized. I wanted to live from day to day again and to be in love with that single breathing moment. But just like Colette, Linda O'Toole had left me too, and it took a long while before I ever got over it. Crazy, mad love . . . Why'd it always have to hurt so bad?

Lucas made a few more calls to Kerry, but still had no luck, so we decided to cruise the streets some more until she got home. We momentarily stopped while Declan grabbed all of our sandwich trash only to jump out in the rain in his crazy loud pink-patterned California board shorts to throw it all away. Right at that very moment, Kerry and Sam passed by on their drive home and noticed the shorts and the crazy spiky hair of Declan Brady.

CHAPTER 10

We climbed high to Kerry and Sam's condo where we watched the evening news and then switched the channel to catch the end of a Chicago Cubs and Braves game while we drank a twelve-pack of Stroh's Beer. My eyes cased one wall of their condo where Sam had exhibits of all of his photography; he had close-ups of budding tree branches and aspen leave silhouettes that starkly contrasted with the straight lines and church ceilings of his cathedrals. Sam's photography reminded me of Ingrid's masterpieces of oil. Sam was an architect. The rain continued outside when a sudden clasp of thunder rang throughout the valley, nature's cathedral, and jolted our conversation in a flash.

"Wow! Now that is one of those cracks that I haven't heard since Ohio!" Decky jumped off his seat on the couch.

When the rain cleared, Declan had to do his laundry which was piling up (this is why he was down to wearing his crazy pink shorts). Luke and I decided to go running and set out on a trail right outside the condo that disappeared into the aspen wilderness above us. As we ran, I was happy at first that the long nights of summer still graced these mountain evenings, but the slowly disappearing light made the greens and browns of the enchanted forest quickly move to a sudden haziness of purple and gray. The air felt cool and clean. The mountain brooks overflowed with the new-fallen rain; they rushed beside the hard dirt path we climbed. An occasional runner passed us by, going in the same direction as the stream, some of them nodding to us in acknowledgment. We ran the three-mile loop that the path took us on, eventually descending and arriving again at the entrance to the condo.

We wanted to be disciples of everything life. In high school, I ran track because my father told me that if I quit the marching band, I had to do something else. Running was the only other thing in life that I was good at, so I pursued it. I could never be the first to hit that tape at the finish line though, for no matter how hard I tried, I always seemed to finish in second place. Because I loved the music of the Rolling Stones, I would play "Gimme Shelter" over and over again in my mind as I ran in all those races . . . be it the quick 220, the quarter mile 440, the half mile 880, or even the cross-country course in Wayland with Roberto Orozco finishing the race ahead of the world. Roberto Orozco was the top runner in New England at the time. I remember him just going off into the woodlands at the cross-country meet finish line like his first-place finish had just been nothing more than an Olympic warm-up. He just kept on running.

On our run in the aspen forest, in between breaths, Luke talked about trying to play team handball when we got to Europe. Maybe, I thought, but really, team handball? Was I agreeing just to agree? Did I really in my wildest dreams ever want to play team handball? No. I wanted to make movies.

After the run, we cleaned up and Kerry, Declan, Lucas, and I went to a few bars in town. Sam stayed home to do architectural stuff. The first club we hit had a jazz band playing, the second bar was a good soft rock-and-roll speakeasy place, the third one had two mirror image video screens playing at opposite ends of the hall, and a fourth place was more like an all-out disco. The unnatural progression of three decades of music was all rolled out in sequence into the night with insanity at the end of it all. Finally having enough, we escaped the crazy disco and in our relief, turned cartwheels in the street, falling right into and then ordering crepes from a roadside cart before heading back to the condo and eventually crashing hard.

Before I hit the floor, I slowly counted my remaining money. I came up with a sobering two hundred twenty more dollars to get me across the rest of the country. I was one hundred dollars into the three-twenty that I had started with. Then there was one hundred ninety-two to get me a one-way ticket to London and only eight hundred left for everything after that. Kerry and Sam would be married in Aspen on Monday. They both seemed to have found the finish line, I thought. Roberto Orozco was resting there.

CHAPTER 11

Friday, August 31, 1984. It had been seven days since we had last seen the beautiful southern shores of golden California.

I awoke around eight thirty in the morning from a deep, dead sleep on the living room floor of Kerry and Sam's Aspen condo with my blankets warm around me and the soft carpet as my mattress. I turned sideways to see Lucas still asleep on the fold-out couch. Declan was nowhere to be seen; his blankets all rolled up neatly and stored on the side of the room. I could hear the chirping of the birds outside; a chainsaw cut through the mountain air and hammers banged at a nearby new homesite.

Someone's vision of paradise was being renovated. Everyone wanted to live here; new homes were going up everywhere.

Sam drew the Venetian blinds in the living room to unveil the majestic mountains above us. Kerry played music in the kitchen as she rattled the breakfast plates and pans, making bacon and eggs for us all.

The rest of Lucas's family was supposed to arrive from Kansas later in the day. There had been seven kids in his family. Anna was the oldest, followed by Kerry, then Faith, Lucas, Kenny, Trent, and Nate. Nate, Lucas's youngest sibling, had died a year before in a car accident. The three older girls all had jet-black hair and Mediterranean skin; they were all beautiful. Lucas's dad had left his family years before. His mom had raised them all on her own on a mere nurse's salary.

We planned on doing the whole Aspen pub crawl again when they arrived in order to celebrate as much as we could: new beginnings, family reunions, the marriage of Kerry and Sam, and the beauty of life.

Lucas, Declan, and I resolved to hike the huge wilderness behind us before the rest of his family arrived. We set out right after breakfast in our running gear, with crazy neck scarves, a knapsack stuffed with raingear (that Sam had lent us), a coconut, three apples, a trail map, and two large containers of water.

The beginning of Hunter's Creek Trail, right outside the condo, started out rocky, and crisscrossed the creek at several points with its wooden foot bridges. It seemed to be a crazy zigzag into the wilderness. At one point we had to cross the creek on a large fallen pine, for the small bridge to the left of it was gone; it had probably been gutted out by the constant onslaught of rising raging water. The sound of water rushed in from every direction as we steadily climbed; the music from this symphony pleasantly filled my ears. This was the freeway hum of the wilderness, I thought. The fresh smell of pines was a welcome replacement to the raw exhaust smell of the real freeway; it overwhelmed my senses. The beautiful mountains were such a welcome contrast to the gray Los Angeles skyline of my past.

I knew aspen trees by their rounded green leaves. Sam had pointed out the crisp, defined leaves to me the night before in the wall photographs that he took. I fancied myself an expert now.

After a slow, subtle climb, our trail opened into a great room; a meadow that was filled with yellow petal flowers everywhere, just like the great poppy fields that surrounded the city of Oz, or that dreaming image of Herb Albert and the Tijuana Brass standing up to their waists in their tuxes. The band on that old album cover looked out at us as we walked toward them. We were in awe.

"Can wisdom be taught?" Lucas spoke like Socrates to Plato and Xenophon. I couldn't tell if he was joking or it was a serious question to engage us once again in a discourse on the mysteries of life.

"Teaching can only guide us; true wisdom must be acquired through experience," I fired back at him, pulling the BS from somewhere, someplace; maybe an old *Kung Fu* episode where the young pupil "Grasshopper" asks the same question of the great master as they both sit with legs crossed and palms upturned to the heavens. Lucas laughed at my answer.

We swam in a freshwater lagoon that was fed by the gurgling stream that we followed. We dove into the wake-up-ice-cold water with our running shorts on. After the refreshing dunk, we shook off and continued up and along the wooded path, veering off the trail for about fifteen minutes in order to explore an abandoned, roofless log cabin that was thick with the overgrowth of decades of brush; the seedlings had probably taken root inside the open structure before we were born. I marveled at this one-time shelter. It had once housed somebody's significant-but-now-forgotten life.

How long had this place been here, I wondered. Years? Decades?

Who had lived here? Were they miners or just squatters? Did they pay taxes? Or just build this place on someone else's land way out here in the country? Why did they leave? My mind constantly worked like this. I was fascinated by people and history and old pictures where I could look at the pocket watch a person was carrying and see if I could picture myself in their skin, just sitting in that parlor as they did back in 1897 or 1913, waiting for the photographer under the black sheet to flash that big flashbulb that he held in one arm so high.

Born into a time
Born into a place
Given a face
On the pavement

I had written these lyrics as part of the chorus of a longer, more intricate verse many years before. It expressed my fascination with history, old forgotten photographs, and the souls that they belonged to. I constantly wondered what part fate had in my being born into the place, time, family, and heritage I had been born into. If I had been born into a Mormon family living in the foothills of the Wasatch Range, would I be a Mormon and a different person today? Or would I be the same person I thought I was now? Would I still be asking questions and still searching for something that felt like the truth, regardless of who I had been born as? How does one's environment affect one's person? I knew that there could never be an answer to these questions though, and this secretly killed me. It made my head explode.

From the roofless structure we moved out and began to ascend the mountainside again, leaving the trail at last and moving straight up, with the landscape growing thicker with shrubs, bushes, and heavy vegetation that made the climb suddenly more difficult. Branches scratched at our bare ankles as we pushed higher. After a few short rests, we made it to a grassy clearing at the top. I was out of breath.

And then we saw cows, several of them . . . Cows just grazing amongst us! Cows at the top of the world! Bovine beasts, these were the sacred animals of all of Hinduism, just grazing on the roof of creation.

"Cows? How the heck did a bunch of cows get up here?" I asked the others in utter bewilderment.

"Surely not the way we came up," was Decky's matter-of-fact reply. He was bent over with his hands on his knees, still breathing heavy, and looked around for answers himself.

Lucas smacked open the coconut on a rock and gave us each a section of the broken shell that held the white moist meat. Sitting on the hillside, I now observed the rolling trail that traversed the tops of these grassy and wooded foothills that we rested on, all the while biting into the white flesh of the coconut and grinding it with my back molars, chewing the cud in a circular motion. The cows must have followed the easier rolling path to have gotten here, I thought as I rested. We had, more or less, come straight up the face from the roofless shelter, and I could see now how the actual trail was a slower and more gradual climb. I wondered if these were, in fact, wild cows, if there were ever such a thing, or if somebody actually owned them and they had lost their way.

Luke and Declan pushed ahead now that we had rejoined the trail, with three of the cows and a threatened bull quickly moving a safe distance away on their approach. The wind began to pick up and could be heard rustling through the leaves of the trees as distant thunder rumbled throughout Greater Aspen. I looked out at the grand cathedral below us. It would not be long now before the rain came, I was sure of it.

Walking swiftly toward the edge of the ridge, I tried to catch up with the others. I took in the view of birches and aspen groves in the valley below the trail. The undergrowth springing out from the ridge was laden with an array of violet, red, white, and yellow petal flowers. A hummingbird flew within a few feet of me, buzzing like a giant queen bee. It flew close enough to sense my presence and hovered there for a minute; its tiny eye studied me as I studied it, before the creature quickly changed direction to disappear over the hill forever. The whirring sound it made as it zoomed away was reminiscent of the aerocar sounds from the *Jetson* space family cartoons.

With the echoes of the thunder and the sudden bursts of wind, I softly sang a Doors song as I walked. The lyrics of the late Jim Morrison were there with me as the rain crept in. His deep voice echoed in the soundtrack of my mind . . . We were all "Riders on the Storm."

The rain came through quickly. We had to take emergency cover underneath some pines overlooking the valley. Lucas took two ponchos out of the backpack and quickly snapped them together to make a tarp that could accommodate the three of us. With the poncho cover now over us, sheets of pouring water hit the plastic fabric hard in a sweeping movement, like a wave moving across the ocean. We sat and looked out at the tiny world below us while the rain came, the theatre of Aspen, a virtual self-contained ecosystem . . . with crashing thunder out amongst the distant heavens, and postcard 3D mountains, two in the foreground and one, snowcapped, in the far distance, encapsulating it all. The stream that we had hiked up wove far below us between the mountain fields, and it seemed so terribly small and distant to me now.

And the high fields that the cows roamed in sort of reminded me of the fields back home in Dracut; without all of that elevation around them, of course. I remembered the long, white, wooden roadside fences out in Kenwood where I would go on my summer runs; the fields out on the farm where my father's aunt Vera lived. Vera and Uncle Arthur had apple orchards and native corn; dairy cows grazed on their neighbors' fields.

Frank used to tell me stories about Uncle Arthur's old carriage house in Dracut (right next to the barn), where he hid his Indian motorcycle in 1938. It had taken him a few years of savings from his paper route to buy it. He'd hitchhike from his house on South Street in Lowell almost every summer day at the age of fourteen to ride the thing. It seemed like such a long trip to me, over the Bridge Street Bridge and down Willard Street into Dracut, all the way to Uncle Arthur's farm. Frank probably smoked cigarettes all of the way there to pass the time (he told us he started smoking when he was thirteen). He probably even skipped school so he could polish and admire his motorcycle all afternoon. I could see Uncle Arthur just laughing at Frank in the carriage house as Arthur walked back and forth about his daily chores on the farm. Arthur never said a word of it to Frank's father (my grandfather) for this was their secret. What a cool uncle old Arthur must have been.

In Aspen, the storm blew over; it had passed quickly. With some distant rumblings of thunder still audible, Lucas set out ahead of us, fast to find a descending trail.

Going down the rocky trail at a good pace, my feet jumped out in front of me, one before the other, almost as if they were acting on their own. I thought of the crazy mountain cows now at least a mile behind us, up so high, and that bull. How lucky we were that it hadn't come at us with its horns thinking we were matadors, or maybe rodeo clowns with our crazy head scarves. The bull always had to protect its wandering herd.

But the girls only wanted the matadors. Could I ever be a matador? Why had I ever gone to California? She was gone now, and I was gone too. I had stared out at her beautiful West through the screened bedroom window in the humid New England night. What had happened to the fireflies that lit the bushes along the driveway of my childhood? What had happened to the tiny blinking lights?

I so wanted to be a little kid again. I dreamed of watching episodes of the TV series *Lost in Space* in the warm living room of my house on Eighteenth Street. In my dream, my mother baked pan pizza for me out in the kitchen; I never wanted it to change. But now, I was suddenly twenty-five. I was afraid and alone in this huge, beautiful world, where hurt seemed to lurk around every corner if you made yourself too vulnerable, and all this blowing-in-the-wind vulnerability suddenly wasn't cute or comfortable anymore.

Thoughts came screaming into me all the way down the trail. All kinds of songs stayed in my head too. There was always a soundtrack playing wherever I went. There was a song from the Alan Parson's Project that this guy Wrench back at UMass used to play all of the time. We called the guy Wrench because he used to steal street signs around campus and hang them up in his room. The song was called "Time." You'd hear it coming from his open door. Every time I heard it, I thought it was the saddest song I ever heard . . . especially when I thought about Colette now, for it was a breakup song and had some really sad, never-see-you-again lines.

I was a third of the way across the continent trying to regain my footing as I quickly descended mountainside trails. It felt like Colette and I were separated by more than the Rocky Mountains and the great western desert beyond them though. The realization that we may not ever see each other again was terribly unsettling. I was alone.

We clamored all the way back to the condo, feet moving fast. Lucas led the way with vocal outbursts of mock Three Stooges calls and the *knuck, knuck, knuck* yells of Curley; yells that echoed in the halls of the great cathedral.

CHAPTER 12

Lucas's sister Kerry told us the night before that Clint Eastwood had once come up to her while she was working out at her Aspen health club. She was bench pressing free weights, flat with her back on the bench, pushing the bar up off her chest, when she looked up and saw him standing there. It was then that Clint said to her, "That's an awful lot of weight to be lifting for such a little girl like you."

Clint Eastwood—the American Matador, Dirty Harry, and Josey Wales—just standing there in the flesh above her, wearing that characteristic, cool, quintessential tough-guy persona. Crazy!

But this was Aspen, mind you, the Rodeo Drive of the Rockies. Everybody big was here, so why be surprised? Why wouldn't we just end our quest right now; settle down and blend into this local community forever?

All three of us knew without even asking that this wasn't our final stop though; it wasn't our call. Decky, Luke, and I had to get somewhere else before we could ever end up in a place like this. We wanted money and fame, lots of it; and happiness, lots of it; and the feeling that we finally found our purpose in life, the reason why we had ever been born. Aspen is a town that is there for people who have already arrived, I reasoned. Just like Clint, Kerry, and Sam. But me, I had to keep on driving; I had to keep on searching . . . pushing for something that only my future self could reveal.

Lucas told Kerry that she should have responded to old Clint with one of the lines from one of his classic westerns. Like the line the bounty hunter who waited outside the western saloon in *The Outlaw Josey Wales* blurted out right before Clint shot him dead. Or maybe say even something more original back to Clint with a macho drawl . . . "Well, a pretty girl's got to stay strong too, Mr. Eastwood!"

"That was so funny when Clint spat on the dog's head after he shot the bounty hunter!" Decky laughed.

We all loved Clint Eastwood movies: *High Plains Drifter, The Outlaw Josey Wales,* and *The*

Good, The Bad and The Ugly. They were all classics for the ages. And then there was Dirty Harry grinding serial killer Scorpio's leg into the turf of Candlestick Park, the playing field of America's football gladiators, where so many battles are fought. Scorpio's back was pinned up against those yard line hash marks. Dirty Harry was crucifying him with his grinding foot while Scorpio begged for his life, just lying there helpless on that chalked off cross. This was American film filled with symbolism and artistic expression for everyone to interpret as they saw fit. This is what I wanted to do some day.

This was why we couldn't work eight-to-five office jobs anymore. Destiny awaited us in film or video. We made our plans to hit the road again after the wedding, for each of our bleeding savings reserves had to last a whole lot longer if we were really going to push that Fairlane and her surfboard across the rest of the country searching. We had to board that plane in Boston bound for London in twenty-four days. I dreamt of finding that sweet sleep somewhere where the sun didn't burn my skin and that beautiful warm light shined inside me forever.

Back at Kerry's apartment, family members were beginning to arrive from Topeka and Chicago. Luke's mother came with his two brothers, Kenny and Trent. Sam's parents and two sisters came in from Chicago. For dinner, Kerry made turkey. It was just like Thanksgiving in August, and it absolutely reminded me of that . . . with wine, beer, potatoes, green beans, stuffing, cranberry sauce, and the room filled with incredible people. The table was dressed with everything as if it was a late-November day.

Elton John sang "Mona Lisas and Mad Hatters" in that little condo just before Sam's dad said grace, and when Elton John voiced those words of thanks for his friends, everyone smiled warmly and looked around at each other as if that moment had been meant for us all.

The thunder raged outside during dinner; God was talking to me again, with lightning lighting up the mountaintops and valleys as the voices roared throughout the hollows of the Aspen night. One crash was so loud that everyone in the kitchen jumped wide-eyed in a moment of sheer wake-up shock. It was a break in the sound track of humanity; it cracked the sound barrier of a glorious life to remind us all of a certain eternity.

"Wow!" Declan was outside in a matter of minutes. He fiddled with the shutter speed on his 35mm camera. He wanted to record the streaks and crooked lines in our night sky by leaving the shutter open. He propped the fragile camera against a rock under the cover of a carport roof and ran back inside. The camera sat there alone, registering a long ten minutes of the fantastic light show.

When the storm cleared, we all cleared the condo. But Declan had to run back inside to put his camera away. After this, we all headed into the night to celebrate. We stopped by Sam's bachelor party at first, but after about twenty minutes there, felt slightly out of place amongst strangers, so we abruptly left. Sam and Kerry had met in Aspen after Luke had moved to Huntington Beach, so Luke didn't know any of Sam's friends who hosted the party. We decided to join up with Lucas's two older sisters, Anna and Faith, beautiful girls who had just arrived from Topeka and Kansas City, who were anxious to explore the crazy night life with us in this surreal moving-picture town; a motion picture happening in real time with plots and twists yet to be uncovered.

In the nightclubs, we drank beer after beer. It wasn't long before I was feeling wrecked again; the music got better as the night went on. Everything was beautiful and mellow, beautiful rock-and-roll music in America's mountain pearl. We screamed to each other on the dance floor just to talk above the din; but in this strange nighttime place, our voices were all at once lost . . . and so were our souls.

Looking around, I saw that all of the people in this one club seemed to be on their own individual islands; they talked in small groups. Some stood alone. They gregariously drank cocktails and puffed cigarettes as if the beer and the tobacco were fuel, sustenance; their lifeblood streams. I watched dust devil spirals of cigarette smoke climb above us to form a huge, mushroomlike cloud that hovered over the dance floor. Below the overhanging fog, the trail of funnels swirled up and around each other to join the ominous cloud; funnels that polluted each other with brand nonsense as they blended together. I watched a girl turn her head sideways from a forgetful conversation; she looked like a lost debutante, blowing her smoke into the air with boredom. Her face told me that she didn't want to be here. The toxic smoke above appeared to be the materialization of our very spirits; for after all, it was the air that we all had breathed. It contained parts of us all. I watched this dreadful cloud continue to grow as it just hung there above the huge room. I watched the stacks of smoke continue to braid around each other below it like dirty licorice, climbing and swirling in the air and finally pushing the cloud out the entryway door . . . moving the mass outward from the club into the narrow alleyway, the mass now trying to find its way out of the madness so it could spread out and pollute the clean Aspen night.

There was a dark-haired guy standing on the far side of the bar silently observing the crowd; he was off on his own. To me, he looked like someone from Lowell's Pawtucketville section. He looked like a young Kerouac, the writer in his prime. I wondered if Kerouac had ever gone through Aspen. What was Aspen even like in the forties? Perhaps it was just some small mountain mining shantytown. Where had I seen this guy before? Maybe he was a friend of Jackie Hillyard's. Jackie was a chef who had lived in Aspen in the '70s, but had long since moved back to Lowell. Maybe I had seen this Kerouac lookalike in the *Lowell Sun*. Maybe he was a celebrity.

"That guy at the end of the bar is from my hometown, I think," I screamed above the din to Decky.

"What's his name?" Declan asked.

"I'm not telling you."

"Why?"

"'Cause you'll make a fool of us all in our drunken stupor," I pronounced.

"The guy's from Lowell, and you're not even going to talk to him?" Declan laughed in disbelief.

"Hey, Lowell!" Declan yelled in Kerouac's direction as the man narrowed his eyes for a moment from across the room to look back at my crazy Ohioan friend. Kerouac now moved in the opposite direction of the room, against the crowd, after he had locked eyes with

Decky. He moved to a new vantage point; he appeared off by himself in a different world. He had wanted to go unnoticed, to avoid interaction and conflict, as if he was studying the room for the same reasons that I was. The guy wanted to be invisible.

With Declan's repeated screams at the poor guy, I finally had to duck out of sight. I was terrified of an encounter now. Who was he? Was he watching us? If I knew him, what would I say to him, anyway? If he was a real person, only uncomfortable conversation would be the outcome, I knew it.

"Lowell, Lowell, Lowell!" Declan screamed into the wild Aspen night as we now exited the bar. We had to move on. The mysterious Lowellian never did acknowledge Declan, though; he paid him no attention, casually watching the rest of the room as we all left. Once out in the night and into the clear air again, I began to wonder if the man was ever there at all. Maybe I had too much to drink. Maybe he just looked like someone I thought I knew. Perhaps he was the great ghost of the famous author himself in another plane, a superimposed one . . . another layer of time itself.

But alas, just like that, he was gone.

CHAPTER 13

September 1st came. It was the eighth day of our memorable journey. I woke up with my face buried in Kerry and Sam's shaggy condo carpet. My rib cage hurt from lying on my stomach all night on the hard floor. I rubbed my eyes feverishly, trying to focus, for in the distance across the room I heard Declan snoring wildly but couldn't quite see him yet. Declan snored in rhyme all of the time; the loud gasps sounded almost cartoonlike to me now. I saw Lucas, asleep, faceup on the couch, beyond the coffee table. My head hurt from apparent alcohol dehydration; there were loud pulsating knocks inside my reeling lobes screaming for some liquid nourishment now. I slowly became aware of where I was. I quickly recalled how I had come to be here.

I sensed the bright daylight filling the room, sunlight showering in on floating dust particles, and reflected on Lucas's own funny observation—*"Oh crap, I'm back here again"*—when he first woke up to the working world back in Huntington Beach. That seemed so ever long ago. We were in Aspen now with no more regrets about our choices in life; we were living out our dreams and searching for purpose again. Yeah, hah!

I heard Jeff Beck's "Cause We've Ended As Lovers" playing on the turntable in the living room; it was a different version of the song. Sam had put the album on amidst the morning stresses of having several people in his tiny condo waking to this new day. After pulling myself up for a moment to look around at all of the empty beer bottles on the coffee table, I focused in on the album jacket, *The Secret Policeman's Other Ball.* It was a cartoon cover of a guitarist in a pink dress and pink top hat. I had never heard Jeff Beck play this piece live. There was a sudden ringing sadness in my head as the weight of the labyrinth of life fully came back to me.

Zane had first introduced me to this song in Paradise Beach, New Hampshire. He said that Stevie Wonder had written the song for his once-true love Syreeta, but Jeff Beck always did the piece with no lyrics at all. Beck just wailed on and on with his electric guitar from beyond that Aspen condo coffee table now. It was truly beautiful. I could only imagine what the lyrics were like as the guitar spoke to me.

Lucas's sister Anna had stayed up late talking with us the night before; all of us had been seated around the coffee table after the mad bar scene. We talked about the crazy times we had in Southern California when Anna came out to see us. We lived in the Newport Beach house then, right next door to Ingrid. We talked about that crazy night that all of us ran down Thirty-sixth Street and dove into the ocean, with Lucas shrieking as he often did—screaming in the winter's night, with the stars all out over Catalina and Jim Morrison singing "Moonlight Drive" from the lonely turntable back at the empty beach house after we had left it. In Newport, I had showed beautiful Anna the poetry I had written and all of my screenplay drafts. I showed her *Fourteen Lines,* a screenplay idea I had. The title was a play on words, a sonnet. It was the story of a cocaine-addicted businessman; it was a hit-rock-bottom-and-recover story about the lonely perils of life. I had written the feel-good ending first, how a beaten man can find the good in life again.

We talked of all of the school courses that could help prepare us for our future no-ceiling careers: Emerson College, film editing at UCLA, TV production at Fullerton, the screenplay courses at Orange Coast College, and the dreams that wouldn't stop bombarding us. Everyone's life was a story, and every story had a lot of good in it. But there were so few storytellers to realize all that good and find a way to touch us with it—to remind us to just have a good time, to change our lives, even though the good was evident everywhere. Life was a beautiful gift that needed more storytellers.

Here in Aspen, my thick journal lay among my things by the coffee table. As I leafed through some of the pages the night before, Anna saw where I had written . . .

A life and a song
The comparison wrong
To realize
To finally see

When a song ends
It can be played again
A life can't be

"What does it all mean?" she asked me.

"I don't know. The complete song is about life and death, I guess," I told her. "You see, we are all rolling through our dog days now, and in your dog days, you never think about death. Not that thinking about death is meant to be a somber thing, though," I said. "It's just nice to be reminded that every waking moment is another chance to make a difference to someone; for life is so finite. We can never relive the past; we can visit it perhaps, but never relive it. The power, you see, is in the free choice of the present."

And it was here at the coffee table that we had crashed.

Another morning hangover haunted me while Bob Geldof and Johnnie Fingers sang from the same *Policeman's Ball* album that Jeff Beck and his guitar had just wailed from. Luke tried to explain to Decky, both of them now awake, the story behind Geldof's "I Don't Like Mondays" as it played.

"It's about this real-life teenage girl who walked onto the campus of a San Diego elementary school one sad Monday morning, right across the street from her house, to blow away two teachers and injure several kids. 'Why did you do it?' the cops asked her when she turned herself in. 'I don't like Mondays; this livens up the day' was her only response," Lucas said.

Think about all of the sadness in a song like that. And it was something that really happened. Was the fate of the two teachers already predetermined when they went to school that day? Where was the choice? Born into a time and born into a space on the pavement of life, they were.

"But the murderous girl was given free will to choose," I could hear my father's arguments at the kitchen table.

"But what of the innocent that were hurt or killed?" I would ask him back. But there never was an answer. Bats flew through our kitchen.

Declan poured himself a large glass of orange juice from a gallon of the stuff in Kerry's refrigerator. "Nectar of the gods!" he exclaimed, downing his large glass of juice quickly, and then jumping back to the container again to pour himself more.

It had only been a few short weeks since the three of us had quit our daily working world grind. The people we worked with, that steady paycheck, that stable career path, the white starched shirts, the crazy ties, the morning cup of necessary coffee . . . All of it was behind us now. No more real jobs, not for me! Back at the circuit board factory, forty-year-old Don White sat on that break room table with a cup of coffee and a stick of that burning tobacco in his hand with his scuffed up JC Penney shoes all over a hard chair. Don White announced to everyone in the room, all my coworkers, that I was a fool to leave the good job that I had in Southern California. "How many kids have gone to chase their dreams, only to wake up one day to find that their money-earning careers have truly passed them by? What a fool you are to leave our circuit board factory!" he said. Meanwhile, he'd go on sucking on his cigarettes and pounding his martinis in the crowded nightclubs of Newport Beach where everybody wanted to be seen, with his rolled-up sleeves and loosened tie. You see, he was living out his dreams—whatever dreams even were.

"America needs people working like me to make it run right!" Don told me.

"Don't forget us when you make it to the big time!" the others said to me on the day I left the factory (everyone except Don White, that is) . . . Some of them wishing they could come along with us, but too afraid, too responsible to truly realize it.

"Making movies, huh?" they said.

"Maybe just telling stories," I said.

Telling stories with the heels of my feet, I scraped the hardened beach sand of Newport Beach. I was always dreaming, writing words and hearts of "I Love You," with the small sandpipers chasing the waves all the while in the background. They ran back and forth as those very waves brought the foamy wash that eventually took all my words away. But the advancing tide also brought sustenance for these tiny birds, and that is what they were after. They kept sticking their long beaks into the wet sand, their heads dipping with indifference, accepting their blue-collar roles, seemingly not caring, not wanting to ask why as they sucked the food out of the ground below. As long as there was food and a job to do, they would never leave. God would always provide. Why couldn't I think this way?

I remembered playing "Giant Step" and other little kid games in our backyard growing up on Eighteenth Street; every kid in our neighborhood would be there. And there was "One, Two, Three, Red Light!" which was kind of like "Giant Step" in that in both games you had to be the first to make it to the cement and granite foundation of Polly Town's centuries-old garage wall that sat beyond our rusted swing set. With "Giant Step," everyone started at the other end of the yard and was granted steps by the "master" at the wall if a question was answered properly. In "One, Two, Three, Red Light!" the kid at the wall would put his closed eyes against the wall and count "One, Two, Three, Red Light!" before turning around quickly. If the children at the other end of the yard were caught moving forward, they would have to move back to the start. In both cases, the first one to the granite wall was always the winner. It seemed that life was no different than "One, Two, Three, Red Light!" or "Giant Step" after all. But why were we always trying so hard to get there, and what was really beyond that wall—something better?

My mind was always a freeway, with every thought another car going by; and every thought held different occupants . . . back and forth; back and forth. These thoughts were always going places, trying to get to that final destination, wherever that may be. So just like that, in a matter-of-fact freeway moment, we had all quit our jobs, for they were jobs that didn't make us happy . . . and we hit the road in order to try to find it all again. Yeehaw!

Ingrid said to us one night in her living room in Newport Beach, "Don't take life too seriously because in 100 years, who is going to care? Everybody'll be gone!"

She was right. Think about it. Every single human being born in 1884 was dead, save for maybe a couple of them. Whatever it was that happened in those great thinking minds of that wonderful year, if not written down or told to others, was now gone forever. I wondered about my second great-grandfather Patrick. I was always putting together the one great story of him that I heard with the stories that I never heard, how he must have worked those rocky fields in rural County Clare, Ireland. What was going through his mind as he toiled? In the 1890s, he was pushed off his land by his English landlord. His wife had passed a few years before in a cascade of sorrow, with many of his children also passing over the years before and after her from malnourishment and disease. So he had to leave his land and head to a strange place called America, an America where his four surviving sons had already gone to live. Paddy landed in the mill city, Lowell, to join the last of his living children in 1898, only to survive a few more years and die on South Street. He was buried at St. Patrick's Cemetery in the family plot with all of my other grandfathers and granduncles after him, lots of them. His name wasn't even on the headstone where six of them were buried; it was just a big stone that read "HOGAN." And think about it, poor Paddy's wife remained in an unmarked grave in the cold rocky ground in a burned down churchyard somewhere back in Ennistymon. There were no stories that any one remembered of her. We only knew her name. Had Paddy taken life too seriously? Perhaps he had little choice. But did anyone now care? All we knew of Paddy was the one great story that had been passed down from my grandfather. That was all that was left of Paddy's life now . . . one great story. There wasn't even a photograph of Paddy, for Paddy was too poor. Just one wonderful story from his distant life. Soon that would be gone too.

"You only fail when you stop trying," my father used to say to me. It was something that maybe someone had passed along to him, perhaps even passed along by Paddy. Frank Hogan had other crazy sayings too. "*He's as Irish as Paddy's pig!*" he'd say. Did Paddy have a pig, I used to wonder. Or was it something that all of the Irish said? How Irish could a pig be? Was an Irish pig different than a German pig? It was sort of funny how those old Irish hated the English almost as much as the Red Sox fans hated the Yankees. My grandmother said it was genocide, you know, what the English had done to them, making them send all of their meat to England and leaving them to eat nothing but potatoes. I figured that all of that hatred for the English wasn't at all good for our family's well-being in the long run. It had made us all angry people.

Paddy and his sons Michael and Thomas died in that house on South Street in Lowell; it was the same house where my father grew up. And Frank's childhood home sat right next door to the huge beautiful granite structure of St. Peter's Church. My grandmother, Frank's mother, attended Mass every single morning at six. In the pews of St. Peter's Church, she burned through her rosary beads, round and round, rubbing them between her fingers, always clutching them, ever so faithfully, day after day. She even had pictures of the bleeding Sacred Heart of Jesus in every room in her house.

Lowell was always behind me and forever before me, like one big raceway loop that connected my future to my past. As a teenager, I used to go on long runs through the farm fields of Dracut; the same country roads that my father Francis had burned through on that Indian motorcycle in the late 1930s. I had heard this story from him many times . . . The day he flew right by my grandfather on Bridge Street while my grandfather was out on his city inspections, with my grandfather not even knowing it was Frank at first. You see, Frank had kept it hidden for so long, the motorcycle that he had squandered his paper route money for. Frank bought the Indian motorcycle when he was fourteen years old and hid it away in Uncle Arthur's carriage house.

"Tom, isn't that Francis?" my grandfather's assistant asked him from the passenger seat on that very day as my father buzzed by them going the other way, a cigarette hanging from his lower lip, hunched forward like Jimmy Dean on his final lap of one of the great races of life. "What a boy!" the assistant laughed.

"What! Such a sin! He's supposed to be in school! Are you sure that was him?" was my grandfather's angry response.

Such a sin! Just like Decky and Luke streaking through the Born-Again Christian revival tent in the big open lot right next to our house a few months before we left Huntington

Beach! Declan told me they ran right down that center aisle and took a left right at the face of Jesus. They ran out the side of the tent and across our lot, right by the grinding oil derrick and right in through our back screen door before any of the revivalists knew what had hit them.

We always loved to judge those Christian extremists who recruited everyone in those weekend tents—the ones with the beautiful homes with the manicured lawns and the BMWs in their driveways—the televangelists on TV. I felt that they looked down on the rest of us. This was such a contrast to the vision of my own grandmother tearing through those rosary beads clutched so tightly in her hands in the silent pews of great St. Peter's Church.

So back and forth it was for me, always asking questions under the big tent. But I needed to get it right; for if I wandered down the wrong path, like the path of the Moonies, for instance, eternity was forever.

"Krishnamurti said that religion is the frozen thought of man out of which they build temples," Lucas proclaimed.

"That's a sin to have been running through that tent like that with no clothes on!" Frank Hogan proclaimed. "Such a sin!"

I often wondered where Krishnamurti would go when he died, and if he was wrong, who was going to tell us?

Consciousness was energy, and energy could not be either created or destroyed. It was physics too, so we had to go somewhere. Even the San Francisco jazzman knew about that. The San Francisco jazzman had even said, "God bless you!"

On the stereo at Kerry and Sam's condo, someone had swapped out *The Secret Policeman's Other Ball* to Christopher Cross, a Top 40 artist, who had just made it big with his song "Sailing."

"Who put on the elevator music?" Decky asked after coming back into the room from brushing his teeth and moving over to his corner of the living room to fiddle with his pile of things.

The television set was on too, with the volume down low and no one watching it. *The Wheel of Fortune,* a game show for prizes and money, aired in the background of our lives. Although I could hardly make out the letters they were guessing, I laughed at the three eager contestants. How silly they looked up there spinning that wheel, smiling, clapping, cheering each other on. Pat Sajak, the host, was standing up there with his Decky-Brady-Crest-Toothpaste smile. I thought about how this whole presentation mirrored the great contest of life itself. Pat Sajak knew we all would do anything to be up there with him; we'd act silly just to be seen on TV. We all wanted a chance to spin that wheel; we all wanted to win lots of prizes and money; we'd follow the rules; we'd smile; we'd wait our turn and falsely cheer the other contestants on. Why did we cheer the others on? We all wanted to be famous, even for a sweet five minutes, if that's all we could get in this life.

I quickly pulled myself away from the TV set now, shook my head, and broke out of the trance, to simply pace the floor and wait my turn to shower in the bathroom. I splashed water on my face in the kitchen sink and brushed my teeth while I waited. After showering, I tossed on yesterday's clothes; a maroon sweater, jeans, and a baseball cap I had been wearing with the Olympia Beer logo on it. It was time to step into the morning mountain air again and immerse myself into cool, refreshing, sober Aspen life. As I stood on the stairway and took full breaths in through my nose, I felt the pain in my sternum that had been with me for over a week now, the pain from the kick of the drunken beer thief who had run down the alleyway of night.

Out in the driveway of the condo, Lucas was under the hood of the Fairlane, frustrated that he couldn't get the engine to turn over. You see, I was never really mechanically inclined and selfishly relied on Lucas and Declan to tend to the upkeep of the car. Walking toward him, I sorted out what I needed to do in my day; I had postcards to be written. That's what was on my mind (it is funny how the postcards that I wrote that day fell behind the couch at Kerry and Sam's condo and didn't arrive in Lowell and California until 1985).

My car was still in Huntington Beach, my 1984 Subaru GL, sitting on a dealer lot on consignment, waiting for the next someone to find it. I didn't have the money now to make another payment on it, so I prayed that it quickly be sold. Oh, if it could only sell quickly, how life would be suddenly beautiful again!

San Francisco seemed so far behind us now. I wondered if the black saxophone man on the street that looked like Springsteen's Clarence Clemons, with his wide-brimmed hat, might be playing his same song of life at Union Square today. Or perhaps he stood on another crowded corner in the city where so many had passed before him.

"If you want to take a picture, you've got to put some money in the case on the sidewalk!" he had shouted at the tourists. "Because in life, there ain't no such thing as a free lunch. It defies the laws of physics, right?"

"Yessir," Lucas had replied back to him.

"Was the sax man quoting Krishnamurti?" I asked Lucas who was still frustratingly buried under the hood of the Fairlane.

"What?"

Even the abandoned castle pavilion we encountered on the changing desert floodplain of Great Salt Lake, all of it, everything from yesterday was deep in the past now. Bugs had smashed against our windshield all across those desert highways of Nevada, huge bug splatterings. I remembered pulling over repeatedly just to wash them off, with water and a rag, like the poor street urchins I had seen at the Mexican border town of Tijuana, who used dirty rags to wash the tourist windshields, just for some gringo coin. We used to dig in our pockets for some change to turn over to them on those Southern California day trips, in a hurt of pity, even though the windshield always appeared worse.

Lucas couldn't get the Fairlane started; he believed the wires from the distributor cap to the spark plugs needed replacing. So from the condo, we walked into Aspen town in the rain. As we walked we again heard the echoes of distant valley thunder throughout the quaint cathedral town.

Once we were in town, the weather cleared. We asked a few passersby where we could find the closest auto parts store. A small variety store cashier, dark haired and hazel eyed, gave us directions to a hardware store a few blocks away. She hypnotized me while she gave Luke directions. I thought about her all the way to the hardware store. And then the clerk at the hardware store directed us to the auto parts store. I thought about the hardware store clerk all of the way to the auto parts store.

On the way back to the car, with the parts now purchased, we stopped for a while to watch a local rugby match. The players scrummed on an Irish green field with beautiful Aspen Mountain as their backdrop. Amongst the spectators lining the boundaries of the field, I noticed a small bearded man with beady eyes studying the three of us as he sipped on a Coors draft that he had bought from the beer tent behind us. An olive-skinned girl stood behind us; she was beautiful. She watched the beady-eyed man study us as I studied her. Her violet sweater and khaki shorts were a dead giveaway to the granola lifestyle she lived and so believed in. She caught me studying her and looked into my eyes. Embarrassingly, I averted them quickly. Another few minutes passed and when I turned again to look for her, the Siren was gone. Maybe I had imagined her.

The Aspen team seemed to be dominating the Boulder team on the field. Lucas had played club rugby and tried to explain the intricacies of this foreign sport to us; the passing, the kicking, the scrum. We saw the teams push as a collective group, the yin and the yang of sport, groveling for possession of that funny-shaped ball. Another small, pretty girl was beside us, her arm locked tightly around her boyfriend. She wore a striped rugby shirt and whispered sweet passions in his ear, but he just looked forward. He seemed uninterested in her. He breathed heavily and was entirely focused on the game. He had a beautiful girl, and he didn't even appear to care. This kept her closer to him, for she was totally entranced in his distant gaze. Love was so complicated. You show someone you care, and they lose you; you show someone you don't care, and they want you. Why did it have to be this way? I thought of my own fall from grace. Colette was lost, and I was locked in my dungeon now, with Jeff Beck's "Cause We've Ended As Lovers" playing forever in the soundtrack of my mind.

After a while, we headed back to the car where Lucas and Declan set to work putting in the new distributor cap. Luke jumped in the driver's seat, turned the ignition key, and the engine turned over easily. *Vroom, vroom!* Declan and I hopped in for the short trip back into town to now look for Lucas's mother, three sisters, and brother Kenny who told us they'd be at "Little Annie's," a small little wooden restaurant named after the daughter of a silver miner back in the late 1870s. As soon as we got there, we ordered up a few pitchers of sweet lip-smacking draft beer and a taco pizza to split amongst the eight of us. Luke's mom didn't have any of the beer, of course. The older, heavyset waitress at Little Annie's, her hair all pulled back and bunched atop the crown of her head, seemed put off by the lot of us as she took our order. Her hair was pulled too tight, I thought. It pulled her eyes out hard and stretched the skin all of the way to her nose. We were eight tourists splitting one measly pizza. I looked out at a wooden caricature of three miners and a lady, presumably "Little Annie" herself, on the wall across from our weathered wooden booth. I thought of "Little Annie" way out here in that crazy West in the 1870s. How Paddy hadn't even made it over to Lowell in 1870, yet this town was here in all of its glory and all these ripping mountains even then. And was this little Annie, the supposed daughter of a silver miner, a real-live person or just a make-believe person because it made for this great story? Stories were the essence of life.

In the booth, Lucas's sister Faith pulled out all of her pictures that she had taken at the Los Angeles Summer Olympics that we all had attended with her just weeks before we left California. She also showed us pictures of the San Francisco Marathon that Lucas and our roommate Jesse competed in on August 9th. Crazy Jesse had run the race without even training for it; he figured that just by riding his bicycle everywhere and playing tennis constantly, that 26.2 miles of pure pavement wouldn't be that difficult to weather by foot. He was always like this. Jesse finished the race in about four hours but really didn't feel too well after that. He lay down at the side of the road at the finish line ready to die; people passing by actually thought he did die. Lucas finished a good bit before Jesse because he had trained to run in the thing. Faith showed all of us the pictures—Luke smiling at the glorious finish line. I noticed that it was a finish line so unlike that childhood memory of Polly Town's wall that I had. Luke's finish line was a magnificent finish line with lots and lots of people behind it. In Faith's pictures, all of the people were happy at that finish line; they all had the appearance like they had been there for eons, all of the people who had gotten there before Luke. Everybody was waiting with warm and open arms. Faith was at Luke's finish line.

As we all began to eat our taco pizza, I now heard classic rock-and-roll music coming from somewhere in the recesses of "Little Annie's Kitchen," from beyond the swinging kitchen service doors, but the sound was ever so faint.

CHAPTER 14

That night, it was a night of everything. Trivial Pursuit with the Coppens family around the round oak kitchen table while listening to an early *Freewheelin' Bob Dylan* and classic Motown, followed by more drinking (at least ten beers' worth in the Aspen nightclubs) while we talked about Shirley MacLaine's belief in reincarnation and the fourth dimension. We talked about all of life being an illusion and other planes of existence like this fourth dimension of hers occupying the exact same space we stood in now. We talked about Stephen Hawking and Albert Einstein and their fascinating study of the dimension of time.

At the condo, Lucas and I talked late into the night with Lucas's sisters Faith and Anna while Declan ran down to the river chasing two Irish girls that had called up to Kerry's living room window looking for Lucas's brother Kenny. Declan tried to fool them and be Kenny, who wanted no part of it, and threw on the same clothes that Kenny had been wearing earlier. He ran down into the darkness to find the girls. He chased their Irish echoes down the trails of night but came back about a half hour later disillusioned. They were gone.

Early in the morning, Declan and I finally crashed, but Luke, his two younger brothers, and his three sisters, all continued talking around the table in the kitchen until six a.m.; they talked lovingly about their youngest brother Nate. Nate had died a year before, going to work at a pizza parlor, driving a lone country road back in Topeka. He had been hit head-on by a carload of drunken girls.

Sunday morning, September 2nd, and the ninth day of being on the road came quickly. I awoke once again in the living room of Kerry and Sam's apartment, but had managed (because of the others talking all night) to have scored the coveted fold-out couch. No more shaggy carpet burns for Mike Hogan, I thought.

We all went to church that morning and after church, we gathered up with Luke's whole family and headed out to a nearby ski resort, stopping once along the way at a McDonald's. I shoveled down two filet of fish sandwiches and a chocolate shake outside the fast-food restaurant, fueling my junk food cravings before our anticipated mountain climb. McDonald's in Aspen . . . It was a stark symbol of the corporate commercialism I loathed, right smack-dab in the middle of God's creation. I thought about the irony of it all.

When we arrived at the ski resort, twelve of us jumped on six chair lifts for six dollars apiece and rode them as high as they would take us. I noticed upon disembarking from the chair at the top of the lift how much easier it was to jump off at the turn without a pair of skis or poles in my hand. From the lift shack, we all had to climb another 100 yards or so to get to the summit.

A sign at the summit told us we were at 11,700 feet. It was a cool forty-eight degrees Fahrenheit and the panoramic summit seating gave us a view of the whole wide world.

Kerry's architect fiancé Sam pointed to the distant mountains, two of them peaked with streaked snow. He told us they were called Maroon Bells. In the breezy air, I thought that Sam said "Marooned Bells" and wondered how they had come to be called that. They were marooned rocky peaks standing out against hills of greens and fallen gray trees. Just like the scene at Tahoe, people were in the air below us, but their winged toys were hang gliders and not the parachutes of the Sierra lake. These hang gliders were just like those that sailed off of the cliffs of Torrey Pines State Beach just north of San Diego, where Colette and I used to hike. I wrote about them one day, inspired and frightened by the thought of the reliance on only the wind to carry you . . . the thought of completely letting yourself go. It was life and death in perfect balance.

Hang Glider
Tattered wind drawn kite
Scream while you're in flight
For the wind's your only sight

Sky diver
Cannot find his way
The thoughts won't go away
The pain is here to stay

Sky glider
Falling, spin away
Cannot change the day
Gray spider, go away

Gray spider
Waiting, cannot see
Although you can't be free
You can't imprison me

Gray spider
Your web will catch the rain
Is it worth it, all the pain
To weave it all again

Hang glider
Scream aboard my kite
Sail with all my might
For a moth flies toward the light

We were on top of the whole world in Aspen. Twelve of us stood quietly and walked around the summit separately, taking in the valleys below. Like architects of the world, portrait painters, we mapped out every river as far as we could see. We allowed the rivers to dip in and around the green foothills freely; we tried to find the mighty Colorado. I imagined the thousand-mile river flowing through the canyon states below us, cutting deep into the centuries, and eventually moving to a trickle through the desert sands of Baja, gasping for life again. How our country looked so peaceful below. There were real lives down there, lots of them; noisy lives, some ugly, more of them beautiful . . . living, breathing, all of them thinking out loud. We gathered ourselves after a while and made it back to the weathered wooden chairs that had brought us up so high.

On the ride down, it started to rain. It quickly turned to a soft sleet and finally a light snow. I was freezing, shivering, in my maroon sweater. Declan was in the chair behind me. We began screaming, both of us, crying to be heard in the biting wind. Just get us through the ride, I thought, for it won't be the last time I ride in a chair lift, freezing cold. There had been plenty of other times; Canon Mountain, Killington. Surely I had been colder than this at times. Sam's sister Elaine sat beside me on the first chair down. She was a Chicago girl who worked as an assistant in a doctor's office. She was blond and pretty; she loved to ski as an alternative to the bar scene, she told me, and loved the Bears and the Cubs. Who didn't love the Cubs? The Cubs shared the same winless fate as the Red Sox; they had their curse of the Billy goat and we had our curse of the Bambino. Beloved Babe Ruth had been sold away to the Yankees in 1919, and after that, we would never win another World Series again.

I stopped at the chair lift turn in order to relieve myself at the halfway shack while the others continued the ride down. When I came out of the wooden building, I was alone, and had to ride the last two chairs down to the base by myself. The clean, beautiful air and the soft snowflakes swirled around me. I took note of the same small stream that I had traced with my eyes from the summit. She still wove in and out of the valley below, disappearing in the green hues of the countryside, only to reappear again further on down the road. With the cold coming at me hard, I sang like a madman into the wind to take my mind off of freezing. I was almost home.

Lucas's estranged father had flown in that morning and was with our group at the top of the mountain. There was an uncomfortable air amongst all of them because of the fact that their dad had left them when Lucas was only eleven; he left Luke's sweet mother to work her two jobs and raise seven kids on her own. Lucas could never forgive him.

I thought about our time in church now to take my mind off of the biting wind. Before the climb, Lucas, Trent, Anna, Declan, and I attended the small Catholic church that Kerry was going to be wed in on Monday. It was a quaint white church in town with beautiful stained glass windows and statues of Christ the Savior and the Blessed Mother adorning opposite sides of the altar. There were lesser statues, probably saints, on either side of Jesus and Mary; and with their painful faces of stone they looked up to Jesus and Mary for golden direction. It had been my first time back in a Catholic church since my sister Kate's wedding a few months before. A visiting dark-haired deacon did the Mass in Aspen. He wore a white robe; he spoke with a distinctive Spanish accent, with muffled words, and was kind of difficult to understand. A young girl and a young boy stood as altar hands on either side of him. The deacon often leaned to either side, as the Mass progressed, reminding the kids of their obligatory duties: "Bring the bread, ring the bells, bring the water, and please get the wine!" After each alert, the boy especially, would jump for a second, regain his composure, and then quickly scamper to retrieve the needed item.

It was necessary for the deacon to drink all of the wine, making sure to take big gulps. Although this wasn't necessarily the right path to salvation, I think it was a prerequisite to deacon-hood.

We had a visiting deacon back at Saint Matthew's in Lowell that was there for about a year when I was a teenager. Deacon Mark was a great guy who loved drinking down those big gulps of wine too. After about six months on the job, Deacon Mark was gone though, admitted to rehab; we never saw him again. He kind of missed his step going up to the altar one day with the chalice all full of communion wafers. They spilled everywhere, and he didn't know if he should bless them again as he picked them up or what exactly to do with them. Deacon Mark fell like Roy Buchanan right off of that stage at the Paradise Beach Casino, and the concert for him abruptly ended too.

But it was Father Cunningham who really missed a lot of steps at Saint Matthews; he was the head of the high school youth group and the consummate pedophile. He single-handedly bestowed more physical and emotional harm upon the youth of 1970s Christian Hill than any man ever had before him or, hopefully, ever will again.

Father "C," as we called him, invited me once with three other kids to a ski weekend in the mountains of Killington, Vermont, but Frank Hogan refused to let me go. At the time, I was pissed, really pissed; I would run away, I thought, because Frank would never let me do anything. But it was Frank's premonition or whatever you want to call it that saved my life, for I never was invited back again, on any trip, with the others. And "C" would keep taking them, tens of them, one by one, and molest them, on those go-away weekends; tennis weekends, ski weekends, or even upstairs in his room in the rectory, or down in the quiet, dark recesses of the Drop-In Center, or in their homes as he visited with their parents and tucked them into their beds at night. "C" always checked in to see how much my friends had grown, God rest their souls.

Look at Father Cunningham
Sitting in his chair
He's happy 'cause our play sold out
If this could happen every year!

We had to sing that song to him at the annual youth group shows. And Frank, knowing that the sin within Father "C" probably existed, but without any proof, could only keep his own children safe, quietly kept his faith and attended Mass with my mother every week. "We need to remember that a priest is still a man, and it's a sin to think otherwise. And it's a sin to run through a Christian tent with no clothes on!"

Now the sermon that morning in the cathedral of Colorado was incomprehensible, maybe because of the strong accent that the deacon spoke with, maybe because of the acoustics in the church itself, or maybe it was just because of my foggy perception of everything around me. I was still hungover, of course. From what I could get out of it, the Spanish deacon spoke of coping with life's misfortunes; he told us about a handicapped boy that carried the Olympic torch in LA and how this had something to do with the union of a man and a woman. Together, they could solve all of life's problems.

I looked around. The church was almost empty. Lucas's younger brother Trent sat beside me in a Zen trancelike state with his eyes closed. A woman with two young children sat two rows in front of us, both kids were about five or so. The girl yawned with a headband of flowers on, and the boy crawled around on the floor of the pew in and around the kneeler, as their mother looked straight-ahead at the struggling deacon.

A tall and attractive olive-skinned girl, who looked about twenty years old, sat further on down in the same pew as the young family. The twenty-year-old's sister, about sixteen, was on her right with what appeared to be their parents at the far end of the row. The twenty-year-old girl cast several mean glances toward the children, probably upset at them for distracting her during the sermon.

I watched them all as the Mass drew to a crescendo, with everyone in the church (except for the young kids and me) lining up to receive communion from the blessed hand of the visiting deacon. Trent handed his trance over to me, I felt, for he got up slowly to join the others in the communion line.

I felt I was outside looking in at a world that I wasn't a member of anymore; I forgot the routine of it all. I could recite the Apostles Creed or the Act of Contrition, all of them, verbatim, yet I failed to listen to what I recited. These were the rituals and prose that had been taught to us from the cradle. I was an outsider, a director, sitting behind the camera as it rolled with a rock-and-roll ballad with a beat all too familiar to me; it permeated my senses as the people took their place and received the perfect round bread wafers one by one.

It was one of those songs that always came into my head. The ballad started out softly and slowly. I imagined getting married myself. The song had a repetitive lead guitar riff that pinged like water dripping into the visual of an open mountain pool. There were ringlets all around the falling drops, followed by the slow buildup of the band's vocals. It was the familiar psychedelic sound of Jefferson Airplane that I heard. I could hear their words . . . the beautiful tenor sounds of Marty Balin with the harmonizing backup of Grace Slick as they sang "Today"; it was such a perfect song for my wedding.

In this secret world in my head, we stood at the altar, Colette and I, as the camera moved out to a wide-angled bird's-eye shot of the whole congregation around us. Like a passage stolen from Thurber's *Mitty*, like Walter himself, I didn't want to ever stop dreaming of how wonderful life could be.

Rack Focus: I was back at Kerry and Sam's church again. My shot encompassed the struggling deacon, the olive-skinned girl, the kids on the kneeler, and Lucas's whole family, and then it all rolled back and faded away. Life was truly beautiful.

CHAPTER 15

It was day ten of our crazy adventure. It was Monday, September 3rd. Declan and I would be ushers. He was up early that morning, right up off of the carpet and bouncing around; he had gotten all dressed up with his striped Goodwill pants, a clean white button-down shirt, and an old black tuxedo jacket with tails. I had a Salvation Army white sport coat with me that Eddie Kinsley had given me back in Newport Beach that I had brought along just for this occasion. I threw on some blue dress pants and a brown button-down shirt, the only button-down shirt that I owned.

"Wow, you look psychedelic!" Lucas's brother Kenny exclaimed as he came into the living room.

The two of us, Decky and I, surely didn't look like we belonged to the rest of them with their rented tuxes and all.

All of us moved at once out the front door of the condo and headed for downtown Aspen. Kerry and the girls had gone off earlier to get ready somewhere private. We gathered at the same church that we had attended the day before, and as soon as we got there, we were warmly greeted by the Spanish padre who magically appeared from the side door.

The padre's homily talked about the love story in Richard Bach's *Bridge Across Forever,* quoting Bach's line about a love that never ends.

Lucas and I were both amazed that the Spanish padre had picked this homily himself, drawing analogies between the love of two people and the love of people for Jesus Christ; plateaus of love, plateaus in life, and just like the same analogies in Richard Bach's *Jonathan Livingston Seagull*, flying higher and higher forever.

Kerry and Sam exchanged vows as about sixty of us watched in silence. Some people were in tears, some were with smiles, some of them, I imagined, reflected on other thoughts in their own lonely hallways. And then there was that one moment when Kerry and Sam kissed that no one in the whole church thought of anything more than pure love. I imagined no one was preoccupied with the complexities of life during that single moment, no one thought about having to go to work the next day. You know how that thought of having to go to work the next day always creeps in uninvited on a Sunday afternoon? The newly married couple exited the church blissfully, now as one. We all stood and watched them outside. After all of the pictures in the postcard-perfect garden with the white wooden steeple, the flowered gazebo, and the majestic backdrop of the greatest mountain range on the American continent behind them, Kerry and Sam boarded a horse and carriage, all Cinderella-like, and rode off to forever.

Lucas, Declan, Kenny, Trent, and I were among the first to arrive at the reception. A tall, blond, attractive woman, probably about forty, with a young girl beside her, sat on the patio outside the hall, close to the beer and wine table. The weathered lines of the woman's face made her more beautiful as she sat there, I thought. She must have loved the outdoors. The little girl was blond like her mom; she was maybe ten years old, and sat attentively at her mother's side.

"Are you from England?" Declan asked the woman promptly upon our entrance, catching that crisp British everything-about-her accent as she spoke to her little girl.

"We are headed that way, eventually, to London," Declan told her. "Of course, after we complete our travels across America, visiting all kinds of family and friends!"

"Sounds like a good time!" she said to us. "Me, I probably will never go back to the UK," addressing Decky. "The beaches there just aren't that nice, and although it is mountainous in Wales, it doesn't compare to Aspen. The all of England is no bigger than your Philadelphia."

"Surely you mean Pennsylvania?" Declan asked. "Philadelphia is only a city!"

"Oh, yes, Pennsylvania," she giggled. "Sorry. Of course it is!" The smack of that accent was ever so perfect as it left her sweet, pursed lips; tea and crumpets, Buckingham Palace and the Queen were here in Aspen now.

I left the two of them conversing on the patio, with the little girl at her mother's side looking up at Decky with her big, sky-blue eyes. I veered inside the open hall, looking for food, quietly observing all of the arriving guests. I looked for the single girls, I hoped, people I had never set eyes on before . . . pretty girls in this single moment of time.

But the reception and the afternoon quickly filled up. Along the white-clothed tables, there was an abundance of food and drink: quiche, crab sandwiches, salmon, meat loaf sandwiches, cream cheese, cake, more cake, champagne, beer, champagne, beer, and more beer.

In the afternoon, Lucas took over the sound system as the grand party continued to roar on. Luke put in his own tape of The Doors and then The Guess Who from the *American Woman* album. I heard the electric guitar and drum beat slowly leading into their classic hit "No Time"; it was another of the many breakup songs that seem to fill up your world after someone leaves you. It was a packing-up-and-leaving song, and it made me sad for a moment again.

But the afternoon kept on burning, and we kept on dancing; we were a moving mass of people, bouncing up and down, pointing and mouthing lyrics, working our way back out onto the patio area where Sam finally got too close to the pool. The brothers Coppens promptly threw him in, with his rented tuxedo and all. Declan, Lucas, Trent, and I dove right in after him; the clothes all went in with us—the crazy-striped pants, the long tux coattails, the psychedelic suit, everything—right into the giant washtub. Luke's brother Kenny threw their sister Anna in; everyone was laughing mouthfuls of chlorine laughter. From the pool we all swam across and spilled into the bubbling Jacuzzi (except for Sam). The regular hotel guests quickly exited when we jumped in, slipping on their pool sandals, grabbing their towels and cotton bathrobes, getting out of our way, some of them with forced smiles in the rush, pretending to be entertained, but noticeably inconvenienced.

We then exited the Jacuzzi one by one with Declan leading the way. He became a caricature of John Belushi from *Animal House*, with wide-open eyes as he sidestepped the hotel lawn. The six of us made our way in the direction of the hotel bar, dripping wet in formal wear, laughing, climbing a four-foot wall, all of us in a line, standing atop the wall, looking down twelve feet to the other side into another beautiful swimming pool below us, and one by one, we tried to muster up the courage to dive in.

John Belushi was everyone's hero; he had died in that Sunset Boulevard hotel just a few years before . . . the hotel right at the bend where the larger-than-life cigarette-smoking Marlboro Man stood. It was right where Sunset Boulevard doglegs left toward the screaming façades of the West. Sunset was full of famous places, like John Wayne's Hollywood home, and the sidewalks of the strip where heroes like Charlie Chaplin once walked decades before we all did, but after this tragedy, the sidewalks of the strip fell silent. And poor Belushi, at the peak of his career, in the castle there, purportedly overdosed on a speedball, and just like that—he was gone.

A life and a song,
The comparison wrong,
To view them from the outside we see,
That when a song ends,
It can be played again,
A life can't be.

"Cannonball!" Decky was the first to jump in the pool. Trent Coppens, with the most perfect swan dive I had ever seen, an Olympic-caliber dive for sure, quickly followed him. Anna, Luke, Kenny, and I jumped all at the same time. Soon, we were all swimming toward the other side of the pool, laughing, gasping breaths between more mouthfuls of chlorine. Our shoes were still on as we slowly made our way toward another Jacuzzi that had a plastic partition between the outside and inside sections of the hotel. We all held our breath and went underneath to enter the other side of an indoor swim-up bar.

We crawled up and sat on the waist-high water stools. We had sat on the opposite side, the dry side of the bar, drinking Bloody Marys with Lucas's dad earlier in the day while "Suite: Judy Blue Eyes," a love song by Crosby, Stills, and Nash, softly played. The sad feelings had crept up on me even then with that music. Love songs were written in lonely desperation by thousands of others with similar stories as mine; beautiful ballads about lost love that expressed this common emotion of our ever-connected human spirit . . . the wailing, the waiting, the desires, the jealousy, the bitter feeling of not being good enough. We always wanted to be loved, and we all shared that terrible feeling of empty rejection when we were left behind.

But now at the wet bar, in the afternoon of life, I was choking with laughter, busting up at myself, so bad that I couldn't control the snot that blew out of my nose. I grabbed a bar napkin, buried my face in my hands, and then looked up to the other side of the bar where I had sat earlier. I saw a sad person in the mirror listening to "Suite: Judy Blue Eyes" and I felt bad for him.

The dry people on the other side of the bar didn't seem bothered by us. Some of them had smiles, but most pretended to not even notice us; we were invisible. The female bartender, Rufus (the same bartender from earlier in the day), turned to the six of us and asked, "What'll it be? Something wet?"

"I'll take a dry martini," Lucas's brother Kenny said, and we all laughed aloud.

That night, we spent our last night in Kerry's apartment before forever leaving Aspen. An Australian film starring Cheryl Ladd played on the television, with a group of us on the couch and floor, too tired and sleepy to even try to get immersed in the plot. No one had the energy to even change the channel or turn the thing off. We were physical zombies; all of us thinking ahead to another place and time.

I lay there on the floor and dreamed about her again. In my thoughts, I had her there for all of time. Dreaming was the comfort zone of life; it was where heaven must be, where the sun warms you and you can lie in it basking all day without ever getting burned. Pleasant, dreamful sleep; the quiet kingdom where the calming waves crash on the shores of eternity, and the sandpipers are happy to just run back and forth chasing them now, for they don't need to look for sustenance anymore.

In that dreaming moment, I was happy and I was comfortable and I was full.

And I would hold onto that thought and the words that I had once heard her say: "I know that I may never be with you again, but I love you."

CHAPTER 16

September 4, 1984. Cruising the mountains and valleys of sweet lifetime, we were eleven days into the journey, a journey born as a simple idea, but unlike so many others, an idea that was boldly acted upon.

In his sister's empty house, Lucas laboriously vacuumed around me. Kerry and Sam were already on their honeymoon, and the others had left for Kansas. With no one left to say good-bye to, we said our heartfelt good-byes to rustic Aspen, the small beautiful ski town in the sky. It was good-bye forever. Denver, Topeka, Kansas City, Oklahoma, all of the other cities of beautiful America still lay ahead of us on the unwritten road. New adventures were out there; we were turning the page. Our next stop would be Denver where Declan's younger sister Megan lived. She was a young professional who had moved out there for a job after graduating from Ohio State a few years before. The plan was to only sleep there for a night and quickly push on toward Topeka.

As the fleeting Fairlane edged its way out of the mountain driveway, I felt a sense of restful and celebratory peace. I had finally surrendered to the great weight of life, at least for a few minutes. I relaxed my mouth and unclenched my teeth and my anxiety lifted for a while.

Weaving over Independence Pass, at 12,000 feet, we witnessed the high-altitude tundra fields of grasses and shrubs. The crisp air gushed in with our windows rolled down and brought on a sudden shortness of breath to me, but it felt good just the same. Meadowlands and greyhound-colored mountains precluded abandoned communes of log cabins overgrown with brush, some of them were roofless, on our gradual way down the mountain to the Midwest. These empty communities were the ghost town bookmarks that solemnly held the places of another time period in our great America, lest we all might forget them amidst our own fleeting lives. Why did they go? Finally, everything grew thicker again in the lower altitudes, and I wearily stumbled into pages of time that would be forever unwritten. I had writer's block now, where a sudden fog settled in and slowed down my copious note taking. I put everything down, closed my eyes, and ultimately surrendered to sleep.

When I awoke, forests of beautiful pines, marching up mountains like columns of the retreating cavalry, surrounded the hillsides around us and threatened us all with promises of scenic forever peace again. The last war was behind us now, for sure, but memories from that war in Vietnam and how she had torn apart America were still evident in the music that we all listened to. Our poor returning veterans had been treated as outcasts by society; it was so tough for them to find work . . . and the politicians . . . They never seemed to help at all, for they quickly forgot about our soldiers and were now anxiously marching on to the next big race. Another bigger war, the Cold War with the Soviet Union, loomed frightfully ahead. The Fairlane would soon enough roll right over the sleeping nuclear missile silos that promised to protect our doom as they lay buried below the cornfields of eastern Colorado and Kansas. Everything seemed squeaky quiet for now, but Russia was the sure enemy in our blind spot, our leaders said. They told us this over and over again. Be ready, for the end of the world might happen with the errant push of a button! Ronnie will be up sleepwalking one night and *Ka-blam!* Good-bye world. It was garbage, I thought, with the Democrats and the Republicans always the ones drawing the hard lines, and everybody else always caught in between it all. Don't get me wrong, I believed that the Soviets were surely capable of doing it . . . Gorby pushing that crazy button, with his own secret Siberian missiles all pointed at us, if he had the chance to, but I also believed in the core goodness of people. Of course, I would fight to the death to defend my beautiful country, but didn't the citizens of Russia feel this way too? How much propaganda were they really feeding us? Ronald Reagan, the president, the ex-governor, the movie star, was running for reelection, and the world still believed he might be a little trigger happy if Gorby pushed him too far. The election and the fate of the free world would all be decided in just a few short months.

I saw the changing 3D depth of the landscape around us as we descended the Rockies into the plains; forests turned to rocky streams that winded through aspen greens and meadows. Autumn leaf gold reigned on the hillsides; hints of red and yellow-colored flowers were spattered by the Creator's hand. It was true beauty in a country so grand.

The scenery took me back to my hitchhiking adventures on Route 2 back and forth to UMass in the late 1970s . . . How those were colorful times. During one of these rides, I was picked up by a lonely philosopher-entrepreneur who spent his days traversing New England in his big white van picking up scrap unused toilet paper from Massachusetts paper mills. The white van gypsy sold the stuff to packaging houses for a quick few bucks. I remembered the guy tried to sell me on his whole philosophy of life as we drove that winding road, as all of the people that picked me up did, for I was always at their mercy for the cost of a ride. What should a young college kid do? I was obliged to listen as payback for their graciousness. The gypsy talked of how every tree of a different color had a right to that color, and they did, and I agreed with him on that. He also said that Catholicism should be the only religion because it was the first religion, and it was there before the Protestants and all the other religions.

"But that's not correct," I timidly spoke out to him from my seat in his toilet paper van.

"What do you mean that's not correct?" he angrily turned to me.

"Catholicism wasn't the first religion," I said. "Jesus was a Jew."

"Well, I will give you that," he reluctantly said to me. "But the Jews had the chance to believe in him! And they didn't!"

The guy was certainly crazy, but for some reason I kept pushing, somehow thinking I might be arguing with Frank back at the kitchen table in Lowell. "But it still wasn't the first religion," I said to him. "I think there were all of those Indian and Chinese religions that came before Catholicism like the Hindus and the Buddhists."

The gypsy turned confused and silent all at once. He didn't say a word as he looked straight-ahead and drove on. When I exited the white toilet paper van, I felt bad for what I had caused in him. I turned his whole belief system upside down. I might have sinned.

"Bless me, Father, for I have sinned." I pictured myself as a boy in the dark recesses of St. Matthew's Catholic confessional; there was a little window with cloth over it so the priest could not see our faces, but he really could. The elaborate wood-latticed confessional door provided the only light inside the little prison booth, and a scary shadow of a man loomed behind the cloth. It was so intimidating; this was a man closer to God than all of us.

"I told an old man that Catholicism wasn't the first religion and shattered his belief system," I would have to confess someday.

"And for that are you truly sorry for your sin?"

"Yes, Father, I am sorry. I just blurted it out without thinking. I was looking at all of the colors of the leaves on the trees of Route 2. I didn't mean anything by it. I thought I was back home at the kitchen table arguing with Frank. I swear it, that's how it all happened," I imagined myself stumbling through it.

As children, our parents had always taught us to clear our plates and eat all of our food; it should never be wasted for there were starving children in China (on the other side of the world). When I was about four or five, I really believed that the Chinese people lived below the deep red dirt in our backyard, all the way through it, clear to the other side. I often tried to dig my way to China out there in the backyard on those long summer days. If I ever was so lucky to dig deep enough and get all the way through, I could take all of my unwanted food off of the dinner plate and pass it down to the Chinese. But I was never able to dig deep enough though. There was always just more red dirt. So the food just kept on getting wasted at the dinner table. Every week I had to confess in the confessional all of the times that I had left food on my plate. One week I had added up a lot of wasted food.

"Bless me, Father, for I have sinned . . . I wasted."

"What? You're wasted?"

"No, I wasted," I confessed to Father Downs. "I waste almost every day."

"You waste what?"

"I waste the food on my dinner plate."

"Is this Michael Hogan again?" Father Downs asked, "For the love of St. Peter!"

My brother Steve was smarter than me. He used to put all those chewed-up pieces of meat in different places, like under the overturned soup spoon on his plate or under the table for Schnopsie, our inbred Schnauzer, to eat. Steve sometimes wedged the chewed meat or liver in the corner of the table, underneath where the legs come up and connect to the top in a spectacular aluminum "V." He was really creative with those pieces of liver that tasted like they had been marinated in chlorine. Steve was brilliant.

The incredible beauty of the Colorado hills pushed back at us through the Fairlane windows as we eased our way closer to the plains. We leaned into the last of the hairpin turns. Pale aqua brush, rusty bushes, yellows, and meadows of purple haze were everywhere.

Bob Marley soon had us bouncing and jamming toward the smoggy Denver skyline. The light of the morning was miles and miles behind us, and the late afternoon loomed just a few miles ahead of us. Salmon-skinned clouds covered the whole sky in a uniform pattern, with glimmering bumps all of the way to the horizon; I had never seen the sky look like this before.

With the city ahead of us, we fiddled with the knob and the snowy radio airwaves. We picked up Magic FM out of Denver, and Gordon Lightfoot's ballad "If You Could Read My Mind" came through.

I listened to this heartbreaking story of a love lost, a song I was very familiar with. It brought out the latent feelings inside; I had been ambushed again. The story tore at me like it was uniquely mine, like I intimately knew the person that this heartbreak was about, almost as if the words had been written by my own hands.

I soon drifted again within the rolling miles. In my Mittyesque daydreams, I segued into our trip being a movie on the big screen. Outside of myself, I watched the three of us in the car, driving toward Denver, with opening credits rolling all over us. The hero is lost (I am the hero). Maybe it ends in New England somewhere; perhaps in a small town in the White Mountains, somewhere off of the Kancamagus, with a roaring fire crackling away in a log cabin and a blizzard raging outside. The girl of my dreams is with me. Of course, in the movie, Declan and Lucas would continue on to Europe or go off to make their own sequel in the last turn of the script. They had probably imagined their own ending anyway.

"You've got to write the ending first," our Orange Coast College writing professor, Mr. Blakely had told us. "The screenwriter must always have his ending in sight. Take the classic *Chinatown*, for instance; there is no other screenplay written more perfectly. It is truly a masterpiece."

The soundtrack was also important. The right music would weave the whole story together, I felt, for, after all, music was the soundtrack of life. Music had a way of igniting fond memories in us all. It could bring back moments in time; you could close your eyes and be back there again.

When I ran track in high school, I played the songs of the Rolling Stones's album *Hot Rocks* over and over again on the parlor turntable each night before a big meet. This is how I would prepare for it. The next day, I'd close my eyes as I silently sat in the blocks waiting for the starter. I was running the 440 at Cauley Stadium. Right there, I tried to hear in my mind the lead-in to "Gimme Shelter" with that crazy clock winding down, followed by Keith Richards coming in with the guitar . . . the rising crescendo of his instrument increasing ever so slowly, and *ka-blam*, with that pop of the starter's gunfire, I would burst out all at once from those nervous blocks . . . and Mick Jagger with his incredible vocals would push me into the raging race.

At the turn in the track, I would cut in, swinging my arms, one arm sweeping in front of my body in order to conserve every ounce of energy. I breathed from my mouth like a blowfish, with arms thrusting . . . *whoosh, who, whoosh, who, whoosh . . .*

Pushing toward the end, pushing hard, seeing blurry people, they were edging closer, and closing in on the finish line . . . all the while, Mick and Keith wailing me through that song and the final seconds of the race. *Gimme Shelter* was the soundtrack to my life's race.

Charlie Donavan would always beat me in all of the races that we ran. I usually took second place ahead of the opposing school. Charlie and I were oftentimes the one and two finishers in all of those articles in the *Lowell Sun*. My mother cut out every single one and stuffed them in a manila envelope that she placed in the back of the china cabinet. They'd all be there someday for me, if I wanted them. When I got to UMass, I told Will Garrity, the dark-haired Irishman from Southie, about having "Gimme Shelter" in my head when I sprinted, 'cause it helped me to focus. But then Garrity from Southie says to me,

"A song about rape and murder helps motivate you?"

"It's not about rape and murder! . . . It's about getting shelter, Garrity; Come on, now."

Why were people always looking through the good to find the bad? Life was this great yarn to me, colored red, white, and blue; it was like a giant quilt made up of all different patches, squares from different places, different people, and different music all pieced together. The human experience was a giant jigsaw puzzle, with jigsaw people connected everywhere. I jotted down something in my notebook as we entered the Denver city limits:

Jigsaw puzzle people
Pieced together
Church without a steeple
Stormy weather

It rhymed. I thought how incredibly crazy it all seemed that everyone else might have these mad thoughts going on in their heads all of the time too. People just like me in similar places but with entirely different observations on life; just like passing cars on the highway and thoughts inside of them always traveling at the speed of light, or whatever the speed of a thought would be.

We cruised through the mall at Sixteenth Street in downtown Denver. The city streets showcased old and new skyscrapers side by side. A black homeless person yelled at us at a stoplight, "Crackers, fucken crackers! Crackers who never cut the poor folk a break! You fucken crackers have stepped on me your whole life! You don't know what it's like to be me, you fucken cracker looking at me!" he screamed in my face. My window was rolled down.

I was sorry for what he said. "Crackers," I chuckled to the other guys. I envisioned a box of Saltines, spoiled past their store date with the individual wax package all squished up and nothing but crumbs left of something that once was complete.

I saw the pristine capital building; its pale white dome heavily lighted in the night. The building was empty; a façade for all of the shenanigans that happen in any political forum. The ragged people outside in its shadows; the homeless in the big cities of America, sleeping during the day, but awake in the night because it was the only way to survive.

On the floor at Decky's sister Megan's apartment that night, I poured over our Rand McNally Road Atlas. We were exhausted from working out, swimming in the complex pool, and afterward, feasting on a delivered pizza. I found the Jersey Shore on the map. From there, I tried to find Medford, New Jersey, where my friend Sandy now lived, but got distracted and followed the turnpike all the way up to Massachusetts; I looked for Pittsfield, Springfield, Fall River, Brockton, the North Shore, and Lowell; I tried to envision the end of this wonderful journey.

Maps were always great for spinning the time and bending your imagination. I remember studying them for hours on end, throwing myself into their two-dimensional topography, going over every place that my eyes could wander, following the rivers to the sea. I looked across all of the Rand McNally cities that we had pushpin-plotted across our vast continent. I realized that each city was teaming with parallel lives, somewhere similar to my own but also very different; people with their own set of schools and sports teams, with many caught up in their own dreams and passions, trying to get through their blessed days. I thought about the infamous sports rivalry between the Red Sox and the Yankees that I had grown up with, and how this same sports passion could probably be found anywhere in America.

Here I lay on an apartment floor in Denver, one of 230 million strong, a single conscious cell amongst many, thinking about my next stop on our gradual move eastward. California was in the rearview mirror now. Huntington Beach, Newport Beach, Costa Mesa, Irvine, Tustin, Fullerton, San Clemente, Santa Barbara; they were all cities that I didn't even know in 1980, but in 1984 brought me fond memories and friendships that I suddenly missed. My friend Sandy had moved from Newport Beach back to Medford, New Jersey, just months before we left.

I looked for Medford on the map again. It was barely a small typeface town; yet, I knew that this place probably meant a lot of things to a lot of people. Sandy had taken creative writing and screenwriting courses with me at Orange Coast. She was tall, thin, and beautiful, for sure. We collaborated on ideas; she was crazy because she could never stop writing. She wrote on her hands; she wrote on her shoes; she wrote beautiful ballads; she wrote on pages that slowly turned into real living medieval heroes and villains. I sometimes wondered if Springsteen had written his beautiful song "4th of July, Asbury Park" exclusively for her as I often hummed those lyrics in my head.

I thought about Jersey people. Most of the guys from Kappa Sig were from Jersey too; most of the wrestling team, as a matter of fact: Guido, Belotti, Caparossa, Sandoval, and Murph. And those fraternity hallways always roared so loud with drunken laughter. I remembered the night that Buddy Love knocked over his rat cage. All those rats, tens of them, all out and scurrying across the fraternity floor. They ran to the holes in the walls; they ran from the light of day, only to haunt us all later on in the dead of night when we came home and flicked on the light switch in our room. We'd always see them scampering. Rats were more dreadful to me than sharks on the open water; all of us had to try to sleep through it all until the board of health finally condemned the place. We had to block out the thought of waking up with one of those crazy rats nibbling away at our face. But beautiful Kappa Sig was gone now. So was that stench of days-old beer in the rubbed out carpets. But sweet memories still lingered of New England springtime blowing reverie through the open windows of that frat house. Sounds of Springsteen rang through the empty corridors of my mind; the sound usually came from Guido's room back there, his door open and Guido's own soft voice accompanying Springsteen's melodic poetry . . .

He sang about Sandy. He sang about Colette. He sang about all of the beautiful girls who forever haunted us all.

CHAPTER 17

September 5th came. I counted out day twelve. Two hundred and forty-nine miles behind us was Denver. We were flying now, already about fifty miles into flat, spacious Kansas. We had thanked Megan for putting us up for the night. Declan had warmly hugged his sister good-bye, and we were off like that. The great stretches of the plains of Colorado had passed; it was hundreds of miles of dizzying yellow fields and lazy-eyed Susans that called to us from the roadside, but we wouldn't fall under their hypnotizing spell. There simply wasn't enough time. Looking at the road bridges in the horizon, we tried to fathom their distance; we tried to guess how far away they were. Lucas guessed four miles, and I guessed fifteen, but it was only 2.8 miles to the first bridge.

"But I thought the naked eye can see for at least fifty miles," Declan said.

Lucas just shrieked in laughter at him, looking ahead as he drove, not even turning to him now.

Monotonous miles rolled by us on the lonesome road; these were the idle times in between the friendly faces and this was always the worst of it all. Memories of Colette played over and over again in my mind; I heard ballads composed of lonely lyrics, spinning sideways in a dream, a boomerang whisked out over the empty fields of Kansas, and came right back in to sit with me.

Her candor
A plaid chair made of wicker
Her soft light may always flicker
Although

The wax turns into liquid
Intrigued without a doubt
Impressionable as something
I tipped it to pour it out
To know

"Can the naked eye see the moon?" Declan asked. And out came another shriek of laughter from Lucas, who then rolled down his window and screamed an ear-piercing scream into the lonely western Kansas sky. He screamed a native warrior's cry; a cry above the silence that he was so accustomed to, pulling the energy from the clouds of the past, and trying to make something significant of it all. We were all screaming forward, breaking into the lazy early afternoon at close to eighty miles per hour, trying to overcome the speed of sound.

After more rolling hills and well into the state on Interstate 70, a wily coyote suddenly ran right across the road in front of us. I was driving now. I tightened on the brakes, panicked at first, then relaxed and eased up all at once. I saw the sly canine scatter to the shoulder. In the rearview mirror, I caught him looking back at us; he was just a little curious, but not enough to know that this big rolling double-ton machine with the surfboard attached to it almost ran him down flat, just like in those old Roadrunner cartoons. The coyote took one last look at us before he ducked into some tumbleweed brush by the side of the road and disappeared forever; he wandered on with his own existence, simply oblivious to his sudden luck to live another day. The country music from the local snowy airwaves played to us, and a radio commercial for International Harvester told us how great it would be to own one: the "Combine Harvester International 1440 of 1984!"

My father, Frank, was a parts man for International Harvester heavy equipment tractors. He once sold their bulldozers and backhoes; he did this for the better part of his blue-collar career. The company's huge, one-sheet, four-colored, glossy calendars always adorned the door to the back shed in our Eighteenth Street kitchen year after year. These calendars ran the whole paneled door of the shed. Behind the shed door, Frank kept his case of ginger ales at room temperature in the sweaty summertime; the shed that led to a further back shed where the old cigarette cards of boxers had been tacked up 100 years before us. Old Man Woodward, who had built the house, had punched the cigarette cards up there for sure; he had punched them up way back in the 1880s, those faded colored illustrations of old boxers, like Joe Coburn and Patsy Cardiff, with their drawn fists up. The cards themselves survived through the winter cold of close to 100 New England years and also weathered the humidity of all of those moist, exhausting summers . . . except now, they had become part of the old shed beams themselves, and could only be flaked off with a jackknife; otherwise, they would have fetched a collector's fortune for me, for sure.

Luke had been reading Shirley MacLaine's *Out on a Limb,* all the way from Denver to Topeka. He talked in the car about chapters twelve, thirteen, fourteen, and fifteen.

"They're the best chapters in the book, Mike. You've really got to read them," he told me.

Shirley MacLaine was all the rage in 1984 with her revelations of past lives and reincarnation. These New Age beliefs centered around the theory that everyone had multiple lives; these "lives" were like rooms in an infinitely large house, and we all passed through them, they said, going from one room to the next when we died—just opening and closing doors, walking throughout all of eternity like this . . . except the next room could be bigger and better than the one behind you if you suddenly became "consciously aware." That was the whole purpose of life, the "New Agers" said . . . to learn, to grow, to be a better person, and to graduate into the next room; sort of like how it all happened in Richard Bach's *Jonathan Livingston Seagull* as the seagull flew to higher and higher planes. Of course, there was the whole "consciously aware" hurdle that you had to get over, I thought. It was magical, I guess, if you got to the next room (your next life) "consciously aware" of it all.

Someone in one of these New Age groups had explained to me that "consciously aware" was the realization of the lives we had behind us, before birth, and to be ready for those ahead of us, after death. Before we were born, we were someplace else, and simply had opted out of that place at the time of death to take on a whole new experience. We didn't necessarily have to have lived on earth; we could have lived anywhere in the universe, they said. We could have been extraterrestrials or even free-floating souls without a body. If we became aware of just who we were before this life and what we had learned in those lives and applied that to our own life, the lives ahead of us would get better and better.

But where did we go if we never became "consciously aware"? Supposedly, we went into another life anyway, but just not aware of any of our past lives. I wondered if I had been Mark Twain. I secretly wished that I was.

"Do you ever wonder if Scientologists are reading this stuff?" Declan asked. "Don't Scientologists believe in extraterrestrials? I sure would never want to come back to earth as a Scientologist!"

I thought back to this one crazy guy in a Scientologist building in Los Angeles. He had the two big Dalmatian-colored mastiffs with him as he tried to convert us to Scientology while we worked as grips for the American Film Institute. He wouldn't leave us alone. He kept on hanging around and talking to us. The Scientologists believed in extraterrestrials.

"Did you know that Jimmy Carter believes in extraterrestrials? He's even seen UFOs!" Declan exclaimed.

I guess it would be kind of cool to have a religion that truly believed in extraterrestrials. I used to believe in them, I guess. There was a day in 1980 when I lay in a hospital bed in Lowell with mononucleosis and scarlet fever, on top of it. I hallucinated in my 104-degree fever about being with the extraterrestrials on Tralfamadore in Kurt Vonnegut's *Slaughterhouse-Five*. I really thought I was there, lying in a Tralfamadorian hospital with an IV going drip-drip into my arm. But then I got over the illness.

I made a wish on a shooting star
I made a wish in a speeding car

People in cars are like people in jars
But people in jars can't get close to the stars
'Cause they're airtight

The New Agers said that there were supposedly millions of planes of existence out there too, and there were millions of beings that looked and thought like us in those other dimensions; millions of other selves like me that had taken the opposite path from a path that I had taken.

"I hope one of my other selves is dating a black girl right now!" Decky gasped. "Geez, I've always wanted to date a black girl!"

Heaven seemed a lot less complicated; there wasn't all of these opening and closing of doors, just one waiting room if you didn't make it all the way—a room called purgatory. You live a good life by being nice to people, and then you die and go to this beautiful warm place called purgatory, and as long as you repent, you never have to worry about walking through the wrong door again. You're done.

"The Jews don't even think there is a hell!" Declan remarked. "Just a longer stay in a place like purgatory, depending on how bad you lived your life."

I kind of liked the Jewish plan. It seemed a lot easier than Catholicism with a little less guilt.

I wondered while we drove along in the car that day if extraterrestrials believed in heaven and hell. We talked and talked on that long ride across America, the miles in between friends and family, for there was so much to talk about, and we never wanted to tire of it. If only it could have lasted forever.

I had once visited this famous medium psychic lady, Morticia Comet, back in Anaheim in 1983 with Dolores the polytheist (from the circuit board factory). When we walked into the place, I saw that Morticia had a waiting room in her house filled with gullible people who each wanted to give her twenty dollars for a psychic reading. Dolores and I were two of those people that day. Morticia pulled each of us into another private room, one by one, and took our money; she turned her eyeballs up into her head and went into a crazy trance, her voice turned real smoky, and she told me that she was channeling a spirit none other than *Seth* himself! I wondered how she could do this if Jane Roberts was the only one who channeled Seth. Maybe channeling spirits was a nonexclusive thing. Maybe anyone could channel a famous spirit like Seth. I bet old Morticia would have channeled an extraterrestrial too, if only I had asked about one.

Morticia Comet told her victims exactly what they wanted to hear. She looked me over; she looked at my calloused hands from weightlifting and guessed that I worked as a laborer somewhere. I told her she was exactly right. We all had come in droves to see Morticia the gypsy lady. We lined the waiting room in nervous anticipation of what good fortune would come next . . . all for the price of a twenty-dollar bill. It was like the sad plight of the lemmings.

On that day in 1983 in Anaheim, the gypsy told me that I had fought for the Confederacy in America's Civil War. I asked Morticia about my hot left foot that was always bothering me when I lay in bed at night. I had fought in the 49th North Carolina Infantry, she said, and had lost my left leg in The Battle of the Crater; that's why I had this crazy hot foot at night. My left foot would continue to turn insanely hot when I lay down to sleep for the rest of my life because of that gruesome battle, she said. The frozen water bottle (to rest my hot foot on so I could relax and go to sleep) would have to stay at the foot of my bed forever. For twenty dollars, Morticia told me that the hot foot would never go away.

"Did I die in that battle, ma'am?"

"No, you lived for many years after it," Morticia told me. Of course, I did!

I also asked the twenty-dollar gypsy if she knew the author Richard Bach, and sure enough, she used to date him! Of course, she did! She told me everything I wanted to hear, all for the price of twenty dollars.

In Kansas, we drove by alfalfa fields, fields of hay and grasses, and steel silos, with cattle in the distance. All of the livestock appeared to be frozen miniatures so far across the fields, frozen yet discernible, dotting the low hills for miles. Here we were right smack-dab in the middle of America, I thought, sailing east with a surfboard atop our car, the three of us braving the seas of waving grains, spellbound, cruising on the greatest deck of the greatest ship of our forever beautiful lives.

Declan had picked up a crazy straw hat somewhere along the route. Lucas and I had no idea where it came from. He pulled it out from his collection of things to wear through Kansas like Huck Finn. All of a sudden, Decky wanted to stop on the shoulder for a single long strand of wheat or some grain to clench between his teeth while we drove into the radio airwave stock calls of a country-accented announcer. We pulled over briefly for Decky to get his fix, and the announcer then proclaimed, "Mayweed at 262, large corn at 292 and a quarter, and soybeans at 629 high!" In the sun, I watched swirls of miniature wind tunnels kicking up on the harvested torn up fields around us. Out of the car, I now sensed the Midwest humidity, the musty and sticky humidity that had slowly overtaken us, mile by mile, deep into Kansas. We had long left the cool, smoggy breezes and urban streets of Denver behind.

Denver was 300 miles behind us. The sea of Kansas roared with waves of rolling green hills; corn and soybeans called the odds against everything now. Time was flying. Four big western states were now nothing but written memories in a notebook; the smoky sand castles of ghosts and gamblers who played their own futures in Winnemucca were gone. The eve of the burly Midwest now beckoned to us to stay close and follow her eastward.

The '80s band Berlin dribbled the song "The Metro" from the radio. It was new music of synthesized sounds, electronic keyboards, and a fast paced tempo; a tempo too quick for Kansas. It didn't belong here. This was the tempo for beer-drenched disco nightclubs in Huntington Beach, I thought, where DJs like Snaggletooth Sabbath sat in dark booths while people lined the packed dance floor smoking their cigarettes. Music for the dance clubs . . . the beat playing over and over as our beach friend Brian Kelly shrieked the corn dog whistle at all of the passersby. If the girls turned to look his way while he shrieked that whistle, he had a chance to take them home.

On that lonely coyote highway in Kansas, we passed a few more fields colored with rusted alfalfa before the landscape finally turned into the hills and trees of Luke's native Topeka.

We had arrived! Topeka at last! Past the city, we pulled into Luke's childhood driveway at dusk. I silently observed the waning light in the smoky rural wind, with the orange sun highlighting a faint five-mile distant Topeka dome; a dome nestled in the forefront of a skyline that slowly sank back toward Denver and Winnemucca and Huntington Beach.

We got out of the car as Midwest screen doors slammed on their rusty wire springs everywhere. There was an unexplained comfort to it all . . . the smell of the last of the August air lingered in the night, somewhat cooling; the monotone buzz of the cicadas went uninterrupted. It reminded me of where we were and where we might have been. The buzzes were close enough to the sounds of my summer childhood to awaken all of the Eighteenth Street memories again. The cicada sounds were different than their New England cousins, however. The New England Dogday Harvestflies had much thicker accents, deep and chainsawlike, accents that extended for a minute or two longer and sounded more like the sounds of engines from minibikes twisting up those Christian Hill streets. The Kansas cicadas were softer yet more succinct.

I wondered for a moment about the biblical plague of the locusts as I looked out onto the cornfields in Lucas's backyard and listened to the emerging night of his Topeka. I didn't know why. Perhaps it was a picture of the Midwest in my mind with swarms of locusts all over the crops from some distant story I had heard. Perhaps it was from the background ringing of the cicadas themselves.

The storms of thorns
Reigned outside
As thick as a plague of locusts

A shelter of comfort
Reigned inside
Where people had turned to their faith

Luke's mother, the sweet matriarch of the Coppens family, was sitting in her living room watching TV when we walked in through the back screen door of her house. His father had long left his mother to raise seven kids on her own. The wire spring stretched and then pulled the door back, making it slam on the threshold, boldly announcing our arrival. I watched the Everly Brothers singing on TV in the reflection of the big picture window across the Topeka living room as Mrs. Coppens all at once jumped up and smiled, then moved quickly to her son. The Everlys were live in concert singing "Bye, Bye, Love."

And the cicadas joined in and sang up from the cornfields that lay just out the back door in the Kansas night. They would never leave, for they belonged here; their sounds had been a part of these regions for centuries, I guessed. They were the sounds of the earth that came before us all, sounds that were with the natives of the plains all the way to the Merrimack, sounds that came with the retreat of the great mile-high cliffs of ice that first exposed these virgin resources of our great, beautiful America and begat all of creation.

CHAPTER 18

Luke's younger brother Trent and his girlfriend Debbie sat in the quaint living room with Mrs. Coppens. It had been a typical Wednesday night for them. I had walked in with my journal in my hand and almost immediately, upon noticing it, Trent asked if he could see it. You see, he was a writer too. I passed it to him cautiously (for I had let him read from it before in California), and he leafed through some of my fresh pages as Debbie sat beside him on the couch. Debbie smiled uncomfortably at all of us.

"If you really want to take your writing seriously, you shouldn't show it to anyone," Trent handed the journal back to me.

"What? Why?" I was confused by this.

"That's what I do. I covet my stuff and keep it from everyone, even Debbie. I'll continue to keep it from everyone for the rest of my life, until I am old and I can't write anymore."

"And then what will you do with it?" I asked him.

"Burn it!" Trent said aloud with animated affirmation, looking up at me with his thick brown curly hair and his heavy eyebrows. He had a serious look on his face, but this was Trent. He might just as well be joking with me; one never knew what he was really thinking.

The Kansas nighttime warm wind blew in through the screen door beside me with a rush. Averting Trent's funny look, I perplexedly turned and looked out through the door and immediately turned my focus to the large thermometer attached to the porch beam that still read a humid eighty-one degrees. It was ten o'clock p.m. Even though it was late, the sunflower state still burned with a fever that wouldn't let go. Beyond the thermometer I still heard all of the cicadas talking in the night, from the cornfields across Mrs. Coppens front yard all the way to the capital building. What Trent was saying to me was crazy.

Lucas kept a journal too. I had glanced through some of his stuff on Interstate 70 coming into Kansas as we drove into the cornfields. I read his notebook in the backseat of the Fairlane as our surfboard skimmed the tops of the rustling cornstalks, surfing toward Topeka.

Lucas wrote of other worlds, other realities out there, on the "other side of the mirror," as he put it. There were multiple planes of existence, he felt, and our present world was only one of those many places; these other planes that were out there were a mere half turn away of the Great Creator's socket wrench. We just couldn't see them, he said, for they existed in another entire dimension. Because of this, these worlds were inaccessible to all who walked among us, layered right over our own world. These different planes took up our same space with other selves living in these other planes; they were just a torque or two off of what we were all like.

Luke's stuff was deep. He had one story of these people from one plane of existence breaking through and coming into this new plane of existence. They traveled faster than the speed of light in several giant ships to get there. It was like bursting through a giant soap bubble. The problem was that when the fleet of ships broke the bubble to enter into the other plane, it caused an atomic chain reaction with the molecules of time, and the whole new world blew up. And there they were stuck in this postapocalyptic place, all of their ships damaged, and no way to ever get home. I thought about *The Planet of The Apes* movie where in that last scene on the beach, Charlton Heston comes up upon a half-buried Lady Liberty. It is here that he suddenly realizes he will never get home—because he is already on earth, but a future earth in another plane of existence, with everyone that he knew gone.

Lucas had another story about the clash of what he called "The Givers and the Takers," a story about two nations going to war.

"It was like two tribes existing in two totally independent worlds," he said, "until the day that one of those tribes discovered the other. You see, the Givers lived in balance with nature and the earth, while the Takers consumed everything and slowly were exhausting the staples of the earth. The Givers were very spiritual, living large and telling great stories around the crackling campfires of night, retelling the great feats of their ancestors. The Takers were materialistic; they came to the Givers' world on great ships, and tore through the land in search of the most valuable resources to send back to the motherland. A great war ensued, and the Takers, victors, forced the Givers to assimilate to the customs of the Takers. And then everything was lost."

"Are you comparing this to the story of America?" I asked him.

I wondered if the warm winds that blew outside in the Kansas night still carried with them all of the stories of America's past. I imagined the great warriors of the plains whispering on the winds of eternity, with invisible echoes of crackling campfires beyond the rustles of the cornstalks. The wisdom from great thinking minds, stories that had never been printed on a page, still rustling on these winds; perhaps they hadn't been lost forever.

"We're still taking," Lucas said to me.

The great nations of the plains were gone. These were great civilizations, civilizations of America's past that stretched down across our beautiful continent and blew into the ancient rivers of the Southwest, through adobe structures of hard-baked mud with outside ovens baking fresh tortillas. These were civilizations that fed into the jungles and cities of the Mayans and the Aztecs; this was our forever migrating humankind, stretching as far as the lands of the Incas of South America and beyond, but now, forever gone. I read that some were wiped out by the diseases brought by the Europeans; most were pushed out by the ever-advancing immigrant tide.

I thought about the great stretches of our continent from Kansas spreading all the way to the Hudson River and eastward, all the way into New England and the Merrimack River Valley, even.

In Lowell, it was Passaconaway, the great chief of the Pennacook, leader of the Pawtucket and The Wamesit nations, who was sheer legendary. He lived on that little island, Tyng's Island, in the Merrimack River where Vesper Country Club now sits. They said there was never a bad thing written about Passaconaway; he was a saint, always working with the white man, well into his hundred years, just so his people could live peacefully.

I wished I was back there in Lowell during Passaconaway's time just to walk around for a few days with him. I dreamed too about journeys throughout the native lands of the Hudson River Valley with James Fenimore Cooper's Uncas in *The Last of the Mohicans*. It was really sad how much Native American history we had actually lost.

And this thing called human conflict was prevalent amongst groups of people everywhere throughout all of history, I imagined. My ancestors wanted the English out of their Ireland. My grandmother told me that the English owned all of the land, but they made the poor Irish farmers pay them ridiculous rent to use it. They were dying over there. Then came the Great Potato Famine, so they had to leave; it was called the great migration of the 1800s. Poor Paddy didn't come to Lowell to conquer; he only wanted to eat again.

So the bloody English were to blame, my grandmother told me. Us kids had been told this our whole lives, just like what old Arnold, the Irish singer at O'Malley's Irish Pub in Paradise Beach, sang every night in his closing song, "The Patriot Game." It was the fault of the English all along.

"I would just burn it," Trent said again above the whispering wind.

"But why do you say this, Trent?"

"For the sake of art, that's all, Mike. For the answer to still be out there for someone else to look for. Lose your ego and burn it!"

Our America was in the crux of the Cold War now. There were two tribes, two superpowers, drawing lines in the sands of the beaches of the whole world. We were aiming missiles at each other, missiles hidden in the silos of Kansas; missiles to defend our freedoms and beliefs; missiles to overcome the enemy for the good of humankind.

I feared again that everything would be lost.

CHAPTER 19

It was Thursday, September 6th, the thirteenth day of our mad adventure across America. I woke up that morning, stood up beside the bed that I had slept in at the Coppens's Topeka home, and immediately noticed that the weird feeling in my lower back that had lingered there before had now returned. The numbness was coming from the area of my back where my kidneys were. I had suffered painful kidney stones back in California the year before; it was all those ice cream cones that begot the kidney stones, the emergency room doctor had informed me. But I had no health insurance to take care of it back then (or, for that matter, even now), so I had to deal with the excruciating pain of having the stones leave me the hard way. I remembered screaming in the bathroom when they hit, and now I feared that all of my drinking on the road might have somehow brought the stones back again.

But after working out with free weights at Luke's sister Anna's club in the morning, the sensations all of a sudden dissipated and I forgot about them once again.

We had lunch at Anna's club, where Anna ordered up all of this food for us; there was sliced turkey on pita bread, stuffed potatoes with cottage cheese, chef's salad, ham, lots of sliced roast beef, and then a small whole wheat pizza that we all split. Decky quietly slipped a ten-dollar bill to the pretty girl behind the deli cash register as the food came rolling out. He was careful to not let Anna see him do this, for she wouldn't have approved of it for sure. Anna insisted that the three of us keep what money we had for our long trip ahead.

While eating lunch, Lucas announced to us all that he had read in the morning paper that Jane Roberts, the author of *Seth Speaks*, had died the day before, on September 5th.

"Really?" Anna and I said in unison.

"Maybe she went to another plane of existence, another life somewhere else, perhaps to another planet," Lucas wondered.

"Maybe she just went to heaven," Declan added.

"Maybe her spirit now sits in a Pacific Northwest bookstore! With burning incense and new age crystals dangling from the rafters, with distant tapes of whale sounds playing in the background," I pictured Trent (who wasn't there) saying to us all.

"But what about Seth? Where did he go? Or is he still floating around out in the cosmos, jumping from body to body (like that crazy gypsy in Anaheim) in order to channel more books to the masses?" I wondered again.

"He didn't possess her; she was just his spiritual medium. There's a big difference between channeling a spirit and a spirit possessing someone," Lucas assured me.

"With Jane gone, what will come next?" everyone wondered.

After lunch, we went to Anna and Laird's (Anna's fiancé) new house for a quick tour of their one-story ranch, with Murphy, their German shepherd barking at us from behind the screen door as we pulled up in the Fairlane. I assumed poor Murphy only saw us in his dog life shades of gray. To him, we were three strangers in a big crazy machine with beautiful, annoying rubber tires that spun in slow, dizzy circles as the car turned the tight corner into his driveway. This was Murphy's domain that we entered; he had carefully pissed out the parameters of his yard, marking the bushes in the corners, and we had intruded.

The bungie cord that held our surfboard down hadn't been adjusted for days; everything was still tight, of course, but for us, the stationary surfboard was becoming a permanent part of the car. We didn't even notice now; it was a rudder in the darkness of night steering us a little left of normalcy the longer we kept it up there.

We had kept close enough to the masses of normal, working humanity to be entertaining to them, though. We needed them, and they needed us. Perhaps our mere presence was a welcome escape for some, but not for poor Murphy.

From Anna and Laird's, we drove to Washburn University to meet up with Laird where he was a defensive coordinator for their football program. We toured Washburn's field house under his guidance. He showed us the indoor pool, its vapors of chlorine gas rising off of the surface in the large open room like the morning fog off of New England's Berkshires. From there, Laird took us into the weight room, where he introduced us to the head football coach who got up off of a bench to shake all of our hands. And then, Laird shuffled us down a side hallway toward the back door of the facility, where a freshman lineman in workout grays rounded the corner and almost ran into us.

"Hey, Coach, did you hear the news?"

"No, tell me the news," Laird responded.

"The landlord sold our apartment. What'll I do? Do you know anywhere that I can live?"

"Sorry, try the newspapers, Bub . . . I'm sure you'll be able to find something," Laird smiled. Laird turned back quickly to us and waved to move forward, like a quarterback that had just avoided a tackle. He moved toward the exit sign end zone.

"Better yet, why don't you just break someone's legs?" Laird yelled after Bub as he pushed the heavy metal handle of the exit door.

Before the door slammed shut, I saw Bub looking back at us sorry and confused. I could tell that he didn't know if Laird was serious or not; I could see the gears turning in his head. He wondered how breaking someone's legs would get him a roof over his head. I felt bad for the kid. I wondered if he would end up breaking the landlord's legs because Coach Laird had told him to.

That evening, we went with Anna and Laird to The Green Parrot, where Kenny, Luke's younger brother, worked as a cook. Gathering around the bar, we had lots of drinks while we waited on Kenny to finish his shift in the kitchen. It was right at that time when this guy named Tad strutted into the bar and came right over to the five of us, all warm and welcoming. We all assumed Tad was Kenny's friend. Anna and Laird kept on buying us all drinks, even Tad. And when Kenny came out of the kitchen at the end of his shift, Kenny assumed Tad was with Anna and Laird, for by that time, Tad had his arms around the couple, hugging them both, and kissing Laird on the head.

Into the parking lot we all went, out into the Topeka night where the cicadas buzzed everywhere. It was dark now, and I imagined in my delirium, walking from a crowded bar into the shift of night that the cicadas were talking to me again, but I didn't know what they were trying to say. We were having the time of our lives, all headed to a friend of Anna's, a lady named Kathryn, who lived on the other side of Topeka, past the golden dome. Tad rode with Lucas, Declan, and me in the Fairlane, while Kenny rode his motorcycle, a Kawasaki Kz1000, behind us. Anna and Laird were in their own car. It was at Kathryn's place, after we all got to talking amongst ourselves, that we soon realized that Tad didn't know a one of us. He was from Canada.

Kathryn was tall, about five foot nine, and appeared to be in her thirties. She had short blond hair and was vice president of marketing at a company that made shoes. Her condo had puffy white cotton ball carpeting throughout all of the white-walled rooms. Declan and I nicknamed it the ivory shoe palace. I wanted to just lie down on the fresh carpet and make snow angels in the middle of the room when we first walked in. My socks rubbed against the soft carpet comfortably, for we all had to take off our shoes at the door. Into the night, Kathryn told us that she was about to go on a two-week vacation to Italy the following morning and had invited us all over to her house for this happy get-together in order to help her stay awake till the morning. She thought Tad was traveling with Luke, Decky, and I and began to talk to him intensely about Europe. In the white-washed night, Tad put his hand on Kathryn's shoulder where she didn't appear to mind. I secretly wondered if Tad would fly with her clear to Italy and marry her on a moonlit night on the gondola waterways of Venice, where they both would live happily ever after.

As the night wore on, we began talking about religion. The volume in the room slowly increased. Everyone was talking at each other and talking loud, but no one was listening. We talked about the Roman Catholic Church, for some of us were still searching for answers, and even though this was the religion that most of us had been raised in, we still had our doubts. As children who grew up in the church, we were never allowed to ask the difficult questions that now harangued us: why no birth control, no premarital sex, no abortion, no divorce, and no free thinking? What about reincarnation and extraterrestrials?

"Because it is a sin," was the answer I had become accustomed to when I asked those same questions growing up.

"Bless me, Father, for I have sinned," I had once confessed to Father Downs back at St. Matthews.

"And what is it that you would like to confess, son?"

"I think I believe in extraterrestrials."

"You believe in what?" Father Downs asked through the dark cloth in the confessional booth in utter disbelief. He always seemed so confused by my confessions. I wondered if anyone else had confessions like this.

"Is this Michael Hogan again?" he would ask aloud. "For the love of St. Peter!"

At Kathryn's house, as we were all loud and talking at each other, someone proclaimed, "God is not only within us, but we are ourselves God!"

"Come on, people can't be God!" Declan raised his voice. "That way of thinking is wrong!"

It was one of those rare serious moments that I ever remembered Declan having. He was upset with the rest of us for our drunken, blasphemous ways. Why must we always slam religion?

"Jimmy Carter's a Baptist, and he believes in extraterrestrials!" Declan screamed. "How do you explain that?"

"There have been many freethinkers through the whole course of history that have been Christian," Tad jumped in to Declan's rescue. "Gregor Mendel, the father of modern genetics, comes to mind."

"If the church preaches to do good, what's so wrong about living your life to do good?" Kenny backed up what Declan and Tad believed.

"What if Decky is Jesus in disguise?" I whispered to Luke, who laughed and whispered back.

"No, I think it is Tad that is Jesus in disguise."

"God bless Tad!" I yelled out to everyone in Kathryn's white apartment. At this, Tad suddenly got all smug and took my sarcastic praise as a sincere compliment. He nodded in my direction and hoisted his beer to salute me. I decided to salute him back.

"God bless Tad! God bless Tad!" we all screamed.

But then Declan, Tad, and Kenny began to talk about sunglasses. They broke off into their own little group, moving to a corner of the living room in the brightness, moving away from the rest of us heathens who were all still gathered in the burning hot kitchen.

We talked and talked all night. The minutes became hours and before long, morning arrived, and Kathryn boarded a taxi for the airport. Tad got into the taxi with her. Just like that, they were gone.

In the stillness of this moment of night, right before dawn, I rode on the back of Kenny's Kawasaki Kz1000 as he blurred through the rural Topeka streets. We were headed back to Luke's mother's house to sleep; it was so late now it was early. The last of the cicadas were wrapping up their diminishing chorus before the morning arrived. "God bless Tad!" they all said to me.

That morning I had a dream about a beach. It felt good; it felt warm, like all of the dreams where I lay on the beach, basking for as long as I wanted. I didn't have to worry about a sunburn or skin cancer for I somehow knew that it was just a dream. The warm and inviting beach had large waves that consistently crashed on the shoreline, but I wasn't afraid of the water. The little sandpipers ran back and forth again, like in all of those other dreams, but they didn't need food; they simply chased the waves. There were no worries left in the world. My body drank in the warm, healing sunlight. In my dream, I feared nothing that was ahead of me in life. It all made such perfect sense to me now. The light was exhilarating.

The warmness began to slowly leave me. In my dream I got up to walk to the shoreline. Declan surfed on a long, wooden board out beyond the breakers as I stood in ankle-deep whitewater writing blurry, incomprehensible words in a wet journal. The journal was falling apart and dropping to the water. Decky, floating on his board out in the water, pointed to two other surfers in the ocean beyond him. The journal had disappeared, and I was on a board in knee-deep water, trying to surf now, but I wasn't able to stand and could only hold the tip of the board. My shaky legs slipped on the fiberglass, and I fell into the abyss. Suddenly in my dream, I sat in a wedding boutique that my sister Kate owned. My brother Steve, my father Frank, and my mother Theresa, all sat with us around the kitchen table that was right in the middle of her store. Elton John came into the store bucking in a wheelchair, doing wheelies; he had a Mohawk haircut.

Maybe the wedding boutique thing came to me because my sister Kate had gotten married in Lowell a few months before. Frank went crazy at Saint Matthews right before the wedding because we ushers couldn't roll out the plastic runner correctly for Frank and my sister to walk down. He pulled out his pocketknife in a mad fury and got down on his hands and knees at the back of the church in his tuxedo, all the while muttering "Jesus Christ" under his breath. He cut off the runner at the back pew just so it would roll right.

And then in the dream I was taking a test back in high school. Time was up, and all of the answers were wrong. It was finals week, and I forgot what classes I needed to go to next 'cause I had skipped them so many times during the semester. I didn't know what I would do to turn in my final papers. I had forgotten my school schedule. I couldn't finish the test I was taking, and the answers were all wrong, and I was crazy frustrated and anxious. I was always in school. It seemed like forever in these recurring dreams where my number two pencil was always breaking. I tried to erase my answers with sweating hands dripping all over the paper. Indiscernible words . . . I couldn't read my answers anymore, and with my fading vision, I suddenly was blind, and everything was so frustratingly incomprehensible.

Then I woke up, breathing heavy, exhilarated, feeling completely happy to be awake and back in Kansas and away from that crazy test once again.

I grabbed my notepad to write down as much as I could remember. The dream seemed like I had been in another plane of existence with another Decky, Kenny, and Tad from Canada. Maybe Tad really was Jesus in disguise or maybe an angel. They were all wearing sunglasses, surfing long boards in heaven.

Tad had said at the bright ivory palace, "To have faith without question is truly a gift." He said this to us right before he disappeared forever in that taxi.

CHAPTER 20

It was noon on Friday, September 7th. The bedroom was foreign to me. I rubbed my tired eyes and slowly came to my senses again. We had slept for two nights in the house where seven children had grown up, seven kids on the outskirts of the wild Kansas plain, with Kenny and Trent the only ones left at home now with their mother. All three of Luke's older sisters had moved out, so there was no need to sleep on the couch or the floor here. Decky and I each had our own rooms. The wire spring pulled taut on the screen door as we walked out into the Kansas morning light. We were leaving again. There were new faces ahead. With winds blowing madly around us, we packed the car up with our scant hobo belongings; everything fit nicely into the neatly organized trunk. Then we said good-bye to two more people in our lives, Luke's mom and his brother Kenny. Luke didn't know when he would ever see them again.

"Stay safe!" Kenny yelled to us, with his mother beside him. She waved to us with her arthritic arm and clawed grip. She then smiled a half smile while Kenny put his arm around her and smiled too. She was happy for her son Lucas, but seemed to be also hiding a hint of deep worry that only a mother can feel. Her kids were adults now, and she had to let them find their own lives, even if it took great distances to do that; she knew that too well. It was only a few years before that her youngest, Nate, was taken from her on that Topeka plain. He was taken from her in the blink of an eye on a lonely Kansas road. He was just a few miles from where she raised him; he was on his way to work at the pizza joint.

The British New Wave band, Tears for Fears' popular song "Mad World" played in the car as we pulled away. I heard the piano keys pounding with repetition after the chorus; key pads striking steel strings. I heard the ringing vibrations going down the scale in sequence at the end of that somber but catchy verse.

Thursday had become Friday, and my car on the dealer lot back on Beach Boulevard in Huntington Beach had a payment that was now two days overdue. I had to wait for the weekend phone rates to call my mother in Massachusetts to see if the dealer had notified her of any pending sale, and if not, I'd have to make a late payment to the bank on Monday. It was money that I didn't have; money for a car and a life that was no longer mine. I wanted it all to go away.

On the way out of Topeka, we drove by Lucas's childhood school. Lucas looked it carefully over and reflected on a time so innocent and simple in his life. Tecumseh Elementary was a school named after the Shawnee Chief Tecumseh, a British ally in the War of 1812. The chief was known for his strength and determination, but was killed by American forces in the Battle of the Thames in 1813. Tecumseh never gave up, Luke said to us.

We went to Anna's gym to get one last workout in before heading to Kansas City, intensely working our chest, shoulders, and arms. I pushed out on the bench press, breathing hard short breaths; it felt like the weight of life itself. We all did overhead presses . . . four sets, and afterward, turned the curl bar inward, four sets again, for we really had to work our biceps.

From the gym we went over to Bennigan's, a chain restaurant, where Anna and her good friend Clarence met up with us. Black Clarence was a notorious local bodybuilder and had even been Mr. Kansas. At the table inside during lunch, Clarence had just finished telling us how he was going to be getting married on Halloween when a woman from behind tapped him on the shoulder. I noticed that she was part of a large group, a big table full of middle-aged businessmen and women who were drinking and yelling with cantankerous bursts of laughter.

"Excuse me, sir, are you Mr. Kansas?"

"Yes, ma'am, I am."

The table behind us immediately became energized with a roar of laughter as she turned to them all wide-eyed with a smile and nodded her head.

"I told you all!" she laughed.

"Can we have your autograph?" a few of the women then jumped up to join her, asking him eagerly.

"Absolutely," said Clarence.

The whole group seemed to be desperately out of shape as they all smoked their cigarettes. They blew their soft clouds into the air around us and lined up at Clarence's shoulder with their papers and pens, smiling and all happy. I watched as the little puffs of smoke curled in the air over our heads before dissipating far above. But Clarence didn't mind. Like a politician with only public service in mind, he smiled, signed every one of those individual sheets of paper, then turned to us with hunched shoulders, shoulders of chiseled rock, and chuckled aloud.

"Comes with the territory, I guess," he laughed, then added, "You gotta take it while you can, 'cause it won't be here forever, boys!"

When we left the restaurant and were out in the parking lot of an early Topeka afternoon, Anna told us that she and Laird might meet up with us when we got to Kansas City that evening, but I could sense the trepidation in her voice. The problem was that the weekends were always so busy at the gym. She knew that this might really be good-bye, but couldn't bring herself to say it.

We hugged her good-bye; there was a tear in her eye for her little brother and his crazy friends. Clarence, the rock of Kansas stood there beside her all the while, shadowing her soft frame and beautiful long, dark hair, consoling her as we pulled away into the blowing wind.

The wind on our way out was blowing so hard that the stop signs on the street corners were wildly twisting and dancing askew. They stressed the steel posts they stood on, bending them back and forth, just like a scene from the *Wizard of Oz*. Good-bye, Topeka. As we drove, the surfboard was suddenly blown to the side of the roof in a fresh burst of wind. We fishtailed down the highway a bit before trying to pull over. It was like driving stolen cars on winter lake ice. I remembered the day when my old friend Ray Champeaux took that Pontiac out onto Lake Mascuppic with all of us rolling around in the back as he turned donuts out on the frozen glass. In Kansas, I jumped from the Fairlane with the car door almost blowing off its hinges, the wind trying to bend the door the other way. I moved the board back and tightened the cord with one more knot to make it more secure and jumped back inside. We then traveled on in the crazy wind, a boat on the river of life, weaving our way all of the thirty minutes to Lawrence. Once in Lawrence, we quickly detoured off of Interstate 70 in order to cruise the University of Kansas, the school where Luke had gotten his engineering degree from.

Lucas graduated from KU in 1982. I knew the university for its basketball team, the Jayhawks, who, with their little blue and red bird cartoon mascot (the kind that resembled a baby version of Foghorn Leghorn), had garnered a lot of national attention throughout the seventies for winning several Big Eight Conference Championships. At first appearance, the campus itself seemed to have a lot of hills and trees, then chiseled rock, sculptures, and clean, beautiful architecture, old buildings, and finally, loads of pretty girls. School had just started up again with a new semester, and all of these beautiful coeds were everywhere, milling about around us with their books in crossed arms, talking, crossing our path, staring at us as we stared at them. We were old guys out of place with a surfboard atop of our vehicle; I sensed that some of the girls might even have felt sorry for us as they quickly looked away. After all, we weren't Big Eight basketball stars; we were telltale gypsies who just seemed to be passing through. And it was there in that very moment, from my seat inside of the moving bubble, that part of me wanted to be back in college again, even back at UMass, not for the academics, but just to be there amongst them all again, with no worries anymore. Anxiety flourished in America's heartland; I wanted to jump out of the car and get lost in the campus. There were hundreds of beautiful girls! And there was always something about that first week of school where no one was in their element yet and just about anything could happen. Blind impulse raged in the campus air, I could sense it. Good things were out there, nothing was routine yet; and for a surreal minute, I was with them all, forever happy in this artificial world.

But we had to go, we couldn't stay. We were moving across America and had to meet Luke's sister Faith in Kansas City by nightfall. It would be another forty minutes on Interstate 70 to Kansas City though. It was 6:00 p.m. by the time we arrived at Faith's apartment in the city. Faith, beautiful, with jet-black hair, just like her sisters, had just gotten home from work and greeted us with that constant smile and endless energy; she was ready to take us out into the night.

And then we were out and driving the city streets with Faith and Lucas. While we cruised, Decky sang "Kansas City" in the backseat next to me. He sure was a happy guy.

Faith took us down Stateline Drive, where Missouri and Kansas stared down at each other with polished mansions on either side of her lonely street. Although times were different now, these houses still harbored the divided memories of the Civil War. Stateline Drive was the epicenter of America, where the East meets the West, where the North meets the South. It had been called Bleeding Kansas a long time ago. Her quiet mansions with empty windows reflected nothing but the setting sky now. The windows looked back at us with sadness, as if to remind us that every story needs to be told for history's sake, lest it repeat itself. The houses so reminded me of Andover Street in my hometown of Lowell.

Andover Street was in Belvedere, on the hills overlooking the bending Merrimack River, where the wealthy mill owners had built their mansions back in America's own pre-Civil War Industrial Revolution. Lowell was one of the planned cities where American industry began, we were told. She was built where the Concord and mighty Merrimack rivers met; she was built on the backs of immigrant workers—men, women, and even children who tried to dig their way to a better life. There, they lay down an entire network of locks and canals in order to harness the water power that raged down from the Kangamangas. The flowing water had powered the giant turbines that ran the cotton looms. It was twelve-hour days for the workers, over and over again. They had to bring their sweat, strength, and determination if they wanted to get paid a measly wage. There was timeless resolve in knowing that some part of me had descended from these very workers. The Irish immigrants that worked alongside the Greeks, the Italians, the Portuguese, and the French Canadians; all of them had been an integral part of this ever-evolving great melting pot of industrialization that called itself Lowell, Massachusetts.

Here in the Midwest now, Stateline Drive turned into a street full of museums, fountains, horses drawing timeless carriages, buggy whips, trolley car buses, and clean, ever so clean, side streets.

"Did you know that there are more fountains in this city than any city in America?" Luke asked rhetorically.

"Really?" I was impressed.

"I think it has the second most in the world, with only maybe Rome having more," he said. "Kansas City was designed and built as a sister city to her."

Before going to the Royals game that evening, we parked the car at a hotel in the city and wandered into a grand party called The Last Summer Bash of Three Years Past. The place was stacked with hordes of people packed into two hotel banquet rooms, with the divided walls on hinges collapsed like an accordion and rolled back on ceiling runners, making two rooms into one grand party. Faith talked our way through the two ladies taking tickets at the door and was able to get us all in for free. The room immediately opened up to crowds of drunks with a lot of white shirts and loose ties. Everyone danced to the disco music of a hired DJ in the corner, with several portable bars set up at different posts. There was free draft beer for all of us! At one of the portable bars, Faith introduced us to three girls that she knew; two were teachers, one was beautiful, but our conversation in the loud banquet hall was impossible. In the noisy silence, we all at once felt uncomfortable and out of place. It was so reminiscent of those Huntington Beach disco clubs that we had so desperately tried to get away from. I suddenly realized too how we were beginning to lose all touch with the working world. Even free beer didn't have enough substance to keep us in the conversation anymore.

"Let's get out of here and go to the Royals game!" Luke screamed above the din.

The Royals were playing the Mariners. The score was tied 1 to 1 when we got to our seats in right field during the middle of the second inning. As I sat down, I immediately took in everything around me; the comfortably reminiscent incredible smell of baseball in the air; hot dogs, beer, and in the quiet distance, the imagined smells of the powerful Missouri spilling watery air from the hills of the upper Midwest into Kaufman Stadium. Yes! It was the weekend, and people everywhere were all happy again. I saw that several small groups of fans celebrated amidst the showers of fountains in the middle of center field. Everyone around us was bubbling with leisure and baseball. These gifts of recreation and camaraderie were the eternal springs that continued to feed weary spirits and helped to keep the working class sane.

Decky discovered that eight cute Gamma Phi sorority girls from KU sat in the row of seats behind us. They were Poly Dollies for sure! And the beer from The Last Summer Bash of Free Beers Past (Decky called it this) helped us three get up the courage to talk to them all, uninhibited, as Faith laughed with us, and we started to tell them about our adventure across America. But we were sadly interrupted by the standup metachronal wave, an infectious round-about stadium event that supposedly originated at an Edmonton Oilers hockey game or an Oakland A's game or a Washington Huskies game, depending on who you believed or which of those three cities you were from. After everyone eventually settled down again from all of that standing up and waving of the arms when the wave subsided, I wasn't sure if the girls were even interested in our story anymore, but we sure were, so we carried on. It sounded so good to me because the ending hadn't even been written yet.

Back in Boston, the Red Sox were having a dismal year, so baseball was falling off the radar and the focus was shifting to football and the Patriots. But here at Kaufman, everyone seemed so excited because the Royals were still in it all. I went back and forth, rack focusing at times, trying to zoom in on the big picture around me; everything was happening at once in the stands and on the field. George Brett wasn't playing due to injury, so by the fourth inning, the Royals were sadly missing his presence. Seattle went ahead 2 to 1 off of an Al Cowen's home run; then 3 to 1 in the fifth with a sacrifice fly by rookie Alvin Davis. Matt Young was still pitching in the sixth for Seattle, but the Royals's own rookie Steve Balboni, who came to the plate all taped up around his chest, crushed Young's slider with two men on, sending it deep into the left field seats.

"Why's he got all that tape around him?" I asked a guy who seemed to be into the game keeping one of those baseball scorebooks in front of me as Balboni rounded the bases.

"He injured his ribs," he told me as he quickly turned back to his game.

The final score was 5 to 4 Royals, with a Quisenberry save, keeping the Royals in a first place tie for the American League West with the Twins.

Everyone in the stadium was high fiving, even us. And then we all started for the exits. In front of me, I watched moving groups of people flow in every direction from the concrete encampment, all at once. It was a departure of the moving masses, not unlike a colony of ants on a melted piece of candy on a hot summer day, disturbed by divine intervention, a stick knocking it away. It was mayhem. We all moved in different directions just to get away from that stick.

By that time, on that day, the Red Sox back home had already been beat 4 to 2 by the Yankees, and although they had acquired Bill Buckner from the Cubs, they were ultimately destined to finish their season fourth in the American League East. Faith's Royals would go on to the AL Championship series against Detroit that year, even though that's as far as they would get.

Once we were back at the car, we headed to Kelly's Westport Inn; it was an Irish pub owned by Randal Kelly, who supposedly was from County Clare. Looking at the old guy moving behind the bar, I wondered what city Randal was from; Ennistymon, perhaps, like Paddy? The crowd and the noise kept me from getting to Randal. It was probably best that I didn't even ask him where he was from, for Randal and his crew worked nonstop all the while, trying to keep the screaming masses full and happy. As they worked away behind the long oak bar, everyone sang with them . . . *"Whiskey! Whack for the Daddy-O! There's whiskey in the jar!"*

Luke ran into a guy named Joshua, an old friend from KU, and called Faith over with excitement to talk with them by the bar. Decky and I began yelling crazy things across the crowded room to see if anyone would pay us any attention, but at first, the noise was too much for anyone to hear a word.

"You're beautiful," Decky yelled out across the bar to a petite girl trying to get the bartender's attention.

The guy standing directly in front of Decky turned around and looked at him with a confused look.

"Whoa, wait a minute." Decky turned to me. "Never got that kind of reaction before . . ."

We tried other lines . . . Declan pulled out his empty pants pockets and at once exclaimed to some girls in front of him, "I've got money falling from my pockets, and I dare you to turn around right now and come out to the car with me!"

But nobody pretended to hear him. After a while, we gathered up Luke and Faith and left Kelly's Westport Inn to walk the Kansas City streets with young people around us partying everywhere. This was a young people's city, I felt.

"Buy some flowers for Jesus," an earthy man on the street corner called to us with people spilling into and out of the bars around him.

"And what will Jesus do with the flowers?" I asked him

"Come on, you guys!" Faith called to us. She didn't want us to start any trouble with the poor guy.

"That's right," the guy looked at me, shouting as he stared me down, "Don't be a wise guy!"

We continued to walk the streets like zombies, blindly following Faith until she took us up an outdoor stairway to another open rooftop grand party. The rooftop was packed with people and loud music. I recognized some of the same people from The Last Bash of Three Years Past, although they carried with them a deeper drunk than they had carried with them earlier. Everyone seemed more obnoxious now. Three girls walked over to us, recognizing Faith.

Ester, Estelle, and Patty hugged and greeted Faith and Luke warmly. We all pushed among the people to find a clearing where we could try to talk. Ester and Estelle were sisters. Faith whispered in my ear that Ester always had a thing for Luke. With this revelation, Decky and I slowly began to gravitate toward Patty, who was exceptionally beautiful too. But Patty, the cunning artist, evaded our ever-obnoxious advances and quickly excused herself to escape to other spaces in the big open room. Estelle was sweet, poor thing, so Declan and I left her with Faith and resolved to yell intangibles out into the anonymous crowd instead of harassing her. Our yells moved past deaf ears though, for it was getting really late, and they echoed off of the rooftop and clear across the distant Missouri into the darkness on the other side of night.

"You look like a nun who used to teach me piano in the fifth grade!" Decky yelled to a group of girls standing about ten feet away from us. Nothing worked. We were lost in America; lost in ourselves; somehow forgetting why we had left it all in the first place. We were too caught up in the drinking, putting the celebration of it all ahead of the experience.

"I think we're back in Huntington," I said to Decky. I looked up, and it was there that the stars of endless creation once again lit the vast open sky above. I looked out across the night as faint Polaris blinked at me. I once again followed her to the outer edge of the open pan of the Big Dipper. Venus still sat by herself alone in the western sky. The reflection off of this whole open canvas above, spackles of white paint on a dark blue-gray cloth, made me realize, once again, how infinite the universe truly was and how, even though I sometimes felt abandoned, that I never really was alone.

And now there was nothing left of the night, so we decided to head back to Faith's. Once at Faith's apartment, we were ravenous for food and ate a whole loaf of her banana bread that she had set out on the kitchen counter. After this, Decky began crawling around on the floor for a while and finally passed out on the carpet, right at the entrance to Faith's roommate Tracy's bedroom. Poor Tracy, who had long been asleep while we were out, had no idea that this type of evil lurked right outside her door.

I rolled on the floor laughing at the sight of Decky's groveling antics outside her door. It was the last thing that I remembered that night. I woke up once in the middle of the night and found myself smack-dab in the center of the floor. Faith, like a nighttime fairy, had put a blanket over me and also put one over Lucas who was passed out on the opposite side of the room. Decky snored loudly under his own blanket at the entrance to Tracy's doorway. Above us all, there was a whole empty comfortable couch where no one lay.

CHAPTER 21

It was now Saturday, September eighth. In the morning light, I dreamt that I was back at the UMass 1977 spring concert with Procol Harum performing on that familiar football stadium stage. Even though the great guitarist Robin Trower had long left the group for his *Bridge of Sighs* album, Gary Brooker, the band's lead crooner, didn't disappoint us under those fuzzy lights at the far end of the patchy green field that day. He was surrounded by people below the stage, on the field, and in the surrounding packed-full stadium seats. These UMass spring concerts had two stages on either end of the football field, each of them set up over the end zones. When one act finished, the stage on the opposite end zone would come to life with a new act all raring to go: Lights, Camera, Action, Boom! While Brooker sang "A Whiter Shade of Pale," I pushed my way through the smoky crowds on the field . . .

I tried to fight my way out of this murky dream and get back to Kansas. The putrid smell of beer was all around me as I groggily walked toward the bright stage lights and Brooker's familiar voice. And then I was awake. What a surreal feeling the dream had been to me; it felt so real, just like it was that very day seven years before.

I drifted in and out of broken dreaming as I lay there on the floor in Kansas City, hearing the sounds of other rock classics slowly fading in and out from somewhere outside the dream . . . all of them sad, sad love songs.

Why did incredible love have to end like this? Would I ever find it again? What was Colette doing at this very moment, I wondered.

The clock in Faith's apartment, out of sight somewhere behind my head, ticked as I lay there—ticktock, ticktock. I imagined it leading up to an imaginary ringing alarm, and then more and more alarms all going off in unison, hundreds of them filling the din of the morning just like it was coming from a Pink Floyd song. And then I remembered that grandfather clock in my grandmother's kitchen ticking endlessly. I was only thirteen. I rolled over to write in my notebook.

The day they took the clocks away
We threw away our keys
And each of our IDs

No more fences, no more gates
No more walls, no more plates
No more bars, no more chains
We looked beyond our windowpanes

Music was the soundtrack of my life. Through all of the good times it played in the background hum of my mind . . . the ups, the downs. How it wrenched at my heart. Was everybody like this? Did everybody think this way? Did everyone wake up with heads full of music and vivid dreams? What was it trying to tell me? What did it symbolize? The music of the morning light weaved in and out of a continuous stream of moving pictures in my waking brain. Was there a message here to be decoded? I thought of those great "interpret your dreams" revelations that everyone talked about. I wondered what I might be missing—the secret to life that others had found while meditating on the mountaintops.

On the hard floor I slipped away again as I tried to remember if my dreams were in black and white, or were they in color? Was it Kansas or Oz? Asleep, I flew in my half-awake and half-dream state now. I tried to float outside of my sleeping self first, then slowly flew up to the ceiling of Faith's apartment. I could do anything now. I was surely asleep again, but this state of awareness was kind of layered like an onion, for I came back down from Faith's ceiling to a Huntington Beach couch where another level of me was dreaming. Crazy. I was dreaming that I was dreaming back in Huntington Beach! Then I got scared. What if I really *was* awake? What if I tried to fly again and jumped out of Faith's second-story window by mistake? I shivered at the concept of not being able to tell my dreams from reality now, fearing that I could actually jump from a window and seriously cease to exist. In Kansas City, I suddenly lay frightened and wide awake, sweating on the floor.

Across the room, Faith was up and going through the cupboards in the kitchen, humming to the music. Lucas had moved to the couch. Decky was still on the floor in the hallway, although his snoring had stopped.

"Do you want to go to the supermarket in Mission with me to get orange juice and other things for breakfast?" Faith asked.

"Yes!" I was relieved.

It was another windy day outside. At the market, the stark florescent lights rained down hard on us at the store entrance; they were beams of brightness that hurt my head. Past the stacked shopping baskets and the cashier stations, a forty-something-year-old lady was handing out pork sausage samples. Faith tried one. I couldn't eat yet so I flatly refused. I was so hungover I desperately had to turn away from the sample lady as she lined up the toothpicks at her little table and looked up at me.

"Sorry, ma'am, I'm a vegetarian," I said to her, hoping that she'd pull the sample from my face quickly before I hurled. Declan had a word for hurling. He called it "Horking." I felt like horking now.

"Then, you better take iron pills, boy!" she yelled after me as Faith and I rounded the first aisle corner. We quickly made the refrigerated section and the orange juice. It was funny how everyone had an opinion on what we all should and should not eat. Everybody was an expert. Everyone wanted you to eat and live like they did, except it was always a meat-and-potatoes existence out here on the wild frontier.

After breakfast we quietly said good-bye to Luke's sister Faith. With her constant travel and free spirit, I knew I could always find Faith. We would surely see her again. But for now, the three of us were alone and southwest bound on Interstate 35, traveling its crooked vein back into the pulsating heart of America. We headed toward Oklahoma City through Wichita. Oklahoma City was where one of Luke's college girlfriends, Fran, lived.

In the Fairlane, it was Luke's turn to drive. He was Sergeant Pepper and we were his Lonely Hearts Club Band. I rode shotgun, and Decky snored in the backseat, perhaps even dreaming about psychedelic album covers and strawberry fields as The Beatles played on the car deck. After a while, Luke switched out The Beatles tape in order to put in a Pink Floyd tape with the children all singing in unison in their song, "Another Brick in the Wall."

As we drove on, I thought about the lyrics to this Pink Floyd song and envisioned that big, cold, stone wall that cut across all of Berlin. I hoped to see it someday. There was always a double meaning in all of this, I felt. These rock stars were our modern-day poets, laying out their observations of life in beautiful lyrics and rhyme, for it to hang out there on the airwaves and after much repetition, someday, sink in. I pondered their verses endlessly. With the music blaring in the car, my thoughts drifted back and forth in the winds while I transcended all of time.

There was the time that Colette and I had seen the movie *The Wall* in 1982. It was a feature film full of animation imagery and music from this same group Pink Floyd. We saw it at the theatre right across from South Coast Plaza. It was a crazy trip through someone else's kaleidoscope mind, I thought. It was a visionary film, the future of music videos, just like MTV. I wondered if I was supposed to have taken some drugs before going into the theatre though, because it surely made me feel like I was on them.

But people tripping out on drugs always freaked out Colette. I took her to see The Grateful Dead at Anaheim Stadium in 1983. The "Dead Heads" in front of us at the concert were all tripped out on acid that day; a freaky guy in front of us with his tie-dyed shirt spun in circles and urinated all over himself without even realizing it. At the time, I thought that this was kind of funny and laughed at the guy.

"Maybe we're not meant for each other," Colette said to me on that day in 1983.

This had been right around the same time as the Red Sox game at Anaheim Stadium where I got into all of that trouble with her. I had given Colette two bottles of Budweiser to put in her pocketbook so she could sneak them past the entrance gate for me, so I wouldn't have to pay for beers in the stadium. On the way in, we got stopped by security. The beers were pulled out, and the cops wrote her up a citation. They took away our tickets and told us to go home. A few weeks later, Colette got a ticket in the mail for carrying the alcohol;

a few months later, she had to appear in court to try to fight the fine. I never even helped her pay for the fine. I was broke. I never even went to court with her because my Mercury Comet with the three gears on the tree wouldn't turn over that day, and there were no hills in California like Eighteenth Street where I could just roll down in neutral and pop the clutch to jump-start the car. Maybe that was the start of my downward spiral.

On our drive through Kansas now, my head was clearing of my hangover. I drank a huge swig from a large jug of orange juice as Luke steadily drove on. Orange juice was life; I wanted to drink it in until the whole bottle was gone (since Decky was sleeping). I took a few more huge swigs of it and wished it could run all down the sides of my mouth. I couldn't get enough of it. I imagined that if I had lots of money, I would buy more orange juice so I could swim in it. All the while, Luke's eyes stayed fixed on the southwestern horizon that stretched out before us. The road was a never-ending ribbon for him that rolled under our hungry wheels as we pressed on, with the pavement feeding the Fairlane's wandering fury once again as she set her sights through those rose-colored glasses affixed to her hood ornament. She set her sights on the distant Oklahoma plain.

> *We were all born into a time*
> *Born into a space*
> *Given a face*
> *On the pavement*
>
> *But the rook was a piece of the sky of night*
> *A pirouette*
> *A spiraling silhouette*
> *Crossed against the light*
> *It was such a mindless flight*

"I would just burn it for the sake of art; the world would never see it!" Luke's little brother Trent had said to me back in Topeka.

I had shown Trent this song that I had written about time:

> *Hour glass*
> *Half full*
> *Grains fall swiftly*
> *And we grow old*
> *Never learning our lesson*
>
> *The answer is simple*
> *Shepherd's told*
> *Life's music*
> *Rewards expression*

"Those words remind me of Pink Floyd's song 'Time,'" Trent told me in Topeka.

"So what are you saying?"

"Plagiarism," Trent coughed under his breath, holding his left hand to his mouth.

"Uh-uh?"

"Everybody borrows without knowing that they're borrowing," Trent said.

"Then what are you trying to say?"

"I'm telling you to burn it! That's all," he said to me before walking away.

I thought he might be messing with me. Trent so liked messing with people. He had really made me laugh when he visited Luke in Newport Beach in April 1984. He and Declan had been in an argument one day. After it all, Declan told Trent that sometimes he was more immature than a young kid.

"You're even more immature than that!" Trent fired back. "You go further back than a little kid!"

"How can anyone be more immature than that?" Decky asked him.

"You're more immature than foreplay! You might as well be the silly thought before it all!" Trent hollered back at Decky.

"A silly thought before it all? What's that supposed to even mean?" Declan asked.

"Exactly!" Trent said to him and walked on out the door.

"Everyone borrows the very words that were taught to them," Trent would say to me. "Don't worry about it, Mike! We all formulate our opinions and our thoughts from what we learn from our parents and mentors, that's all. Don't worry about it; someone else will someday take whatever they learn from you. So be very careful what you write down. You don't want to be responsible for too much change in this world," he said. "Your job is to go through this life as an observer."

"Why?" I wondered.

I was lost. Was he still messing with me? And what would ever become of Trent? Perhaps he would go to live on a mountaintop and would take a vow of silence never to speak again for the rest of his days—because that was art in its truest form.

The blue vein, Interstate 35, took us west again toward Wichita. It was as if the wind and the road didn't want us to ever leave that side of America. With the sky all funny and overcast, it didn't seem like any particular season to me anymore . . . neither summer, nor fall, or anything in between. Where were the hot and dry Indian summer canyon days of Utah? There was nothing but crazy static air everywhere now. I noticed a man and a woman up ahead walking down the shoulder of the lonesome highway; they had two bags in each of their hands. There were no thumbs in the air; they simply looked down at the dusty shoulder as they walked. Their clothes were ragged, worn out by the years of dirty asphalt rubbing against them. They had hard features due to their exposure to the raw elements over the years of dripping time. Luke didn't seem to notice them as we two roared right on by. Declan was still sound asleep and snoring in the backseat of the car.

Bales of hay dotted the windblown fields for miles on either side of the interstate.

"What is that stuff? Is that wheat?" I asked Luke.

"No," he said to me, "it's hay . . . Did you ever read that short story in school *The Three-Day Blow* by Hemmingway?"

"No. Why?"

"With the wind blowing like this, it kind of reminds me of that story. It's a story about the wind blowing hard for three days, and all the while that it blows, these two main characters keep on talking about life while they are drinking whiskey in a cabin."

"I wonder what Hemmingway is trying to say?"

"I'm not sure," Luke said. "At the end of the story, one of the guys decides to try to go back to his old girlfriend . . . 'cause he realizes 'nothing is ever finished' . . . I'm sure that there's a message in there somewhere."

"I like Hemmingway," I said. "One of my favorites is *The Old Man and the Sea*. I love that book; I love it because it's so short."

Luke laughed.

I used to hate reading and would obsess on the margin on the left of the bookmark getting bigger as the margin on the right disappeared. I'd obsess on it more than the story that I was reading.

"Yeah, it is weird with all of this crazy wind!" I announced. "What if it's the dawn of another Dust Bowl?" I watched the dirt devils kicking up on the plain. "Like *The Grapes of Wrath* during the Great Depression with the Joad family!" I said.

I remembered Henry Fonda on that black-and-white big movie screen. The Joads' old packed car driving across the California border with their Grandma dead and falling off the back of it before they ever got there. It was classic.

"I wonder if this blowing wind has affected Decky's behavior," Luke said to me laughing, "A good sleep is never finished!" he chuckled as Decky continued to snore in the back.

"We can write a new story, *The Three-Day Snore!*" I proclaimed.

"It's a boring read that just makes people sleepy," Lucas laughed a whoop again, turning momentarily from the road to wipe his mouth with his hand.

"Those people walking there back on the highway, do you think they are like the Okies leaving their land, like the ones from the *Grapes of Wrath?*" I asked him.

We were homeless like them, I thought, but only by our own choice. Perhaps these poor people arrived there differently, going from home to home of family and friends, sponging, skating, amassing unpaid debt, wearing out welcomes, moving on, and finally with family gone, they had to walk the highways for another town, disappearing into obscurity, the uninhabitable plain, with most of America too busy to notice because they were all off chasing their own dreams. Just like the Brookers in Tidebrook, I thought, these poor people were everywhere; perhaps they were the Brookers of the West, not having the wherewithal to know any better. They were right smack-dab dead center in a burgeoning dust bowl thousands of miles from paradise, forgotten forever.

"I didn't even see them," Luke said to me. "Back there on the highway?"

I wondered if they had been apparitions. I had walked the streets myself for a few days back in Paradise Beach after we had all been thrown out of our apartment back in 1977.

Zane, Robert Hillyard, Nick MacNamara, and I walked the streets with bags of clothes on our backs, afraid to call home and tell our mothers we had been evicted. We had nowhere to go as we walked to the doors of our beach friends and asked if they could take us in. Sometimes we'd go on "clothesline shopping sprees" during the night, to find a new pair of shorts to wear. We walked through the beach neighborhoods after midnight, stealing other people's things, threads that had been so innocently hung out in the cool air to dry. One night, Nick MacNamara wheeled a bicycle beside him that was left unlocked behind a porch.

"What if we get stopped by the cops?" I freaked out. "Do we just run?"

"I'll tell them we were just evicted from our apartment," Nick said to me. We were no-good thieves.

When I hung with Ray Champeaux's gang back in Lowell, we even stole cars. During those days, Ray would pop the lips off of the steering column ignition with a flathead screwdriver, stick the screwdriver into the wiring there and pull out all of the ignition guts, then stick the screwdriver back in, turn it slowly, and fire it up. Mercury Montegos and old Pontiacs were Ray's specialty. I was only fourteen years old when we went on our first joy ride all the way to Paradise Beach from Lowell.

Ray sang "Midnight Rider" from the Allman Brothers as he drove there, taking the back roads through Kenwood, Methuen, Lawrence, Newburyport, and Salisbury. We cruised coolly through the marshes of the Brookers and sailed into the sweet salt air of Paradise, finally there. Life seemed easy for us cheaters. For a fleeting false moment, it was pristine.

Ray Champeaux sang as if he were Greg Allman himself, singing "Midnight Rider" and riding all high and mighty in that stolen car all the way home . . .

One morning after one of those great rides to Paradise Beach in 1973, my sister Kate jumped off the phone and yelled to my parents at the breakfast table, "Dad! Someone stole Lisa's parents' car last night!"

Frank was aghast. He was disgusted with the growing crime in our neighborhood. Unbeknownst to him, I was involved in it all. It wasn't long after that, though, that Ray got caught. You see, his thirst got to be too much. He started taking it in big gulps, having to steal a car almost every night, and the slope got real slippery for him. He wanted more and more, but he was sliding fast. Ray finally fell off the stage. The cops were out patrolling the shopping center parking lot one night and caught poor Ray with his screwdriver in the ignition of a purple Montego. Luckily for me, I had walked from that job. And then Ray went away for a while, but that's a whole different story.

"What a shame! What a sin it all is! Do they know what they're doing?" Frank asked aloud.

"Do you believe in karma?" I asked Luke now on the never-ending western plain. "Like, if you do something bad earlier in your life, will it somehow come back to you in some form or another and haunt you forever until you have made good again?"

"Well, heck, yeah!" Luke said to me, all wide-eyed and turning from the wheel. He looked at me to wonder what I might come out with next.

The sun was now breaking through the windy Oklahoman horizon.

"Stealing a car is a sin," Frank looked me in the eye and told me that morning back in 1973. I never told him it was Ray and I, though. I never told anyone.

So here, karma was staring me down eleven years later. All of these sins and countless others had stuck with me . . . petty thefts, our clothesline shopping, the wood from the neighbor's barn that we stole to build our dream clubhouse, the cars, everything was mounting here now. Was it a simple case of Catholic guilt? I was doomed forever until the day that I could bring myself to kneel down on that cold maroon padded rail in the shadowy depths of the confessional booth in St. Matthews, until I gave it up to the dominant priest behind the little cloth window. Sure, I gave up the light stuff to Father Downs, like wasting my food and my belief in extraterrestrials, but never gave up the heavy-duty stuff to him. And God forbid ever having to give up the heavy stuff to the likes of Father Cunningham!

Look at Father Cunningham
Sitting in his chair
He's grinning 'cause we've all sold out
This always happens every year!

Luke shoved in a cassette tape that our friend Vandy Vanderkampf made for us. Vandy worked for the *L.A. Times* as a writer; he got the job right out of college when he came out to California from Minnesota, because he was such a brilliant kid, always writing articles in the opinion section. Vandy had opinions on everything. The tape was a collection of music that Vandy had mixed and given to us before we left Huntington Beach that night. It was all of the new stuff going from the late '70s into the '80s, the new stuff that everyone listened to now. Decky and Luke listened to this new kind of music too. Decky loved it, and so it rolled with us through the lonely plains now. There was some older Bowie on it, but mostly the newer groups like the Go-Go's, R.E.M. and U2. It was okay music, I thought, much better than disco.

The Human League, one of these British new pop groups on Vandy's cassette, had a hit song that came up as we drove. I listened closely to this metaphorical tune that I had come to know. It was called "Mirror Man" . . . In the repetitive verse, as I listened closely to the words that I had heard so often, it now sounded like the singer was trying to put distance between his relationship with someone else; a lover perhaps? The singer promised to change, while the cute girls singing in the background just "oooddd" and "aahhhd" on and on. Who was the mirror man?

Our Huntington Beach friend Vandy was a guy who drank in life the same way that Decky did; he was always excited about everything, especially new music. He had such a thirst for it; he loved this new sound. He believed it was going to be as big as rock and roll. It was the natural progression of music, he told us. The disco bandwagon had faded quickly. It fizzled in a puff under a ball of silver and glitter in 1979, but rock and roll continued to live on. This new stuff was a derivation of rock, Vandy said, and he gleamed with it as it rolled out on L.A.'s KROQ. That summer, Vandy camped out all weekend at the US Festival in San

Bernardino just so he could see all of those bands perform live: The Police, The Ramones, Oingo Boingo, The English Beat, The B-52s, and The Pretenders. This new music defined the '80s for Vandy. He probably heard it in his head all of the time, like at a Minnesota Twins game or even at those "Golden Gophers ice ha-key games."

For us, with this blossoming age of MTV and music videos, this new music brought on new and endless possibilities to express ourselves in a new kind of film medium. Every time I saw that image of Neil Armstrong landing on the moon with that psychedelic MTV flag, I dreamed of writing and directing a new music video. We were going to do it in England!

A coyote lay dead on the cold shoulder of the Oklahoma road while a hawk in the near distance stood alert atop a rolled bale of hay. The hawk waited for his space back, for our car was roaring too close to the dead carcass. The hawk seemed content to wait until we passed, and as we did, I saw in the rearview mirror his resolve to fly back down to the road to resume his purge of the fresh roadkill, wings ablaze and talons jumping. Crops of yellow-petaled flowers randomly graced the shoulder of the desolate fields; they looked like baby sunflowers. Miles and miles of lime green and rust brown prairies stretched to the east and western horizon behind the flowers. In the distance, I saw purple grazing cattle, some looked miniature again in rolling hills. Our country was vast and beautiful. We had tied a pair of sunglasses that we had found in the salt flats of Utah to the hood ornament of the Fairlane, and I looked out at them now through the windshield as they took in the road ahead.

I longed for another day where I would roam these roads again comfortably with a 35 millimeter camera or even an 8 millimeter as a director taking black-and-white pictures of the gray beauty that the open road of America and God had created. But there was lots of distance between those days. I had to get through this long journey first. And then my crazy mind jumped the mad track again beyond the panorama of the beautiful rolling hills and went dark with thoughts of tomorrow and my next car payment for a car that wasn't mine no more. The Subaru that still sat alone back on a lot in Huntington Beach.

I changed tapes, in and out, listening to one or two songs at a time to get my mind off of it until we were only sixty-eight miles from Oklahoma City. It was six o'clock in the evening with patches of blue sky and the sun blazing hot, burning the crazy clouds away. She also had finally chased away the blowing wind for good.

Caprissi, Taboo, and I had rolled through Oklahoma City on Interstate 40 in 1981 in my red three-on-the-tree Mercury Comet. First gear was down left, then clutch, second gear was up right, then clutch, and third went straight down from there, where we cruised all the way through the cowboy city without stopping. I remembered those never-ending prairie plains approaching the city on either side of the dusky night in 1981. We had never been this far west back then, but had nothing but eyes for California, and wanted to keep moving on.

And now in 1984, I would finally stop here. We were already well south of the Kansas border, with Interstate 35 dropping straight down from Wichita. On the Rand McNally map, we were just a little past Highway 134 and Perry, Oklahoma. I anticipated running into Interstate 40 again as I looked at the colored map paper booklet. It would be a night in *Marlboro Country* with Luke's friend Fran from Topeka. I had flashback visions of the giant

Marlboro cowboy cutout on Sunset Boulevard where Belushi had died.

Decky was awake in the backseat, fresh again, but now I was growing weary. My head rolled back until it snapped my sad eyes wide open again. I had cowboy cutout random dream thoughts bleeding in and out of reality. In the far distance, across the weary fields, lay the Oklahoma City skyline, and all at once, an opening in the cloud cover allowed the sun to come raining down on it, like a spotlight pointing us to the right place. It was a vision of someone's paradise. Another hawk out over the field was flying toward the distant light beam with a small bird, a sparrow, attacking it as the hawk tried to avoid it. The hawk flew in broken, choppy, errant half circles with the tiny sparrow nipping at its tail.

"Look at that little sparrow chasing that big hawk out there!" I said to my friends.

"Yeah, hawk probably took its baby," Luke said.

"Is that a jay hawk?" Decky asked.

"Probably," I said. "What kind of hawk is a jay hawk, anyway?"

"It's really just a mythical bird," Luke said, "But you can call it whatever you want to call it, I guess, if you want to think that a jay hawk really exists. Maybe we can imagine it a real bird."

"Okay, then, it's a jay hawk!" Decky said matter-of-factly.

"I think the term came about around the time of the Civil War, with the Jayhawkers opposing slavery," Luke continued. "I think I learned that in history class."

It must have been around the same time as Bleeding Kansas, I thought. Life was beautiful and cruel all at once.

A light from the heavens illuminated the distant city while a tiny sparrow chased a powerful hawk for something it valued more than life itself. The sparrow had no fear of the dominating hawk as the hawk continued to fly higher and further into the distance. The sparrow flailed hopelessly behind, but he never gave up. They both eventually disappeared into the light.

"Do you think it's karma?" I asked.

"Naw," Luke said, "karma only exists in your world!" He laughed at me with another sneer. "What, do you think that the sparrow had it coming to him? There is no such thing as evil in the animal kingdom."

Red dirt and green grass rolled out from under the roadside ahead of us, but it soon turned to a sudden vast stretch of charred fields on both sides of the interstate. It was evident that there had been a sweeping fire, maybe just days before, for the smell was still in the air. The embers must have jumped the asphalt in a rush, burning bushes and all the grasses in its desperate path.

Wildfires
Forests burning down
Embers on the ground
Fields of succession

We arrived in Oklahoma City at seven o'clock. It took us another hour to find Fran's apartment. We climbed the concrete stairs and entered the small apartment that was hidden away behind a main drag Holiday Inn. It was a simple slice of middle-class America, just one street over from the fast lane.

Fran was a cute, petite girl with a short, black hair bob. She gave Luke a big warm hug as he walked in through the door ahead of us. She had left Topeka after KU to take a job as an assistant fashion buyer at Dillard's Department Store's main headquarters. The way she was dressed with her tight black spandex miniskirt when she greeted us could have told us this. Fran politely bowed her head to Decky and I. Decky reached both arms around her to give her a big hug (the same way that Luke did), which made her blush and laugh. The apartment was neat and plain, a one-bedroom flat with a small living room, a fold-away sofa, a few tables, an easy chair, a magazine rack, a radio, and some unhung Vogue prints on the floor against the wall.

Decky and I decided to leave the two of them alone for a while. We took the Fairlane out to explore and hit a grocery store past the Holiday Inn to shop for the ingredients to make our famous spaghetti, California style. We found tremendous disappointment in the produce section, for there were no avocadoes. We wanted to throw the avocado pit into the sauce like we had done before in Newport Beach. We had convincingly come to believe that the mojo from the pit would give the sauce the great taste that was rivaled by none.

Back in Fran's small kitchen, we, unfortunately, had to work with what we had; no avocado pit, and for cookware, at first using the top of a popcorn popper for a noodle strainer while cutting vegetables gingerly on the corian countertop without a cutting board. Then we searched through every cabinet and drawer for a can opener before finding a small key-turn portable one that worked just fine on the tomato sauce. And then we dined with spaghetti and wine and listened to a jazz station, KOCC, from the small radio in the living room. I was happy and full. Luke pushed at my bloated stomach and laughed aloud.

Suddenly, I began sweating, feeling sick from overeating and wanting for the outside air. I abruptly left the apartment, ran down the outdoor stairs, and began walking down a side street that lined the highway. The great Interstate 40 and her moving vehicles buzzed madly beside me. A brilliant electrical storm was taking place out in the distance toward the east. The clouds along the dark horizon were lighting up with animation; it was another theatre experience somewhere else. The clouds' silver linings at an instant were highlighted, illustrating beautiful hope in the ever-present storms of life. I saw a single streak of lightning break into multiple veins that cut across the sky in a horizontal fashion, a reaching branch, followed by many flashing lights that were hidden by the dark eastern clouds. The access road that I was walking on suddenly dead-ended, and I was now all alone. I had to turn around.

When I got back to Fran's apartment, I felt better. We all jumped into her convertible Volkswagen for a tour of the city. The bright red bug was a perfect ride for this pretty girl. The cool night air blew through her black bobbed out hair with Luke beside her riding shotgun and Decky and I riding in the back like two little kids.

Stone and glass skyscrapers shot up around us; these were the monuments that the beam of light had pointed us to earlier. They were an urban exclamation point in the plains of the cowboy west. We drove past parkways, hotels, a theatre, and sculptures standing all alone. The streets seemed all quiet and desolate for a Saturday night. We passed a renovated high school and a worn-out bus station. I envisioned all of the people in the last century who had waited at that bus station for their ticket West, some who eventually made it to California and some (like Grandma Joad) who never did. We drove by the capital building and the solemn federal building. Toward the outer edge of town we saw abandoned warehouses lining the barren streets. And then we saw him. Here he was! The same larger-than-life cutout of the Marlboro Man. The exact same guy stood there on the edge of the plain. It was the same façade that stood giantlike at the Sunset Strip right outside the castle hotel where Belushi spent his last night on earth. The Marlboro Man seemed more at home here as he looked down upon us in the red bobbing bug as we turned around to head back into town now, his stirrups and ten-gallon hat up high. He was lighting up that cigarette so convincingly, as if to tell us that if we smoked Marlboros, we might look as good as he did some day.

"Where are all the nightclubs?" I said aloud over the wind to Fran as she drove.

"Oh, we have them like any other big city," she said. "You know, there's cowboy bars, rock and roll, punk, meat markets, whatever you are looking for, scattered all throughout the city."

"Where are the meat markets?" Decky wondered aloud, but no one answered him.

But then the spaghetti and wine hit me again. I started feeling sick. I, all of a sudden, felt that I needed to lie down. My head drifted into thoughts of my Subaru sitting back at the dealer lot in Huntington Beach. What if it didn't sell? What about my bank payment? What about the insurance payment? Where would the money come from? The pain in my back started up again; the numbness came from the area where my kidneys might be. I felt my kidneys pressing against me from the rigid backseat of the red VW bug. And now, anxiety with the endless stress that came from my crazy imagination filled my being. I didn't want to end up like Kerouac's *Dean Moriarty* had ended up down in Mexico, alone and abandoned on the side of some railroad track. The wind in my face brought water to my eyes. I never wanted to be in debt again.

Richard Bach, who authored *Jonathan Livingston Seagull,* had written somewhere that in anything we perceived as a problem, there could actually be a lesson in it. In his fictional reference to a great book, he said that when you opened that book and put your finger on a random paragraph in it with a problem in mind, the passage that you pointed to could be the answer to your current dilemma. Was the great book that he referred to really the Bible, I wondered?

By the time we got back to Fran's apartment, I was feeling a little better. I crashed on the pullout sofa bed. Decky slept on the floor, and Lucas slept with Fran. But Fran's cat Dillinger was an irritable monster the whole night. He attacked my arms and legs when they fell off the side of the bed. I had half dreams of Dillinger bumping around below me and walking the back of the sofa all night long.

Decky, frustrated in the early-morning hours, thought about sticking the cat in the freezer. He shouted this idea to me from his position on the floor, for all he really wanted was a few hours of peaceful sleep and Dillinger would not leave him alone.

CHAPTER 22

Sunday, September 9th. We showered early and said good-bye. I ate several pieces of a cut pineapple that Fran had prepared as we headed out the door.

It was my turn to put gas in the tank. At the gas station, I reached into my bag that had been stored in the trunk of the car to grab the mileage notes that I had been logging since our departure. The odometer read 72,680 miles now. It had started at 69,500 miles in Huntington Beach, sixteen days before. It was amazing to me that we already had logged over 3,000 miles. I squeezed the nozzle handle on the hose in order to get every last drop into the tank for the long journey ahead. The gallon numbers slowly churned down, stopping at 12.8 gallons. Spin, Cherries, Cherries, Orange, Nothing. Good-bye. It was $14.10 out of my pocket, just about $1.10 per gallon of gas.

> *The party is over, the wine has been drunk, more barrels of oil on back order*
> *Seven veiled sisters hold out their hands at the front of a line,*
> *Worth more to the desert than water*

The Fairlane was refreshed now. While I finished filling the tank, Decky had squeegeed the windshield clear of all of the splattered insects that had run into us on our journey across the plain. We were now ready for Interstate 40, all 678 miles of it; we would try to make it all the way to Nashville by nightfall.

We would try to go from the west to the east in a day. And out on the open road beyond the city, as we pushed further east, we were fully prepared to witness the terrain changes, fully desiring to turn those pages from stretching western plains to hilly eastern woodlands. I longed for the early colors of autumn and to see the leaves changing; I looked forward to those once-familiar images of home.

The vast morning sky was gray and overcast with September gloom. Decky and Luke began working on the second loaf of banana bread that Faith had given to us back in Kansas

City. They broke off hunks and corners into their hands, pulling it from the plastic wrap that had so neatly held it all together; the crumbs fell on their clothing and onto the seat of the car around them. We were immediately surrounded by nothing but farmland and old abandoned Creole barns, with the grazing cows out there watching us again. Further out there was some scattered marshland here and there as we pushed further eastward, amidst now desolate roads that disappeared into the hills of an ever-lamenting America.

"Luke got his monkey scrubbed twice last night!" Declan screamed to all of Oklahoma with the windows rolled down and the stale Midwest air blowing in and around us. "That crazy cat! Fucking Dillinger! I was ready to take his ninth life last night!" he added. "Dillinger almost went into the freezer with the ice cube trays and the TV dinners!"

Luke laughed. "Dillinger almost met Smith and Wesson, did he?"

There were hitchhikers every few miles on this long Oklahoma stretch. A man, perhaps in his fifties, open mouthed and wearing a baseball cap, looked at us going by as if he was looking back at his own fleeting youth. We were a moving picture of who he was, thirty years before, riding in a '49 Hudson on an adventure that would never end, perhaps getting too caught up in it all and never going home. Out there on the highway he looked at us as if he suddenly realized that life had sorely passed him by. I wondered about the places that he had been and the stories that he could tell us, but thought it better to not stop for him. I figured that he might be too old to be a Vietnam vet but maybe too young to have fought in World War II; maybe he had been in the Korean War, or simply a member of a lost generation caught in between it all. Everything material he had ever cared for sat in a weathered duffel bag at his feet on the side of the road now. Where have you been, old man? I wondered if I might be looking out at a future version of me.

On the highway between Henryetta and Checotah we crossed the bridge over Lake Eufaula. A speedboat passed under us with a group of happy people aboard. I saw three beautiful girls with their boyfriends who pushed the air from their faces so confidently. Here were six other lives rolling in a tangent direction below us while Casey Kasem and his weekly Top 40 radio broadcast counted down the top songs of the week as we cut above them in the car.

Springsteen was on tour all across America. Anna's fiancé Laird told us back in Topeka that Springsteen would play eleven long days in New Jersey. We might try to see him in concert if we got there in time, although money might be an issue for us. Tickets for The Boss would be pricey, for sure. Maybe we could surf with our bungie cord surfboard along the shore when we got there instead. We'd send out postcard greetings from Asbury Park, postcards that looked just like the album cover.

The morning clouds stayed with us and light sheets of misty rain started to come down by the time we got to Clarksville, Arkansas, but it was here that we began to finally see some real trees. The confederate gray forest of the South in the barely visible rain surrounded us. We saw groves of forlorn trees in a misty foggy cloud that extended back from the road; it was a cloud that sat at ground level right atop our earth. The thickness seemed to go back forever, through this deep, mysterious southern forest, a vivid color grey, with ghosts of soldiers of another time, *Red Badge of Courage*-like, still dwelling within the dreamy past of it. The pine needles on the forest floor, seemingly soft, a blanket in time, invited all of the weary . . . those that had walked here as ghosts for over 100 years, to lie down and finally sleep forever.

The gas needle on the dash fell from full to empty quickly. We stopped in Clarksville for Luke to take his turn and fill the tank back up. He stood out at the pump while the price wheel turned. I wondered if the song by The Monkees, "Last Train To Clarksville," was a song about this place. We were at the blanket heels of the Ozarks. Was it about another Clarksville in another state? Maybe there were lots of Clarksvilles out there across America. The hit had risen to the top of the Billboard charts in the late sixties. It was about a soldier going off to Vietnam telling his girl to meet him in Clarksville 'cause he wasn't sure if he would ever return from the war.

As we pulled away from the station, Decky fiddled with the radio dial. He briefly got some reception, KINB; it was a broadcast chasing after us all the way from Oklahoma City, but it faded forever after only a few minutes. The airwaves were filled with static now, broken and pulsating waves of snow, throbbing like a heartbeat, but then they slowly faded away too. We pushed further into the state of Arkansas toward Little Rock. Decky refused to give up as he continued to try to work the dial. After more fiddling, he finally settled on a country music station where Sam Cooke's "A Change Is Gonna Come" broke through softer roars of static. The white noise eventually gave way to the somber melody, with the clarity of the tune coming into full reception.

I looked out from my backseat window and felt a pit of horror in my stomach as the arches passed by, McDonald's golden arches, with their large, bright, familiar yellow plastic "M" trademark on a tall post hanging high over the beautiful dark green backdrop of the hilly Ozarks. Decky twisted the dial again, for we were drawing nearer to Little Rock, and there was a better chance of finding more stations. He landed on a clear DJ announcer who talked about the 20th Annual Arkansas State Horse Show.

I thought about Herb Albert and the Tijuana Brass standing in that pristine meadow of yellow flowers again, that empty album jacket just sitting beside the parlor turntable during my Eighteenth Street teenage years. Decky finally gave up on the dial and the airwaves and now resorted to the tape player. He put in Lynyrd Skynyrd's "Freebird" and "Sweet Home Alabama." I tried to focus on a stack of Topeka postcards on my lap as I sat in the backseat of the car, methodically addressing them to our friends Henry, Brian Kelly, Ingrid, and my parents. The road and the endless day droned on and on. We guessed all of the states that border each individual state, figuring that Tennessee bordered more than any other; we counted nine states that touched Tennessee. All the while, Lucas determinedly drove further. In the afternoon, the sun finally broke through the clouds of the Arkansas sky. I finished a postcard from Carl's Pharmacy in Aspen that Decky and I would send to Brian Kelly. I felt hungry again, not having eaten much since the pineapple for breakfast and likened my diet to that of a python, stuffing myself for just one huge meal every twenty-four hours. Perhaps I would do it again tonight, like I had done with the spaghetti. Perhaps I might overeat again and even feel sick. Life was all about this.

We talked about taking German lessons in Europe, just for something to talk about. We listened to more rock and roll from Luke's collection. After ten hours of mad driving, we finally saw the great bridge, and drove across it, watching the massive brown water river pass below us. It was the great Mississippi River! It was the great river that splits America into the East Coast and the West Coast, the river of Lewis and Clark. Mark Twain's Tom Sawyer and Huckleberry Finn may have paddled on a raft somewhere below us, traveling throughout America's real and imaginary past. My mind seemed to be everywhere at once during the crossing; it transcended all of time. I felt the essence of the South, with the great Memphis skyline off to the right staring the tiny Fairlane down as she approached her. We crossed over the "M"-shaped scaffold bridge, the Hernando De Soto. It was named after the Spanish explorer who was buried beneath the body of the river somewhere, although some believed he wasn't here but buried at the bottom of a lake back in Arkansas.

There were signs on the side of the road for Tupelo, Elvis's birthplace. The signs beckoned to us to venture down Interstate 78 where we might see where Elvis grew up in a little white one-room house, and the place where he bought his first guitar. But we resisted the temptation because we were sick of driving, and Luke's friend Clark awaited us in Nashville.

In Memphis, we stopped for more gas, and paid $1.03 per gallon this time. I noticed a distinct Southern accent coming from the jumpsuit-wearing attendant as he spoke to us. His drawl was so much like the TV show and movie characterizations that we all had come to know. Was this the Deep South? Or was that place a little bit further down below us? Perhaps it was just Mississippi and Alabama, neighbor states of Tennessee that were the "Deep" part of this South; I wasn't sure. Alabama was infamous, of course. It was where George Wallace, Lynyrd Skynyrd, and Atticus Finch from *To Kill a Mockingbird* all came from. I liked that book *To Kill a Mockingbird* because it was so easy to read.

It was funny how people seemed to mock the South a lot, and its stereotypes. It was all about cotton and tobacco sometimes. Remember those rednecks in *Deliverance*? That banjo-playing hillbilly that sat on his rundown porch could play acoustics like no other. We dreamed of Southern Belles, the great football rivalries of the SEC, sweet tea, Georgia peaches, fried green tomatoes, and stacks and stacks of Waffle Houses that took up more real estate than the golden arches ever would.

But the dark memories of slavery also hung in America's closet, and recently, the long march for civil rights. Dr. Martin Luther King Jr. had been assassinated in Memphis. I noticed the late-afternoon sun throwing shadows across these downtown streets. I thought about what Dr. King said the day before going out on that motel balcony . . . He had been to the top of the mountain and had seen the Promised Land—"*God's Will Be God's Will.*" He didn't fear any man because he had "*seen the glory of the coming of the Lord.*" It made me sad. Here we were in Memphis. It was a sad chapter in the great unraveling American ball of yarn. How hatred existed in someone's soul just because of the color of another's skin. It was only thread and cloth on the outside, yet people couldn't see past the suits they wore to see what someone was like on the inside. We fought wars over the color or style of our suits, without even realizing it was never our choice to wear them in the first place; we were born into them! People even segregated themselves into exclusive groups because they wore the same suits. How silly it all seemed. Why so many would never grasp the stupidity of all of it . . . Heck, we were a bunch of idiots.

I wondered now, if Alabama was considered the Deep South, then what about Florida? But the Yankees had infiltrated Florida in golden droves in the fifties and the sixties, so perhaps Florida wasn't Deep enough anymore.

I remembered going to Daytona Beach in 1980 during my senior year at UMass. Five of us drove twenty-four hours on rotating shifts, all in one car. We went 1,200 miles from Massachusetts to Florida in one shot. It was my first drive through the South. One of the guys I was with got nabbed for speeding in South Carolina, and we had to follow the cop to an off-road courthouse. We had to pay cash before the cop would let the guy go. When we finally got to Daytona Beach, we talked to a barefoot hillbilly in a pool hall that had never worn shoes or a suit in his whole life. I used to imagine that as the picture of the South.

But, alas, here in 1984, we were in Memphis. We had 200 more miles of rolling green hills on Interstate 40 before we would get to Nashville. We stopped at a roadside variety store where Decky bought a piece of fried chicken for seventy-four cents just to try it out. Luke and I ate the last of Faith's banana bread and what food we had left with us. We split a banana. I took an apple, and he took a plum.

Listening to Aerosmith now on the tape deck, we pushed on into the cool early-evening searching for Nashville and country music. On the rolling ribbon of Interstate 40, a few occasional houses, nothing more than wooden shacks, appeared through the thick trees. The rolling landscape changed from thick pines to leafy, deciduous colors, to rare fields of alfalfa, before ending with a few grazing cows along long, flat stretches of the road. Even though it was still Sunday night, my mind was already on Monday and the calls I would have to make to the auto dealer and the bank in the morning.

It was 8:30 p.m. when the lit-up city skyline of Nashville came into view from our creeping position on the interstate. Country radio stations ambushed the dial at the outer city limits. Billboards were everywhere; some highlighted the 1984 Tennessee State Fair, another the infamous KZ100, a billboard featuring Willie Nelson, then more with Barbara Mandrell in concert and advertisements for her One-Hour Photo.

We were only eight miles from Clark's house when we ran out of gas. When I had tucked it under a hundred miles outside of Nashville we were still showing above a quarter of a tank. How could I be so stupid to let that needle go down to nothing? I must have lost track. Everyone was quiet when the car choked repeatedly, stuttered with multiple jerks forward, and then came to a sad final stop. We sat there in the breakdown lane of the interstate. Decky and I quickly changed from shorts to jeans and set our sights on a Texaco sign about a half mile in the distance. It was down through the shoulder trees along the highway, so we begin to hoof there on foot. Lucas stayed with the car.

"I should have pulled over. I saw we were close to running out," I whined to Declan.

"Sometimes the needle will go below the empty hash and get you a few more miles;

sometimes it won't. It's funny like that," Decky said.

We had run out of gas in the Fairlane before, the three of us, on a weekend trip from Huntington Beach to Las Vegas. Luke had been at the wheel that time. It was right at the California-Nevada state line. We had climbed up and through the mountains on Interstate 15. It was the darkest night of the year. The Fairlane coughed and sputtered bone-dry right as we crested the top of the desert grade. Thinking quickly, Luke shifted into neutral, and we rode that mountain almost all the way down to Nevada at near roller-coaster speeds. As we neared the state line, the lights of Whiskey Pete's, a great casino oasis, sat out there all alone. But the desert road eventually flattened out, and the casino was still miles away. The Fairlane slowly decelerated from seventy to fifty to thirty to ten to nothing, and then the three of us were out and pushing it from the middle of our desolate stop to that glittering mirage that we saw on the Vegas backlit horizon. Southern Nevada has the only night sky in the world where starlight comes from the sizzling hot desert floor. In the Nevada desert, Luke threw the driver's side door open. He pushed with his right arm on the steering wheel while Decky and I pushed with our backs to the bumper. We tried to get traction with our slippery shoes on the warm asphalt; we rocked her through mere inches at a time. We pushed for not more than a few minutes when this old guy (he looked like Sam McCloud, Texas Ranger) in an old Ford pickup came up right behind us and yelled at us to get back in the car.

"I'll push you all the way to Whiskey Pete's! Get back in there, fellas!" he cried.

Sam McCloud pulled right up to the bumper, and then he pushed us all the way! When Sam pushed us down the exit to Whiskey Pete's, he hit his brakes and backed his truck off. We rolled right on in and up to the gas pump. Sam McCloud waved a passing wave good-bye to us in Nevada.

"Hope you win the big one!" Decky yelled to him as he drove off. Some people are saints and go through life always doing good for others. I couldn't understand it.

Now in Nashville, there was no great mountain with a steep grade to ride all the way down to salvation. In the grand scheme of things, in this great plan, I figured everyone's allowed to run out of gas at least once in their lifetime, but we had already used up our free pass.

"Am I stupid?" I exclaimed to Decky as we walked down the lonely exit ramp in Tennessee. We ducked under a concrete overpass and hiked a quarter of a mile over a worn dirt footpath through brush and the invading kudzu in order to get to the station that we had seen from the interstate.

Decky and I approached two attendants who stood out in front of the pumps. One guy was about six foot four and wore an old faded green T-shirt and a pair of ragged bell bottoms; the other guy was as small as I was and wore a greasy Texaco jumpsuit.

"Do you guys have a container that we can fill with a gallon of gas? Our car is broken down out there on the interstate," Decky said to them.

"Talk to that fella over there closing up the garage," the big guy said to us, pointing to an old guy with a light scraggly goat beard. The old guy was dressed in a greasy T-shirt, high water jeans, a pair of climbing boots, no socks, and a worn-out Atlanta Braves baseball cap.

"Here, take this old plastic container. You can keep it," old Goat Beard said to us as he poured water from the container before handing it to us.

"We're just going to put in a dollar 'cause we'll be back with the car for more," I said to him.

"Put in $1.04," he said to me as we walked back to the pump. "That's your cash discount."

Decky carried the container, and we trudged off into the darkness. We took the same shortcut up the frontage road foot path, under the bridge, and over the guard rail to the spot on the interstate where we had just left Luke and the car. But Luke and the car weren't there. We were befuddled. This was the same road and the same spot where we had left him. Confused, we started back to the gas station again, but walked by way of the road, with cars speeding by us all the while, our backs to them as they came at us off the soft shoulder. As we neared the station for the second time, down in the clearing under the station lights, we saw Luke and the car. The hood was open, and Luke was bare-chested and bouncing around underneath it.

"I've never seen that done before," Decky said aloud, "getting a car to start without any gas. How did he do it?"

"I pushed it to the off-ramp, cruised a little, then pushed it some more," Luke told us as we got nearer to him.

Inside the station, I bought two six-packs of Schaefer beer. Luke filled the tank and then tried to call Clark from a phone booth in the corner of the lot. He couldn't reach him. We jumped in the car, but now the car wouldn't start, so we had to push it back under the brighter station lights. As the Fairlane rolled back, her right side front bumper unintentionally scraped a parked Ford pickup truck.

"What do we do?" I whispered to the others. "Do we tell them?"

Luke and Decky both shook their heads silently. We couldn't. Besides, it was just a little scratch, we assured ourselves.

We looked over through the darkness to see if any of the three attendants had seen what had just happened, but none of them had noticed. But four black teenagers were pulling out of the station in a VW bus, and they saw it happen. They looked at us, the car, and then up to the surfboard in scratch-your-head wonderment as they slowly pulled away.

Under the lights, the scraggly bearded attendant brought out a battery charger and plugged it into an outside outlet, hooking it up to our battery before turning it on.

"Black California plates, heh?" he said to me while running his check. "Y'all going to school out here?"

"No, just passing through visiting friends. We're on our way to Boston," I told him.

"That's an awful lot of miles for an old engine like this," he said to me.

"But it's only got 73,000 on it now," I said. "Luke bought it off of an old lady that kept it in her garage for years."

"Oh, I didn't realize she only had 73,000 miles on her. Never mind, then," he apologized. "You know, I've been as far west as Denver. I went to auto school for about four months out there and even got job offers out in California and Arizona at Anthony Rigatelli's

$69.95 Tune-Up Time!" the goat-beard man said. "I'd really like to go back to Denver some-day," he suggested as he continued to work under the hood.

"Do you want a beer?" I asked him. I drank from an open can of Schaefer as he worked beside me.

"No, sir, not on the job," he told me. "Go ahead and start her up," Scraggly Beard signaled to Luke who now sat behind the wheel.

Lucas cranked it up, and the Fairlane turned over right away. She was all raring to go now.

"Heh, heh, we sort of put the fire back in that old baby, didn't we?" the bearded attendant laughed out loud, lowering the hood and wiping his hands on the rag that hung from his back pocket.

"Thank you!" I shook his greasy hand.

"Have a good one!" Decky laughed as we jumped into the car, thanking the three of them again. We were on our way, full of gas and full of life. We all had a cold can of Schaefer to celebrate.

Decky yelled out one last yell to Old Scraggly Beard as we pulled away, "Hope you win the big one!"

Lucas screeched a one-pitch laugh as a sudden feeling of déjà vu overcame me. Scraggly Beard had helped us just like Sam McCloud had in the Nevada desert. We had scratched the truck in his lot, and I had this pit bull guilt again. Bad karma would be coming back now for sure, I thought, with just more penance to pay some day. But the wooden confessional box built from stolen boards from the neighbor's barn was too far gone. We were quietly pulling away after having shredded across old Sam McCloud's Ford pickup, ignoring our demons instead of confronting them head-on.

"Oh-oh," Luke said shaking his head as we drove away, almost as if he could see right into my troubled mind. "Mike's feeling all guilty again."

But what were we supposed to do?

We arrived at Clark's about thirty minutes later. His apartment was just on the outskirts of Nashville. On the couch off to the right of the doorway, his friends Hannah and Kirk got up to greet us when we walked in. Kirk was a KU alumnus and Hannah was Kirk's sister. She was a tall, pretty blonde with green eyes and long, curly hair. A thin layer of makeup covered her broken-out complexion. Luke vaguely remembered Kirk, who also lived here in Nashville now. He was studying for his master's at Vanderbilt, he told us. Hannah had been a sales rep at IBC here in town but had just recently quit her job. She was headed to Colombia, South America, she said, on October 1st, with a one-way ticket to see her boyfriend who lived there. Hannah hoped to never return to the USA. Clark had cooked a whole chicken for us, and we were grateful as we stacked our plates with food in the kitchen.

After dinner, Luke pulled out the videotape that he had brought along on our journey. It was a videotape that he had shot on a rented recorder back in Southern California. He popped the tape into Clark's VCR for everyone to watch. Here, we watched as Luke interviewed people back in our lonesome kitchen in Huntington Beach. You could see gas pipes sticking out of the wall beside the refrigerator. The pipes looked for a stove to plug into, but our landlord never gave us a stove. I tried to hear the oil digger on the tape, the constant hum that we had become accustomed to coming from our backyard, but couldn't hear her at first. She had stopped silent the night that we had left, but on the tape, she should have been still humming. The video recording now moved toward the back of the house as Luke rack focused through the back screened-in porch and, sure enough, there the digger was, just dipping her head up and down behind a chain-linked fence enclosure. Luke cut back to an eight dollar and sixty-two cent royalty check on the kitchen table that had been made out to the landlord from some oil company. We had opened it by mistake. We assumed it was for the rights to dredge for the crude. On the tape, Luke interviewed everyone at our house party. He asked them about life on the coast; he asked them about the constant hum of the oil digger; he asked them if they believed in the afterlife. Luke was chronicling the American dream. It was a short documentary on videotape. Tape was a much-easier medium to record on than film was, he felt. This would be the first of many documentaries to follow, for this is what we were all going to do, Luke told Clark, Hannah and Kirk; we were going to make it big someday for sure. But the tape abruptly ended and Hannah and Kirk got up to leave. Kirk still had homework to do, he said, and Hannah had to get ready for South America. As they left, Hannah wished us good luck in our travels, and we wished the same for her.

"Hope you win the big one!" Decky yelled to them both from the second-floor apartment door.

"And when you're in Europe, don't forget to visit Scotland!" Hannah yelled back to him.

We drank into the night, eating chips and dip and anything else we could find in Clark's lonesome kitchen cabinets. Clark played cards with us into the approaching Tennessee dawn, a crazy card game called Bourgeois. We drank to Pete Townsend and the Stones blasting on the stereo; we pounded down one beer after another. They went down just like water and spilled out of the sides of our mouths. After cleaning the chip bowl dry, I ran my finger around the sour cream and onion container in order to get every last bit of it. The beers kept going, and we never thought about what it all was going to feel like when we lay on our backs and watched the spinning starry world crash around us after the lights went out. I tried to sleep, but the bed spins made me crazy, and I had to throw my leg off the edge of the couch. I wished the world would stand still.

CHAPTER 23

Monday, September 10th. It had been seventeen days.

Another morning in another city. I woke up and momentarily did not know where I was. There were sounds familiar to me, though, Steppenwolf (the lonesome wolf of the steppes) sang "Born To Be Wild." The music coming from Clark's stereo slowly built to a crescendo.

"You always have to put on an album side; there always has to be tunes playing if you're anywhere near the stereo," Gary Pare from Paradise Beach (when I lived there with Zane) used to say. "No matter if you're just waking up to help that hangover or just getting in from work, it should be automatic. You always need to put on a side to relax. You always have to have music—because music is as bad as the ocean, man! Music is life!"

Here in Nashville, all dressed up in a shirt and tie, Clark sat at the kitchen table and nursed his own hangover. I noticed that he was balding, like me, and also stood at about my height and build. I was Clark in a parallel life, making morning sales calls. It was some other random universe. I noticed his audible Kansas drawl. Clark had a degree in mechanical engineering, just like Luke, but he had moved to Nashville for a sales job in GM's robotics division. He told us that he hated every minute of it. Clark was doing what he thought he had to do. He was out on his own, renting his own furnished apartment, two bedrooms, for four hundred dollars a month. Clark was living the bloody American dream.

Clark's sales calls made it into my hangover sleep while I lay on the couch. I was in and out of half dreams. It was a scenario of robotic arms on factory show floors with someone narrating in the background. It was all about automation and the future. The average production bled into something called lemonade horsepower, and it all replaced a workforce who wanted to go bowling, because that is where the dream ended.

"Help yourselves to anything in the apartment. I'm off to work." Clark left us.

"And Mike," he said before he left, "you can use my MCI work line to make those calls you need to make to California."

"Thank you, Clark."

So in my morning depression, I called the Subaru Sales Manager Ernie, who lamented that there was still no sale on my consigned vehicle that sat on his lot on Beach Boulevard in Huntington Beach. Even though he had promised that he would have it sold in under a week, he didn't have a crystal ball, you know. He sang his well rehearsed ballad to me. Three weeks had gone by. I tried two phone numbers that I had for the bank, but both of them rang and rang and rang with no answer.

I agonized for several minutes there at Clark's kitchen table about making yet another car payment. Finally, I traded Decky one hundred and eighty-five dollars in American Express traveler's checks for a personal check that Decky had to write to Bank of America. It was almost like playing Monopoly, except I had nothing to show for the money I just spent. There would also be an insurance payment that would be due in another few days if the Subaru still hadn't sold. It was sand slipping through my fingers. A plane ticket to Europe was hinging on how many grains would be left when we got to Boston. The Subaru was my sad addiction. I had wanted that new car when it first looked out at me from the lot earlier that year, but now, just a few months later, I couldn't get rid of it. I wondered what old Ernie had listed my car for. What kind of profit was he making off of me?

Clark came back for lunch, and we listened to the Stones again. We spun their *Big Hits (High Tide and Green Grass)* greatest hits album from the sweet sixties. At the table, Clark and Luke reminisced one last time about all the good times at KU, for the past was now gone and everyone was moving in different directions. They may never see each other again.

When we left Clark, we navigated north toward the on-ramp to Interstate 65. We traveled through Kentucky, and I slept in the back all the way to Louisville. It was such a slow and comfortable sleep. It was one of those forget-all-your-troubles sleeps, a hover-outside-your-body sleep. It took me all the way across the big murky Ohio River into Indiana, and I felt rejuvenated when I finally awoke.

And so we continued on and rode that sweet crazy Interstate 65 all the way through the farmlands of Indiana. We drove on toll roads where road construction was happening everywhere. I watched teams of road crews rejuvenating these superhighway veins that connected every city in America. Potholes banged on our wheels on the frontage detour roads, divots knocked at our alignment as we searched for places to rest. We were moving forward on the zigzag line that had been marked on the Rand McNally Road Atlas, the line that eventually would lead me back to Lowell.

Right around the Interstate 44 exit sign for Shelbyville, Indiana, a sudden impulse overcame Decky, who reached into his things and pulled out Ohio Max's lost pot pipe that Mary had given to him back in San Pablo, California. This was the same pot pipe that Decky was supposed to return to Max in Columbus when we got there. I watched as Decky swiftly cranked on the handle on the front passenger window. The raw cornstalk Indiana air blew in, and he heaved the pipe out the window with the arm of the lefty ball player that he had once been. We both watched the pipe bounce once off the shoulder and down the side ditch and out of our sight forever.

"Why'd you do that?" I laughed.

"If it truly has a mind of its own, let's see if it can get back to Max in Ohio now!" Decky said to me, all wide-eyed and convicted.

"The weirdest thing happened, guys!" I imagined Max saying to us back in Columbus. "I pulled over to take a leak on my way back from Indiana, and I looked down, and right there in the ditch at the edge of the cornfield was my pipe!"

There were truckers at a truck stop in Rensselaer, Indiana, just wandering about. They had nothing but miles and miles of open road separating their present state of being from the future. A few of them talked on the side amongst themselves, trading handles and road stories. CB radio smack was their only other social outlet, I thought. They were on a forever-moving journey, a map occupied by their lonely big rigs and their changing precious cargo. I imagined the commonality of their running into a long forgotten acquaintance on these pit stops. It was a marvelous sophisticated subculture with its own language and its own rules.

As we closed in on Chicago, we roared through Gary, Indiana, the birthplace of Michael Jackson and the Jackson 5. It was music videos like Michael Jackson's *Thriller*, a John Landis directed sci-fi music video, that had got us all pumped up about making this kind of stuff in the first place. *Thriller* was all the rage on MTV, when it had been released in late 1983. The video, just like Landis's film *An American Werewolf in London,* had some pretty cool special effects. But Gary, Indiana, seemed like nothing more than an old steel town on the lake now. It didn't appear that anyone was home; they had all moved out west. American industry was shipping offshore where labor was cheap. It was a somber state of affairs.

Decky and I rummaged through our collection of tapes (three boxes of them). Luke slept outstretched on the back bench seat. To burn the time, we had decided to randomly select a tape without looking at the title, pop it in the deck quickly, play at least three songs on it before we could pull it out, and then repeat this by popping in another. We had to do this until we hit the city limits. Decky went first, pulling Joe Walsh, Boston, and Meat Loaf. It went okay. Then it was my turn, and I pulled the David Seymour Band.

"Who is the blasted David Seymour Band?" I asked Declan. Of course, it was one of his Cleveland bands. I jumped to pull the thing out of the cassette deck. I had to break the rules.

"You can't break the rules of this stupid game!" Decky said laughing.

I ejected the tape and dug into the box looking for something else. I pulled out *Foreigner* and played a song that had lyrics that I loved, "Starrider."

I loved the thought of all of the stars out there in the vast night sky and "Starrider" took me there. I thought back to the millions of blinking lights in the Utah night sky. What were they really? Suns? The ever-expanding cosmos, the great unknown, and the answers to all of life's crazy questions were somewhere out there too, I felt.

In my head, I went back to California again to Torrey Pines State Park with Colette and the hang gliders launching off of the cliffs. "Starrider" rhymed with hang glider.

Hang Glider
Tattered wind-drawn kite
Like a moth flies toward the light

I wanted to soar back to Aspen, too, but Aspen now seemed like a whole lifetime ago. I wanted to be marooned on her peaks again, revisiting all of the emotions and desires that I left there.

Gray spider
Cannot find his way
The thoughts won't go away
Is the pain just here to stay?

"That's bloody plagiarism, Mike. You stole the melody!" Trent had said to me back in Aspen. And then the hang glider crashed.

CHAPTER 24

We arrived in Chicago about 11:30 p.m. I checked my log notes with the gas mileage and odometer readings as we searched for another gas station. We turned a clean 74,000 miles just as we rolled up to the pump; seven, four, zero, zero, zero. Spin, Cherries, Cherries, Orange, Nothing. Good-bye. Isn't it crazy how everything in life is about numbers and formulas? They're the only things that make absolute sense in the world. Luke shelled out $12.92 at the island window for 12.1 gallons of gas ($1.06 per gallon). The tank was full again.

And the oil diggers hummed everywhere to satisfy the world's all-consuming petro thirst. They dipped indifferently out in the desert sands of the Arabian Peninsula; they sank deep into the turquoise oceans off the coast of Venezuela; they were everywhere; they were in the North Sea of Scotland, even in Texas and Alaska. I wondered if the lone digger in the backyard lot on Sixth Street in Huntington Beach was still sitting silent. In my mind she was.

When I was fifteen years old, I siphoned gas up on the hill on Eighteenth Street into a five-gallon plastic container. In the middle of those 1973 October nights, Ray Champeaux and I would go from car to car outside the apartments at the edge of the dark Eighteenth Street woods. Gas prices had gone from $.36 per gallon to $.40 per gallon that year, and we needed to get gas for our nightly joy rides. While parents sat in front of their TV sets watching Archie Bunker and McCloud Texas Ranger, I was shoving a rubber hose down into some poor soul's gas tank. I remember I got a mouthful of gasoline once and had to spit it out quickly. My friend Ray boasted that it tasted like a shot of whiskey, 'cause he had downed his father's whiskey before, and it was horrible like that. Karma would come back to get me someday for stealing people's gas; Luke had told me so. I was the sparrow being chased by the jay hawk on the open Oklahoma plain, flying erratically trying to avoid repentance, but the hawk, so big and overpowering, was dangerously closing in on me. The hilly woods of Eighteenth Street rose up above a field of marshlands and the frozen stick tunnel of my childhood. This was the infamous stick tunnel that we had to all crawl through in my juvenile skating days, the tunnel of sticks that led to the timeless Paul's Pond. In the short days of winter, we would crawl through with our skates on our back, our hockey sticks too, in order to get to the endless fields of ice, frozen paths between the rows of marsh weeds, a labyrinth of sorts that would all ultimately lead to the beautiful pond. But that's a whole different story.

I watched those numbers spin on the pump in Chicago, like it was some sort of jackpot in some wild dream. These were the seconds and minutes of life, the passing of time, numbers spinning away as they added up faster than the second hand spins on the grandfather clock. Life was fleeting, where a written sentence was only good before the period. The power of choice was in the present moment for sure.

I thought about America's dwindling energy woes as those numbers turned on the one-armed gas bandit.

The party is over, the wine has been drunk, more barrels of oil on back order
Seven veiled sisters hold out their hands at the front of a line
Worth more to the desert than water
And the days are getting shorter

Decky's friends Colin and Xander lived in an apartment in the city. This was what I envisioned Chicago to be. It was an old brown stone building just like the buildings in Boston . . . These faces of stone that lined the streets breathed centuries of past tenants' souls, tenants who had come and gone, spirits living within the same walls of these hundreds-year-old structures forever, lives that had walked these city streets, over and over again. This was the Windy City, the beautiful Midwest city on the lake, the home of old-time gangsters like Al Capone and the likes of bootleggers who once defined all of prohibition itself. It had everything you looked for in a big city. This was the home of the Chicago Cubs and of Wrigley Field. I sat for a few moments in the brown stone courtyard amidst walls of crawling ivy taking notes.

Decky knew Colin and Xander from Ohio State. Colin worked for AT&T and had been in Chicago for about a month now; he left Ohio after his longtime girlfriend had dumped him. He told us that he needed to move away from everything that reminded him of her. Xander was an accountant for Peat, Marwick, and Mitchell. He had been working for them in Chicago for two months now, but like all of the other friends we had encountered, secretly wished he could come with us on our adventure. The stress of this postcollege job in a new city was driving him mad. He was losing his hair and his mind.

We sat in the rented $800 per month apartment living room with its Victorian high ceilings, cracked plaster walls, and old hardwood floors, drinking beers and screwdrivers, listening to Al Jarreau on Xander's new high-fidelity stereo system. The stylus rolled against the pressed vinyl tracks of the record. We sat through the cracks, pops, and idiosyncrasies of it all. The stylus sifted through every audible scratch, mere bumps and potholes that strangely enhanced the good sounds of life, this beautiful medium called music. It was the sweet sound of substance. I felt the richness within me, the instrumentals and vocals emanated from the two floor speakers on opposite sides of the room. They rolled and collided with each other and then came at us and hit us where we sat on the couch—it was incredible. We might as well be right there in the studio with Al Jarreau himself as he recorded this crazy track, for that's how real it all seemed.

"We are the hippies of the modern era, the beat generation of the '80s!" Luke proclaimed with certain happiness. He toasted Colin and Xander. It was happiness and a sense of freedom that no workingman could ever know.

CHAPTER 25

It was Tuesday, September 11th. We had been on the road for eighteen days.
"Love makes you stronger," Ingrid said to me in my dream. I awoke at ten thirty in the morning. I didn't feel so well. We had been drinking beer with shots of vodka and screwdrivers before bed. Xander and Colin had gone off to work hours earlier. Luke and Decky were slow to rise like me.

"Stay positive," Ingrid's boyfriend Howie yelled up to me from under her fig tree back in my dream. "Fear only exists in our heads! Life is too great, too beautiful! Don't ever try to miss a minute of it!"

"You need some 'hair of the dog' that bit you! That'll chase those pains and the whole hangover away!" other voices inside were speaking to me now. It was what everyone used to say on those mornings after at Paradise Beach or after the all-night parties at UMass.

"'The hair of the dog' that bit you, just take a sip to ease the hangover, make it all go away, only a few sips, maybe even a whole beer will do the trick, but be careful; never take more than a full beer in the morning, lest you may really slip and end up a full-fledged alcoholic someday. Then the party never ends." I remembered the alcoholic beer sages going over the drill repeatedly to me.

I thought about the age-old rhyme that we'd recite to figure out the night's drinking routine: "Whiskey before beer, no fear; beer before whiskey, risky."

With my own pitiful pitfall of the night before I rhymed: "Screwdrivers and beer, plenty of fear . . ."

Thoughts were flooding into my head. Had I relieved myself in a drunken stupor outside on the brownstone at the base of Xander's building last night? What was I doing outside by myself? Maybe I was finally turning mad. I vowed to not have another drop of alcohol until that evening. We had about twenty-four hours to experience Chicago, and I desperately wanted to be sober.

We left Xander's and walked to the corner of Demming Street and Clark. We were bus-stop bound, for we wanted to head downtown to see the famous Sears Tower. At the bus stop, an elderly lady, probably homeless, dressed in various layers of white clothing, slipcovers over old furniture, fished frantically through the metal meshed trash basket nearby. After a sigh of relief, she settled for a soiled section of the *Chicago Tribune*, brought it over to the bus bench, and sat sadly beside me, bringing with her a poignant smell; it was the overpowering smell of the lonely streets. She began studying the newspaper with intensity. I wondered if she was actually reading.

As she studied, I studied. I studied the hard lines of her weathered profile while she sat there looking at the pictures in the paper, turning the pages crisply and succinctly, almost like she was sitting in the living room of a Victorian parlor in old New England. I looked at her white, straw, unkempt hair, greasy and matted back over the top of her head, combed only by her cracked fingers, and I was suddenly taken aback at how much her features reminded me of my own grandmother, Lillian Hogan. I thought back to my own grandmother's house in Lowell, all of her framed pictures of the sacred heart of Jesus in her hallways, the grandfather clock in the kitchen.

"Bless the Beasts and the Children"

I remembered that poem on a dorm room poster. It was written under the picture of a great bison standing in the middle of a prairie. The poster hung in the room of our friend Buffalo. Someone had taken it off of a wall at Fitchburg State College while we ravaged the campus on one of our weekend road binges, rolled it up and tucked it under Buffalo's giant arm while he was asleep, maybe because of the Buffalo in the picture, or maybe because of the kindness of the giant beast.

The bus pulled up to our bench in Chicago, and we boarded with my grandmother. Strangely, she had the exact change for her fare. She brought the newspaper on board with her and sat by herself up front, impervious to the changing world around her. Luke, Decky, and I walked to the back of the bus; the many faces of the lonely looked up at us as we passed them by. I saw sadness in my nana Hogan's happiness while she sat there up front; she was comfortable, excited for this brief warm moment as she traveled through life. Who knew what the future would bring for her? Did she even think as far ahead as the cold Chicago winter that loomed out there in the months ahead of us? Probably not, I thought, for it seemed that the comfort of the bus ride was all that she needed, all she had. Bless the beasts and the homeless.

The bus ride lasted about a half hour. We got off at Adams and followed our stretching necks toward the tallest building in the city. At the top of the Sears Tower we walked around and checked out the panoramic skyline of the great Midwest and the enormous Lake Michigan. It must have been an ocean to the Native American Potawatomi with its marvelous shoreline. We looked out at Indiana below us, Michigan on the distant purple horizon, and Illinois and Wisconsin pushing out to the great north. The city, from a hawk's-eye view, was much the same as any city skyline view . . . Boston from the top of the Prudential

Building, or Manhattan from the top of the World Trade Towers, or earth from heaven.

At the base of the building we bought a few postcards at the tourist stand and wandered into a nearby bookstore. Bookstores were always a safe haven for me, timeless places graced by the likes of Mark Twain, Ernest Hemmingway, and John Steinbeck. You could cross dimensions by reading the thoughts of the great writers; their light was still amongst us. You could be right there with them, your own problems on hold, shelved away until you stepped out of the trance of the written pages. I often tried to see beyond the words and put myself into their mind-set as the great ones recorded their thoughts. What were they thinking of? I had to get lost in order to find myself. At the entrance, I walked by end caps filled with books on Einstein's *Theories of Relativity* and Frank Abagnale's *Catch Me If You Can*. Luke headed for the New Age aisle and looked for the new book by Richard Bach, *The Bridge Across Forever*. It was still only out in hardcover.

"Maybe I'll buy it in New York if it is in paperback by then," Luke declared. Then he pulled *Seth Speaks* by Jane Roberts from another shelf.

"I still find it kind of strange that she just died," I said.

"But the spirit is infinite, Mike," Luke said. "She's somewhere else now in full consciousness. I'm going to buy this for my own road copy."

I looked on the bottom shelf at *Out on a Limb* by Shirley MacLaine, another book that Luke had with him on the road. I noticed that Shirley was staring back at me from the cover, the sunset behind her highlighted her stark red hair. She stood there in a white pullover and put me into a trance. I moved back and started to walk away, but Shirley's eyes followed me. She continued to stare me down. I had to leave the aisle.

We ate fast food at Wendy's and took advantage of the free salad bar refills. From there, we moved on to an old record store, where we looked through collections of albums for about an hour, perusing the greats of rock-and-roll history. I wondered if my own apple crate collection (shipped via UPS) had made it back to Massachusetts yet as I stood there flipping through the covers in the store. Covers of The Beatles, The Yardbirds, Blind Faith, Cream, The Doors, The Stones, Carly Simon, Gordon Lightfoot, and Don McLean. "American Pie" was certainly Don McLean's magnum opus if ever there had to be one. I was in the eighth-grade when it was released. I had heard that this magnificent ballad was purportedly about Buddy Holly, Ritchie Valens, and the Big Bopper perishing in a plane crash in Clear Lake, Iowa, in 1959. Nothing in McLean's lyrics said anything about the event. The poetry, they said, told it all.

Lost in the record bins, I continued to finger through the stacks of album jackets like a music junkie. I remembered hanging out at fourteen years old in the music department of Truitt's Department Store on Bridge Street in Lowell just like this, looking at albums, reading their back covers for hours in order to stay out of the winter cold. Back then, the crotchety department store manager eventually got fed up with Ray Champeaux and me; he chased us out to the parking lot and the dirty snow.

"Beat it! You guys don't have five bucks between you!" he shouted at us as we got outside the doors.

"*Thwappppp!*" Ray Champeaux hurled a slush ball at the old store manager as he was standing there.

"I'll call the cops on you little bastards! I will. I better not see your faces in here anymore!" The old man yelled as we laughed and ran away. That was 1972.

In 1984, it was liberating to be able to walk out of the Chicago music store of our own free will. In 1984, it was liberating to be able to walk out of the Chicago music store of our own free will. Of course, we didn't buy anything, not so much as a simple cassette to play in the Fairlane. We needed to squander every cent for essentials like beer, food and gas..... and maybe an occasional movie.

Luke and I wanted to see *Gremlins,* Spielberg's new film that was showing just a few blocks away. Decky wanted no part of it; he still needed to absorb all of Chicago. We could watch a film anytime, he told us. We let him go. I wanted to see the special effects and to study the screenplay itself. There wasn't a lot of time to do this if I was going to be making these films someday. Thinking back to my screenwriting classes at Orange Coast College, I sat down in the dark theatre with Luke and had the full intent of noting the plot points throughout the entire film. I even had my notepad with me. So I sat there resolved to look at my watch for the timed twists, as if through the director's eyes . . . the fade-ins, the fade-outs, the cuts, the rack focuses, all of the camera movements, the dialogue, and maybe even the lighting. But it was only a matter of a few minutes before I was completely immersed in the story on the screen, forgetting my commitments. I got lost in Spielberg's amazing knack for special effects. These gremlins were little magical creatures, small animated puppets that turned evil when they were allowed to eat food late at night. And it was weird, for exposure to water seemed to make them multiply, but exposure to sunlight made them die. The credits rolled, the lights came up, and my notepad was empty.

Decky caught up with us outside the theatre all exuberant, and we all jumped on the train toward Fullerton Street. En route, with a firm grip on the floor pole, I noticed a beautiful girl beside me in a business suit. She wore a wedding band and casually read the advertisements posted over the seats of the train; she studied the faces below the ads. I followed behind her as she went from face to face; I quickly looked down to the floor when she abruptly turned to catch me. She gently smiled. Across the car, a tall, bearded, bald man talked to another short, bald guy with glasses on. He told him about his bookbinding night course. It was obvious; the men showed affection toward each other, almost as if they were flirting. The tall guy pulled a book out of his blue backpack, all thick with empty pages. It was bound for his class. He told the short guy how it had taken him two hours a night over the last three nights to complete the thing. Love was in the air; it was all around me. But Collette was still gone.

Somewhere around Fullerton Street, the three of us jumped off and walked about a mile eastward toward a convenience store where we bought orange juice and eggs. We then went to a liquor store right next to it in order to buy three six-packs of beer.

This liquor store was a weird, peculiar place; it was almost like I knew everyone inside her doors. It was very surreal, almost dreamlike. When we walked in, I noticed a tall, thin androgynous David Bowie lookalike on the phone in the corner. Richard Pryor's double bought lottery tickets at the counter and old Willie Mosconi, the pool shark, stood behind me in line. But it was a hard-featured, white-haired, seventy-year old Irishman on a stool behind the counter that haunted me the most. He looked just like Grady, the usher from St. Matthews who worked at Nealon's Packy on Bridge Street. Grady always sat on that same low stool right inside the front door of Nealon's, greeting everyone as they entered. Grady made beer deliveries throughout the city of Lowell all of the time, delivering beer to the masses; he was an extremely hardworking old man. He delivered beer up until the day he died.

I can't stop thinking
That Grady's dead
With his murderer still at large

They hit him
With a baseball bat
Behind St. John's garage

I can't stop thinking
That Grady's dead
What constitutes this fear?

To kill a man
On hallowed ground
For delivering a case of beer

I can't help but think that Grady's dead
His funeral was sad
Two small girls stirred as a casket passed
And cried for their granddad

I keep hoping
That I'll see him again
On his stool inside the door
I never said good-bye to him
Take my order just once more

On his deliveries, he always carried a brown paper lunch bag full of small bills in order to make change for people. It was a bitter cold January when the murderers did it. It was a setup; two punks beat him to death, luring him out to a remote place behind the hospital so they could steal the cash that he carried. When the police found Grady, he still had a tight grip on that bag and all the money was still there. Grady died without ever letting them get a hand on it. God bless him.

And here in Chicago, old Grady was back. He said to Richard Pryor at the counter, "Shit, Deacon, when you win the lottery, you'll have to write a book on how you did it!"

"Man, I ain't writing no book. I ain't telling anyone how I did it!" Richard Pryor laughed and turned to me.

When I got up to the counter, Chicago Grady smiled just like he knew me. I couldn't believe how much he looked like the real Grady, more than anyone had ever looked like anyone else before. I had this warm feeling that he was well again, but had to keep telling myself that this really wasn't him.

"Three six-packs? Is that all?" he laughed aloud with me.

Decky had a theory about how so many people looked alike. He believed that there were only so many formulas for a face out there, so they all had to be repeated everywhere about humankind, all over the earth, probably several hundred times, maybe even thousands of times. Outside the liquor store, Decky reasoned with me that this was the real reason that David Bowie, Richard Pryor, Willie Mosconi, and Grady from Lowell were all there with us in the small Chicago neighborhood.

Maybe there was something more to it all, though, I wondered. Perhaps it all was a sign. Maybe Grady was an angel appearing to me. There were so many of these empty pages in this freshly bound book of life that needed to be filled, I thought. There were so many things to think about and to talk about. Every day was a blessing, every day a chance to be good to someone.

We got back to Xander and Colin's place about six thirty. Colin was at the turntable. He was home from work when we walked through the apartment door, juggling some classic rock-and-roll platters, pulling one off, putting another on, and turned to greet us with a "Live-In-Concert" LP in his hand.

"Tunes, tunes, tunes, gotta have my tunes!" Colin warmly greeted us. He looked just like Gary Pare from Paradise Beach flipping those albums.

It was still only four thirty in the afternoon back in California. It hit me that I could still try to call the bank back there about my ongoing car-payment dilemma. I grabbed my notes and jumped on the phone to Bank of America. At first, the nervous customer service representative had a panic attack about how they were supposed to reach me if they didn't get paid. I gave her my mother and father's number in Lowell, telling the girl on the phone that Lowell was where I was ultimately headed.

"Don't worry; I'll pay it, calm down!" I told her. "Who do you think you're dealing with?"

When Xander got home from work, we all ate dinner and drank the three six-packs of beer that we had bought. The old "hair of the dog" that bit me made me feel happy for a moment, especially the sound of that first crack of the tab on that aluminum beer can. We sat around the living room and talked about all kinds of things while eating dinner. The movies, great books, our love of rock and roll; we were the traveling bohemians of the modern era. Luke explained to Xander and Colin how eating well and working out throughout our trip was key to our survival in this bohemian life. We were determined to never work an eight-to-five job again; we might even shave our heads to wander the streets of Europe when we got over there, although I wasn't sure why. We talked on with Colin and Xander about Decky's love to jump into the middle of all of the tourists' pictures as we traveled through these places of America. He wanted to be in everyone's photo. He wanted to be looking out at them when they developed their film, smiling with that big Decky Brady smile. There was also Decky's secret desire to swim in as many bodies of water as possible across our great country. We would all swim in Lake Michigan on our way out of Illinois, we said.

But what were we going to do tonight? Where should gypsies go? The Chicago nightclubs were calling out to us, this beautiful night full of beautiful women. Two beers into the night already, I daydreamed about hundreds of beautiful women and how empty life would be without them. I wanted to be forever a part of this great big beautiful unraveling reel of America. Where was the girl of my dreams? Did I know her? She was alive now, breathing, out there somewhere in the never-ending universe, perhaps a faint beacon in this huge, impenetrable, star-filled night. She seemed really far away from me now, but deep down, I knew that the light really did exist.

Bananarama's "Cruel Summer" played in the cab on our way to Rush Street. It was a popular new music '80s song by a hip all-girl group from England about lost love. The black cabdriver, Sonny, talked to us about his eighteen-hour days while "Cruel Summer" played. He owned his own cab and was going to buy two or three more he told us, for he was a businessman and he was living the great American dream. Sonny told us how he loved talking to each and every one of his customers to learn as much as he could about life.

"Three of us here are gypsies, and we are never going to work again!" Luke told him.

Sonny just smiled and nodded back to him, looking in the rearview mirror at all of us. "Well, boys, I've never heard that one before!" He laughed.

Sonny believed that you need to work hard every single day of your God-given life if you want to make lots of money.

"I ain't never gonna retire, boys! God willing, I'm gonna work till I drop!" Sonny smiled a gold-toothed smile at us, and we all smiled back, exiting the cab now to the crazy sounds of Rush Street.

"Hope you win the big one!" Decky yelled to Sonny as he pulled away into the bright night of life.

In a disco club on Rush Street, we were confronted with a wall of loud music upon entering. Tears For Fears' Top 40 hit, "Shout" faded into a song by The Romantics "That's What I Like About You," and we talked louder in order to be heard across the roaring sound. Cigarette smoke floated everywhere; it was camping in the workingman's leftover business suits. Some workers wreaked stronger than others. Bright flashing lights came down from above and trailed across our faces. Xander made his way to the bar and bought all of us endless beers. "Rock and roll will never die," I yelled out to Xander, toasting him gleefully. Alcohol was the well of happiness here, and everyone drank from it.

Beer brought on the good times and the bad. I talked to Xander and Colin at the bar about how I considered myself a happy drunk, although sometimes, I found myself getting into pitiful skirmishes. But it was never my fault. Of course, there was the beer fight at our going away party in Huntington Beach. The cooler of beer that had been stolen from us and the bandit's kick to my sternum, with full bottles whizzing by our heads, giant cocktail missiles, and pitiful me on my ass as the hoodlums ran into the alleyways of night. And then there was the fight in the backseat of Brian Kelly's Mercedes that I got into with Michael Lewis. We were all on the way back from Sean Tarrytown's brother-in-law's San Diego mansion party (he supposedly used his yacht to run marijuana from Baja to San Diego). The fight started between Michael Lewis and Eddie Kinsley. I just happened to be sitting in the middle of them. With our arms locked, Michael Lewis landed an upper cut to my lip that bled out all over Brian Kelly's backseat. Brian Kelly had to pull over somewhere near San Onofre. We pulled over right where the coyotes, the immigrant smugglers, pull over in broad daylight. It was right before the Camp Pendleton Marine checkpoint. A sign on the side of the road had the words "CAUTION," with a cutout silhouette of a man, a woman, and a little girl running in flight. You see, the coyotes often ran to their trunks here to let their cargo out. These poor bastard immigrants were on their own to run across the freeway to the beach or into the hills of the desert. Sometimes they would run across the freeway and get killed. They had no voice, they had no choice. They were only looking for a better life. On that night, Michael Lewis and I shook hands right under that ghostly sign and crawled back into Brian Kelly's backseat and behaved the rest of the way home.

In Chicago, we left the disco place and walked through two more dead clubs on Rush Street; both had a few buzzed stragglers holding up the bar, just standing around waiting for something to come their way on a Tuesday night. I was six beers into our night and cruising now, with the open night bohemian air ahead of me. I had no care or concept of time anymore. Xander and Colin had to work in the morning, but both vowed to press on and show us more. We stopped into the Clark Street Ale House after a $2.80 cab fare that Colin picked up. A drunk patron told us while we stood there ordering five draws and five baskets of popcorn that the place used to be called the Stop and Drink; it had been a local watering hole all the way back into the late 1800s, you know, those years that were sometimes referred to as the gay nineties, during the times of brothels and burlesque shows.

"It was always a drinking spot. The long bar along the south wall over there is new, but the trim and the ceiling panels are all original," he told us.

"How does he know this?" Xander turned to us.

"Maybe he's a vampire!" Luke whispered to us all.

The trim that was high above us was elaborate. It reminded me of the hand carved grooved wood around the doorways in my parents' house on Eighteenth Street, our sweet Victorian house that Old Man Woodward had built in the late 1800s. Woodward lived there until the day that he died in the late 1950s. We were only the second family to ever live there over the span of almost 100 years. Woodward left behind all of his hand carved awls, drills, and wooden planes in an old tool chest in our cellar for me to discover. And his ghost still rocked in his invisible rocking chair at the foot of my old bed upstairs. When I was a kid, I was convinced that the creaking hardwood close to the window had to be his ghost, for my mother told me that when they bought the house in 1960, that an old rocking chair was in that very spot. I wondered if his ghost had ever gone down into the cellar to look at his old tools. Some summer nights, the floor would just creak away as I looked out from my bed across the fireflies along the edge of the driveway and beyond the darkness of the Merrimack River Valley out toward California. I always tried talking to him, but he just rocked away.

"You look startling!" Decky yelled to a pretty girl passing us by in the Ale House. He yelled to another, "You look like a nun who used to teach me piano in the fifth grade!" Nothing was working for him.

Xander called to me across the Clark Street Ale House, across the din of loud patrons and forgotten conversations. "Hey, Chrome Dome, order me and yourself another draw. I'll pay for it!"

Later that night, we all stopped at the same convenience store we had been to earlier in the day to each buy our own pints of ice cream before stumbling back to the brownstone apartment complex. I shoveled down a whole pint of rum raisin in the living room before passing out on the couch.

I dreamed about gremlins. Gremlins were little magical creatures that turned evil when they were allowed to eat ice cream late at night. Exposure to beer made them multiply, but exposure to sunlight made them die.

CHAPTER 26

It was now Wednesday, September 12th. We had been traveling for nineteen days. I woke up early on Xander's couch and immediately saw my two friends strewn across the floor below me. When Decky and Luke awoke, we decided to take a run, to go about a mile all the way down to the sandy beachfront of Lake Michigan in order to dive into the dirty water. It was Decky's dream to do this, and we badly needed to wash off the crazy ghosts of the night before. It was cold, ugly water at the shoreline, yet so refreshing. We waded in a few feet and dove into the low-breaking waves of the great ocean of the Potawatomi.

Back at the brownstone apartment, we said our good-byes to Xander and Colin, who were in the throes of their own morning depression, like millions of other Americans. They had to go to work. I remembered the mental preparation, the grooming, and the solemn walk to the car every morning; it was a routine that we three weren't a part of anymore. It was so foreign to me now that even the disdain and bitter feelings that were associated with it had all but left me, the old thrill of "working for a living."

We were back on the road by ten thirty. A cabbie cut Decky off just as we tried to find our way east out of the city. Decky tooted the horn and flipped the cabdriver off, and the driver nonchalantly flipped him back "the bird" in response. With the windows rolled down now, a strong smell of exhaust permeated the busy thoroughfare air. The sulfurous aroma smelled like hard-boiled eggs.

"I get it," Decky said aloud. "That's the way they communicate around here!" With another accentuated hand gesture out the window, he yelled to the cabdriver, "Hope you win the big one! That's how I communicate!"

We wanted to be Columbus bound. Luke, our copilot, manned the road atlas; he tried to look for the big streets, picking eastbound roads at random until we could get to the interstate that we had come into the city on. In the crosstown traffic, passersby were tooting at us and rolling down their windows to tell us that we had tennis shoes and shorts hanging from the back of our car.

"Thanks," Luke yelled back from the passenger seat with a wave of his hand. "We're just drying them off; we swam in Lake Michigan this morning. It's Decky's fault!"

On the interstate, we passed three guys in an old red Dodge pickup truck, riding three across in the cab, with a camouflaged canoe hanging out of the tailgate. They were wearing army greens and browns, the same color as their canoe, and looked over at us in amusement when the Fairlane passed them on the left. Our laundry was hanging out the trunk and our canoe, the surfboard, was still bungie-corded down on top. I wondered where these soldiers were headed. They were three parallel lives on the road not taken. Maybe they were going to Fort Wayne. Did they think we were fools? The waves weren't big enough to surf Lake Michigan. We were the idiots that they were training to defend. I nodded to them from the backseat, and all three nodded back politely.

There were middle-aged men and women all dressed up on the interstate, going to lunch, going on sales calls, on their way to meetings, who knows, some seemed unnerved and uncomfortable. A van drove by with some disabled adults all seated attentively inside. A pretty blond woman, their trip chaperone, had both of her hands tense on the steering wheel. She looked from side to side across the wide road as she tried to change lanes. Blessed be the disabled and the children; they have no voice; they have no choice. In kindergarten, Miss Lansing told us that kids with Down's syndrome were closer to God than anybody else in the whole world, and that's why we should treat them with kindness. That was when you could talk about God in school. We used to say prayers for them before class every morning.

A blue late-model Ford station wagon cruised by us in the right lane. Two thirty-something ladies had two small children seated in the back. The kids pointed to the surfboard and appeared to ask questions to their mothers, but their mothers kept on talking to each other, never venturing from their bubble, never hearing anything more than the sound of their own voices while their radio played . . .

People in jars
Stay away from the stars
'Cause they're airtight

In Merrillville, we transitioned from the 65 and traveled southeast on Interstate 30, through the farmlands of Indiana. We passed cornfields with the overpowering smell of manure and all kinds of heavy farm machinery. The roadside billboards advertised wholesome milk. These were the baby-blue highways of America, I imagined, where native corn and whole milk were the lifeblood of these communities, staples that would ultimately feed our great nation. We were now blazing through the center of the country like a twister, I felt, leaving in our wake family and friends whose lives we were privileged to touch once more. We had infected all of them with our sickness, I secretly knew it. We exposed them to our restless search for something, for life. But the oil derricks had to keep on pumping somehow, despite our lack of responsibility, feeding the thirst of prosperity, working on overtime while we played, humming in the background of progress. The oil derrick in the Huntington

Beach backyard lot had stopped, though. I was certain she still wasn't working.

It was a humid day in Indiana. A bee flew by, buzzing around me and then carried on while I sat at the truck stop just outside Fort Wayne. The air was cool, fresh; the high blue sky streaked with stretches of cirrus clouds, all of them curving and holding onto our beautiful earth like an omnipotent pair of cupped hands. Truckers were greeting each other with their customary nods as they jumped from their rigs. They loaded up with their road ammo in the store near the pumps after also relieving themselves. It was just like back at the earlier truck stop we had driven through in Rensselaer. I likened the truckers to highway cowboys; their rigs complemented the freight trains on the lonely plain, running food and goods, back and forth all over the country. These road warriors were always in touch with the underlying pulse of the nation.

Crossing the Indiana border, the lyrics from Neil Young's song "Ohio" at once came marching into my head. This song was the anthem song of Kent State that told the story of the 1970 college kids that had protested the U.S. invasion of Cambodia. They were gunned down by the Ohio National Guard. Neil Young's emphatic repetition, a line about the four that died there, laid into me, over and over again as we crossed the state line. This was all I had ever known of Ohio before I met Decky.

Sure . . . Caprissi, Taboo, and I had cruised through the state once before in the darkness of the night, border to border, Pennsylvania to Indiana, on our way out west. But we had never stopped, save to get gas once. In the light I now noticed that we were surrounded by cornfields and random rustic barns here and there, a countryside reminiscent of rural New England. One barn in the distance had an old tin windmill beside it, the rusty blade turned ever so slowly in the humid wind. We exited from the 30 onto Ottawa Road, Route 65, and headed south to Lima. I read the road sign and enunciated "Leem-a" like the bean. Decky laughed to tell me that it was pronounced "Lime-a, like a lime." When we stopped again for gas, five farm boys came out of the station laughing and pointing to the surfboard on our car.

"Which way to the beach?" one of them said, laughing, with the others busting up beside him.

I pointed eastward toward the flat horizon with green stalk cornfields stretched out in front of us farther than any eye could see.

"We left California, and we seem to be a little lost," Decky held out his open palms as he walked toward them, wearing a wide-eyed grin.

The farm boys laughed, all of them, and directed us to the 117 South, another tributary road, where we picked up the 33 into Columbus. The 117 South reminded me so much of the back roads of Dracut and Methuen that I even pictured the hundred-years-old carriage house of my father's uncle Arthur out there, somewhere, just like it had been in Dracut. Maybe it was next to a dilapidated barn with Frank's 1934 Indian motorcycle hidden somewhere in its depths.

We tried to pick up music on the radio but could only find a weak Stevie Wonder singing "I Just Called to Say I Love You." This made me think again about Jeff Beck's "'Cause We've Ended as Lovers" from the *Blow by Blow* album. The guitar took a breath as it sobbed when I played it in my head. It echoed in and out; it kept pulling at me. It was amazing that all of humankind shared a similar connectedness when confronted with moving music. It tore at everyone's core being in much the same way, I was sure of it, bringing back inner desires that were once a part of another distant moment. The beat of the music would take me somewhere else, a place in the past, old feelings of love, happy memories from yesterday, and then sudden feelings of sadness, for now it was gone. Music was the language that spoke to us all and told us that we were uniquely human. I still missed her.

Throughout the din and the flatness of the western Ohio landscape, there were outbreaks of occasional sanity, oases of majestic green trees in the middle of abundant life-bread cornfields. From the distance, a monster tractor approached us on a small winding road. It passed loudly behind us as we moved quickly by it in the opposite direction, the loud roaring sound trailing the machine by a few seconds after the beast had already gone by.

"Boy, what a big mother!" Decky exclaimed.

"And the tractor he was driving in was pretty big too!" I responded smartly.

Luke elicited a loud shriek of sudden laughter, the response that the road itself had come to know, one that was so characteristic of Luke's whole being.

Decky fiddled with the radio dial and happily found what he had been searching for, WMMS, "Home of the Buzzard!" Cleveland Rock Radio! We continued to drive along another country road alongside a small river as dusk quietly approached. With our windows rolled down, the slow marching hum of the crickets came with dusk, trying to bring the day to a close; they sang their love songs in unison to each other, millions of them, all along the tall grasses of the Columbus roadside. We took in the sounds of the late afternoon, to drink in all of Ohio State, for we had landed.

Once on campus, Decky took us first to the football stadium and had us climb to the top of the bell tower to take in the early-evening view. We watched the sun setting peacefully on what was now the forgotten west; the distance between the bell tower and the orange-pink horizon appeared so great to me that it was hard to believe it was the same west we had just shuffled across. And there was nothing but a warm and calm purple darkness out toward the east. The breeze up at the top was light and relaxing, with the smell of the fall air igniting old memories of more cornstalks and maple leaves. I looked out on the canvas of surrounding trees, the leaves that would soon turn colors and fall to the campus corridors below us, and imagined crowds of students shuffling through them; the greens of summer gone. I imagined thousands of students marching to home football games, classes, midterms, the bitter cold of the Ohio winter, and ultimately, those dreadful final exams. Neil Young's "Ohio" played once again in my head.

From the bell tower we walked amongst the tree-lined parkways of the campus. Hazy purple light from the onset of night caused the faint shadows of the trees to trip the paths and eventually disappear. On the right was a pond with a shooting fountain and summer algae stagnating all along the edges of it. We walked by old Ohio architecture, university buildings, searching for some sign of student life, longing for a connection to the world that we had once been so much a part of.

"It's weird how every college campus is like its own little world," Luke said. "You know how they all have their own school colors, traditions, culture, beliefs, a sense of individual school spirit . . . all of them tiny islands unto themselves."

"Hundreds of random colleges with their own mascots like Brutus the Buckeye," I said. "Come on, Decky, how can you have a fierce and intimidating chestnut as a school mascot?"

"Be careful how you talk about Brutus," Decky warned. Decky told us that back in the day at an Indiana away game, the Indiana fans stormed the court and flattened poor Brutus the Buckeye after the game. They got him on the floor and started punching and kicking him, trying to pull off Brutus's big head. Poor Brutus was all laid out on the court trying to hold onto that huge papier-mâché chestnut head while getting kicked in the ribs. It was funny and sad at the same time.

We were anxious to move on but decided to hit one of the local pizza joint happy hours, Papa Joe's, on our way out. A homeless black man sat on the stoop on the side of the restaurant.

"How you guys doing?" he asked.

"Fine, thanks, how about you?" I quickly answered as we passed on the sidewalk behind him.

"Can I ask you something?" he followed it up. "Can you spare any change?"

Luke reached into his pockets. "Well, I got a quarter that I can give you," he said. We were all three homeless ourselves, I thought, but Luke still selflessly gave to the homeless.

"That'll be just fine. God bless you," he said to us all, taking the quarter swiftly from Luke's outstretched hand as Luke bent over to hand it to him. The black man half stooped back to his comfortable seat on the curb.

It was strange, I thought, that it was always the ones on the bottom of society, with all the misfortune that life had dealt them, who still had all of this faith left in God. They never blamed God for their circumstances like some of the more fortunate did; they never walked out on God like the rest of us. Was it because God might be the only hope left in this crumbling world? Some called it the point of sweet surrender, when the only way back to sanity is to accept where you have fallen and ask someone for help.

Papa Joe's was filled with young people, crazy, returning college kids, with school not yet in session, celebrating a new semester as the Top 40's music roared inside. From the corner jukebox, sounds echoed off the walls loudly as we pushed our way to the bar in the center of the restaurant. Decky ordered a pitcher of *"Hoody Gold"* with three mugs. There were six big guys standing in a huddle at the bar right next to us when Decky passed the empty mugs to Luke and me. Two or three of the guys were wearing red Buckeye sneakers. They had five real cute girls around them, trying to break their way into the guys' conversation, but the guys were too into their strategy talk about the week's upcoming game against Washington State; they paid the girls no attention. Luke, Decky, and I were just plain invisible to everyone.

"I don't think they're big enough to be football players," Decky yelled over to me.

"They're just tiny girls, Decky, of course not!" I yelled back to him.

"That's what I was thinking." He scrunched his nose and moved on behind the linesmen's backs, always keeping a firm grip on our pitcher of beer.

As I said, no one noticed us because we were invisible. We were too old for this crowd. We quickly downed the pitcher of Hoody and prepared to cut out to Decky's hometown, Cuyahoga Falls, for there was nothing left for us here. Neverland had forever changed. The girls all around us talked amongst themselves, shrouded, protected in their bubble. We sadly realized that the past was quickly fleeting; this wasn't Decky's Ohio State anymore. All of Decky's college friends were long gone, off somewhere, working their grown-up jobs now. We had to move on. We laid the empty pitcher and the empty mugs on the bar. No one turned to watch us leave, for they remained in their own separate world, so sheltered, so naïve, so happy.

Out at the side entrance, our homeless friend awaited us with two white compatriots seated on the stoop on either side of him. These were three parallel lives to ours, just hanging on to that bottom rung. They were definitely on a different journey than we were, I realized, just outside the bubble, but, for as fallen as their lives seemed, I strangely wondered if they had secretly arrived, sitting right at the front of the line at the gate. The homeless all had a certain peace about them that I wanted to possess. I was searching for a way to surrender to this wholeness that the three seated on the curb now all seemed to hold onto. They seemed so calm in their being. God would take care of it all.

"Hey, buddy!" one of them yelled at Luke as he approached.

"No, no, I already hit him," our old black friend quickly told the others.

We all laughed at this and bid them all to have a good night.

"Stay warm tonight, my friends," Luke said to them when we passed.

"God bless you," the black man said, yet again.

Pulling out of the parking lot in the Fairlane, I waved to the curbside angel, who was still sitting on the stoop, smiling, taking a brown bag hit from his bottle of Mad Dog 20/20. He nodded his head and winked to us.

"Hope you win the big one!" Decky yelled out to him from the open window.

We were northbound on the 71 toward Akron and Cuyahoga Falls. Decky assured us it was only a mere two and a half-hour drive. We were restless. We longed for the home cooked food and comfort of Cuyahoga Falls.

In the distant days ahead, perhaps in a week, we'd be going through my college town, Amherst, too. I worried that UMass would be a similar experience to Ohio State, with everyone gone and all grown up.

It was late by the time we arrived at Decky's parents' house in Cuyahoga Falls. We were well tired of playing "guess the name of the next song" on the radio. Decky seemed to always win. WMMS, "the Buzzard," faded in and out before finally just going dead with white noise.

"I wonder if she's gone off the air for the night," Decky said. "We should be getting a stronger signal, not a weaker one. After all, we are driving toward Cleveland . . ."

CHAPTER 27

We arrived at the Brady house late. Everyone was asleep when we got there, but Decky's parents had left a key for him under the front door mat so that we could let ourselves in. Decky was one of five children growing up in this rural neighborhood in Cuyahoga Falls, Ohio, but now, his youngest sister Molly was the only one left at home. The rest of the Brady kids were spread out all over the country. Decky's oldest brother lived in Washington State; his sister Maggie was the next oldest and now lived in New Jersey; Decky was right in the middle, then Megan who was a year younger and who we had visited in Denver, and finally Molly. On Taft Avenue there were bedrooms for each of us, and it wasn't long at all before all of the lights were out. It was a peaceful sleep.

Thursday came. When we awoke in the morning, Molly greeted us as we came downstairs. She was the only one home now for the parents had already both gone off to work. Decky's dad, "Crazy Legs" (I loved referring to him as this) was a chemist at Goodyear in Cleveland, and his mom, Bridgie, was a dietician at the city hospital. Molly sat at the kitchen table reading as we clanged around her. She was a junior at Ohio State, where we had just come from, but her semester and move there wouldn't start for a few more days.

After breakfast, we ran for a few miles through the neighborhoods and tried to sweat away the ill feelings associated with several accumulated days of drinking. On our run, the houses on Decky's street and throughout all of the area jumped right out of the '60s at me; most were two-story Capes; it was like running through the Hollywood set of *Leave It To Beaver* for me. The housing development had been built for the families coming to Ohio who worked in the growing rubber industry back in the early years. We pushed for about three miles through the territory of the Cuyahoga (the name translated in Native American meant "*the crooked river*"). During our run, Decky reminisced about his childhood in these suburban streets with community quips and bits of nostalgia along the way with his narrative. He showed us the trees he used to climb and where they all swam at the Old Mill, and how they played tennis out on Wilhelm's street all of the time. He spoke of endless nights of flashlight tag and the tale of god-awful "Rex's erection," a tall cement eyesore tower built by some guy named Rex that didn't seem to serve a purpose but could never be torn down.

In the afternoon, Decky and Molly took us over to the Blossom Music Center. We went to the outdoor stage area and looked out from under the large overhanging roof toward a surrounding panorama of a belt of graded green lawn that served as seating. It went all the way back to the beautiful dark green tree line, the forest beyond encompassed nature's cathedral. A group of stagehands were preparing the place for Cindi Lauper who would be performing that evening. Decky explained to us that because the stage area was wooden, it provided for some of the most superb acoustics ever heard in an outdoor arena. I looked out to the open area and imagined myself up there performing air guitar for the masses . . .

His tools are vocal jewels, he sings
A harvest, running springs
A band silhouettes the stage
A lion outside his cage

When lights come on
His symphony is born

"Are you traveling with the show?" Decky asked a crew member carrying extension cords to the stage.

"No, but he is," the man replied and pointed to another bearded guy working next to him.

"Oh-oh," the bearded guy said to the first. "Now you got me in trouble."

We didn't bother with him. We walked out from the stage area and passed a black, superfluous, curvy, marble sculpture inscribed with words that said something like "The Language of the World is Universal." It was a clef symbolizing the gift of music. I at once realized that this inscription illustrated everything that I always believed the definition of music to be. Rock and roll truly was a gift to the world. I knew that. My poetry expressed it all.

And we would grow old
Before ever learning our lesson
If not for the sound
That soothes it all
It's music that facilitates expression

"Burn it!" Luke's brother Trent joked that these words should be burned into flakes of floating embers. "Let it blow away on the wind; that will be a true expression!"

From here we went to Virginia Kendall Park, a wide-open place the size of several foot-ball fields, probably like eight of them. At the edges, it was surrounded by a forest of trees. When we got to the trees, we followed a wooded path to the famous Ice Box Cave. On the way there, the beautiful sunlight came in from far above us, her light cutting through the dark canopy overhead in a series of individual laser beams angling to the earth, strings of a harp, evading the tops of the giant trees that struggled to keep it all themselves. There was the smell of dampness here; the faint sound of the nearby river provided a soundtrack for the changing season; the leaves showed with their colors that ever so gradually they wanted to change from greens to reds to oranges to yellows and rusts, for it was the end of their sum-mer stay. Red leaves were beginning to collect on the ground around us, oak leaves, while acorns, green mosses, and lichens graced the rounded and cut rocks off of the path. These were the coral beds of the upper world, I thought, rising above the land ocean's floor, slowly building on a foundation of past years that were layered over the cold earth. I looked upon these layers of decomposing matter, reflecting on all who had walked along this path. There were memories buried within the leaves from these pages of before. Small green plants and bushes covered the remainder of the forest floor, dwarfed by taller pines and oaks and all other things of a more simple and primitive beauty.

Wildflowers
Constant changes in our flora
The ever-changing aura
Fields of succession

Plants
Growing into leaves
Begetting taller trees
Fields of succession

Wildfires
Forests burning down
Embers on the ground
Fields of succession

Attitudes
States of mind
Somehow realigned
To justify one's way of living
Over and over
Fields of succession

Thinking
Thoughts forever changing
Friendship rearranging
I am the rain forest
No longer the desert
Fields of succession

We walked to the base of the giant ledges; it was a monument of cut stone, with cliffs and drops between varying planes of elevation, all of it cut by erosion, the simple forces of water, water that flowed for centuries unheeded. All the way up, the rock was covered with moss and sporadic outcroppings of bushes and trees that sprouted up out of anything on the rocks' surface that closely resembled earth. Sometimes it almost seemed that the bushes grew from the rock themselves. A chipmunk ran by, disappearing into a wooded hole in the ground, and the birds called out to the forest, warning nature of our rapid approach.

I felt alive as if I walked the very pages of James Fenimore Cooper's *The Last of The Mohicans,* sensing life through the forest as Uncas had, drinking it in, imagining that this place in Eastern Ohio was probably very similar to the terrain of the early 1800s' Hudson River Valley. We had so much to learn from the signs of nature, so much that others had known before us. It was crazy to think that we had left it all behind somewhere on the road to progress.

We walked down the last outdoor corridor to Ice Box Cave. There were thirty-foot granite walls on either side of us, with the sky still our ceiling, but the walls, like the initial separation of the continents, almost looked like they had been perfectly broken apart for our passage, one ledge the opposite three-dimensional jigsaw puzzle piece to the other.

Inside Ice Box Cave, the sudden drop in temperature was clearly evident and hence, explained the name that Decky called it.

"I wonder who named it," I said.

"Had to be someone who was around when the Ice Box was invented," Luke guessed, "I don't know, 1800s?"

"I wonder what the Cuyahoga called it then?"

The mouth of the cave was about ten feet by twelve feet and once past the entrance, two narrow passageways cut back into the darkness.

Decky had brought a small flashlight with him from home and flipped the plastic switch on, and it at once brought immense light into the small space in front of us. The walls of the cave were full of moisture; the drip, drip echo into the few inches of water on the floor could be heard from all around. Fallen trees, laid down by humans before us, were there for walkways, and we proceeded deeper into the passageway on our right, pushing to where the walls began pushing back at us on both sides now. We were like clay in a vice. Decky put the light overhead and showed us the still twenty to thirty foot high ceiling in the cave, before instructing the last in line, Molly, to turn around and head out and around the corridor on the left.

"If there was an earthquake right now, we'd be gone," Luke said.

"Gone and smack-dab into another life?" I asked him.

"Not me," he replied.

"What? What do you mean?" I wondered why.

"I might not come back right away," he laughed.

"Don't you want to come back as a fat old lady riding in a big old Cadillac with Texas license plates? Like the one we saw in Colorado riding next to her husband?" I asked him. They towed an Airstream trailer through big old America and threw their McDonald's trash wrappers onto that clean mountain air highway when we passed them. It made me sad, just like in the '70s commercial when the Native American turned to a camera to shed a single tear when someone threw trash out of their car on the side of the highway.

"Naw, not anyone like that, although I don't think it matters," Luke said. "It's just another physical experience."

"Wouldn't coming back as that lady we saw in Colorado be like taking a step backward?" Decky seemed confused.

"What's the fun in coming back here anyways? I mean, to come right back to this space and time?" Luke answered. "I will probably go to another time and place way out there in the future!"

This was how our conversations sometimes would go. Poor Molly sat silent in the backseat of the Fairlane on our way out of there, looking out the window the whole time. I wondered how crazy she actually thought we all were. What had happened to her brother, and why was he traveling with these two lunatics? She didn't utter a single word.

After dropping Molly off back at home, the three of us walked one block over from Taft Avenue to visit Wilhelm's parents, Sadie and Bill Schmidt. Wilhelm was Decky's neighborhood friend who had followed Decky all the way out to California but opted to stay back in Huntington Beach and not go on this adventure with us. His parents had heard from the Bradys that we would be coming through town and wanted to have us over for dinner. Out on the wooden deck that Wilhelm's father had built, we feasted away on grilled steak, potato salad, and fresh-cut vegetables while Decky flipped through the pages of three photo albums that he had brought along with him. From the pictures on the pages, he chronicled our West Coast exploits with Wilhelm.

Bill Schmidt loaded our plates with steak from the grill. He was a retired buyer from Firestone Rubber. He told us that he had started as a mechanical engineer but had moved to the purchasing department many years back for the excitement of it all. O Ohio! The rubber she made that fed the great machine of Detroit, those turning wheels of progress, the great American auto industry, and how it now seemed with all of the jobs leaving such a bitter wreck! It remained a mystery if the jobs would ever return.

"Eat it up; ain't no good warm!" he told us as he came by and piled the steak on our plates.

His own steak was already gone. He always ate his steak alone before eating anything else.

"The potato salad can wait because that stays cold all of the time," he said.

Bill and Wilhelm had built the garage that stood off of the back deck to the right of where we sat. And sitting there in a moment of quiet observation, it immediately occurred to me that Bill had the same thirst for living that his son had, a blanket of hope for all of humankind. I marveled at how Wilhelm always seemed to be happy, taking anything that was thrown at him, and always spinning it positive. Wilhelm broke out in song and dance during the strangest of moments; he became crazy when crazy wasn't allowed, screaming and twisting to "Incense and Peppermints" by The Strawberry Alarm Clock, a one-hit wonder '60s band with their psychedelic tune whenever it came up on the oldies stations.

Wilhelm often threw his arms madly about him on his way to work at the circuit board factory on a Monday morning, falling to the apartment floor as he sang, and then he would calmly get up to walk out the door, just to make us all laugh.

"Wake up, people, it's a new dawn!" Wilhelm screamed in Huntington Beach on the weekends, with most of us hungover under the morning marine layer fog, as he banged the kitchen pots and pans before making pancakes for everybody. This was Grace Slick's famous scream during the Woodstock dawn, he told us, right before she and the Jefferson Airplane launched into a frantic rendition of "Volunteers."

On the back deck at the Schmidt house, Luke, Decky, and I talked into the night about our crazy adventure across country. Three and one half hours later, we managed to finish all of Mr. Schmidt's Stroh's beers (at least two six-packs' worth). Bill Schmidt had helped with this while his wife Sadie just laughed and laughed.

"Eat it up; ain't no good warm!" Bill told us again.

By the time we left, there was thunder in the Cuyahoga Valley. How I had missed the thunder of the east. Those loud roars first started when we had crossed the great divide of Utah, and by the time we had gotten to Aspen, the thunder was everywhere, just like the thunder of my childhood. In another time, I would have imagined it was the voice of God himself. When I was young, my mother would freak out and unplug the television set during those New England booming storms. One grand storm she even herded us kids under the cover of the dining room table until it passed. Perhaps the Cuyahoga Valley storm would bring in cool rain.

Back at Decky's house, we finally met his parents, Bridgie, and old crazy legs himself. Decky's dad, Walter, ran track for Boston College. He was so fast going around that indoor field house track (they say his legs churned like bike pedals on a crank set) that someone had come up with this funny nickname that stuck with him. After school, Walter moved out west to Akron to work for Goodyear as a chemist. It was in Akron that he met the West Virginian girl of his dreams and began his family of seven. The TV rolled the whole time in Decky's living room. *Cheers,* the Boston Bar-based sitcom, was on. From their armchairs, Walter and Bridgie invited us to have a seat, but the Cleveland night life awaited us, Decky told them. We really couldn't stay; we had to get a move on, for Big Jim and his wife Elaine, old friends of Decky, awaited us.

Big Jim had a partnership in a landscape construction company in Cleveland, and Elaine was an accountant. They had been married for five years, had married during college, and lived in the country suburb of Boston Heights. When we pulled up to the driveway, Big Jim's Massey tractor sat dormant in the driveway; it stared us down as we jumped from the Fairlane and headed for their front door. I wondered if the intimidating beast might even bark at us like Murphy had back in Topeka. Once we were inside, we all sat around another TV set with *Hill Street Blues*, the American cop drama on. No one seemed to be watching it as Big Jim and Elaine took turns ripping on Decky; they laughed at his crazy haircut. It just stuck up into the air like it was constantly charged with balloon electricity. All the while they blurted out the high school and college quirks and quips that were uniquely Decky's own.

"Hope you win the big one!"

Things got so funny that Big Jim even decided to shut *Hill Street Blues* off and put on WMMS so we could listen to rock and roll. Luke, Decky, and I drank the Rolling Rock beer that we had brought, while Big Jim and Elaine stuck to their Stroh's Signature brew. Jim and Decky talked about their Catholic high school geometry teacher named Clint Eastwood; he drove a Harley to school, held Hot Wheels 500 races in class, let his students use his dartboard, and even had a stereo system and funky modern furniture in his classroom. And now old Clint was a principal and the head football coach of another school, always living up to his name every step of the way.

"And in *The Outlaw Josey Wales* he spat on the dog's head!" Decky laughed.

Big Jim told Decky about the people who had won state lotteries since he had left Ohio. There was some sort of TV special on that talked about what they all were doing now. Elaine and Big Jim bickered back and forth about the details.

"Most of them are in prison now for overspending," Jim said. "Some eighteen-year-old, after winning, flew down to Florida to buy two kilos. Got bagged!" he said.

"Now that John Belushi had it all," Big Jim went on. "He was really going places, but he blew it, too, literally! He was allergic to the stuff!"

"Yeah, such a pity," I said. "At the peak of his career, right in that hotel on Sunset Boulevard, he overdosed, and just like that, he was gone."

"He blew it in this life anyway," Big Jim again said. "He's probably in another dimension by now, who knows?"

Luke and I were aghast, surprised that Big Jim just said this.

"I've died before," Luke said to Big Jim, testing Big Jim now for more insanity.

"Oh, you have, have you?" Big Jim replied, "Well, I'll tell you there's been many a morning when I've been so hungover, I've thought I must be dead too!"

Luke shrieked in laughter.

CHAPTER 28

Friday, September 14th came.

I dreamed that I left my body again. Up into the air above the room I ascended. I was out on Taft Avenue in Cuyahoga Falls, floating upward. My gravity was gone; my spirit rose quickly while my conscious mind watched my sleeping body back on the bed fifty feet below me. I got scared for I thought I was ascending too quickly, so I anxiously jerked into a half-awake paranoid state and with that, my spirit came crashing back through the bedroom ceiling and was thrown back abruptly into the breathing body mass that so temporarily was mine. I woke up and wondered where I was, now fully alert in the middle of the night of life in a cold, dark room in Ohio, with my forehead and chest soaking with sweat.

"You blew it," I told myself.

And in the morning light, I went running with Luke. We ran lightly first, then we sprinted for 100 yards, ran lightly again, sprinted again, ran lightly, then sprinted one last time before stopping to catch our heaving breath. Decky and his dad Walter had gone off to play tennis.

Luke and I ran the neighborhoods of Decky's past. We ran right by Cuyahoga Falls High School as the students were getting out of class. We ran into a peaceful cemetery as the wind rustled through the wet trees; the breeze soothed the moist granite headstones; it gently touched the chiseled names of once living souls. I read some of them aloud—"Kelly, Thatcher, Montgomery"—all of them once breathed and felt emotion as I did. There were hundreds of them. Their physical bodies (or what was left of them) now in the cold earth below us; our breathing flesh was the only thing that now separated us from them, for only their spirits still lived. And the earth that our sneakers treaded on was now the stark barrier between life and death. I thought about how the phenomenon of time itself separated the breathing from the dead. So many in our great race had come and gone, and we would one day join this great movement, for life was always fleeting, and there was no escaping it. Were they still asleep under this organic blanket of roots, leaves, grasses and moss? Or were they someplace else? Perhaps they were now in a much better place.

At one point as we paced steadily through the vast cemetery, I wanted to stop, for we were lost and I needed to rest until we could get our bearings again. My mind went errant. Everyone below us was connected to someone above, I thought. Through the generations we were all somehow descendants of peasants, kings, great chiefs, and skilled hunters: live, grow, die, be reborn. This was the amazing cycle of life. How complex it all was. But all of us living were still chasing this fleeting beauty called life. With advancing age and our ultimate infirmity certain, would we ever let go of the belief that we had something over those who came before us? God would show us all in the end that we were merely human too. All of the great books were the only thread that loosely held all of our histories' humanity together. And no one was ever spared, not the great kings, not the famous actors, not even the presidents. How easy it was to mock God when we were living. What secrets did the peaceful souls before us now know? I wondered as I panted there, all hunched over, carefully looking for signs. There was a fallen tree branch on the road in front of us; a squirrel ran over a forgotten grave marker buried under some leaves. Perhaps it had a surname that was the same name as mine.

"Come on, you puss!" Luke pushed me. I was panting and out of breath. We both immediately realized that we needed to get to the other end of the cemetery. We needed to look for Thirteenth Street and then Jefferson. We were going in circles. We began to run at a good pace again. Eventually, we spotted the familiar big blue water tower of yesterday on the hill that overlooked the tennis courts where Decky and his father were volleying.

After a slow climb over the crest of the hill, we sat comfortably and watched the Bradys volley to each other on the court below us. I was still winded. In my high school track years, my coach, Mr. Malloy, always pushed me to go farther, faster; he pushed me like Luke had just pushed me out of the graveyard.

"Come on, Hogan, let's go. Move! Get up there!" Malloy screamed at me as he paced the inside of the old track at Cauley Stadium. With newspapers in his hand, he swept the air along with the folded sports page as I came to the rounded corner. He half-smiled in loving disgust as he walked alongside me wearing a long tan raincoat and brown fedora hat. "Get up there with the rest of them!" he bellowed. He sometimes had his glasses off and clutched in his other hand, jogging to stay even with me as I gasped, showing me that I was hardly even moving.

"Come on! Will you get up there!"

I was always on that gravel track dying, lost in a world of my own pain, plagued by the terrible challenges of a sixteen-year-old, dreaming of the girls who ran on the other side of the field as I played the same Rolling Stones song over and over in my head so I could forget about the pain and reach the finish line . . . "*Gimme Shelter.*"

One more lap, I thought on those days, seeing a definite end to my pain the quicker I could finish this bloody run. Cutting into the turn, I swung into it with my arms. I huffed like a blowfish with every arm thrust . . . *whoosh, who, whoosh, who, whoosh* . . . the song playing over and over and over again in my head . . . If that was all I could focus on, if I kept the tune in my head, it would all soon be over.

And that is how I got through every race. Now, in 1984, Coach Malloy was a regular down at Tabor's in Lowell, where my friend Richie sometimes tended bar. Yeah, good old Richie. Richie had almost come out to California with Caprissi and me after putting the idea in our stinkin' heads three years before . . . good old loveable Richie. He told me in his letters now that Coach Malloy sometimes asked about me out in California from his comfortable end seat at the bar.

"How's old Hogan doing? What's he doing now?"

And they said that just like old "Crazy Legs" Brady, Coach Malloy was quite the runner in his day too.

"They used to call him 'Feets' 'cause he was so quick," my father Frank told me over and over again. "Feets Malloy," the pride of Lowell.

Luke and I sat atop the hill under the water tower. I wondered if old "Feets" had ever run into the likes of "Crazy Legs" at a Boston track meet during the '40s, like maybe back when the Sox played with Williams, Pesky, and Dom DiMaggio, like the same year as the '46 World Series.

"Crazy Legs" volleyed a tennis ball back and forth down on the green clay court below us with Decky. Those legs still worked madly, as if they still wanted to be that crazy track star of forty years before, I could sense it.

When they finished, "Crazy Legs" drove us all back to Taft Avenue again, where Luke, Decky, and I jumped in the Fairlane to go pick up Decky's processed photos at a Fotomat parking lot booth. Later on, we showered and had dinner at the Bradys. Decky's mother made lasagna; she served a big salad and poured everyone around the table a big glass of wholesome milk, for after all, we were all seated at the table of America's heartland. After dinner, we went out again with Big Jim and Elaine, picking them up in the Fairlane. Big Jim's tractor still sat in the front yard of their Boston Heights home and stared us down again as we approached. It was intimidating and eerily silent. All of us packed in the car, Luke and Big Jim up front, and headed north toward Cleveland.

"We're off to the great North Coast of America!" Decky exclaimed.

On a wooded two-lane road, reminiscent of the back roads of my youth that we used to drive around in, Luke decided to stop at a roadside bar. We all walked into the bar from the rainy Ohio night and immediately encountered a contingency of craning curious locals whose eyes stopped what they were doing and fixed on our grand entrance. All of them were dressed in jeans and T-shirts, most with long hair, with rock star lookalikes everywhere in the crowd. Bob Seger, Ted Nugent, Grace Slick, and Janis Joplin . . . They were all there. I spotted them. The bar silence was deafening at first, but then their eyes stopped at Big Jim and methodically they turned, one by one, back into their own worlds again . . . rock-and-roll music, cigarettes, local sports, and liquor. I was happy that Big Jim was with us, for without him, we may have had trouble, for we were in the middle of a wooded nowhere, between Akron and Cleveland, where everyone knew everyone, and no one goes into other people's neighborhood bars—except if you were us.

This place was worlds away from the college bar of Columbus and further away from the Huntington Beach disco clubs of August. We had entered back into a simple time again, a time before all of the charades. These were Ohio's finest working-class heroes. They didn't care how they might appear to us on the outside. They weren't interested in trendy styles or trendy people; they were simply out to have a few beers and listen to juke box rock and roll on a rainy Friday night.

We all sat down at a picnic table next to the jukebox by the door. There were names scratched into the table, all kinds of stuff, like: "Betty and Dean '78," "Bill and Delores were here—1981." Some little heart scratches were etched here and there, some profanity, and a loud "Ricky SUCKS." *Poor Ricky*, I thought. There was a basket of popcorn that had been abandoned on the table by someone before us. All the while, Deep Purple's "Smoke on the Water" rattled the black base front of the large jukebox beside us. Decky grabbed the old basket of leftover kernels and darted to the center bar. He came back quickly, bouncing with three fresh baskets of popcorn.

"Do you know what this song is about?" Decky asked as he put down the baskets. Big Jim was still at the bar asking about the availability of bottled Stroh's Signature while Elaine was already on her way back to the picnic table carrying two pitchers of regular draft beer.

"No," I replied.

"It's about the time that Lake Erie was burning, The great North Shore of America! Fire on the water!" Decky laughed.

"Oh yeah, I think I remember hearing about that. Maybe you told us before?"

Bahhh, Bah, Bahhh, Bah Bahh, Ba-bahhh, Bah, Bah, Bah, Ba-bahhhh, the sound of that heavy guitar permeated our space. I imagined it might be as heavy as the film of filth that had caught fire on Lake Erie. I suddenly looked around and took notice that the whole bar seemed to be tapping their hands and rocking their barstools to this crazy riff. Heads rocked back and forth as people looked off into space, thinking back to their high school days. There was casual conversation here and there. I heard people discussing the Browns already having lost two at the start of the season. Denver would be in town this weekend; maybe they could get a win. Someone in the corner near the restrooms was lamenting about another disappointing Indians season while someone else spoke up. "What about Len Barker's perfect game in '81?" But others just resigned to tap their hands and shake their heads to the good old rock and roll that played above all of the background sports talk; a sound so uniquely akin to the true identity of what was Cleveland.

Everyone in the whole bar looked familiar to me, even though I had never met a single one of them. I was fascinated by this phenomenon. Were there never enough faces to go around the whole world or what? Maybe they were all ghosts. Besides Ted Nugent and Janis Joplin, there were others around that had a strange resemblance to the people I had grown up with. There was a Ray Champeaux lookalike standing over at the bar and staring me down; next to him was someone that absolutely could be my friend Dukie's older brother. Lones was here too, except maybe a little bit shorter with darker hair, but those same big old inch-thick Coke-bottle glasses, and just like Lones, at the smack center of every important conversation.

Luke punched a cover of "Brown Eyed Girl" by Jimmy Buffet using the white buttons of the juke box. The machine's robot arm moved up and back, finally grabbing the 45 from the catalog stack to place it onto the turntable, which was partially hidden from sight. How I loved that Van Morrison song no matter who was singing it. Heck, I loved listening to my own voice sing it.

Once both pitchers of beer were gone with the red popcorn baskets empty, we collectively decided to get out of there and proceeded to stumble into the dizzy drizzly night, leaving the people in their rock-and-roll bubble behind. As I turned back to watch our forever exit, nobody even turned to watch us leave. We were invisible again.

We drove on, approaching another big city in the middle of America with a crazy surfboard attached to our car. When we got close, Big Jim and Elaine pointed out Cleveland's Terminal Tower to us. Its older architecture was completely illuminated in the sky of night with brilliant light reflecting off of the clean white stone of the building. It was a glowing iron whose white-hot color contrasted with the cooler, newer buildings in its immediate vicinity.

"It used to be the tallest building in the world before the Empire State Building was built," Big Jim told us.

"What was the tallest building in the world before Terminal Tower was built?" Luke asked.

"Who knows? The Tower of Babel?" Big Jim answered with an optimistic chuckle.

I had learned about the Tower of Babel in catechism at St. Matthews as a child, a tower built by one people after the great flood with the desire to all speak one language. What's the harm in that? Here the story was coming back to me from somewhere out of the thick, drizzling Cleveland air, with Big Jim the storyteller.

We drove through The Flats, and along the Cuyahoga River we saw a red iron swinging bridge that sat sideways in the darkness; it appeared to wait patiently for a passing barge before it could swing itself back and lock into place. The small bridge paled in size to a huge arch bridge of columns of white concrete and steel that crossed above it, a greater bridge to higher levels, higher planes running above The Flats. Without crossing the swinging bridge, we found ourselves in a rundown section of town and a local joint that Big Jim had wanted to take us to. Inside was a long, narrow bar running the length of the floor and a big group of Clevelanders congregated around the far end, where there was a dart board. I noticed that the clientele were mostly working class, some blue collar, like those at the roadside bar we had just been to, but there were a good mix of others a little more dressed up, with some wearing collared shirts instead of their T-shirted brethren. In a general sense, I noticed that the professional-dressed city folk had less weathered features than those in T-shirts beside them. They were polished and smooth with bigger paychecks, bigger egos, and a lot more to lose in life than the group throwing darts at the wall.

As we ordered drinks and tried to get settled, I took a step back and studied my physical surroundings further. A short, stocky, thirty-something bald guy at the bar talked to the others in my group about Europe. Big Jim slowly peeled away from this debacle, dismissing the overwhelming know-it-all that attempted to hold onto us all. Jim was an eddy in the tide, motioning to me to walk with him toward the cooler dartboard gang assembled at the far end of the bar.

"You don't know how lucky you all are, the places you'll stay, the people you'll meet, pages of stories that aren't even told yet," the guy engaged Decky, where poor Decky couldn't get away cleanly. I chased after Big Jim, but my feet momentarily stuck to the spilled beer floorboards. I thwack-thwacked away. It made my exit more noticeable to the midnight rambler.

"Yeah, that's why he's sitting here in Cleveland," Big Jim said to me when I caught up to him.

Big Jim and I stood near the dart area. We had soon cased both levels of the place and now stood at the bottom of the wooden staircase in the corner and patiently waited for the others to catch up with us. But the mad bald fisherman had cast his loose net over them now and held them steady within his earshot as he droned on and on.

I saw Luke test the loose net from afar. He was first to break away and come over to us, leaving just Elaine and Decky behind. We talked for a minute about Luke's little brother Nate while Big Jim snuck to the side of the bar for more drinks. Young Nate died a year earlier while on his way to work at his pizza parlor job; Nate flipped pies there. He was driving along a lonely two-lane Topeka country road and was hit head-on by a carload of drunken high school girls who themselves ended up with nothing more than a few scratches and bruises. It was an incredible tragedy for the whole Coppens family because Nate, being the youngest, was always so loved by everyone.

"And why is it that the drunk drivers always live?" I asked aloud. "How is that fair?"

"I don't know . . . because they're loose I guess. Their bodies are all relaxed instead of their stiffening up. I've determined that life is not always about what is and isn't fair," Luke answered.

My father Frank had always reasoned that the unexplained and the unfair was all the more reason to believe that there had to be a higher place, an explanation for it all. There had to be an ultimate peace that would finally be revealed on that certain day of reckoning. "That's where it's all going to come to you! *Thwack!*" he told me. "So you better listen up!"

Luke talked to Jim and I about the two Annas in his life. Anna his cute sister and another Anna, a girl he had met before we left California. "At the end of all this, you might go back there and marry her someday," I said to him. While we talked, a disc jockey spun classic rock and roll throughout the club from a partially hidden booth up on the second-floor landing.

"Maybe . . . You never know what's ahead for us all," Luke agreed.

In the corner near the dartboard, a map of the state of California hung on the wall. Newport Beach was boldly circled with harsh pen-marking graffiti that notated boldly "*Mae was here!*" I wondered why the map was even here. No other maps on the walls were evident, just this one California map at the far end of the bar. If Mae was there, why did she ever come back to Cleveland? Was she visiting Newport Beach out there? Did she own this bar? Or was she just another drunk patron? Perhaps she was living with some guy named Kilroy now.

After we heard Bob Dylan's howling cries for grace in "Saved," the DJ put on The Who with "Love, Reign O'er Me." The man in the booth worked autonomously through the night; his selections were his own. I could see that he was having a blast as he talked to himself up there, mixing records. The rain and the crescendo of The Who's song slowly rose to the level of the crazy crowd amidst puddles of random conversation. It rained hard outside too. The beer was taking hold of me now; I could tell for I began to sing loudly and turned to stare out the window at the pouring rain on the empty street outside. My thoughts were a freeway inside of my head; The Who's Roger Daltrey screamed to me. I sang aloud with him in the crowded bar, but no one wanted to listen to me. I could hardly hear my own beautiful voice above the din. The guy in the booth put on "Heartbreaker" by The Stones next. It was a song about a kid being shot down in New York City by mistake, shot down with a .44 by the cops, Dirty Harry style. I thought about the hard rain outside and how Neil Young and Waylon Jennings were supposed to be playing tonight at The Blossom Music Center back in Cuyahoga Falls. Would they still play? Luke, Big Jim, and I talked on and on about this. Someone in the bar mentioned that Cyndi Lauper only had 5,000 in attendance the night before because of the weather. I wondered what the almighty snobby stagehand thought about that. Who's afraid of the rain anyway? After all, this was Cleveland where rock and roll reigned hard! Elton John would play tomorrow night on that beautiful rainy outdoor stage, but sadly, Luke, Decky, and I'd be gone.

We hopped across the river with our lonely group to another crowded bar. The swinging barge bridge this time allowed our passage to the other side of the city in the wet darkness. It must have quietly moved into place while we were drinking in the dartboard bar.

I was certainly drunk now and barely remembered a doorman that took a dollar off of me as I entered; my poor fleeting memory had stalled.

"Why is it only a dollar?" I asked the big guy.

"If you want to play you gotta pay! Nobody rides for free!" the big man said back to me and then chuckled aloud in a reminiscent San Francisco dream.

Inside now, Decky and I bounced around with our usual pickup lines while Luke played Pac-Man in the corner by himself; he had inadvertently hit the "one player" button instead of hitting the "two player" button when he started the game. Joining him for a moment, we decided to count scores, a turn at a time, instead of playing each other in the game.

While Luke gobbled the Pac-dots on the video maze during his turn, Decky walked up to a girl wearing a red double-breasted-style vest to say, "I see you're double-breasted tonight!"

She was aghast. I thought she might smack him at first, but she simply walked away indignantly.

"You look like a nun who used to teach me piano in the fifth grade!" Decky said to another cute girl standing by the bar as she rolled her eyes at him and turned abruptly away. "Gosh, there's something about that line that always gets them going! I almost had her! Did you see it!" He turned to me laughing.

Soon a girl appeared over Luke's shoulder and began to watch him play Pac-Man. She had beautiful shoulder-length brown hair and brown eyes. She stood there alone in the night, a Van Morrison siren, but just like that, Decky swooped in like a hawk and started to talk to her before I could even stumble in her general direction.

I immediately noticed that she had a French accent. I overheard her respond to Decky with a smile. I moved from Luke's opposite side now and tried my best high school French on her, slurring my speech, trying desperately to roll my drunken Rs.

"Je m'appelle Mike."

"My name is Colette." She wasn't impressed with my French. And her name was Colette!

In broken English, Colette proceeded to tell Decky and Luke that she lived in a village outside of Paris. She was traveling America and was staying at youth hostels throughout the continent. She had been with some friends here in Cleveland, but she was moving on now. She had a bus ticket to Chicago, and from there, would go further west, eventually to Los Angeles and Newport Beach.

"Say hello to Mae for us in Newport Beach," I said.

"Que?"

"What is your impression of America so far?" Decky asked her.

"Why do the French hate Americans?" I obnoxiously blurted out over Decky's shoulder. "Is it because of the Cold War?"

"No," she said, "I'm not sure how you would say . . . your arrogance?"

And with my arrogance still lingering there, Colette decided to say good-bye to Decky and walk swiftly away. I said good-bye to Colette as she walked into the crowd, but she didn't turn back. Here I was invisible to another Colette, I thought. Why? Because love didn't reign anymore. It would rain cool rain again someday though, I figured it had to, but when? Was I really that much of a jerk? All the while, the hard Cleveland rain still pelted the street in blowing waves outside.

"Must be, how do you say, my arrogance?" I turned to Luke. "You look like a nun who used to teach me piano in the fifth grade!" I yelled after Colette. Luke shirked his characteristic laugh at this. Decky seemed mad that I had chased Colette away. Again.

While Decky drove Big Jim and Elaine home that night to Boston Heights, Luke and I fell asleep in the backseat of the Ford. The cool, cool rain fell hard as I slept, banging like hard hail on the roof of the car. It rained all of the way to Taft Avenue.

We arrived at Decky's parents' house about two o'clock a.m. A note on the counter left by Decky's mother Bridgie said that our friend, Eddie Kinsley, had called from California while we were out. Being it so late, I thought I'd wait until the morning to call him back.

The three of us raided the kitchen cabinets, opening the refrigerator repeatedly to pull out food. Luke laid sheets of white bread on the counter while Decky filled them all with ham, then placed all of the sliced cheese from a thick Kraft Singles package on each half. I moved down the line of open sandwiches and filled them with gobs of mustard before we put the top slice of bread over them all. The gremlins had returned. It made perfect sense to me now—it was the exposure to water that made them multiply.

CHAPTER 29

Saturday, September 15th, the 22nd day

Bridgie made everyone pork chops for brunch and cooked up lots of vegetables from her backyard garden: cabbage, carrots, tomatoes, broccoli, and cucumbers, all cooked in olive oil. And, of course, there was homemade lemon meringue pie for dessert. I asked Bridgie how broccoli in her garden grew, and she brought me over to the kitchen window that overlooked the backyard.

"See the back left corner of the garden?"

"Yes."

"Well, come up to the first yellow flower and do you see the green leaves below it?"

"I see them."

"Well, the broccoli grows in the middle of the leaves. You can pick it off, and it will grow again, just as long as you keep the leaves intact."

From the kitchen window I looked out past the broccoli and through two yards to see the back side of the Schmidt's green garage, the garage that Wilhelm and his dad had built ten years before without a permit or plans. And there to the left of it was the back deck where we had sat.

I thought of all of the things Wilhelm's father had said to us that night when we sat on that back deck drinking all of his Stroh's beer.

"Eat it up; ain't no good warm!"

I thought about poor Wilhelm all by himself out on the West Coast now. What would become of him? And all of my other friends I had made out there like Brian Kelly and Sean Tarrytown. The consummate funnyman, Sean Tarrytown was transitioning to another engineering job up in Northern California. He left the comfort of the circuit board factory for more money. With his move from the beach, I wondered if we would lose contact with Tarrytown forever, because that's usually how those things went. I also realized that these last three weeks of travel had only been but a few pages in my wonderful life. It was such a short snap of the towel, yet, we had reconnected with so many friends, and we already had so many great memories of this trip: Zane and Maureen, Roni, Anna, all of Luke's family, and many, many more. Would I ever see any of them again?

There were so many chapters ahead for me too. This journey wasn't a linear thing, though; it wasn't like having to get through a long book. I had to keep telling myself to get inside of every moment along the way. Life was about the power of the present, for the present moment mattered more than anything. Heck, it actually dictated what would happen in the future when you realized this simple notion and fearlessly acted on it. I wasn't simply reading through the written pages of *War and Peace* or another long work of art, with thousands of pages to turn and the burning desire to gauge the marker to measure how far I had to go to finish. I didn't have to get through anyone else's written words. You see, here I actually was, the writer.

Our plans were to drive straight through to Philadelphia. The hard Cleveland rain had stopped now, and light drizzle graced the afternoon. As we readied to leave Taft Avenue, the cool air with that clean smell that fresh rain often brings with it was exhilarating. A low fog hung above the moist asphalt of the streets of Decky's old neighborhood. Bursts of sun broke through the fast-moving throws of white and dark clouds. The sun's bright silhouette outline appeared to me like a ghost behind a rolling cloth sheet. In the driveway, Decky's little sister Molly prepared to leave for Ohio State. Molly sang to the music, a song from The Kinks that blasted out of her bedroom window as she made her happy trips back and forth from the house to her car, packing it with her full crates and clothing. Her first day of school was Wednesday, the 19th, but she was moving back to Columbus today. This was already her junior year, Decky quipped to us. She was the last Brady left in college. Poor Molly was going to be a chemical engineer.

Philadelphia was next for us where we were going to spend a night at Decky's older sister Maggie's place. Maggie's apartment was situated just outside the city in rural New Jersey. She was away on business, but her husband Jimmy would be expecting us in the evening. From there, we would move on and visit Sandy, my writing friend from California. Sandy had recently moved back home to help her family out since her brother had been framed for something he didn't do and sent to prison. I had promised Sandy in a letter that I'd have a screenplay synopsis to her by the time we landed in Jersey. This was an exercise to keep us both focused and on track with our individual goals, for Sandy would, in turn, have me critique a screenplay synopsis of her own. When I had left Huntington Beach, I had a few ideas and thought there'd be plenty of time to come up with a complete screenplay synopsis while we crossed the country, but now, I realized it was too late. It had all gone by so fast.

"Don't shelf that cocaine story idea just yet," Decky said to me. "Why don't you just give her that one?"

Fourteen Lines was the name of the screenplay. It was a story that I had started at Orange Coast College about a businessman crack addict who carried around a pocket mirror and a Swiss Army Knife. I based the idea on some of the stuff that I had seen while I worked at a company called IBC in 1981. The sales professionals in suits at IBC spent their evenings in and out of Newport Beach Happy Hour powder rooms; they'd sometimes even offer me lines to snort in the empty break rooms of the workplace during the day, but I always nervously refused. Because of this, I was ostracized from the sales group overnight. All of them were up-and-coming executives with too much money to spend, living in the sweet spot of life, that beautiful lap of luxury, Newport Beach, California. Disillusioned with it all, I left IBC and stumbled into the street again. This led to the ketchup-and-white-bread sandwiches and the attempt to work the Hollywood intern jobs before my last desperate circuit board factory gig.

I had come up with this title *Fourteen Lines* to symbolize a lot of things, with fourteen also being the number of lines in a sonnet. *Fourteen lines* became fourteen lies in the end. My main character was a person a lot like myself, only older, a future me who had made all the wrong choices; he had become addicted to crack cocaine. He was an executive who had it all without ever knowing it, without ever being happy; he was always chasing the next great thing. He forgot how to breathe in life, to drink the whole glass of orange juice and let it run down the sides of his face. He blew it all by snorting powder up his nose.

"You've got to write the ending first," our writing professor, Mr. Blakely, always said. "The screenwriter must always have his ending in sight. Take the classic *Chinatown,* for instance. There is no other screenplay written more perfectly. It is truly a masterpiece."

So I wrote the ending first. It was beautiful . . . a beaten man finally finding the goodness in life again.

A good screenplay, like everything in life, was mostly in the formula, Blakely said. Just like life itself, if you could master the routine of it all, the rest was easy. A screenplay formula, just like a math formula, was a simple series of clear-cut steps. After all, didn't everything in the universe ultimately have a sense of order to it? Introduce the characters and the situation in your setup, throw in your hook, establish some resolve in the midpoint, after the midpoint build it to a crescendo-like climax, followed up by the final twist where everything falls into place, and then, smack—you finish with the happy ending, the good wins over the bad, and love always triumphs. Like a well planned event, he said, everything in a good screenplay could be carefully spelled out in a linear sequence, there was an order to it. Of course, you needed the vision too, Blakely said, but once you had that, the easy part came—a standard blueprint to put it all out on, the sweet, passionate unraveling of everything and anything.

"A writer's vision flows from the power of the present moment!" Blakely exclaimed. "When you are in it, you will know it!" That was the line of his I loved the most.

But sometimes a good visionary probably needed a good screenwriter too. I wondered if it was ever possible to be both. I scratched my head and wondered if someone could also have a well planned life just the same as a well planned event. Something always seemed to come along and screw up the plans.

The odometer read 74,481 miles. We stopped on our way out of Akron to fill the tank with fourteen and a half gallons of gasoline. Luke paid $15.10 at the pump, and we were once again on our way. With Interstate 76 all rolled out before us, we headed east toward the Pennsylvania line. Fields of wildflowers, with yellows, scarlets, greens, and browns, stretched out beyond imaginary stanchions as they aligned the sides of the big asphalt carpet that went forever to the eastern horizon. Further along the road, off to the right, I noticed that a field of sunflowers had captured an oil derrick, overrunning it with beauty as the oil digger still tried to pump away nervously, droning on amidst an onslaught of climbing vines; its very existence was threatened by this gradual manifestation of nature. The bright colors of life were slowly overtaking the grays of a once-determined progress.

Before Youngstown, the 76 rolled into Interstate 80, where we continued on into western Pennsylvania. Pittsburgh and all of Steeler Nation sat below us to the south. I had never been there, however, we had no time for it now. We would stay on the 80 eastward all afternoon. Seas of tall green mossy grasses adorned our peripheral field of view, with speckles of violet flowers everywhere. We were running furiously through the poppy fields toward Oz, looking for the great city beyond the horizon. I felt dreary.

The wildflower
Will always grow free
The world should let it be

The candle
Needs oxygen to burn
Takes in everything to learn,
To grow

I once knew the wildflower, I thought, but now she was gone. I still held her in my memories, though.

A rainy, damp, refreshing smack of East Coast autumn hit us head-on, right in the windshield, as we listened to Gordon Lightfoot sing "Carefree Highway." There were many seasons along this roadside, I observed, some still stuck in summer with no signs of any changes and some way ahead of autumn, almost barren, with the rest of the landscape around us at various stages in between. It was like one of Ingrid's ever-changing paintings. I remembered she had a rolling landscape masterpiece that changed from left to right, where winter had to find a way backward through fall and then summer in order to get to spring. I looked hard for spring again, but saw no signs of her. I noticed red, orange, and gold-leafed trees all intermingled with the stable firs of a certain December.

"I can't wait to get to Europe to have sex!" Decky screamed out of the open window of the car and then turned to me to say, "And you can quote me on that! This trip has been some trip!"

We crossed over bridges on Interstate 80 where I immediately experienced the great perception of depth. Faraway rivers hundreds of feet below us nestled in deep green wilderness roared with the spirits of ancient voices. With one bridge came vertigo and sweating palms. I had to avert my gaze upward again to steady myself on the three-dimensional hills across the valley. There were several hints of coal country beyond the hills, and trees were now everywhere across the landscape, covering all of life's colors. It was so different than the subtle browns and yellows of the now-distant American West. On the right side of the car, I counted seven hills in sequence, just like standing dominoes. The low western sun behind us caused them to throw shadows on each other. The weight of the eclipsing darkness from one cast longer shadows upon the next in line, but these were such futile attempts for darkness to take each of these hills down, I thought, for even though I had never been here before, I innately knew these hills had endured the night for centuries and would never fall. They would still stand tall in the morning, for sure.

Wild green grass that graced the sides of the road turned shades of purple and rust browns as we pushed on. The failing light played tricks with the grasses' hues; hints of orange still burned on the grass tops, like embers, as the disappearing sun tried to ignite them all one last time, but tragically, to no avail. For any who doubted the return of daylight, the night beckoned them to not be afraid of her ominous illusion anymore. It was a peaceful blanket, she promised, and the morning light would certainly be magnificent, like no other light you have ever seen before.

We tried cutting from I-80 from Bellafonte toward Reading, all the while looking for the mad turnpike. Maybe it was Route 147? Maybe it was Route 61? We traversed small Pennsylvania towns of yesterday, and I had visions of bearded Amish gentlemen riding in horse drawn wagons beside me. I saw mountains to our right now that had already swallowed the orange setting sun. Dusk. A barn stood in the distance with silver and gray fields before it. Everything was quickly losing its purple now. It was a crazy time study; the colors moved fast to black and white, with the only movement in this still life that of color itself. And then the roads curved and winded for another 174 miles.

We drove on into the night toward Philadelphia and eventually crossed over the Delaware River toward Voorhees, New Jersey, where Decky's sister, Maggie, and brother-in-law, Jimmy, lived. It was midnight and another 120 miles by the time we arrived there. Jimmy was the only one home, for Maggie was traveling out West on business.

"Eat it up; ain't no good warm!" Mr. Schmidt had said. This was the life that the darkness had promised.

CHAPTER 30

Sunday, September 16th, it had been twenty-three days that we had been on the road. Decky's brother-in-law, Jimmy, told us all about Springsteen's "Born in the USA Tour" that he had been to at the Philadelphia Spectrum the week before. "The Boss," he said, "played from eight o'clock until one o'clock in the morning. Throughout the whole show, there were waves of arms and hands in the air, with bodies surfing across this whitewater wash of people, bodies slowly getting passed toward the stage, as if they were riding atop invisible surfboards!" All their minds were driftwood while Bruce pulled pretty girls up out of the audience to dance with them in the dark.

"This guy will be sold out forever!" Jimmy exclaimed. "It was the best rock-and-roll show I've ever been to! . . . Across the sea of people some large signs in the audience proclaimed, 'F Michael Jackson, we got The Boss!'"

Springsteen was everything, and this was New Jersey, where he had gotten his start. I thought back on how Buddy Love used to play Springsteen's *Live at Winterland* bootleg over and over again back at UMass in 1979. "BackStreets" echoed throughout those empty fraternity hallways with Guido always singing the loudest to The Boss's song.

Buddy Love got so excited when we played that album, that one night at the fraternity while he danced about to it, he knocked over his overcrowded rat cage, and all of those rats ran mad to the holes in the walls, running from the light of the night. The rats haunted us for months after that. Every time we flicked on the light in our rooms, we were scared to see one of them scampering for the walls. When I tried to sleep, I had to pray (The Lord's Prayer) endlessly just to take my mind off of them, just to block out the thought of a rat crawling across my face in the darkness.

One spring day before graduation, the Board of Health condemned the fraternity building because of all of those rats and the deplorable conditions of the house itself, and we all had to move out. I had such sweet memories of the stench of beer in those old, worn-out carpets, the New England springtime blowing reverie through broken screens, my stereo speakers behind them, screaming back toward the campus with sounds of Bruce Springsteen on a sunny afternoon.

In Jersey now, Luke, Decky, and I, after spending a short night at Maggie and Jimmy's, were quickly moving again. We noticed a small-town, boarded-up movie theatre with frontage signs that called out "For Sale" right off of New Jersey Highway 61. The price was a mere thirty-five thousand dollars. It was an indication of a sad, disappearing rural America; it seemed that everything had to be in a strip mall now. Who would ever buy a one-screen movie theatre that just sat out there in the boonies all by itself? Everyone was moving west to California, chasing the sun, anyways, chasing a better living; that is, everyone except us.

"Last night was *Highway 61 Revisted*," I said to Decky.

"If this is the road that Dylan wrote about, I feel that poor guy's pain. After this drive, I never want to visit it again," Decky replied.

"Hopefully, no more bloody drives after yesterday," Luke echoed.

We only had six more hours if we wanted to go straight to Massachusetts, but we still had people to see between here and there. Besides, as Luke said, there would be no more bloody drives. Our next stop was Medford, New Jersey, to see my writing friend Sandy. It was only about thirty minutes away.

A disc jockey on Philadelphia's WYSP proclaimed that Tina Turner actually bought a new fur coat every day . . . and then the DJ played "What's Love Got to Do with It?" He came back on the air after that and told us that Prince brought purple rain to wherever he went. I jawed around on the meaning of his words and realized how tough it must be to be a DJ, always trying to come up with clever things to say.

We headed due east on Interstate 70 and an old green Maverick passed us by; it was like the old Maverick that my friend Richie Clark used to drive. The Maverick also had a very similar body style to my old three-on-the-tree red Comet that was buried somewhere back in California now.

It was late one night in 1977 when Richie and I were headed back from Paradise Beach, New Hampshire, and he lost control of that Maverick. The first time he lost control that night was right as we got onto Route 495 from the beach. You see, Richie fell asleep at the wheel. I was sleeping beside him and woke up on Route 495 in a panic as we veered onto the dirt shoulder of the highway. The rubber tires hit the soft sand, and thankfully, jolted Richie out of his sleep and back into wakefulness. *Ka-bling*! A mile marker reflector that we had hit head-on flew up over the windshield.

"Gotta stay awake, gotta make it to the boulevard," Richie kept saying to me that night.

But by the time we got to the boulevard near Lowell, which was another half hour away, Richie had succumbed again to the sandman. Wide-eyed, I awoke to the loud screeches as we crossed into the opposing traffic lanes. Luckily for both of us that night, it was so late that no cars were around. But just as we crossed the lanes, I saw the river. Oh crap! I looked at the stationary guard rail on the other side of the road that was now in front of us. Behind it was a good-bye steep drop into the rushing Merrimack River. I thought in a fleeting moment that Richie and I were going into the river that night! And then, *Ka-blam*! We hit the guard rail head-on and bounced right off the heavy steel barrier. The car spun a flying one-eighty degrees before coming to a dead stop on the edge of the steep grade. The front end of Richie's Maverick was really banged up, but the guard rail had saved us; it was the only thing between us and the cliff that looked down on the rushing dark water below. Richie quickly regained his senses as we sat there on the rail and he tried to start her again, but she wouldn't start. The bent and twisted steel rail hugged the right side of the Maverick so close that I had to hop over the driver's seat and jump out Richie's side to escape the car and the moving water below me.

In the quiet darkness in that 1977 night, Richie and I pushed and pulled tirelessly at the weary car to get her off the rail. When we finally got her bumper untangled, we pushed her back across the empty lanes of the road. The Maverick's front end dragged and scraped the asphalt, fighting us all the way. When we had her over by the side of the highway near the hill at First Street and out of the way of the Pawtucket Boulevard, Richie tried to turn the ignition one last time to see if he could get her started, but she wouldn't kick over. She just choked and coughed; steam gushed from her radiator. Richie and I buried the Maverick there at the bottom of Christian Hill on that night. There were cuts on our heads, cuts on our knees, but we were happy to be walking and alive. We were sober again and drank in the dawn with enormous gulps, letting it run down the sides of our faces as we walked slowly home. We were very lucky that day.

Now here in New Jersey, Luke, Decky, and I noticed that the Maverick on the New Jersey 70 had a surfboard affixed to her roof just like we did, and it was clear that she was headed to where this road ended; the infamous Jersey Shore. Luke tooted the horn and hollered madly at the long-haired teenager driving. The kid looked over nervously at first and then looked up to the surfboard on the top of the Fairlane and smugly gave us the "thumbs-up" sign.

"Yes! All right! There we go! From ocean to ocean, coast to coast, we've seen our first signs of the Jersey Shore!" Decky yelled. "Our crazy surfboard finally looks normal again! Yes!"

It was about three o'clock in the afternoon. From a payphone, Sandy gave us directions to Tuckerton Road where she was going to meet us. I called the directions out to Luke. "From Main Street take Stokes Road until we get to Lenepee Trail. Stay on Lenepee Trail for about a mile until we see Tuckerton Road."

Once we rounded the corner to Tuckerton Road I spotted her, standing on the street corner outside of a brand-new Toyota, with two little kids, Rachel, about two years old, and Roxy, about five, bouncing around in the back of the car.

She was beautiful standing there. She wore a red flannel shirt and blue jeans, country-like, the beautiful New Jersey sun studying the perfect lines of her face. When I saw Sandy there, it made me realize how much I missed Colette. How I longed to touch her lips ever so softly with my index finger again, run it over her beautiful cheeks as she closed her eyes gently, run the bridge of her perfect nose forever.

Luke looked ahead at Sandy and before we all got out of the car he said aloud, "Is there anything ever more beautiful?"

The light of the world touched her face as she stood there; it highlighted her cheeks. We all were breathless. It had been a long time for the three of us. She was such a wonderful contrast to the darkness of the weary road we had been traveling.

I had visions of Colette. I missed her. My heart was racing; it felt as if it were going to rip the fiber of my flesh and shirt to show itself again. It trembled in the soft New Jersey afternoon, for nothing could ever be more perfect than being in love again.

"I am enjoying this moment! Drink in her beauty!" Luke whispered to Decky and me.

Time had stopped. I felt the slow motion around me as I reached out to give her a hug. I wished it was Colette; I wished it could be forever.

Sandy had us follow her first to her aunt Theresa's fruit stand where her aunt gave us several bags of free fruit for our journey ahead. It was all fresh, all tree-picked. There were peaches, apples, and pears, right out of a line of just picked wooden baskets on the old wooden stand. The fresh breeze off of the roadside orchard scented the air with memories of a carefree life. There was a cat in a rocking chair out in front of the stand that opened one eye to look us over; it didn't seem to trust us at all. Decky immediately had a premonition. When we got back to the car, he told us he had a horrifying flashback to Luke's friend Fran's cat Dillinger in Oklahoma and thought that this cat might really be Dillinger, the cat who had tormented him so all night long. Decky was spooked by this . . . The cat looked just like Dillinger! With this karma, I thought back to the distant night where we had been clawed and tugged at.

"Dillinger almost went in the freezer that night, I swear it!" Decky exclaimed.

We left the stand and followed Sandy to the house that she was babysitting the two little girls at. The lonely street that the two-bedroom house sat on didn't even have a street sign. Once we all were inside, we sat around the kitchen table where we talked away the rest of the sunny afternoon.

Taking Decky's suggestion, I brought a copy of my *Fourteen Lines* synopsis in with me. I suddenly realized it was a poor excuse to hand over to her, for Sandy knew that this was the same synopsis I had been working on back when she was in California with me. She simply smiled when she saw the title.

"His is a good one!" Decky spoke up, not knowing that Sandy had heard about the idea before.

Now, Sandy's synopsis was a Romeo-and-Juliet love story, she explained as she laid out the neatly typed pages before us. It was about a poor boy from a labor union home that fell in love with the daughter of a big business owner. The girl's father's company employed most of the people in the tiny East Coast town, but the business was dead set against the union coming in. Because of this, there was violent bloodshed at the climax of the screenplay, with the two lovers caught right in the middle of it all.

"That sounds like a good one too!" Decky proclaimed at the old wooden table we all sat around.

We talked about our trip; where we had been, the people we had met, the places we had seen, the sheer loneliness of the transient life, and the longing for the next stop in between the long stretches of road. Sandy listened with big wide eyes. Deep inside, I could see her reeling, going back to her own lonely travel across our magnificent country all by herself.

"My sister called from Hawaii the other day," Sandy said, "and the first words out of her mouth were, 'I have some bad news for you.' So I gave the phone to my aunt and said, 'You take it!' But Aunt Theresa gave the phone back to me saying, 'You take it!' . . . I was scared and screamed into the phone back at my sister, 'Gabriella, you first got to tell me that no one died, and then I will calm myself!' And my sister screams back, 'Calm yourself, girl! I was only going to tell you that Ryan broke his arm!'"

This was the simple girl that Sandy was. We talked about religion. Sandy had moved in with a born-again Christian roommate in Medford who preached to Sandy daily about how everyone that didn't repent for their earthly sins would go to hell someday. The two little girls that Sandy babysat ate graham crackers at the table beside her.

"But what about my aunt? Or little Roxy? They surely can't go to hell like you say," Sandy had said to her roommate. "Roxy knows no bad; she was born an angel."

"It's too bad that these people give religion such a bad name," Decky spoke up.

I told Sandy that Decky and Luke had streaked through a Christian Revival tent during a service in the big park across from our house in Huntington Beach just a few weeks before we left California. Her eyes got wide again.

"But they meant well," I said, "they just did it for a laugh."

All evil was an illusion, I felt. I didn't want to think about hell or a wrathful God any more. From the little bit that I knew, Jesus showed nothing but compassion for the sick and the poor outcasts, the prostitutes, the beggars and the thieves. My image of a kind God just didn't fit in with the wrathful God of the Born-Agains.

All the while, the two little girls, blond and blue-eyed, innocent and beautiful, sat there intently watching us, just taking everything in. Roxy had cerebral palsy. Her eyes turned inward; she wore heavy glasses. Her bright little mind was housed in a body that couldn't work right, with nerve signals misfiring and not knowing how to tell her muscles to move without having to exert some great effort. It was something the rest of us took for granted, like breathing or sleeping or anything that was life. There was so much that we didn't understand. Why should any disease or even death scare us like it did? We were eternal spirits, and somehow, every single experience here on earth had to have a reason, something we could learn from.

It quickly became time for Luke, Decky, and I to move on. I told Sandy that we might try to stop by in the morning before leaving New Jersey, but I knew we wouldn't be stopping by; it was all a part of the formality of everything. You just couldn't walk out of someone's life forever without trying to see them one last time. But it just wasn't possible. I knew right then that this was good-bye forever, and Sandy knew it too. "And be sure to thank your aunt Theresa for all of the fruit she gave us!"

"Oh, and I brought you this book," I told her reaching into my bag now, "*How to Write for Television*. You can have it." It had been a book I had bought to figure out the formula for sitcoms, but I decided after reading it that I really didn't want to write for this medium after all, for I loved the feature film format too much. Sandy thanked me for the gift.

On the way out of the swinging screen door, Luke whispered to her, "Thank you for being the prettiest thing I've seen in such a long time."

We jumped into the Fairlane, and I watched Sandy one last time as she still blushed from Luke's compliment; she held little Rachel on her hip. Sandy opened up the door and waved good-bye to us all. Roxy's taut, turned arm reached out below Sandy's, her small fingers stiff and clawlike. She tried to wave good-bye with her other hand, grabbing Sandy's leg tightly; Roxy's own little legs buckled at the knees.

And somewhere in another place Springsteen sang that beautiful song to her . . .

And then they were gone. We cut back toward the 295, northbound, to take the turnpike. We put the "Born to Run" tape into the tape deck, for it was only appropriate now. As Springsteen sang, I thought about the saxophone player in San Francisco who had so reminded me of the Big Man Clarence Clemons, himself. The Big Man was The Boss's right-hand man. San Francisco was so far gone to me, on the other side of the country now, but the black man with his black, wide-brimmed hat still played his song of life on that crowded corner as the nameless and the famous continued to walk on by. I just knew he was still there.

"Because in life, there ain't no such thing as a free lunch!" he yelled out to us all.

The sun set behind us. We headed eastbound on Interstate 195 toward Asbury Park, Southside Johnny, Tom Petty, and the New Jersey Shore. Bright orange and pink plastic slides grew above the trees on the side of the road. I think it was an amusement park. Nature's edges were superimposed around it; the trees pushed by it all to engulf the highway, and the wilderness came right up to the edge of the road and looked for a safe place to cross. This wasn't the concrete and smokestack New Jersey that I had envisioned, but a beautiful land waiting to be discovered again.

At a Texaco station off the side of the interstate, Laird's mom Tina met up with us. At first sight, I immediately remembered her from Kerry and Sam's Aspen wedding. Laird, Anna's fiancé, had called ahead to his mom from Topeka to tell her of our passing through. It was Tina's idea to have us for the night. She wouldn't have it any other way; after all, Luke was a part of her family now. She was divorced, happy, and full of life. We followed her to her small apartment a few miles inland from the shore where she had prepared sandwiches, cheese and crackers, a big jar of pickles, and had some cold Molson Golden Ale for us. We camped in the living room watching the NFL highlights of the Chiefs and Raider game while we ate her food. After that, we watched *Monty Python's Flying Circus* and a *Star Trek* rerun, "The Doomsday Machine." It was about 10:00 p.m. when we decided to head out to "Gary's Bar" on Tina's suggestion. Luke invited her to come along, but she laughed at this, thanking him and advising us that we were better off to go it alone. "You don't want to be seen with someone as old as your mom now, do you?"

We really didn't mind, and we told her that, but she politely refused. So we walked into the quiet neighborhood bar in the dark of the night, three happy travelers.

"If everyone in the world was like that," Decky spoke aloud of Laird's mom as we walked into the bar, "just think of it . . . There'd probably be no wars!"

CHAPTER 31

Monday, September 24th.

It was eight in the morning, and I awoke to the comforting, greasy smell of eggs, bacon, and warm butter-soaked toast. I wondered if I was home again. At the small apartment kitchen table, we huddled around large glasses of orange juice and full plates of food. The dreams of the night before dissipated with the folding of the convertible couch and packing of our few things once again for the road ahead. After breakfast, Laird's mom gave us directions to the aching Jersey Shore that we wanted to visit before heading north.

After a short ride eastward, we pulled over in a roadside neighborhood whose streets were lined with small summer cottages. We had found the shore! This was the other end of the continent that we had just come so eagerly across, the right coast of America. It had only taken twenty-four days to get this far! My first glimpses of the roaring ocean were incredible, just as I had wanted it to be. We walked over a rickety wooden walkway between two beachfront houses to access the beach. Sand dunes and tall outcroppings of weed grasses greeted us everywhere. I quietly looked out at the angry, turbulent Atlantic that was now in front of us. The wind was blowing wildly as we began to run barefoot on the soft and weary sand northward with the waves crashing a few yards from our feet in their choppy defiance. We first ran on the steep slope that abruptly dropped to the water, but quickly decided it was too difficult a grade, for it was high tide now and the wind was mad in our faces. It was too much work for the effort. I wondered if this feeling was somewhat akin to what little Roxy felt as she grabbled with the challenges of cerebral palsy. The visit to Sandy of the day before came back to me. We moved closer into the crashing water washes; the wet ground was harder than the sloped sand, and even though we had to withstand moments of knee-deep surges that halted our progress, we decided to battle and tough it out down there. The cold, engulfing, crashing white capped water made it more of a game for us.

Even the sandpipers were scarce on this abandoned autumn shoreline, although some of these friends still appeared, almost haphazardly, during our jagged run, as if they were lost from the rest of their species and perhaps still searching for another summer. Had they flown in with the errant gusts of a Northeastern wind coming down from Nantucket? I didn't know if the species was even migratory, but just like all of the beaches that I had lived on in my life, such as Huntington, Newport, and Paradise, I was always fascinated by these little creatures just the same. They were my peaceful friends. Winter was eminent. The gradual grade of the tidelands was disappearing for the little birds, and with it, all of the sustenance beneath it. All of the tourists were gone from the cold, abandoned beach; all of them were off somewhere else following their own migratory patterns. Perhaps some were still chasing the sun somewhere.

With the wind hitting us now with biting blasts, we decided to only go a little farther, as far as the pier, which was now about 100 yards away. Once there, we tried for the jetty which was about 100 yards beyond the pier, and it was there that we stopped. We then set out to run back at a much-easier pace, with the wind at our backs now. At the rickety wood path entrance we had started from, we found our shoes again atop the high sand. They were slowly becoming buried in the angry wind, getting heavier and heavier with the passing time.

The sands of the hourglass
Where already this sentence is old
Only to be retold
In their memories of gold
As they think about the past

Tina had run out and bought a dozen Dunkin' Donuts. Back at her tiny apartment, we were greeted at the door by the smell of freshly brewed hot coffee. There were jelly donuts, glazed ones, cinnamon, chocolate, plain, and bear claws with that crazy frosted crust that you could gnaw off in little pieces. I filled a large mug with steaming coffee and poured in a lot of real cream and loaded it with three spoons of sugar, stirring it all up and dunking the bear claw into it until it became so soggy that it almost broke off in the cup. The sweet coffee dribbled out of it and rolled down my chin as I put the whole piece in my mouth, barely able to chew. The sugary syrup coffee at the bottom of the mug was like dessert. Why did things so bad for you have to taste so good?

We said good-bye and headed north on the Garden State Freeway, the New Jersey Turnpike, where the crazy booming skyline and the Lincoln Tunnel finally appeared out of nowhere and shot us into New York City. We parked on Fifty-fourth and Eighth in a twenty-four-hour parking garage. Ammonia-like smells lingered in the side stairwells; the urine-stained concrete walls called out a certain form of urban expression. This was the life-scrawling graffiti of the poor homeless. We boarded the E train southbound. It was ninety cents to ride. We ended up at the World Trade Center with her beautiful twin towers looking straight down on us when we climbed the stairs out of the underground tunnel to street level. From below, the towers appeared to shoot up to heaven.

Atop the observation deck, I panned the great island that was spread out below me now, this grand island of Manhattan, with the Hudson River on the left and the East River on the right. I thought about how all of it had been traded for goods worth twenty-four dollars back when the Lenape lived here some 350 years before us. I looked to the distant purple hazy horizon; I knew it was a vantage point that the Lenape never had, lest they never would have let their island go. We looked out and tried to determine which states and how far we could see, Connecticut to the northeast, New Jersey to the south and west, and all of New York State to the northwest.

"I wonder if that is Massachusetts up there on the horizon," I said.

"Can the naked eye see for more than fifty miles?" Decky asked. "Isn't Massachusetts more than fifty miles away?"

The Statue of Liberty sat out on tiny Ellis Island to the south of us all on her own; Lady Liberty looked so small now below us. I remembered that climb years before into her windowed crown. I looked out to the north again all the way out to Central Park, the green rectangular beauty of it all, surrounded by such a vast city. I embraced all of the architecture below us, the Empire State Building, The Chrysler Building, tons and tons of concrete and steel all filled with moving people, beings, everyone thinking something different, individual cells making up one beautiful earth organism. We were atop the largest city of our kingdom in an amazing double-helix structure 100 stories high that had been built by mere men. I remembered seeing all of the old pictures of the construction of the thing, with the workers sitting on beams of iron and eating their lunches, welding without a net, never afraid of falling, like ancient cliff walkers, absolute masters of their domain. Our vantage point was like having a hawk's-eye view, the same as the view of Boston from the top of the Prudential Building or Chicago from the top of the Sears Tower or precious Earth from the heavens above.

At street level again we walked up toward Greenwich Village. On the street outside one of the taverns was an Australian photographer taking pictures of "Series S" fire hydrants. Everyone was an artist here, everyone had a script, everyone sang on Broadway. The streets teamed with thought. The next big thing hung there right under everybody's nose, although I wondered what artistic value a "Series S" fire hydrant might have. It could make a good coffee table book someday perhaps.

"Hope you win the big one!" Decky said to the photographer.

We went into the tavern that the photographer stood in front of, but we found it almost empty, because for everybody else, even in Manhattan, it was still a working Monday afternoon. I remembered a Greenwich Village bar much like this one that I had been to in 1979 on one of our UMass weekend road trips where we walked in on none other than David Peel performing his infamous song, "The Pope Smokes Dope."

Now in 1984, this tavern that Luke, Decky, and I stumbled into had the same peanut shells all over the bar floor that David Peel's bar had. There were buckets of peanuts on the tables too. You could shell them and throw the shells all over the place if you wanted to. We began shelling and eating the peanuts, for this would be our lunch. Peel's song came in . . .

The pope smokes dope, God gave him the grass
The pope smokes dope, he likes to smoke in mass
The pope smokes dope, he's a groovy head
The pope smokes dope, the pope smokes dope

Maybe it was the same bar, I couldn't tell for sure, but it kind of felt like it. What had ever happened to this guy, David Peel? Wasn't he a friend of John Lennon? That would be really cool if we could meet up with him again, I thought.

Back in 1979, after me and my UMass friends left the bar that day, my friend Jake jumped down on the subway tracks in a drunken stupor to retrieve a bouncing token for his fare. It was the simple cost of life itself back then.

"Jake!" We screamed for him to scramble to the side of the tracks and jumped to pull him up and out, as the light on the front of the fast car quickly approached from the other end of the tunnel.

"What were you thinking?"

"It was the only token I had," Jake said. "The pope smokes dope."

Now here we were in 1984. Behind the long oak bar again, a beautiful bartender tended our large, thirsty-size drafts. As she poured them from the tap in front of us, she talked to a thirty-something-year-old man sitting down at the end stool with a briefcase beside him. She talked to him about Broadway; the man blew smoke from his cigarette toward us all. He wiped his runny nose with the side of his hand. She was a therapist, I thought, stroking his ego all the while. I watched her craftsmanship. She quietly listened to his dreams. How many stories had she already heard today? Was he a Wall Street guy? He wore a shirt and a loud tie, with a coat overhanging the neighboring stool, as if to piss out his own territory. He rolled his beady eyes at us while he talked to her; perhaps we were cramping his style.

"When I make it to the big time, come see me," he said to the bartender as he threw down a five-dollar bill and left. She only smiled and then turned to smile at us. No words needed to be said; she was good at her job.

After drinking our beer and filling up on hundreds of peanuts, we exited the little tavern and descended to the train. People on the bouncing car studied us as we studied them. A man walked through the length of the car, handing out worn and printed cards that told us he was deaf and dumb and that he was looking for a donation, any donation that we could spare. When the train stopped, we saw him again. He reappeared magically, coming through quickly, picking up the cards that had been left on the silent seats, left there by the dumbfounded passengers. He got off at this stop and jumped into the car behind us. As the train started again, I watched him repeat his routine in the next car; he would ride all day, I thought, collecting donations. This was a hard job in and of itself, working the masses, a sort of survival of the fittest. It was a manifestation of his entrepreneurial spirit in the big city.

"It must be really hard keeping your mouth shut for an entire day," Decky whispered to me.

I remembered this one guy in Hollywood who used to walk with a limp and one crutch all the way up Sunset Boulevard, hobbling up the busy side of the street like a robot, asking everyone methodically at the outdoor restaurants and shops for money. You'd see him later walking down the other side of the street, the crutch gone, with a perfect stride, counting his dollars and coins. It always seemed like such hard work to me.

"He must have gotten better!" we used to say jokingly to each other every time we saw the guy in the late afternoon counting his money.

"I wonder if we are going to end up that way," I said to Decky.

"I got it! You can be deaf, I'll be dumb, and Luke will be blind!" Decky turned to me shaking his head. "We'll just have to find Luke a pair of dark glasses, and we can lead him around, and he can ask everyone for money and explain our situation to them!"

From the train, we walked fourteen blocks all of the way to Times Square, looking everywhere for a Woolworth's, for at some point, we had to have ten-minute head shots done for our international student ID cards. We eventually settled on having them done in a quick stop photo booth. I looked so frightened in the photo that was taken of me. Did I always look this way?

In Times Square, we approached a crowd that surrounded a team of break dancers who moved rhythmically on the street corner. It was the last few minutes of the dancers' performance. A shoe box came through the crowd for donations, and we carefully passed it along. A jazz band played on the next block with another open trombone case for tips. There were clenched hands everywhere in the crowd, sudden movements and empty faces. Luke and Decky threw all of their loose change into the case. All I had were dollar bills and travelers checks. I couldn't part with those dollar bills, I thought. I was a gypsy myself, just roaming the diverse streets of this grand civilization.

"God bless you!" the trumpet player said to Luke.

In the late afternoon, we sought the refuge of another movie theatre, paying three dollars apiece to see the newly released *Ghostbusters*. The film was set in New York City, a paranormal city terrorized by a host of ghosts and the giant *Stay Puft Marshmallow Man*. Professor Blakely back at Orange Coast College had taught us that everything in a screenplay was a formula, so just as I had attempted to take notes in *Gremlins*, sitting there in the midtown darkness, I studied the probable setup and the hook with my open notepad. The movie started out where Dan Aykroyd and his associates lose their jobs and open up a ghost hunting office in an old fire station. This was followed by twists and turns that uncover demons and a gateway into a whole other dimension. The whole thing culminates in scenes where the ghostbusters are finally let out of jail to battle Gozer, the evil god from another world. In the end, the ghostbusters cross their zapping proton beam weapons and seal the open portal forever, annihilating the Marshmallow Man. Good wins over evil, and the ghostbusters are redeemed as true heroes. Casey Kasem even made a cameo in the movie. I would have to make a cameo appearance in my own movies someday too, I decided. I had read that my hero, John Belushi, was supposed to be in the movie, but he died while Dan Aykroyd was still writing the screenplay. I wished that Belushi was still here. He made us all laugh; he was always larger than life, even larger than the Marshmallow Man,

I thought, but just like that—he was gone.

From the theatre, we spilled along the midcity sidewalk, just like we had back in Chicago, but people were everywhere here, moving busily around us; the bloody workday was over. We ducked into a nearby bookstore to get out of the bustling crowd. Inside, I leafed through a "Best of Photojournalism" picture book and marveled at the dimension of time that stood still in these old photographs, these ghostly images of light on paper. Ever notice how glassy-eyed everyone looks in these old pictures? Kind of like my Europe Student ID photo. I focused on the pocket watch chain coming from an old conductor's pocket. I tried to picture myself in his skin. I tried to be him in my crazy mind. I stood there on that train platform back in 1891, watching the funny photographer fiddle under a big black bedsheet as he held up a giant flashbulb in the air and cracked it in my face. Flash!

Born into a time
Born into a place
Given a face
On the pavement

Just outside the doors of the bookstore, a crew taped a commercial starring a chubby blond actress from the TV Show *Dallas* as we tried to integrate back into the moving masses of the passersby. We lingered there for a moment, huddled behind a group of curious on-lookers, just to see who exactly this actress was, but she was unrecognizable to me. Despite its huge popularity, I never really watched the show *Dallas* and neither did my friends, so we quietly broke away from the crowd after a few minutes. We headed to Fifty-fourth and Eighth to pick up the old urine scent that we had so fondly left behind hours before . . . Those familiar stairwells of the parking garage that led to the resting Fairlane. The Fairlane still sat quietly in the garage. The surfboard was perfectly intact on top, for there was no real reason for anyone to steal a surfboard in Manhattan. You couldn't even pawn the thing, I imagined. It was my turn to drive, so I started her up and exited the garage now and headed northbound out of the city. Central Park quickly came up on our right as nighttime swiftly approached.

We first cruised through the low light of Harlem with some of the black people that hung out on the street corners looking back at our strange vessel in reckless wonderment. As the blocks went by, on the lonely streets outside of our bubble windows, I noticed now how the city had changed from the largely lit storefronts of lower Manhattan to this heavy look of quiet desolation. We all had abandoned them here.

In 1980, a group of my friends from Lowell took a road trip to New York City with our friend Dukie who had played football for Columbia. You see, Columbia University is situated just on the outskirts of Harlem. Dukie had just graduated that year and had this new Volvo station wagon that he wanted to show to all of his underclassmen friends who were still back at school. When we got to the university, we parked on the outside of the enclosed campus and went upstairs to Dukie's old dorm room to grab his friend Grinder. Of course, Dukie had to show Grinder his new car.

In that few minutes that we had gone upstairs back in 1980, all of our things were stolen from the stupid Volvo, right there on the streets of Harlem. The thieves had quickly pulled up the knob on the driver's side door with a screwdriver and a bent coat hanger, probably the same way I had seen Ray Champeaux do it so many times back when we were both fourteen. With all of our things stolen now, we had to wear the same clothes for three friggin' days. The thieves had even taken our toothbrushes. The funny thing as I think back to that time is that we really didn't give a damn. We still had a blast despite it all. It was such a simple beautiful time, I thought.

In 1984, as Luke, Decky, and I sat there stopped at the traffic signal now, I suddenly felt afraid. On either side of the street, curious eyes looked out from the small groups they were in; some of the people pointed to the surfboard, some of them laughed, some of them figured we surely must be lost.

"Mike, just avoid any eye contact," Decky said to me. "Pray for green, and if that green light doesn't come, just floor it!"

"Come on, green!" I muttered under my breath.

But the stupid light wouldn't change. The green wouldn't come. So I anxiously floored it at once through the red and drove as quickly as I could through blocks and blocks of empty streets. I soon found the FDR Freeway, but even so, realized I was desperately lost and quickly exited a tunnel to the 289, somehow going back all the way to the Brooklyn Bridge. I wondered if we could ever find our way out, caught in the same vortex that the ghostbusters had been caught in. New York City would not allow us to leave. But then a sign for the 95 North appeared, and soon, we were on the 91 and were able to cruise through Hartford. We finally made it to Springfield by three in the morning. We neared Amherst around four o'clock and there, in the predawn darkness, I witnessed, once again, the sweet rolling beauty of the early-morning Berkshire foothills. They were awakened in my memory. Blue light appeared over their ridges from the east; it was a brand-new morning. Childhood dreams came back to me. We were in Massachusetts again! *Spanky and Our Gang* sang "Lazy Day" on our radio. Then James Taylor sang about the dreamy Berkshires. I was exhausted.

I had traveled this road, the windy Route 9, so many times before. I had often hitchhiked the edges of North Hampton and Hadley to UMass as an undergrad. We were soon on the UMass campus where the fog's dreamlike arms in the morning darkness hung over the campus pond in a pastel watercolor that reminded me of a distant painting by Ingrid. We passed wearily by. The Fairlane climbed the hills of Central, a dorm community, and quietly pulled over behind Baker House. A campus cop passed by us on the hill, but unlike the butte roads of Utah or the billowing fields of the Midwest, there was no cause for alert; we seemed to blend right in, even with the crazy board atop our car.

Our morning was finally sound. We slept for about an hour and a half until five thirty a.m. I slept in the front seat, Luke was in the back. Decky had rolled himself up in an old plastic sheet (with his sleeping bag inside of it) that he had pulled from a Dumpster that was outside of Baker House. Decky positioned his plastic cocoon in the front of the car, all wrapped up beneath the grill and the warm radiator.

When I awoke a few hours later, I saw Decky bouncing outside of our windows. "That was the greatest sleep I have ever had!" He jumped at us. "I put the piece of plastic sideways against the blowing wind and rain, and I was so warm!"

In the daylight, I rubbed my eyes and saw that this college community that I had once lived in so comfortably was completely foreign to me now. We tried to find my past, but on this barren Tuesday morning, just like in Kansas and Ohio, just like the schools of Luke and of Decky, there was nothing for me here anymore. Where had they all gone? Buddy Love had disappeared. I hadn't been good at all about keeping in touch with the rest of them.

From the hill outside of Baker House, I pointed out the landmark red brick library to Luke and Decky, all twenty-six floors of it. It could be seen from everywhere on campus, shooting up high in the middle of rural New England, a pinnacle of our educational aspirations. I told them about one terrible suicide off of the top when I was a freshman, and how everybody yelled at the poor soul from the ground to jump. From the edge so far above, the guy vanished for a few moments. Little did we all know that he had disappeared only to get a last good-bye running leap. Seconds later, here he came catapulting off of the top in slow motion, waving his arms frantically like a stuntman in the movies. He came down fast at all of us in the dispersing crowd, crashing terribly in a life-ending halt at the base of the building on the smack-hard pavement. Sad silence rippled through the crowd around me as his clump of lifeless, broken bones rested there. Everyone backed away. Everyone was aghast.

"Even the suicides off of the Golden Gate Bridge break hard on the cold water, as if the water itself is cement," Luke told us.

I wondered that day as I looked on the poor soul's lifeless body if he was still there with us somehow, watching us all as he ascended to the heavens.

"It's a sin to commit suicide," my father Frank used to say.

"You can't fly with just one wing!" Decky exclaimed, quoting his alcoholic friend Max from Ohio.

"Do you think Max's pot pipe has made it back to Ohio from Indiana?" Luke laughed.

I had walked the UMass library's twenty-six-floor stair wells once, reading all of the graffiti on the walls all of the way up, the musings of higher learning. I remembered Nietzsche's famous quote, "God is dead—Nietzsche," just pen scratched there on the wall in the high floors of the tower. And below it, someone else had written, "Nietzsche is dead—God."

It was still way too early for students to be making their way to their morning classes. We drove by the athletic fields on the western edges of the campus. Beyond these fields the farmlands of rural Amherst reached out all the way to the Connecticut River and out toward Smith College, an all-girls school. My college friend Jake stole a bus on the way back from Smith College one wild night in 1978. The driver stopped the bus in a maddening snowstorm because six of us were hanging from the floor poles and ringing the buzzer cords, screaming and crazy drunk.

"If you don't settle down, I refuse to drive any farther," the driver protested. He opened the bus front door and walked out to stand in the blowing snow on the side of the lonely road with his arms folded in disgust. The bus was in the middle of nowhere, there was nothing but farm fields and whiteout snow in those miles between the two college towns.

With the bus driver now out in the cold, Jake suddenly ran to the front of the bus, hopped in the driver's seat, shut the door, pushed the start button, and abandoned the defiant driver right there on the side of the road. The other passengers on the bus immediately freaked out at what was happening, themselves now subjects of the takeover, screaming, "What are you doing! Are you crazy! Let us off! Let us off!"

Two hundred yards up the road, Jake opened the door again and let about twenty people out in the middle of nowhere, the rest of the innocents, and closed the doors with just the six of us inside now. We were all mad, laughing and drunk on the ride of our life in the middle of a blizzard. *What has he just done? We are so screwed!* I thought.

We rode right into the center of Amherst that night where Jake grounded the bus in a snowbank close to the police station and city hall. The six of us piled out of the bus and scattered in six different directions, mad directions—run for your life places, trying to find a way back to sanity and reason, like rats out of Buddy Love's cage running for the cracks in the walls, trying to get out of the light of night.

There I ran in 1978, on my own, cutting into the turns and backyards of the Amherst neighborhoods, a few miles of them, remembering Coach Malloy, running hard, swinging arms, breathing from my mouth like a blowfish with every arm thrust . . . *whoosh, who, whoosh, who, whoosh* . . . with The Rolling Stones all the while singing in my head . . . "*Gimme Shelter*" . . . I was running the race of my life and had to find a way back home.

Pushing, pushing, seeing blurry, edging closer, I was closing in on our warm dorm in the northeast quadrant of the campus. I played that song over and over again in my mind. I heard the haunting ghostly guitar play of Keith Richards; I heard his heroin addiction coming through it all. I heard the harmonica and those piercing background vocals, the crazy high notes of the irreplaceable Merry Clayton, her screaming voice reminded me how I so needed the shelter of the dorm, the shelter and comfort of finishing the race.

I loved that song more than no other. If the age of rock and roll had to be defined by just one song, this was surely that song. But now, everything was gone. We were crazed youth back then trying to find ourselves. We'd go to the football games where we would purposely sit in the section behind the marching band and snap beer caps into the moving tubas every time they turned our way. There were Thursday nights at the pub, or pickled eggs and whiskey shooters at Barselotti's, or heated basketball games in the Boyden Field House, with yells and chants whenever we played the University of Rhode Island, "U-R-I, U-R-I, U-R-I-N-E!" There was UMass lacrosse, the game of the Native Americans, or the infamous UMass spring concerts, with the likes of The Allman Brothers, The Grateful Dead, Procol Harum, The Kinks, and The J. Geils Band. It was at UMass that Buddy Love sprang Barney the beagle from the dog pound down the road, that crazy full-moon howling night where Buddy broke into the building and opened all of the dogs' cages. I'll never forget that beautiful sight of Buddy Love running up that long driveway holding Barney in his arms with 100 dogs running up the driveway right behind him, all of them barking with craziness and freedom. It was right out of one of those Disney movies.

And all of the parties at Smith College we had gone to in those four years . . . There was the time my Lowell friend Richie Clark hung crazily from the outdoor Christmas tree lights in the snowy Smith Quad while coeds screamed from windows at him or the time he hung across the outside of a Volvo screaming for his dear life with his crutches in the air as four pretty girls kidnapped him and sped away. There were the early days at Kappa Sig when I got caught after storming the house as a pledge. They placed me on the front porch facing the campus on a picnic table turned on its end. I was bound to it, on display—naked in another deafening snow morning while students walked to their classes. But here in 1984, as we cruised by in the Fairlane, Kappa Sig was all boarded up. Everything was gone.

Luke, Decky, and I left the campus in the Fairlane and drove north up the foggy armed reach of rolling Route 202, over the early colors of wooded foothills. The clouds of rural Worcester and the Quabbin Reservoir could be seen below us from a scenic vantage point.

We were on Route 2 eastbound now. We would be in Lowell in two hours. I had heard volumes of travel stories when I used to hitchhike to school on that same two-hour route. This was the road that the lonely philosopher-entrepreneur picked me up on. Was he still driving these roads years later with his big white van still all filled up with toilet paper? "Every tree of a different color had a right to that color," he told me.

And there were the hippies that threw Robert Hillyard and I out in the hard rain in 1979. They picked us up in their Scooby-Doo van during a crazy New England downpour of heavy thunder and cracks of tree-splitting lightning; two women, two men, and one little girl. The hippies drove a few hundred yards and asked us if we had any weed, and when we said, "No, sorry, we don't," they pulled right over and opened the side slider and the "Shaggy" character told us, "Then get the fuck out." They were children of love, but I learned solemnly that day that sometimes even love will not let you ride for free.

A gay theatre guy drove between Boston and New York City during one ride and told me all about his affairs with Jim Nabors and Rock Hudson. It was the first I had ever heard of Rock being gay. Rock Hudson took pictures on the red carpet with Ronald Reagan in June of 1984. And now the world has just learned that he has this dreadful disease. It would not be long before Rock would be gone.

We were close to the Lowell Connector now. I had driven this route so many times before. I remembered I'd have some beautiful girl from Belvedere on my mind when I drove that newspaper truck for the *Lowell Sun*, but I was always too afraid to ask her out. I wondered if I'd see the misty fingers of fog coming up from the valley of the Merrimack again. We'd once again cross that river toward Centralville.

Morning earth
Knee-deep fog fingered dawn
Purple horizon
Darkness gone

Distant city castles
Pink and smokelike hue
I watched the sky turn
From starlit to blue

Bright still moon
Beneath the native forest's streets
The ongoing battle
That daylight defeats

From a newspaper truck
Gray to green with color
I opened my eyes
To see the dawn of life's umbrella

When I drove a newspaper truck for the *Lowell Sun* in 1981, the Sunday morning routes were always the best. Downtown after midnight, all of us drivers would line up outside the press room along the canal where all the trucks were parked; winter steam rose from pipes that jutted out into the canal just above its murky water. From the alley, we would watch through the windows as the presses started and the papers came rolling out on the lines along the ceiling of the distribution room, Sunday editions sandwiched between two rolling belts. If Owen the floor manager walked out and suspected that you were too wasted to drive, he'd pull you in and you'd be stuck in the distribution room all morning, stuck on the lines throwing in inserts into the loose newspapers as the papers fed down to the floor level. The bundles at the end of the line would all be stacked and tied by machines, with labels for the paper boys on brown wrapping paper inserted on top. We would load all of the trucks up out on that ice-cold canal, most of us buzzed from Saturday night alcohol.

Kevin, the cigar-smoking big boss, would do a last-minute sobriety check on his drivers before letting them go out into the world; there was always one or two of us that got sent home. If you got sent home twice, you'd lose your job. The veteran drivers had shown me all of those country rural routes through Lowell's surrounding towns: Westford, Chelmsford, Littleton, Ayer, and Fort Devens. They taught me how to roll a paper with one hand, drive the left-hand side of the road in the dawn of night, and stuff the rural newspaper mailboxes without ever taking my foot off the gas. One driver, Edmund, one afternoon in Ayer, raced a freight train down a frontage road and weaved in and around the closed railway gate with its red flashing lights just because he didn't want to wait ten minutes at the crossing. I was training with Edmund that day and that was surely one day that I almost died. When we finished our route early, we got to meet up with the other drivers at Kimball's in worry-free Westford and eat ice cream in the melting New England summer sun. Edmund and I got to eat a lot of ice cream that day. I let it run down the sides of my mouth. It was that wake-up call to simply living that I will always cherish the most.

Decky and Luke were asleep as I bootlegged onto Route 495 North. It was seven thirty in the morning, and I was now in the middle of rush-hour traffic, surfboard on my back. I was almost home with 75,480 miles logged on the weary car. We had nearly 6,000 miles of beautiful America behind us.

CHAPTER 32

And here it was Tuesday, September 18th. Luke and Decky were awake now, sitting up in the car. I drove madly, focused like a weary runner on one of the last legs of a twenty-five-day race across beautiful America. We were nearing the end of the first half of our great expedition, I thought, the one I had dreamt about for weeks upon weeks back in Huntington Beach. I had no idea where it all would ever end, and that was okay.

Approaching Lowell from Route 495, I jumped onto the very familiar Lowell Connector, a four-lane highway that dumped right into Lowell, ending abruptly at a red light. There we were immediately thrust into the neighborhood where everything began for my family in America; we were a block away from the sacred ground where four generations of the Hogans had lived, an Irish-American lineage that started with my second great-grandfather Paddy. As we veered down South Street, right off of Gorham, I looked out at the bare grassy ground beside the back entrance to St. Peter's Church. This was where the family's old duplex tenement house had once stood. I had only seen the house in black-and-white pictures, of course, for it had been torn down long before I was ever born. I remembered that in those photographs, the house always appeared so tiny to me, for it was forever dwarfed by the huge St. Peter's Church on its right. It was a mere blade of grass in the giant cathedral's shadows. My father told me that the right half of the house was always rented to boarders, other immigrant families in the early days, while the Hogan clan all lived on the left side, three generations of them. I looked and saw that huge St. Peter's stood alone now, all by itself out there. What had happened to her parish and their faith? No one came to Mass anymore. Sometime in the 1950s, the family house was sold and torn down, along with a whole line of other houses all the way down the street beside the church. They were replaced by a development of yellow brick apartment buildings that stretched along the South Common toward downtown. St Patrick's Cemetery was behind us, just a few miles down Gorham Street in the other direction. This was where all of the family funeral processions ultimately ended.

The whole time that she lived beside the church, my grandmother Lillian Hogan attended the six a.m. Mass every morning at St. Peter's. She always carried around a full set of rosary beads with her and sometimes could be seen whispering prayer after prayer as she moved her fingers from bead to bead. She prayed for us all. I don't think I ever saw her without those worry beads wrapped around her hands, her calloused fingers running through them one by one as she recited her daily prayers. The simple repetition of her prayers seemed to help to wipe away the worry of the misfortune of generations. God and St. Peter had helped all of them get through their hardest times.

I knew their stories well. My great-grandparents Michael the baker and Mary the servant had purchased the original South Street house just a few years after they were married in the 1890s. Mary had left Ireland in the late 1880s to wait on the wealthy English of Boston. Michael came over a few years after her. Back in Ireland, they had lived amongst the rural farms of Carrownaclogh and Ballynahown, near the town of Ennistymon. They knew each other in childhood, but were never really close because of their five-year difference in age. But in America, like all of humanity who seeks to find the company of comfort, they met up again in blessed Lowell and soon married in St. Peter's. Mary was older than Michael, but through decades of census takers knocking on her door, she had managed to become younger than him. In the late 1890s, Michael left Lavery's Bakery (owned by the famous Brennan family) in order to open up his own bakery on Central Street. It was then that he sent over for his widowed father Paddy . . . Paddy who couldn't read or write, Paddy the dying farmer. Paddy had wanted to die with his surviving children. But in order to do so, he had to leave his poor deceased wife (and all of the others) in the cold rocky earth of Ballynahown; they were all buried in unmarked graves next to a burned-down parish church near Ennistymon. Paddy had to leave them forever.

I wanted to someday tell their story and the stories of all the mill immigrants. I wanted it to be a movie. There were so many pages that I wanted to write; some happy, some sad, all of them screaming screenplays, moving pictures of the everlasting human struggle—the same struggle that transcends all of the races and all of the ages.

Michael the baker died of consumption at thirty-six, and my own grandfather, Michael's eldest son Tom (who was just a young teenager at the time) was immediately thrown into a tougher life because of it. He had to drop out of the tenth grade in order to support his poor mother and his three siblings. His two sisters would eventually leave the house to become nuns. It's funny; Luke and Decky thought that my father Frank looked exactly like one of his auntie nuns in an old picture that I showed them. Some even wondered if it was my father actually wearing a nun habit, trying to fool around, maybe a Halloween costume or something, but it wasn't. Frank would have definitely thought that would be a sin to do such a thing.

"Impersonating a nun? That is such a sin!"

Not long after Michael the baker died, my great-uncle Johnnie was the victim of a terrible accident. He was only sixteen years old. On Friday, October 23, 1914, the *Lowell Sun* nightly headlines read: *"Men Frightfully Injured in Gas Tank Explosion—Welding Gas at Vocational School Exploded with Terrific Force."*

In the Fairlane, Luke, Decky, and I were back on Gorham Street, and I continued to absorb the past. I looked out at a city of ghosts now, generations and generations of them; a paperboy on the curb, a beat cop with his London-like bob hat walking amidst horses and buggy whips on cobblestone streets, people riding on a crowded cable car, and the sacred heart of Jesus there amongst them all, in the rosary beads of my grandmother's hands, never leaving their side, just walking there with them.

These old cobblestone streets carried the constant traffic from our endless worrying minds; cars carrying different thoughts from different time periods that passed our family's DNA down throughout the generations, from Merrimack River footpaths, to horse drawn carriages, to my grandfather's Hudson, to Frank's Indian motorcycle, and now to the Ford Fairlane that I was sitting in.

All of humanity always traveled the same roadways, I figured. And those rounded polished stones that still showed on some of those streets, laid there by what are now buried hands, were a constant reminder to me that death was certainly for real. No matter what, there was no escaping it, and I would have to sit one last time in the dark confessional booth sooner or later. God would eventually take us all in the end, and there was little comfort in trying to believe that getting to heaven (if you were a believer) would be easy, because the dying part of it really scared me so.

Luke, Decky, and I went all of the way down Gorham Street. Over to the right I looked out at the old neighborhoods of the Portuguese, the Italians, and the Greeks. Just beyond these neighborhoods were the choppy banks of the Concord River, where the Colburn School sat, the red brick elementary school where John Nance punched Miss Murphy in the stomach before running down the old wooden stairs and out into the cold truant streets of spring. Miss Murphy, with her strong around-the-corner perfume scent and her inch-thick caked-on makeup gave poor Nance ten hard whacks of the ruler that had pushed him over the edge that fateful day in 1966.

Beyond the neighborhoods and the river I looked up toward the hills of old Andover Street, the old land of the Wamesit that seemed to stretch back to forever. They were still there somewhere; I wanted to believe it.

We doglegged left onto Central Street. I looked up at the empty windowpanes of what once was Bob Noonan's Music Studio, up over the old Rialto Bowling Lanes. Noonan's name was still all in stencils in a semicircle on the windows in 1984, even though that floor of the building had been vacant for many years. Bob Noonan had the thickest gray hair I had ever seen on a human being. As his student, I had to learn "Flight of the Bumblebee" on the clarinet, sitting in the lesson chair through it all as the metronome ticked behind me; the ticktock of it always reminded me of eternity. Would the lesson ever be over? The lesson lasted from the third grade all of the way into high school, but then I got in deep with Ray Champeaux and his gang, where playing in the marching band wasn't cool anymore, so I quit it all. It seemed like it was just a few months after that when Bob Noonan and all of that gray hair dropped dead of a heart attack. I wondered if at suppertime he ate those big hunks of butter like my grandfather had on the night that he died. I wondered if his wife had to run to the cupboard to get him a shot of whiskey, so that it might make him feel better.

The excitement of being home rushed within me. I took a right at the light at Prescott Street now where I pointed out to the guys the *Lowell Sun* building where I had worked in 1980. That was my last Lowell job before sweet California. The truck alley that we used to line up on was around the back, running the length of a somber canal that cut under Merrimack Street and continued on toward the large cotton mill complexes. These beautiful man-made canal waterways ran everywhere in our city; they had once powered the wheels of progress.

Passing through Kearney Square, I looked to the left up Merrimack Street all the way to city hall and took it all in again. In the Pollard Library during the 1970s, I would pore over many of the old *Lowell Sun* microfiche films from 1914. It was in the library that I had first learned the exact details of the fateful gas explosion that my father's uncle had been in. I built it all back up in my storyboard mind, brick by brick, adding imaginary dialogue to the fantastic story, adding to the words that had already been quoted where I needed to, in order to fill the gaps. The series of articles from the *Lowell Sun* laid it all out for me. All I had to do was to bring it to life . . .

There in a gloomy October day in 1914, poor Johnnie Hogan hovered between life and death in a bed at St. John's Hospital. At the Lowell Hospital on the other side of town, the boy's teacher, Clarence Letourneau, merely twenty-six years old, was also near death.

"What negligence! The teacher should have known better!" my great-grandmother Mary cried, lamenting in that thick Irish brogue to her eldest son, my grandfather Tom, who, at seventeen, was the man of the house. Mary was one to hardly ever show emotion, but what had just happened to her fourteen-year-old son had really broken her.

It happened on a fall afternoon in a bustling mill city. A conscientious and eager student, Johnnie Hogan had stayed after school to work with his teacher on one of those beautiful machines, an automobile, but just in a few split seconds, everything went crazy, changing the path that they both were on forever. It happened right there in the basement of the Mann School on Broadway Street beyond city hall. Johnnie and Clarence tried to make sense of something they actually knew very little about.

The *Lowell Sun* said that from his dying hospital bed, Clarence the teacher told the investigators in a fog, "I am not sure if it was due to ignition or concussion." And as he came in and out of the ether, the teacher asked his own wailing mother, "Whatever happened to the boy, Mother? Is he going to make it?" Clarence lay there, with no penicillin discovered yet, delirious, trying to surmise in a dreamy painful stupor what had ever happened to them.

"These are the streets where four generations of my family lived," I said to Decky and Luke as I drove on. "When we were young, my father Frank often cruised these neighborhoods, holding all of us captive in his Plymouth station wagon, telling all kinds of stories about his altar-boy days at St. Peter's School, his cherished Uncle Johnnie, his beloved Indian Motorcycle, and the beautiful girl he met right up there at the five-and-dime soda fountain after the war."

"On my knees in front of the acetylene tank, I don't know if after turning the valve on, I had ever turned it off." Johnnie came briefly out of his hospital delirium in 1914 to tell the police investigators who questioned him.

"Load the newer oxygen tank to sixty pounds of pressure, Johnnie," Mr. Letourneau told him in the basement of the school.

Putting the match to the welding gun, Johnnie tried to regulate the flame. He went to the 250-pound acetylene tank and turned the valve wide open. But the flow of acetylene was stifled and could not find a way to vent in the small pinhole at the end of the welding gun. So it followed the path of least resistance and went straight into the oxygen tank. It turns out that the welding gun was missing its fine wire screen, so a mad flame followed the acetylene and flashed back with it all the way to the oxygen tank. Rats in a tunnel.

"Kaaaa-blam!!!!!!!!"

The loud blast was heard for at least a mile, past the Old Worthen, past city hall, all the way out to the Boot Mill yards. And with that, people immediately filled the surrounding streets, all curious, anxious, all of them trying to see what had happened and willing to help in whatever way they could. Luckily, all of the students had been dismissed from the Mann School earlier in the day. The force of the explosion shattered all of the windows of the school and blew out the cellar stairs. Everything in the basement was demolished. When the janitor on the first floor saw the first sheets of flames shoot up from the cellar and heard the screams of the injured teacher, he immediately jumped down the hole in the floor where the stairway had been. The janitor saw Clarence the teacher, his right hand hung to the wrist by strings of flesh, escaping up the back stairway and ran to him where he was able to help him to the street. An ambulance rushed poor Clarence away as everyone looked in horror at the burns about the poor man's face and remaining hand.

The fixture on the building supporting the electric light wires caught fire as the fire in the cellar raged. But no one knew that Johnnie still lay downstairs under the rubble. When the fire department got there, Fire Chief Sullivan jumped into the pit and over to the demolished brick wall that once supported the welding machine, for he thought that he heard a faint sound, a murmur of faint *please-help-me* life. Sullivan frantically began pulling off bricks from the fallen wall and all of the fallen debris. He dug at the source of the covered moans and found young Johnnie lying there, Johnnie-come-lately, Johnnie-left-for-dead.

Johnnie, missing an arm and a leg, was picked up out of the rubble by the fearless chief who hurried him out to a Good Samaritan, Mr. O'Donnell, in the crowd outside. Mr. O'Donnell had a brand-new automobile.

"Please get this boy to the hospital!" Sullivan begged him. Therein I pondered the coincidences and ironies in all of life.

After O'Donnell sped off, Chief Sullivan went back into the fire and debris to retrieve poor Johnnie's missing arm and leg beneath the still moaning rubble. When he found them, Sullivan took the bloody left arm and left leg to the hospital, the loose parts of Johnnie all wrapped up in rags, the limbs of life that would never live again.

In an early November morning in 1914, Professor Letourneau died. His parents were devastated at losing their only child, for he had lived at home with them and supported them, giving them six bucks a week. Clarence had supported the three of them with his salary of five hundred dollars a year. And just like that, he was gone. The *Sun* said that the parents of Clarence Letourneau were left with nothing. There was an undertaker's bill for $152.50 and a hospital bill for $12.80 that someone would have to pay

In the ensuing weeks, Mary Hogan's son Johnnie slowly recovered, cheerful in his hospital bed, talkative, passing his time reading and sometimes even singing out loud, his voice bellowing everywhere throughout all of St. John's.

"When Irish Eyes Are Smiling, sure 'tis like a morn in spring.
In the lilt of Irish laughter, you can hear the angels sing."

In the aftermath of it all, my great-grandmother, Mary Hogan, sued the city of Lowell for $50,000. The great trial of *Johnnie Hogan vs. The City of Lowell* went on for years.

From the front of the courtroom, Johnnie's lead council, Mr. Donahue, proclaimed, "I don't propose to go into the gruesome details of the accident, but will ask that young Johnnie take the stand."

I could see young Johnnie, armless and legless in the days of 1916 as he struggled to attain his balance, unassisted by any prosthesis or crutches, bouncing like he was on a pogo stick, balancing one side to another in the silent courtroom, with ladies in the gallery sobbing and wearing big floppy-colored hats and all of those nineteen sixteen crazy costumes, with World War I still raging out in the Atlantic and the Boston Red Sox still winning the World Series, and Council Donahue, so Jimmy Stewart-like in his poise, saying in a loud, booming voice, "Go ahead! Stand up, Johnnie!"

And as Johnnie jumped toward the stand, Donahue announced to them all, "The pain and suffering that this boy has had to go through would move the stoutest heart! He became the victim of an accident that took the sunshine from his life and wrecked the castle he had built for the future!"

I wondered if Donahue's visions of a castle looked anything like the Chateau Marmont on Sunset Boulevard, the one that was right next to the giant Marlboro Man cutout. Or maybe a giant abandoned plastic castle boat marina on the lonely floodplain outside of Salt Lake City or the fairy-tale fiefdoms that rose up from the plateau badlands of Utah. The buttes themselves looking much like the interstellar drawings that were illustrated amidst clouds. Maybe it was a centuries-old Irish castle where kings had once lived. Maybe Johnnie himself envisioned the castlelike homes of the mill owners up on Andover Street when he heard those words, homes high on the bluff set against the pink and stacked sunset backdrop of the glimmering Merrimack River.

In the end, Johnnie was awarded $5,000, but because Johnnie was still a minor, the money had to be signed over to my great-grandmother, Mary Hogan.

"On his eighteenth birthday, it will be my intention to make it over to my son John, so that in the event of anything happening to me, his rights will be secure," my great-grandmother proclaimed in the *Lowell Sun*. And then she took the money and added another tenement to the South Street home. That is where my screenplay would end.

Johnnie went on to live another thirty years, of course, driving the stick and the clutch of the very machines that begat his path, with his one arm and one leg moving from the steering wheel to the stick shift, from the clutch to the break to the gas, so quickly, so smoothly, for Johnnie was born to drive. He'd drive the country roads of Dracut in his 1938 Chevrolet Rumble Seat with the top down, his nephew Frank (my father) bouncing beside him, while Frank the dreamer thought about the soda fountain and a beautiful girl he would marry someday. The yarn of four generations made this great quilt of my life.

In the Fairlane, driving in Lowell in 1984, I showed the guys the building on Bridge Street where the barbershop of another great-grandfather, Henry Hughes, had once been. It was a taxi stand now. Across the street was Fran's Fruit Stand on the corner of an old complex that once housed a lot of the Boot Mill working girls. The complex had been converted in the forties to low-rent apartments, all just standing silently there in a row, looking back at us gauntly as we passed them by. Ghosts moved back and forth along Bridge Street. I saw Charles Dickens visiting in the mid-1800s. Edgar Allen Poe walked by us toward Merrimack Street; he was here as part of a lecture series and was set to give a poetry reading at the library. I saw Kerouac himself darting across Kearney Square toward Arthur's Paradise Diner on the Boot Mill Canal. Ray Champeaux used to call the diner "Arthur's by the Sea." This place was famous for the Boot Mill Sandwich, made up of home fries, eggs, and sausage, all in between a big buttered bulkie roll. The Triple Boot Mill Sandwich was enormous; if you finished it, you would be so full, you'd feel sick. The old diner railcar sat there now and looked down upon its reflection on the shimmering green canal. There'd be days where Ray Champeaux would jump over that iron railing to crawl back into the canal and explore the locks and underground secret passageways; he'd disappear over those heavy gates that held back the great walls of water from the mighty Merrimack. Ray would call to me from the darkness to follow, but I was too afraid to follow, afraid that I'd slip and fall between the old rusty gears fifty feet below the gates, jamming up the wheels of progress forever.

Gordy Scott, Billy Caldwell, and I were cutting through the Boot Mills parking lot one morning back in high school when a high school teacher, Mr. Yawkey, fell right on his face in front of us. On the icy ground, his briefcase flew toward us, spilling everyone's test papers as it spun out of control on the ground. Yawkey's face and hands were all scratched up and bloody as he flapped there like a fish on the ice. The three of us ran over to pick him up, but we couldn't get him to stand. Yawkey kept slipping and falling and mumbling incoherently, like the four of us were all part of some great vaudeville skit. Yawkey was a mess that day.

"I don't understand," I said to Gordy. "What's wrong with him?"

"Don't you see it?" Gordon said to me as he and Billy grabbed at the guy to hold him straight, "He's freaking wasted!"

Gordy had me run to the school ahead of them to get Mrs. McMahon out of home room so I could tell her what was going on back in the parking lot.

"I'll take care of it," Mrs. McMahon assured me. "Don't let him back in the car!"

But just as she said this, Gordon and Billy rounded the corner in the old high school annex.

"He wrestled free from us and high-tailed out of there in his stupid car," Gordon told us. "He's gone! The freaking drunk!"

From downtown Lowell, Luke, Decky, and I drove onto the Bridge Street Bridge and crossed into Centralville. I looked out at the Boot Cotton Mills on my left, just empty shells now. All of these old brick buildings were now a lifeless fortress that formed a battery around the inner city, lining the south banks of the murky and treacherous river like the walls of a one-time great kingdom. On the bridge itself, I looked up and saw a vision of my old friend Ray Champeaux. Back when we were kids, Ray used to run to the top of that old iron bridge for kicks; he was like one of those fearless native ledge walkers out on the cliffs of the Wild West, or an old skyscraper laborer, a worker in an old *Life Magazine* picture who ate his lunch out on the steel support beams of the World Trade Towers. The walkers and the workers were all nameless now, but nevertheless real people who once had real lives like the rest of us. Ray skipped as he ran those two-foot wide girders in my vision, running the whole length of the bridge, above all of the curious cars, while people looked up and pointed at him as they honked on their horns. *Look at crazy Ray run the rafters! Has he gone mad? He's going to fall and kill himself!*

Heading north on Bridge Street we passed Nealon's Package Store where Grady the clerk had worked all of those years. But like I told you before, Grady was brutally murdered. The door of the package store was now ajar; it appeared as if no one was inside at all. How tragically sad the murder of this nice man all seemed to me now. From Nealon's, we went on to pass by St. Matthews where I first thought I had heard the voice of God. I had heard those magnificent rumblings of thunder when I was a child, the thunder that turned out to be mere people rising to their feet in the main church above us. I could still hear the priest high on the altar shouting, "Praise be to God!" as we passed by the church now. I secretly wished it really had been God back then making those sounds, for life would be all so easy now. And the pedophile Father Cunningham from St. Matthew's was now locked away somewhere being reformed. They say that in the end, he finally asked God for forgiveness. All I could think about was that silly song that we had to sing to him during the CYO musical in 1975.

Look at Father Cunningham
Sitting in his chair
He's grinning 'cause we've all sold out
This always happens every year!

Luke, Decky, and I were pushing deep into Centralville now. I headed toward Dracut. We passed Gage Field, a huge hill that led to playgrounds up on our right and McPherson's, another playground down toward lower Centralville, on our left. Lots of my teenage beers had been consumed at Gage where we usually hung out in the evening hours. A little past Gage Field, I made a right on Eighteenth Street where I climbed the hill toward my child-hood home. I pointed out what we always figured was Kerouac's *Dr. Sax's* castle to Decky and Luke; it was the Victorian-style house that sat atop the elbow of Whitney Avenue as Whitney took a turn eastward to run parallel to Eighteenth Street and alongside Gage Field. I imagined Kerouac's *Great World Snake* eerily looking down on us from the tower windows as we slowly pushed up past him and on up Eighteenth Street.

Before long, I was pulling into my parents' driveway.

"We are here!" I shouted aloud.

From the screened-in porch, my mother jumped up to greet me and delivered the sweetest words of freedom I had ever heard.

"Someone from the bank called to tell us that they received the payment check from the Subaru dealership and that your car was sold. You are all paid in full, they said!" She yelled down to me even before her kiss hello.

No more worries! No more earthly possessions! I was well on my way!

Nighttime descended upon us quickly. We talked anxiously around the dinner table, telling my parents all about where we had been. After supper, Luke, Decky, and I went downtown with my sisters Ciara and Kate and another friend Donny Dubois. We walked the length of cobblestoned Middle Street in search of old acquaintances. Here and there we pushed our way into crowded bars before finally ending up at trendy Pollards. Inside, the bar was packed for a Tuesday night. Everyone looked familiar to me, some I knew but didn't really know, but nevertheless all my people; they grew up here like their fathers and grandfathers before them, and most of them would never leave. Decky recognized people in the bar too, he told me, even though he had never been to Lowell; they were all just a part of his theory that there were only so many faces to go around.

"You look like a nun who used to teach me piano in the fifth grade!" Decky yelled across the noise. He was invisible.

But the noise was too much. We decided to head back to Centralville to see my friend Liam who tended bar at The Tavern at the Bridge. The Tavern just sat there alone on the north side of the Merrimack River on the VFW Highway and Bridge Street, right at the doorstep to Centralville. It was the final stop on the usual crawl home from downtown for one last cold one. It was where all the locals drank quietly; one last drink before everyone entered the spin zone of sleep and said good night to the physical world. The Tavern was called The Spindle Pub in the seventies, but new ownership changed the name to The Tavern in the eighties. We all still called it The Spindle though, and as we walked around the side parking lot to enter through the front door, I looked across at the now quiet VFW-Bridge Street intersection where I noticed that someone had laid a fresh bouquet of cut flowers on the southeast side of the road, right at the curb where the old lady had died.

The only person I had ever seen killed with my own eyes was right there, right at the bridge. Gordy, Billy, and I had been walking home from high school one winter afternoon in 1976. From the bridge, we started to approach this poor old lady who waited there for the light to change; she was standing at the crosswalk when smack out of nowhere a mad car gone awry screamed across the boulevard and killed her. When the late-model car hit her, the impact alone sent her flying about twenty feet in the air and just like that, her lifeless body landed on the sidewalk before us. It was so sad, right in the dead of a Lowell winter, with the icy Merrimack just cutting along far below us, ice-sheeted shores breaking off to rushing ice-cold water at the river's edge as her body lay on the sidewalk at our feet, lifeless on the dirty, slushy snow, old footprints packed about her. The poor old woman had gone somewhere else before she ever hit the ground. There was nothing we could do. We were frantic as more people arrived. The color of the car that had hit her was a blur, and just like that, it was gone.

"Did you see the car? Did you get the plate?" a man in a mechanic's uniform called to us as he knelt beside her, touching her head.

"No, uh, it was red," my high school friend Gordy said.

Blood came out of the side of her mouth on a patch of virgin snow by the poor woman's head. She was somebody's grandmother, I thought, as we watched and waited for the ambulance to come. She had survived the Great Depression, childbirth, World War II, and everything else around it, and just like that, someone had come along in a fleeting flash and killed her.

Back there on that day in 1976, I wondered if she hovered above us as the moving river's water rushed below and a clean sheet of sparkling ice broke away free, moving to the open water and joining the beautiful current.

You just have to believe in heaven after seeing something like that.

CHAPTER 33

Wednesday came.

Even though I slept up in my old room, I dreamt that I was downstairs asleep on the living room couch. I dreamt that I was back in high school again on some lazy afternoon. It was a dream within a dream. I had them often, cascading dreams, collapsing on each other like Russian Matryoshka dolls; each dream was an empty wooden casket that opened within another wooden casket, and I couldn't wake up until I found a way to free myself from all of them. Even though my spirit was forever awake, I felt my body now was a stone. I tried to roll off of the couch I thought I was on, but I couldn't. I tried yelling out to someone, to my mother, who, in this dream I thought was watching soap operas, but my tongue wouldn't work; the nerve signal was blocked, and I could only murmur faint, forced moans. I finally remembered to surrender to it all. You see, to prove to my sleeping self that I was, in fact, in a dream, I had to test the bounds of physical limitation and try to do something impossible. I had to try to fly. Complete surrender was the only way to ever awaken. So I jumped up in the air in my dreaming wakefulness and floated and propelled with no gravity at once, all the way across the room and up toward the ceiling. With this discovery, I now became immediately relaxed and regained my confidence. I could do anything! I slowly moved toward the windows of my parents' house. I moved freely now, bumping into the living room wall and pushing off. I was a spaceman. I flew into the kitchen and then out through the back screen door and up over the neighborhoods of Christian Hill.

It wasn't long before I was out over the September choppy Merrimack. I pushed myself up still farther into the starlit sky above me, suddenly looking down with no fear, feeling liberated, looking down on the beautiful, abandoned mill city in the warmth of the real New England night.

The mill city changed rapidly below me as I traveled back through dreaming time. The mills quickly disappeared and changed into the beauty of a forested countryside, with the same old characteristic bend in the river that had always been there. It had always looked like an upturned horseshoe from the sky; the southward flowing Merrimack curved back upward and held Centralville like a great hand holds a beautiful dove. From there, the river continued its flow northward toward peaceful Paradise Beach and the distant New Hampshire sea. High above it all, I hovered there for a few moments and imagined that I was back in the time of the native nations. I suddenly stood on Tyng's Island in the middle of the river, face-to-face with the great sachem Passaconaway and his own magical dreaming spirit. I noticed an early English preacher, right there beside him while all three of us said nothing to each other, silently surrendering to this still peace. Then I pulled slowly away from them, upward again, and watched as the two great men stood effortless in the rising waters. The water soon overtook the island they were standing on and flooded all of the surrounding towns. The upturned horseshoe was gone.

I finally awoke from it all in my old room upstairs. The dreams were gone. At the foot of my bed the floor creaked away. Old Woodward's ghost was back in his invisible wooden rocking chair, I thought. The familiar creaking sound was nevertheless a little spooky, but I wasn't afraid. After all, this was still the house he had built back in the 1880s.

Downstairs in the kitchen that morning in 1984, I talked Decky into running the back roads of Kenwood, Dracut, with me, just like I had done during my days in high school. It didn't take much convincing with Decky.

"I'm ready. Let's go!" he exclaimed.

I had a regular-five mile route that I would run on weekends. When I ran in the fall, there were always fresh smells of native corn from the small roadside stands along this route. On this morning with Decky, I counted the wooden posts of the old fences along the stretch and remembered the frequent childhood rides with my father. Peculiar clouds danced across the lower stretches of sky like errant white brushstrokes curling from some great canvas of the Creator. The signs of October's soft footsteps were out there too, for they were evident in the gradual changes of color in the hilly landscape ahead of us. Out there in the distant hills of Dracut, I imagined Uncle Arthur's weathered carriage house alongside his barn again. I only knew it from a black-and-white album picture taken during a 1930's summertime. The structure had fallen down sometime back in the '40s, but I thought I could always smell the dusty, humid air that came from inside of it just by looking at that old picture. The buzzing sounds of the Dogday Harvestfly mixed into the roaring sound of a motorcycle as the loud bike came up from behind us. As Decky and I pushed along these old roads, the motorcycle passed us quickly and weaved its way into the quilted countryside. I imagined my father and his motorcycle forever riding out there too, somewhere where he was young again.

That evening, I finally reunited with Richie Clark at his apartment in Pawtucketville. Dukie, Bessisso, and Whacko were there too. Lots of people came out to celebrate my home-coming that night. It was crazy. There was lots of beer, cases and cases of it, with wicked talk of days ahead and days gone by. My younger brother Steve and his friend Dan, my younger sister Kate and Sully, Sophie and Dylan, Dukie's sister KJ, Frankie Tabor, Abby (a girl who pulled me drunk out of the water of Lake Mascuppic one night when I fell off of Gordy's boat), Aidan Maloney, and even my old California travel companion Sal Caprissi, all showed up to see Luke, Decky, and I off on our great adventure abroad.

It was such a wonderful life.

CHAPTER 34

Thursday came.

My lifelong friend Billy Caldwell was getting married on Saturday. So Thursday night, we all gathered at the Spindle Pub (The Tavern), about twenty of us, to take him out for one final roaring drunk before his big day.

Decky, Luke, and I were the first ones to get there that night. Little by little, the others came and eventually we all assembled as a group toward the rear of the long bar. Billy, looking all surprised, and his brother Cliffy, soon arrived, and we all hooted and hollered out Billy's name when he walked through the big red door in the front. The coolers clanged, and the taps poured. As the mood of the occasion slowly grew, we began to discuss the long night's plan, everyone with arms flying about in the dank, dreamy darkness, everyone cavorting, mingling, and moving in random groups of three. Some of us leaned on the walls outside of the bathrooms and against the Pac-Man machine while a neon Budweiser sign flashed in the window above us. Car light reflections from the VFW Highway ran madly in the big window in a streaming line, one after the other, mostly heading eastward on the boulevard. As the cold, bottled, longneck beers grew in our hands, I listened intuitively to the sound of nothing for a few moments. It seemed so peaceful to me. It was just like the old days again, I thought, and in my anxious excitement, it felt like maybe I had never left Centralville at all.

The plans were finalized. Our first stops would be a few of the nicer establishments along Market and Middle streets, like Pollards or the Dubliner, and later, we would head back to Central Street where the real people were, Charlie McIntyre's Pub.

Charlie McIntyre was one of the nicest guys in the whole world. Billy played on his softball team along with Richie, Sully, and Dukie, and Charlie had wanted to see us all that night. If you met him, Charlie was a big and burly guy with a steel keg of beer for a stomach; he was the baddest men's club softball pitcher in all of Middlesex County. At the pub, drinks for the softball players and their friends were always on the house, especially after a win, so much so that Charlie fell deep into debt over the years, and consequently, his vendors slowly began to cut him off. In the latter days of the pub, there were many discussions that he had to have with the delivery drivers out in the dark and damp side alley, just to find a way to pull off a little more credit, just to get a few more kegs delivered, the lifeblood of his friends. Like all good things, however, the kegs were drying up, and time was quickly running out.

That night, after one of those regular beer vendor alleyway discussions, Charlie came back in through the side door and announced to everyone, "Sorry, we're all out of Miller beer indefinitely, but we still got free Budweiser!"

And everyone in the small place cheered, "Yay!"

At the pub, a heavy lady, maybe in her middle forties, was terribly wasted; she sat at Charlie's bar slobbering, talking to herself, murmuring moans, with her eyes half-closed, burying her head for several minutes at a time. I noticed the poor dear was missing two front teeth and had the characteristic nose of W. C. Fields. She raised her head to sip a free Bud draft from a pilsner glass and then quickly jumped up to go to the ladies' room, talking inaudible gibberish to me as she passed. As I stood there all alone, she snapped a bark in my face before turning away and then continued on toward the crowded restroom corridor.

Two skinny, T-shirted, middle-aged men, drunk, with bluish blurred-out tattoos all over their thin, boney arms, moved in toward her seat near the bar, bickering over their lady friends who seemed to also congregate in that long restroom corridor.

My sister Kate's boyfriend Sully pointed to a scruffy little guy sitting all by himself at a two-seater table by the six foot-by-six foot platform dance floor, and told Luke, Decky, and I that the guy was a Vietnam vet. "He has seen terrible things; I think someone said he was one of those guys that they dropped into the Viet Cong tunnels to ferret out the enemy. After a while, the guy just went plain crazy and had to be honorably discharged."

I took it all in while looking around me, wondering at the beauty of this grand carnival of life. These were mostly the descendants of the streets of Lowell, and Charlie had taken them all in. They had been a part of this inner-city culture from the times of our grandfathers; they were descendants of America's Great War veterans, descendants of the cotton mill laborers, the tired and the poor who had been shoveled to the streets by everyone else. All of the jobs seemed to be moving to the south or overseas, and there was nothing left for them to do. These were my brothers and sisters, these sad descendants of Galloway.

All the while we were there, the front door was kept wide open by a brick with the cool September breeze blowing in from back Central Street. I walked around with a Budweiser in my hand as I observed everyone. A tall lady, with long dark hair, probably in her midtwenties, with terrible dark yellow teeth from apparent heroin addiction, swore at no one as they walked through that door. She yelled out into the open night air after Charlie, even though Charlie stood out of earshot behind the bar inside.

"Hey, Charlie, call me a cab!"

"Okay, you're a cab!" some wise guy yelled back at her.

A group of three big ladies with their skinny alcoholic men companions were gathered near the dance floor. All of them smoked cigarettes and whispered into one another's ears.

I imagined that they talked about the softball group stag party that had just invaded their establishment.

At the bar, I noticed a short-haired, thin, handicapped man seated alone at the opposite end with a severely deformed arm. Three small fingers extended out of his short arm; the arm itself was about half the length of his good arm. He smiled at me and worked the thirsty, draft beer quickly with the little arm.

"This is my good arm! It's closer to my mouth!" he gleamed at me with happiness.

Back at the restrooms, a big black lady with a short tight Afro told another in the recesses of the dark corridor, "I have nothing in common with him so he can go fuck himself!" She looked out toward the dance floor. Out on the small platform dance floor, two thin black men danced to the disco juke box, one wearing a beard and a Red Sox cap, the other one bald. The bearded man pointed to the bald man dancing, laughing aloud, and said, "Never mind her! He's got nothing in common with himself!"

With all of this going on, a surge of patriotism came out of nowhere. I don't know how it all started, but it was as if someone close to the door, perhaps the lady still yelling for a cab, had wrangled a sudden wave of unity that blew in from the ancient city night. Perhaps it was a leftover chorus from a 1945 Victory Parade that marched down Central Street. It had been floating out there for decades, just waiting for this night. Within a few short minutes, everyone was singing "God Bless America!"

I remembered the 1980 U.S. Hockey Team victory and a similar feeling of national unity after their improbable "Miracle on Ice." And now, at McIntyre's Pub, everyone, including the vet, the lady that had been sleeping, Charlie, the people who had been fighting in the corridor, all of them began to sway and sing, with arms locked around each other; no one had a care in the world. I reached over to the guy with the deformed arm who sat in the corner and put my hand on his shoulder to join in. We were soon swaying and singing loudly with all of America. His little arm hoisted his mug of beer.

Here in tiny McIntyre's Pub on back Central Street, the world was immediately overcome by the rapture of beer and song; everyone had become one. We were misfits, all of us; spirits resonating in the real world, one single gigantic strand of DNA that wrapped around the whole room. Everyone remained arm in arm, braided, and sang as loud as they could scream. The great chain of life grew and fed off of itself and soon moved outward from the pub and spilled into the narrow alleyway and street. On the street, hands stretched out to grasp other hands, but the singing soon died down and people unwillingly broke away and eventually disappeared.

As he had done before, Charlie had thrown his tethered lifeline out from the pub into the lonely Lowell night to save us all. McIntyre's Pub was always a different glimpse of beauty and madness, all rolled up into one that life will sometimes show you. It was always fresh and exhilarating to me. I was grateful to old Charlie for this. With everyone singing and locking arms and singing "God Bless America" like that, it seemed like such an incredible moment in time.

How many more dive bars across America were like McIntyre's? How many here had chosen this path that they were now upon? Was there a greater purpose to it all? Truly, this could never be the end for some of these blessed souls. Where would they all be in a few years? There should always be such a comfortable place for the tired and the poor like this. Were there places in Lowell like this throughout the late 1800s and earlier part of our century? How I wished I could walk every corridor of time in order to find out. I got momentarily lost in the verse of Edwin Arlington Robinson . . .

> Miniver Cheevy, born too late,
> Scratched his head and kept on thinking;
> Miniver coughed, and called it fate,
> And kept on drinking.

We poured out into the night from McIntyre's, Billy in tow, singing, jubilant, headed to O'Jay's. From O'Jay's, we went to the Lokai to drink crazy-colored fruit drinks and eat the carnation garnish that came with them. Billy's brother, Cliffy, and I ate two or three carnations each before we left to end the night at Towne Pizza, where I showed Decky and Luke how to eat greasy cheese steaks at two in the morning, just like we used to do on our way home from the bars before I had ever left for California. My friend Liam threw a slice of pizza at me from across the joint, for we all teased him for trying to talk (he was incoherent) to five girls who were ordering something at the counter. The slice bounced hard off of my shirt collar and fell to the floor.

I looked at the upright slice on the dirty floor and wondered about the five-second rule and if it might still be good enough to pick it up and eat it.

After a few minutes, I picked up the slice of pizza and started eating. It was still warm. It was delicious.

CHAPTER 35

It was already Friday the 21st of September. We would be leaving for London in three more days. I thought about how quickly this matter-of-fact journey of just setting out of Huntington Beach to take a huge risk and move to Europe, our crossing the map of America first in a mad zigzag stretch to visit all of the multiple acquaintances of life, had abruptly come to an end.

When I awoke in the morning, I was madly hungover. I hated feeling this way. I thought on how this addiction bred the bitter morning withdrawals like this. "It'll get you when you aren't looking," Frank said. "A drink here, a drink there, and before you know it, you're falling off the stage of life and wondering, 'How did that happen?' Just like that, you're gone."

But I still wanted to be the rock star in the night somehow. I needed to drink, I wanted to drink, I continued to convince myself. My head was pounding now though; it was crying out, hurting from the lack of hydration that the alcohol had usurped from every cell during the long hours of the night. I really had to find a way out of the pain of it all. Downstairs in my parents' kitchen, I found some temporary solace by hitting the orange juice hard. I drank lots of it. Some of it fell out the sides of my mouth as I swigged from the bottle. I passed it to Decky and wiped my mouth with my sleeve as Decky began swigging lots of it too. We both finished the whole freaking gallon of it.

Later in the day, Luke and I ran seven miles into Kenwood, trying to shake off the rest of our demons, trying to sweat it all out. We absolutely had to feel good again, for my friend Billy and his fiancée Christina's big wedding was this weekend. During our run, we promised ourselves not to drink for the whole day. We'd stick around the house, we said.

That evening when my father came home, we had a massive kitchen table discussion just like old times.

A big wooden antique bench with a mirror attached to it (just like the evil queen's from SnowWhite) sat out in the back shed just beyond the opened paneled door in the kitchen. The bench was one of the pieces of furniture that had been left behind by Old Man Woodward. In fact, there were a lot of really cool antiques that he had left behind when we had moved there in 1960 'cause there wasn't any place for Woodward's antiques where he was going. You see, Woodward died in that house.

From my seat at the kitchen table, I looked over as my mother closed the back shed door. A large, single sheet International Harvester calendar hung the length of the door. Frank worked for International Harvester and always hung that sheet so he could dream and wonder about the days ahead, to see a whole year laid out before his eyes. He always had his two-week vacation at Paradise Beach circled in July; that was what he lived for. And, of course, there were all of the three-day weekends and holidays circled too. As I sat there, I just looked at that whole door that was filled with 1984. The calendars from years before had come and gone, all of them with those two weeks circled, practically the only two weeks in the whole year that really mattered to Frank.

Schnopsie, the crazy gray miniature schnauzer, was penned behind a childproof gate that separated the kitchen from the pantry. He always barked at intruders; he barked at us and tried to get at us as we talked that night, turning his head sideways as he lunged over the top of the little gate. I talked on and ignored him, and this really pissed him off. He had drawn blood on me once before, so I dared not ever try to be his friend again. But my father loved him, understood him, and openly admitted that Schnopsie's aggressive nature must have had something to do with how he had been bred. Something must have gone awry with the breed. Miniature Schnauzers were supposed to be gentle dogs. And what were they to do with him now anyway? Frank and Theresa surely couldn't give him up, for no one would want him; he might end up at the pound.

"Imagine the three of you trying to retell the story of your trip in thirty years. I bet you that your stories will all be very different," Frank said.

"Kind of, I guess," I answered.

"Yeah, everybody is looking at the same experience from different angles," Luke affirmed him.

"What about the New Testament, then?" Frank asked. He had to get that in.

"Matthew, Mark, Luke, John, and Peter wrote their own accounts of Jesus' life in their own books thirty years after Jesus died. Isn't it remarkable that their stories were so similar?"

Frank had said it before, endlessly. I remembered those kitchen table arguments over the years, and he would always end it with this, for he knew that this was the only thing that I couldn't come up with a good argument against. How could a handful of people write the exact same story thirty years later?

"I want to bring attention to the fact that Mike has already cheated on his thirty-year story, Mr. Hogan, because he has been writing it ahead of time. He has been taking notes the whole way across country!" Decky said aloud. Frank laughed.

"Did you know that Jesus was the first nonviolent revolutionary?" Luke said, quoting to Frank something Stephen Stills had said on the *4 Way Street* album.

With that, Schnopsie snapped; he lunged half of his body over the two-foot high child gate before falling backward onto his two hind legs in a convulsive spill in the slippery pantry. The dog bounced back up and turned his head sideways to chop again at all of us. He was bedeviled now, a feral animal that needed to be calmed. Luke tried to calm him by reaching his open-palmed hand over the top of the gate, but Schnopsie seized the moment and lashed at his outstretched hand, immediately drawing blood. Luke pulled his arm back over the gate in a snap while Frank jumped up from his seat at the table to run over to them.

"Bad dog! Bad, bad dog!" Frank snarled at Schnopsie, while my mother jumped the gate to grab a wet cloth from the pantry so she could treat Luke's poor bleeding hand. From the ball of his hand, blood rolled off Luke's wrist as he raised it perpendicular to his body. It dripped on the kitchen floor. My mother cleaned the wound quickly with the damp rag and then dressed it with some Neosporin-type ointment that was in the pantry first aid kit and finally bandaged it all up. Schnopsie cowered in the corner. Something must have gone awry with the breed, they said.

After a while when things calmed back down, Sully came to our back door to pick up my sister Kate. We had planned earlier that day to all head up to Sully's mother's house which was a mile away, up by the Christian Hill reservoir on the top of the hill. Frank and Theresa would go with us too. It was a tradition; we'd go up there for coffee and dessert on Christmas night and other special occasions. And on this last night of a calendar summer, we celebrated at Sully's mother's house with a great feast of Boston crème, lemon meringue, apple and cherry pies as we drank tea and coffee and talked about Luke's bandaged hand and everything in the world.

After it all ended, we stuck to our promise and all went back to the house on Eighteenth, for there would be no partying for the three of us tonight. We desperately needed a full day of recovery, for Billy and Christina's wedding warm-up was going to be Saturday morning up at Gage Field.

My apple crate of favorite albums that I had shipped from Ingrid's in distant Newport Beach now rested by the old turntable in the parlor. Before bed, I leafed through the whole album collection slowly, contemplating what I should play. My fingers landed at first on *Wings over America* and then carefully lifted the cover of the turntable. I pulled the large vinyl disc out of its dust jacket. With the pushing of a button, the stylus jumped up and jerked over, then dropped down into place and slowly ran the groove of "Picasso's Last Words" followed by Paul Simon's classic interpretation of "Richard Cory."

Edwin Arlington Robinson was one of my favorite American poets. As I listened to Simon's lyrics, I marveled at how he had so cleverly taken the poetry of Robinson and put it to this music. Paul Simon changed the poem ever so slightly, adding his own verse, a crisper, modern picture of the magnate that Robinson had envisioned. And poor old Richard Cory . . . In the end, money didn't have one blessed thing to do with the happiness that he sought. And just like that, he was gone.

Edwin Arlington Robinson told us:

So on we worked, and waited for the light,
And went without the meat, and cursed the bread;
And Richard Cory, one calm summer night,
Went home and put a bullet through his head.

CHAPTER 36

Saturday the 22nd of September. It was Billy and Christina's wedding day. As I awoke, I tried to remember what I had just found in my dream. It was something peaceful; it was hidden in plain sight; it was beautiful.

I wondered if heaven was like this, when the sun warms you, a place where you bask all day in the light without ever getting burned, a quiet kingdom where the calming waves crash on the shores of eternity, where the sandpipers are happy to just run back and forth chasing the shoreline, a place where they don't need to look for sustenance anymore. I didn't want to leave Lowell but knew I had to. We had two more days here before we would have to leave for London. The sand was slipping through the hourglass more swiftly now; at least, it seemed that way, for there was only a little bit left in the picture I saw. In London, we'd surely have to flip the hourglass over again.

After breakfast, Luke, Decky, and I headed out to Gage Field, where we met up with all of the others. We began drinking beers at nine in the morning. We stayed there awhile, a group of about thirty of us, and filled up that big oil drum trash can near the basketball courts with lots of aluminum can empties, making one-handed basketball shots from several feet away. It had always been a tradition for us, going all the way back to high school days, to drink heavily at Gage Field before the big event. These were the flowing fields of our youth that we had grown up in, filled with green, green grass and wild dandelions. Across the horseshoe road that held all of the playing fields, right near the baseball diamond, sat the bubbler of eternity. Outside the basketball courts, near our parked cars, we spilled warm bottles of Budweiser everywhere and celebrated passages of time; these were our fields of succession. After a few hours had passed, we collectively planned our drive to the wedding ceremony, for it was a long drive to Danvers. We loaded up the cars and began the parade. The old Fairlane fit right in, with her stoic surfboard still attached, finding her place in the gala procession of Mustangs, Buicks, Chevys, and Cadillacs; it was a caravan of cars leaving the horseshoe-shaped road that was always turned upward. We headed by way of Andover, toward the North Shore of Massachusetts and eventually arrived in Danvers.

We found the church with minutes to spare and as the cars pulled into the parking area, people began to file in. I couldn't hold my kidneys any longer and ran through the backyard of the church to take a leak on the ten-foot high row of bushes that surrounded the property. Timmy Finnegan was doing the same thing when I got there, watering the shrubs in a circular motion and seemingly deep in thought; he was singing a song and looking up at the perfect sky with its perfect puffy clouds moving slowly across the blue backdrop of the upper atmosphere of the whole world. The sweet smell of stargazer lilies came from the church's surrounding garden. Suddenly, coming right through the bushes, an older man with silver hair appeared. He had come from the adjoining yard.

"Oh-oh," I heard Timmy say as he quickly zipped up. I danced around a bit to cut my own stream short, wetting my psychedelic suit pants in the process. After that, I turned quickly to make a clean getaway, but I was stopped by the older man's words.

"No, it's all right, I am not angry," the man spoke out at us both as he stood there. "People relieve themselves on those bushes all of the time. Are you in the wedding party?"

"Not in it, but going to it, yes," Timmy said to him. "Thank you for understanding. We had to really go!"

"Enjoy the ceremony," the man said to us as he walked away, quickly retreating back through the bushes that he had come from.

Timmy and I quickly ran to the front of the church to go in. We slipped by the assembling bridal party and quietly hustled halfway down the aisle to join the rest of our large group on the right-hand side of the church. When we sat down, the minister entered from a side door and walked over to stand at the head of the church with the groom. I looked over to Timmy Finnegan in amazement. The minister was the same man we had just talked to behind the church! Timmy's eyes were as wide as mine, and he shook his head with a silent grimace.

The traditional bridal chorus from Wagner's *Lohengrin* began, and the march was underway. This was the bridal song of 100 years, I thought. I transgressed time seeing Frank and Theresa, my grandparents, great-grandparents, and people all the way back to Jesus getting married to this song.

Billy stood there up at the altar. With everyone situated up there, the minister began to speak. In his sermon, he talked about the everlasting bond between two people, a bond that could transgress all of time.

A young woman with two young children sat two rows in front of us, both of the kids were about four or five. The little girl yawned while the boy crawled around on the floor. The mother looked straight-ahead. An olive-skinned girl, tall and attractive, probably in her midtwenties, sat further on down in the same row with a teenage brother on her right and what appeared to be their parents at the far end. The pretty girl cast several smiling glances toward the playing children.

I watched them all as the service drew to a crescendo. I was outside looking into a beautiful world, this ritual of Western life that had been with us forever. I was a movie director again, sitting behind the camera as it rolled with a rock-and-roll ballad all too familiar in the background of this crazy dream. The ballad started soft and slow. I dreamed that it was me and Colette up there. In my mind, there was a soft guitar riff, and then the electric guitar came in with a sound akin to the pinging of water. The sound became a visual of ripples in an open mountain pool, followed by the beautiful tenor sounds of Marty Balin and the harmonizing backup from Grace Slick as they sang "Today" in my head. It was such a perfect song for a wedding. I could hear the words . . .

In this dream we stood at the altar, Colette and I, as the camera moved out to a wide-angled shot of the whole congregation around us. My whole family was there, but then it all rolled back in a snap and faded away. Like a passage stolen from Thurber's *The Secret Life of Walter Mitty*, I couldn't stop dreaming of how wonderful my world could be.

I woke up to the sounds of clapping hands. Richie had started the clapping and the whole church followed his lead. Cheering, we all watched the new couple and the wedding party pass, and we slowly spilled out of the church behind them into the warm and comfortable New England sun. It was, after all, such a beautiful life.

Of course, our Christian Hill group of thirty or so went back to the church parking lot to drink again. Surprisingly, we had gone the whole service without a drop! In the parking lot, some of us now jumped into O-Dog's van in order to escape the gaze of the Protestant traditionalists getting into their cars around us who scorned the simultaneous cracks of the aluminum can tabs in the open air. Billy's pretty sister joined us for a time in the van while we drank. I had dated her in high school, but she was married now. Her newlywed husband Jack was with her, but soon was giving her the eye roll to leave. They both had to catch up to the rest of the wedding party to partake in Billy and Christina's wedding pictures.

After a few more beers, Luke, Decky, and I, along with the others, disembarked from the van to head for the reception hall for more celebration. The place was a few miles down the road, adjacent to a country club, with the perfect green golf course spread out behind the golf pro shop and restaurant. Billy, Christina, and the whole wedding party were all out on the surrounding grounds when we arrived; Billy looked over and laughed at his crew of drunk friends while the fidgety photographer moved them all around, trying to get the perfect shots that would last for all of eternity and transgress all of time.

Inside, I looked around at the large room dressed with several round tables, each having centerpieces of small glass bowls with three or four goldfish swimming in them. You see, Billy's parents owned a pet store on Market Street in downtown Lowell. The fish bowls were his mother's idea. It was a great setup before we got there.

We were all only seated for a few minutes when my friend Dukie reached into the bowl at the center of our table and handed me the poor little flapping, floundering fish.

"I dare you to swallow it whole, Mikey," he said to me.

My sister Kate (with Sully beside her) and all of the other girls at our table began to wince with disgust as they looked at the poor little fish. I popped it into my mouth, closing my eyes at first. I thought back to my chewing on the carnations at the Lo Kai just days before this. I grabbed my open beer, took a big gulp, and with it I felt the unfortunate fish wriggle past my Adam's apple and go on down. There was a mixture of loud laughter, amazement, and total disownment coming from everyone who had witnessed it. The sad thing about it all was this now caused a ripple of cause and effect throughout the whole room. A pebble had just been thrown into a calm pool of water. We were Gage Field people from Christian Hill. We ruined weddings.

Dukie laughed at my actions affectionately. "Mikey, I know I can do one too 'cause I swallow cling peaches like that all of the time!" he screamed aloud.

With that, Dukie pulled another fish from the small glass bowl and put it in his mouth. Everyone in the whole room was either aghast or laughing at us now. I grabbed for the last fish in our table's bowl, because now it was a competition. Dukie had opened it up. I gagged as the small fish slithered down this time. One table over from ours, Richie had watched us both and decided that it was his turn to do one.

"Waiter, there's a bone in my fish!" he yelled out to Dukie and I before putting the small fish in his mouth to swallow it down.

"Whooa!" He shook his head, closing his eyes as he did so. "At first, I thought I was going to barf!" He laughed to his whole table.

The madness ignited around us. Everyone had a Gage Field joker at their table that wanted to try it. A small growing group of us began moving to the adjoining tables, reaching into the centerpieces, trying to eat them all, beat the others, grabbing the orange, black, and white fish, and putting them into our mouths one by one.

"How many can we do?"

"I didn't know the dinner today was going to be surf and turf!" someone yelled at us from one of the distant tables. We continued laughing. Decky and Luke tried at least one on their own. I continued to move about at the back of the room, looking for fish, disrupting the whole order of things, right as the wedding party came in and began to assemble at the head table.

Like a wave of lost karma, the dark skies opened and all of the spontaneous laughter switched to silence at once. It wasn't funny anymore. I stood there with a goldfish in my hand, three tables from where I was supposed to be seated. At the head of the hall, Billy's mother was angry. I was eating up her centerpieces; I was ruining the special day for everyone. This wasn't funny. She stood up to look at me and then to Richie and just shook her head in disappointment at both of us.

"Oh-oh." I looked over to Richie. We both scattered back to our seats and sheepishly sat down.

I had just made an ass of myself in front of everyone. I wasn't sober. All the while in my head, The Stones and Mick Jagger raged with the "Monkey Man" soundtrack. Did other people have songs constantly playing in their head?

I was the monkey man.

CHAPTER 37

On Sunday, September 23rd, the Patriots played the Redskins at home. It was Tony Eason's first professional start. He had come off a week of stepping in for Steve Grogan against Seattle and orchestrating the largest come-from-behind win the Pats had ever seen. Frank was all ready for the game the week before. I think he may have even circled September 23rd on the International Harvester calendar that hung on the back shed door.

This week, on our final full day in America, Luke, Decky, and I decided to watch the game at Richie's apartment. The Pats didn't score until the third quarter on a thirty-eight yard Eason to Starring touchdown pass. But they wouldn't get another touchdown for the rest of the game. In the end, the Pats lost to the Redskins twenty-six to ten.

After the game was over, we left the surfboard at Richie's apartment. He would keep it, maybe make a coffee table out of it, he said, a coffee table that had started on the shores of Huntington Beach and surfed the waves of Kansas, Oklahoma, and Indiana; a coffee table like no other before it.

Monday the 24th came really quickly. It marked thirty-one days of being on the road for us. Our journey in America was over. It was an incredible story, but like all great stories, these amazing chapters of life have to end sometime. I quietly sensed another great journey that was now ahead of me. That same anxiety that I had back in Huntington Beach began to well again. We were leaving our great country, maybe forever, with our one-way tickets to London purchased and in our possession now.

On Eighteenth Street, we said our final good-byes to my parents and the sweet Fairlane. Luke parked her resting at the far end of the driveway. She would sit there in the event that Luke would return, through the changing seasons, through the heaps of fallen leaves, and the onset of winter's snow. If Luke ever returned, he would need a means to get back to Kansas, or Alaska, or wherever else, and the Fairlane had done right by us. With the bungie cord and surfboard gone now, she looked so naked and abandoned there as we rolled out of the driveway and turned to go down the street in my sister Kate's boyfriend Sully's car. My older sister Ciara drove with us too.

We left Lowell the same way we had come in. On the way out, we passed Arthur's Paradise Diner. We passed by the abandoned barbershop of the most famous barber of Lowell, my great-grandfather Henry Hughes. His mother had been a beggar right there in Kearney Square in the late 1800s. She was buried in Edson Cemetery in a pauper's grave without a headstone, my grandmother Lillian used to tell me.

> Born into a time,
> Born into a place,
> Given a face,
> But now forgotten.

Had the famous barber tried to help her? I would never know. He had to raise eight young children on his own. Lillian was one of them.

We drove down Gorham Street toward the Lowell Connector. There was a woman named Mary Jane Gannon who died on Gorham Street in 1908, pulled under an electric car, right there in front of St. Peter's Church where she had just gone to confession. Mary Jane was Lillian's other grandmother (not the pauper grandmother). My twelve-year-old grandfather Tom saw it all happen from South Street that day. Mary Jane had tried to step up on the car, but the conductor closed the door too quickly, and she was thrown under the wheels. She was pinned there for two hours; had both legs amputated by the car before it was all over. My grandfather Tom watched as people went crazy around her, trying to lift the car without a jack. Tom looked into Mary Jane's eyes as she lay there right before she died. I wondered if she hovered above him as he looked toward the church and said a silent prayer. You just have to believe in heaven after seeing something like that. You see, Mary Jane had just gone to confession.

Life was so random and coincidental, I thought. Tom, who had stood there in 1908 as a kid and looked into Mary Jane's dying eyes, ended up marrying Mary Jane's granddaughter, Lillian, fourteen years later. It was strange how the paths of true love seemed to always crisscross.

"There's no such thing as coincidence," Luke said to us all in the car.

I said good-bye to empty St. Peter's Church and South Street. I thought about my own uncle Mike. In the early 1950s before I was born, Lillian made him break his engagement to the only woman he ever loved, a Protestant. It was a few years after the breakup in 1954 when poor Mike died of cancer. It had come on so sudden. My grandmother blamed it on the deplorable conditions of the war. But I wondered if his will to live had been taken from him when he had to give the girl up in order to honor the wishes of his parents. I wondered if, in fact, it wasn't cancer at all but simply a broken heart. I wondered if Uncle Mike was somewhere now with his Protestant bride.

We jumped on the Lowell Connector, Route 495 bound. I remembered the stories of old people that are married for fifty years who die within hours of each other, leaving the earth together to find another chance in another place, a beautiful place where the sun is warm but never burns the skin, and people paddle out into a starlit ocean, sitting atop their surfboards in the beautiful sparkling darkness to worship the silence.

My mother was given up for adoption as a newborn in 1924. I was fourteen when Theresa found her birth certificate in her adopted mother's cold flat after the funeral. A single mother's name on a birth certificate, that's all there was . . . A name we didn't know, and it was at the bottom of a dresser drawer tucked beneath marriage licenses and forgotten linen.

I always wondered about those nameless and faceless grandparents of mine. Was my mother born of a love that knew no bounds? But why had they given her away? Was he a Protestant?

Good-bye, Lowell.

We drove south on Route 93. Approaching Boston now, I looked over at Bunker Hill Monument from the bridge. The granite obelisk thrust into the blue skies of Charlestown on our left as it always had. I remembered Ray Champeaux and I took the train out of Lowell as kids all the way to North Station one day with the desire to climb that tower. He had taken a crisp twenty-dollar bill out of his mother's open purse to pay for our tickets. We had skipped school. It had been an icy climb that day for both of us. We exhaled fits of running steam into the cold air as we counted those 294 granite stairs all the way to the top. We thought it was the stairway to heaven. At first, as we began to climb, it seemed like it would never end, but once we got to running them in an exhilarating full sprint, it ended so abruptly. From those little cut stone windows at the top, I peered out across all of Boston, looking down while I imagined the ghosts of the early New Englanders hundreds of feet below me, ghosts who were fighting the British on the ground, ghosts who had once been breathing aloud like me, gulping at life, fighting to the death for what they stood for . . . ghosts whose memories lived on.

I pointed out the white steeple of Old North Church to Luke and Decky, just visible to the south, jutting up over the water beyond it, a church that had been so much a part of so many historic rides, rides that were alive and seemed to last forever. But the steeple quickly disappeared out of sight like everything else material, as fast as a passage of a book or the burning of a simple match. I pointed out The Prudential Tower, off to our right, overlooking Fenway, where the Red Sox would be returning from Baltimore and playing the Blue Jays later in the day, with no chance at making the playoffs, for Detroit was so far ahead in the AL East that the rest of the games didn't even matter anymore. Boston Sand and Gravel, a permanent landmark of the working class, sat there as it always did, that big yellow sign on a ghostly gray steel building, right off the raised highway next to Storrow Drive, and then we disappeared down through the tunnel underneath all of that water, toward Logan Airport, leaving all of the generations that I came from finally behind.

Generations upon generations of Irish Catholic guilt, generations of perseverance and love, and generations of everything else that came with it. This was my burden and my gift. God knew the sequence of each of our lives like the written pages of a novel, from beginning to end, but here I was in the moment, in the midst of these pages with the free will to choose whatever would be written tomorrow. And I knew it.

My heroes, the great writers, comedians and musicians, like Kerouac, Belushi and Roy Buchanan, transcended all of time with their poetry. Some had very tragic courses with destiny, some had an untimely demise, but all of it could never undermine their passion for everything in life while they walked. They drank life in, and it poured all out the sides of their mouths, and it spilled all over everything. Alcoholism and addiction didn't have to be the trade-off for passion and genius. I knew that Kerouac's *Dean Moriarty* had never died. Somewhere in Mexico, a lonesome horizontal ladder made from abandoned railway ties stretched for hundreds of miles across the arid desert until it found lush green vegetation and the warm sunlight of eternity.

Paradise was within us, in Luke, Decky, Colette, all of my friends, my family, all of the people that I always knew, and all those that had touched me across our beautiful land. And the truly great ones allowed us to breathe as they did every time we stepped into their pages. I could feel them; I could drink in life the way they did and cherish the opportunity to struggle every day in order to keep from falling, lest I fall into my own unwritten pages in my sordid old age without ever registering a word.

In the end, I didn't burn it all like Trent had wanted me to. I always had it with me. I had written the ending first. It was beautiful, a beaten man finally finding the goodness in rich life again. There was a warm beautiful beach there where the sun always shined.

And in the blink of an eye, Luke, Decky and I were flying at thirty thousand feet. And just like that . . . We were gone.

There was this brilliant bright light right after that very last vision of her. She was with me now. Colette was beautiful, standing there, red plaid shirt and blue jeans, country like, the beautiful warm Orange County sun studying the perfect lines of her face. I touched those lines one more time just ever so softly with my index finger, ran it over her beautiful cheeks as I closed my eyes gently and ran the bridge of her perfect nose forever.

The End

CREDITS

Lyrics to "The Pope Smokes Dope" PERMISSION & COURTESY OF DAVID PEEL ARCHIVES